"*To Outwit Them All* keeps yo
of espionage, love, and intrigu
loyalty to the Crown, Betty F
during the American Revolution. A real look at ordinary citizens risking it
all to do extraordinary things. A must-read for any Culper Spy Ring fan and
lover of suspense." —**Margo Arceri**, Culper Spy Ring historian and founder of
Tri-Spy Tours

"The most intriguing, edge-of-your-seat historical fiction I've read in a long
while. Wirgau's authentic-for-the-period writing, impeccable research, and
great attention to historical detail brought daily life during the Revolutionary
War and the Culper Spy Ring vividly to life. Through *To Outwit Them All*, I
walked the British-occupied streets of New York City through a Patriot spy's
eyes, ever aware that one wrong move could be her last. Once begun, I could
not put this book down. Brilliant." —**Cathy Gohlke**, Christy Hall of Fame
author of *This Promised Land*

"*To Outwit Them All* is a dive into an intense period of American history
peopled with fierce Patriots and dedicated Loyalists surrounded by the might
of the British army. The story weaves around the life of Betty Floyd—whom
many believe to be the illusive 355 of Washington's Culper Ring—and her work
as a spy for the Continental Army. Author Wirgau includes many historical
figures and events throughout the novel, drawing the reader into the life and
times of the Revolutionary War. A must-read for all fans of early American
historical novels!" —**Pegg Thomas**, multi-award-winning author of Path to
Freedom series

"Vividly presented, it makes the reader feel as if we are there, reliving the
years of the war. It reawakened my love for the period of occupation and the
brave residents who risked their lives for American independence." —**Karen
Quinones**, historian and author of *Theodosia Burr: Teen Eyewitness to the
Founding of the New Nation*

"Peggy Wirgau has done it again! Her latest novel, set during the American
Revolution, tells the story of one young woman, Agent 355, who overcame
a disability and her own fears to make a difference. I literally could not put
this book down, staying up much too late each evening to read just one
more chapter. The fast-paced storyline and well-drawn characters were that
compelling. *To Outwit Them All* is a beautifully crafted, well-researched, and
inspiring story. It is a must-read!" —**Taryn R. Hutchison**, award-winning
author of A Cold War Trilogy

"Set in the City of New York in 1779–1780, *To Outwit Them All* is the story
of Betty Floyd, a clever and alluring patriot spy who cavorts with British
generals to learn their military secrets. She draws none other than Major John
André into her spell. Or is Major André deceiving Betty? This thrilling novel

combines the sweep of history with the intimacy of a woman's perspective. Fans of the television drama *Turn: Washington's Spies* take note." —**Katherine Kirkpatrick**, author of *Trouble's Daughter, Redcoats and Petticoats,* and *To Chase the Glowing Hours*

"Peggy Wirgau's novel *To Outwit Them All* introduces the reader to the life of socialite Betty Floyd, who becomes the only female spy member of the highly secretive group known as the Culper Ring during the American Revolution. This story is a captivating page-turner as Betty maneuvers her way through the British-occupied New York City social scene, risking her safety to gather relevant information for George Washington's troops. It is truly an enjoyable read." —**Jeanette Minniti**, author of *The Only Way Home*

"*To Outwit Them All* is a meticulous portrayal of life during the British occupation of New York City during the Revolutionary War. Through Betty's eyes, we see the worst of humanity in the inhumane treatment of American prisoners while British officers and the city's wealthy Loyalist class hold opulent balls and parties. Welcomed into elite society, Betty seeks to use those connections to serve the American cause; she enters the dangerous underworld of the city's spies. A single mistake would mean imprisonment or, worse, death.

"Author Peggy Wirgau draws the reader into her fascinating novel *To Outwit Them All* with compelling characters, inspired by true events. Set during the American Revolution, this poignant story expertly blends conflict, romance, and cultural elements like no other. Steeped in impeccable research and riddled in suspense until the end, Wirgau's vivid imagery adds depth to the story, making it a must-read." —**Becky Van Vleet**, award-winning author of *Unintended Hero*

"*To Outwit Them All* is a captivating and action-packed tale based on the history of the Culper Spy Ring that aided the Patriot cause, its members risking their lives in enemy territory—British-occupied New York City. Wirgau brings a fresh (and much needed) female perspective on a conflict that could not have been resolved without the contribution of women at all levels of society, many of whose identities or full roles have been lost to history. In the character of Betty Floyd, Wirgau puts forth a candidate for 355 ("lady" in Culper code) and animates the world of espionage in New York during the American Revolution. Deftly navigating two worlds, Betty's conversations with her contact and cousin, Robert Townsend, are so persuasive and lively that one will be inspired to learn more about the Culper Spy Ring and its crucial role in the Revolution." —**Justinne Lake-Jedzinak**, PhD, Director of Education and Public Programs at Raynham Hall Museum

To Outwit Them All

Deceiving the enemy is
a dangerous dance.

Peggy Wirgau

THE STORY OF THE LADY IN GEORGE WASHINGTON'S SPY RING

IRON
STREAM
FICTION

Birmingham, Alabama

To Outwit Them All

Iron Stream Fiction
An imprint of Iron Stream Media
100 Missionary Ridge
Birmingham, AL 35242
IronStreamMedia.com

Library of Congress Control Number: 2025930855

Scripture quotations from The Authorized (King James) Version. Rights in the Authorized Version in the United Kingdom are vested in the Crown. Reproduced by permission of the Crown's patentee, Cambridge University Press.

Cover design by www.BookCoverDesign.us

ISBN: 978-1-56309-796-6 (hardback)
ISBN: 978-1-56309-790-4 (paperback)
ISBN: 978-1-56309-791-1 (eBook)

1 2 3 4 5—29 28 27 26 25

Dedicated to my family

*And to all the brave women of the American Revolution
whose names we will never know.*

Acknowledgments

Many thanks to the following who helped make this book possible:

Everyone at Iron Stream Media for believing in this story and working to make it the best it can be. Special thanks to Senior Editor, Susan Cornell.

My friends in American Christian Fiction Writers and Historical Novel Society for their encouragement, ideas, and inspiration. Special thanks to Christy Hall of Fame author Cathy Gohlke and author Mary Hamilton.

Those who have patiently answered my questions and helped me locate just the right bit of information. Special thanks to Caren Zatyk at Smithtown Library's Long Island Room on Long Island and Maureen Smilow for researching the Floyd and Townsend families.

Karen Quinones, for bringing Revolutionary-era New York to life through her tours and videos, sharing in my excitement in giving a voice and identity to 355, and suggestions on the manuscript.

Kim Childress, for her friendship, help in navigating the writing world, and unwavering encouragement to keep writing.

My husband, Matt, for his enthusiasm and patience as I revised a thousand times, constantly telling me to "make it better," and the never-ending tech support.

Almighty God, for all He is and all He does, and for giving me the courage and words to write the books that are on my heart.

Peggy Wirgau
October 2025

Preface

Several years ago, I came across a list of influential women in American history. One stood out, known only as 355. As a member of the Culper Spy Ring during the American Revolution, she repeatedly spied on the British, passing on valuable intelligence to General George Washington. Despite much speculation as to who she was, her identity remains unknown to this day.

Wanting to know more, I began researching Culper Ring activities and who the experts thought 355 may have been. The theory that made the most sense to me suggested that she masqueraded as a Loyalist living in British-occupied New York. What better way to infiltrate the enemy and learn their secrets than to socialize with their officers, particularly John André, the British Director of Intelligence? This seemed to fit with Culper leader Abraham Woodhull's letter he wrote in 1779 regarding his trip to New York and a "lady who will outwit them all."

In the book *George Washington's Secret Six*, authors Brian Kilmeade and Don Yaeger suggest seven possibilities as to 355's true identity, one being Betty Floyd, cousin to Culper member Robert Townsend and the niece of William Floyd, a signer of the Declaration of Independence. They list the evidence pointing to why Betty may have been 355 but also give possible reasons she might not have qualified.

There is much we will probably never know for certain about Betty Floyd. But in examining what we do know, I wondered, *What if?* Although this is a work of fiction, it's my hope that this story will help you wonder as well and consider the possibility that Miss Betty Floyd was indeed 355, the Culper Ring's mysterious lady.

Part One

Preamble

If anyone had asked for my opinion when it all began, we never would have had any sort of revolution. We colonists would have continued to live quiet lives and counted our blessings as King George III's royal subjects.

Yet, when the seeds of muffled discontent slowly bloomed into outspoken anger, the wild dream of building a new nation sprouted among men and took root. In due course, we entered a hellish war deemed impossible to win.

I was invited to participate, to do what only I could do, or so it seemed. Gradually, that wild dream became my own, and despite my numerous faults and missteps, I pursued it to the best of my ability.

There are those who attribute my efforts to others or even dare to say I did not exist. My only desire here is to put those misconceptions to rest.

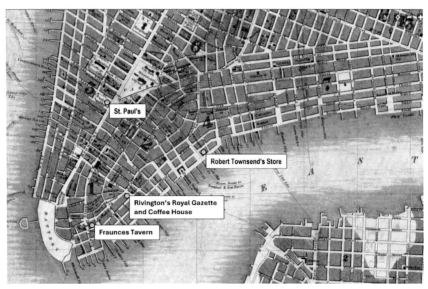

Partial map of old New York, with locations Betty frequently visits in the story.

One

Another rat, black as ink, scuttled past my foot and off to the shadows beyond the prisoners' cots. I flinched as I sponged Lieutenant Christopher Martin's forehead.

The high fever had finally lost its hold on him. "Pardon the rats, Miss Floyd."

I determined to make light of the situation. "How are any of you expected to recover when you're forced to share these fine accommodations with the former tenants?"

He glanced toward the cold stone wall where water seeped in from the previous night's rain and vermin managed to come and go. "They must wonder what became of their old victuals."

The cramped room in Rhinelander's Sugar House—now a prison for Continental soldiers—had forever lost its sweetness. Long empty of sugar and molasses, the odor of disease and urine permeated the air, burning my eyes.

I stood to fetch the pitcher of murky water and poured a bit more into the basin. In this room, where I wiped brows and held cups to parched lips, prisoners were deemed the fittest and thought least likely to succumb to their illnesses. If they recovered and were exchanged or paroled, would they go back to their regiments? Or would they recognize the futility of fighting a war they could never hope to win?

Returning to the lieutenant's cot, I studied his face in the dim light from the barred window near the ceiling. "With your fever down, your cheeks no longer match that neckerchief you insist on wearing."

He fingered the red scarf bearing the image of George Washington, the hope of the Patriots—or treasonous rebels, depending which side one took. Pride shone in his eyes. "They'd have to kill me for it, Miss Floyd."

I had little interest in their general. Despite the British military's takeover of our Long Island farm three years ago, I saw no reason to wage war over some of the colonists' desire for independence. Apart from Uncle William serving in the Continental Congress and signing that Declaration three years ago, most of the Floyd family remained loyal to the Crown.

My mother and twelve-year-old brother were the exceptions. They sided with the Patriots yet were careful to keep their views to themselves. I remained far more interested in adjusting to my new life in the city than in politics or the rumors regarding when Britain would put an end to the war.

"Please, shall we drop the formalities?" I seated myself on the stool again. "You may call me Betty, for mercy's sake." I'd been at his side during the worst of the dysentery. That seemed enough reason to warrant his using my Christian name.

"Thank you, Miss Betty. And call me Christopher." He shifted toward me and rubbed the back of his neck. "I'd be a dead man if not for you."

I dropped the excuse of a sponge in the basin of water I held in my lap. "You can thank me by getting well. No doubt they'll require your cot for another poor fellow soon, so my guess is they'll release you." I hoped that would be the case, for his sake, even if it meant saying goodbye.

He reached for my deformed left hand, the hand that caused most to recoil. My instinct was to pull away, yet there was a sincerity in his touch that made me hesitate.

He wrapped his fingers around mine—the thumb and forefinger that Providence had seen fit to give me. "If they do release me, may I write to you? Unless there's another—"

The guard near the doorway, Mr. Crankshaw, rapped a large stick against the stone wall. "You there." He pointed his stick at the lieutenant. "Keep your filthy hands to yourself."

As if such things meant anything to him. Crankshaw was with the Loyalist militia and new to the prison, but not to me. What a shame to see such a disgusting man in charge of these unfortunate souls.

Curious eyes turned our way, followed by the usual crude remarks. I'd grown accustomed to their language, along with the rats. Neither bothered me as much as the sense of entrapment that gripped me behind the prison walls, even though I could walk out the door any time I chose.

Crankshaw rapped the wall again. "Quiet, you fools. I can have the lot o' you whipped, and don't think I won't."

I rose in haste, sending the basin to the stone floor, the water trickling away in every direction. As I bent to retrieve it and grab a rag, I spoke to Christopher in a muffled voice. "He is rather loud, but I'd venture to say he's harmless."

"I heard he was demoted," he whispered back. "We call him The Crow. He thinks it his duty to squawk at us."

I set the basin and sponge under Christopher's cot beside his shoes, which had more holes than leather. Governor Tryon's raiders had captured him and twelve other men in New Haven earlier in the summer. By the time he and his fellow soldiers were transported all the way to New York, dysentery had grabbed hold. Only half had recovered, including Christopher.

What if I consented to him writing to me—the daughter of a Long Island Tory landowner corresponding with a rebel Connecticut blacksmith? Mail was regularly searched, and any hint of spying on either side was cause for trouble.

I straightened. "It's nearly time for me to leave. Try to rest. I'll return as soon as I can."

He raised a brow, wanting an answer. He was certainly more of a gentleman than many a Loyalist. What harm would there be in a friendly letter?

Crankshaw turned his back to swear at two men bickering over a dropped chunk of bread.

I leaned close to the lieutenant again and whispered. "In case you're paroled before I return, you may post a letter in care of my cousin, Robert Townsend. He has a shop near the wharf—Oakham and Townsend."

Christopher's eyes glistened. "I hope to write soon, Betty."

My mother's small frame darkened the doorway. A frown

crossed her face as she tied her hat ribbon—a good indication of how difficult her work had been in the next room, where she nursed the occupants about to leave this world within days, if not hours.

I weaved my way between cots toward the door. Perhaps some cakes would cheer these men, if I could find a way to sneak them in. And an extra one for Christopher.

Crankshaw gave my mother a curt nod. Below his right eye twitched a telltale black mark of syphilis. "Why do you trouble yourselves here on such a fine day, ladies? Surely you must have better things to do."

"We are making ourselves useful, *sir*," I said, stepping toward him. "What else can one do during this ridiculous war?"

A note of recognition, like a wispy cloud, crossed his fleshy face. "You should stick to the parties, Miss, and amuse the king's officers."

So, he recalled seeing me at the party. But did he remember the details of our brief encounter?

"You find me amusing, do you?" I patted his protruding, red-jacketed chest with my left hand, just to watch his eyes bulge.

Mother wore an air of authority Crankshaw lacked. She cleared her throat and drew herself to her full height. "If the army would provide a semblance of care for its prisoners, there would be less need for us to visit. As it is, these men are ill and far from their homes. And they are still British subjects. It's the least we can do to bring food and give them a bit of comfort." She turned on her heel.

I called back over my shoulder as I followed her out. "A pair of rat traps are sorely needed. Please see to it."

Men hollered and applauded while Crankshaw banged his stick. I caught a glimpse of Christopher, his wide grin briefly lighting up the dismal room.

Pulling our skirts in, Mother and I stepped through refuse strewn along the short hall. We stopped to wash our hands in the bucket of water near the door, using our own cake of soap.

"At least someone remembered to go to the well," Mother said. She carried the basket that we'd brought with us that morning, filled with what we could spare from the pantry and medicinal herbs from our struggling garden. We'd included the usual sausage as a bribe for the sentry on duty—a worthwhile expense.

Outside in the warm sunlight, we shook our hands dry, and I pushed my sleeves past my elbows as high as I dared. A deep breath of fresh summer air eased the sensation of captivity.

"We're here a handful of hours each week, yet I feel as if *I'm* imprisoned each time," I said. "I cannot imagine being unable to escape."

"Indeed," Mother said. "We are blessed to be able to come and go as we please."

A driver turned his two workhorses into the side yard between the prison building and Mr. William Rhinelander's home. They pulled the dead cart, as it was known, ready for the prison's latest casualties.

Rather than look at it, I studied the weeds encroaching the path to the road. "Were there more today?"

Mother hastened down the path. "Eight died overnight. I spent all morning sewing them into their blankets."

Two

I followed her across the road to where the tall oaks offered their shade, thinking of the eight men whose bodies would soon be tossed on the cart and driven to a burial pit beyond the city.

"The war seems so far away most of the time," I said. "Yet here at the prison, I'm reminded of its reality."

Mother slowed her pace. "Oh, 'tis most assuredly real. If it were not so, we would still be on our farm." She glanced in my direction. "Elizabeth, I appreciate your joining me on these visits. You've been most caring and patient."

I couldn't help but smile. "The men are so appreciative of anything I do, no matter how awkward I may be at doing it."

"But must you be so contrary with the guards?" Her tone hinted at frustration.

"Me—contrary?" I sidestepped a mud puddle. "You've said yourself they must be put in their place when they deserve it. And that Crankshaw fellow deserves it."

"What do you mean?" She lowered her voice but spat the words. "Has he acted inappropriately?"

Two officers heading our way tipped their hats as we turned the corner at Rose Street. One stared a bit too long, and I hid my left hand in the folds of my gown.

When they passed, I explained. "Do you remember the party that Celeste and I attended, honoring the new regiment taking up their duties in New York? Crankshaw came with other lower-level soldiers."

Mother grunted. "Go on."

"He asked me to dance a minuet, which was a surprise in itself because he doesn't look as if he could dance at all. Then when he saw my hand, he was suddenly attacked with a fit of dreadful coughing. He hurried away, and I thought he might truly be choking. That is, until he and Celeste joined the other dancers on the floor."

Mother normally kept her anger to herself, unless one of her children suffered ridicule. "How dare he?" She raised her basket skyward. "A miraculous recovery."

"That wasn't all. When the music ended, he reached for Celeste's hands, appearing to count her fingers."

Mother let out a growl. "Shameful."

I clutched my apron, cringing at the memory. "And a minuet doesn't involve touching hands at all."

"Even so—"

"Thank heaven for Celeste. She marched off and left him standing in the center of the floor. He only embarrassed himself. No wonder he's a lowly prison guard. I disregarded the whole incident, but I couldn't resist reminding him of it today."

After twenty-one years of being viewed as stupid, cursed, or contagious due to my deformity, I endeavored not to allow such slights to upset me, but there were times that called for a mild retort. Today had been one of those times.

"I'm thankful you have such a loyal friend in Celeste," Mother said, "and you have every right to be angry. However, I'm afraid you're too harsh with your words at times, my dear. It's unbecoming a lady. And I do wish you would think carefully before attending the military's social functions. The majority of those men are not to be trusted. Remember the way they treated us."

I'd heard the same argument more times than I cared to count. "Of course, but please don't concern yourself. The parties are quite entertaining and the one advantage I can see to having nearly the entire British military residing under our noses. That was the only time when anyone acted less than gentlemanly."

Mother cast me a look to say she doubted that was true, and she was correct. Men were seldom gentlemen at parties, most notably military men, and certainly not when the rum and champagne flowed freely.

We stepped around loose stones on the uneven walk and passed large ivy-covered brick homes, their entries framed with roses or determined daisies baking in the heat. Not many streets away across Broadway, a good part of the city still lay in ruins, due to the fire of three years ago that destroyed countless houses and shops.

It was an accepted fact that Washington's army had set the fire as they escaped New York, avoiding a bloody standoff with General Howe's men. Our street and its homes had remained beyond the reach of the fire's path. I couldn't imagine where else we would have gone when our Long Island property swarmed with redcoats, and we were forced to leave almost everything behind.

Mother pulled a handkin from her pocket to pat her perspiring forehead. "I suppose it's a possibility you will meet someone decent among all those officers, even if they are British—someone who recognizes your fine inner qualities as well as your beauty. It may take time, due to . . . your circumstances." She pressed the handkin to her neck. "But please use discretion. It isn't appropriate to be seen at every gathering."

"There is no need to remind me of the *circumstances*." I extended my left hand. "And we don't attend everything—only when Celeste receives an invitation. I'm fortunate that she brings me as her guest. Regardless, I won't be getting married for a good while. Certainly not until the war ends."

We passed a house where a woman dressed entirely in black bent over her broom as she swept her wooden stoop. She returned my nod with a suspicious scowl—the typical reaction among elderly city dwellers dealing with military occupation and the spies that could be anywhere, and probably were.

"War or no war," Mother continued, "you must consider your future. We had quite a struggle after your father died, even with your Uncle William's help."

"But we had the farm to run and workers to care for. Now that we're here—"

"We're barely better off, with what your grandmother left to us. You may not think you need a husband today, but you will."

We turned down our street. "How unromantic—to marry for financial reasons."

"Ah, romance is fleeting, my dear. You must also be practical."

I peeled damp stray hairs from my neck and tucked them under my cap. Certainly, I was aware of the need for a source of income. And marriage was a high calling, with raising a family an expected goal of most girls from the time we received our first doll. I was no different. Yet in my heart, I longed for more—to do something important or to *be* someone in addition to a wife. But whatever that could mean was as far off as the shores of England.

Then the old voice hissed from years ago.

Who do you think you are?

We reached our home, a narrow three-story tucked under an enormous elm tree that shaded the house in summer. Fortunately for us, the British had overlooked the place during their takeover shortly before our arrival in early October of 1776.

Regardless of their immediate need to find quarters, Mother surmised the occupying forces hadn't been interested in a house with a loose front step and missing shingles. Cousin Robert had offered to repair them himself, but then he and Mother decided not to give the military a reason to change their minds. Although Alice, Grandmother Sharp's companion and housekeeper, would never have allowed them in the door.

Alice met us at the top step and reached for Mother's basket as we followed her inside. "Come in, Miz Margaret, Miss Betty. Lemonade's in the parlor. How be the men today?"

"Most are doing as well as can be expected," Mother said. As was her habit, she refrained from speaking of the dead prisoners. She lifted a fan from the hall table and fanned her face with eyes closed.

A pleasant breeze blew in from the open door in the pantry at the end of the center hall. It helped to cool the first-floor rooms, even on the hottest days.

I removed my cap and wiped my face and neck. "Where is Joe?"

"He helpin' Mr. Townsend at the store with a new shipment. But he said to tell you he done all his readin'."

At seventy, Alice still had the energy of anyone half her age. Grandmother had freed Alice some years ago, yet she'd chosen to stay and care for Grandmother when she could no longer feed herself or climb stairs.

The same day that British soldiers informed Mother of their

plans to billet themselves in our farmhouse, Alice had sent word of Grandmother's death. Mother then made the decision to leave the farm and return to her childhood home. Three days later, she, my brother Joe, and I packed our trunks and made our way to the city. When we arrived on the heels of the fire, exhausted and apprehensive, Alice had welcomed us with open arms.

She hurried to the parlor off the hall and poured cups of lemonade for us from the pitcher on the small table. I held the cool pewter against my forehead.

Mother took her cup. "I'm going up to rest, but I'll be down shortly. And we'll help with the stew. There should still be a bushel of root vegetables in the cellar."

Alice gave Mother a reassuring wave. "No hurry. Turnips and carrots are already simmerin'."

I dropped onto one of the worn green velvet chairs and removed my shoes. The thick rug welcomed my perspiring feet. "Turnips and carrots again. Oh, what I would give for all the fresh fruits and vegetables on our farm. We can hardly obtain good seeds now."

Alice placed the pitcher back on its trivet. When Mother's bedroom door clicked, she said, "A shame the farmers outside the city can't sell us some o' their harvest. I hear Washington's men won't let 'em." She shook her head. "And all the people in those tents in Canvas Town, they got nothin'."

Alice always had a way of setting me straight. "I'm glad we can share a little with them. We are managing, thanks to the privateers and the neighbors." I waved toward the back door. "And our garden, when it cooperates."

Alice's gaze softened. "How be that handsome lieutenant?"

I tasted the cool lemonade, unsure if I wished to change the subject. "I never should have told you about him. But to answer your question, his condition is improving, and he's bound to be on his way any day."

"The sooner he leave that ol' sugar house, the better." She pointed a finger my way. "But you don't need to be gettin' caught up with no soldier."

"Alice, I don't believe you. You and Mother want nothing more than to see me betrothed."

For once, she let my comment go unchallenged. She pulled two letters from her pocket and handed them to me. "Mr. Townsend had this delivered today, and Miss Celeste had their girl bring the other."

On the front of the larger folded letter, I recognized the crooked handwriting.

Jacob, at last.

"Best hurry and hang that gown in the sun," Alice said. "We don't want any sickness in this house. No use in temptin' trouble."

"Yes, of course." I grabbed my shoes and broke the familiar red *CW* seal on the smaller message as I headed for the stairs. What could Celeste wish to tell me that warranted a letter?

Celeste Walker and I had been friends ever since our fathers became acquainted years ago in Setauket, and our mothers met during a church function. When Mr. Walker's wine import business grew and the family moved to New York City, I thought I might never see Celeste again. But in six months' time, everything changed, and we moved as well. Now we managed to see each other often, especially since her invitations to military functions had increased.

> *Betty,*
>
> *A last-minute invitation has arrived for a party tomorrow evening at General Clinton's headquarters, and I trust you will wish to attend with me.*
>
> *I have it on good authority that Major John André is expected. Knowing this, I may not sleep!*
>
> *I'll send Marcus with the carriage at two o'clock to bring you here so that we shall have enough time to dress and style our hair together.*
>
> *Yours,*
> *Celeste*

She would be absolutely rattled if, indeed, Major André attended the party. As General Clinton's new Director of Intelligence, he'd only been in New York a few weeks, but rumors of his fine attributes had spread across town like butter in a hot skillet.

I would go, of course, for no other reason than to calm her nerves. Mother would understand.

Major John André

Three

Celeste and I spent the next afternoon dressing and primping for what might prove to be the most lavish party of the summer. With her younger sisters running in and out of her bedroom, we coaxed our hair into piles of curls and pinned them high, then donned our formal frocks and their accoutrements. It was all rather exhausting, but fun, nonetheless.

"Are you sure you don't want to walk?" I asked her. "'Tis not far."

She grabbed her gloves from atop her dressing table. "Now, Betty, do you wish to arrive perspiring before you even dance? Besides, Marcus is ready and waiting."

Celeste viewed her move to New York and the coinciding British occupation as the opportunity of a lifetime. She would likely find her future husband amid all those young and not-so-young bachelors serving the king. But as I told Mother, I saw the invitations as an entertaining diversion, not a means to an end.

As the pumpkin-orange sun sank behind the trees, we stuffed our wide skirts into the Walkers' open carriage. Marcus, the family's lifelong slave, climbed up to the driver's seat, and Celeste and I chattered like chickens for the short ride to One Broadway, formerly the mansion of Archibald Kennedy, and General Washington's after that, but currently General Clinton's headquarters.

New York City was a crowded and well-guarded military garrison in the middle of a ghastly war, but that hadn't stopped General Clinton and his staff from making it the center of colonial high society. Anyone in the city who was not in support of the Crown when the British occupied it had abandoned their homes and left town (with the possible exception of Alice). The wealthiest of those who remained considered it their solemn duty to entertain the king's esteemed officers. New York, we were told, had never seen such gaiety.

Aside from the entertainments, the general mood was one of cautious optimism. People tended to accept the inconveniences brought on by the war: shortages, mail searches, soldiers in the streets ready to arrest anyone on suspicion of spying. Most took it all in stride and went about their business. But in the coffeehouses and taverns, constant rumors circulated regarding the war, fed by questionable stories in the *Royal Gazette* and broadsides ranting over one thing or another.

Our carriage passed the Bowling Green and the black iron fence surrounding it. Even though it is now a quiet park with visitors enjoying a stroll, I tried to imagine when King George's statue had stood in the center, and the night not long before our arrival when a crowd of rebels led by the Sons of Liberty tore the entire thing down and dragged it away.

Fort George and the grand homes along Broadway came into view. I turned to Celeste. "Whatever did we used to do on Long Island for entertainment?"

She fingered the embroidered tucker peeking out of the bodice on her mint green gown. "Thank goodness our mothers insisted on dance lessons for us. Little did they know where we'd put them to use." She patted the beauty mark she'd applied near her mouth. "What do you think?"

I studied her powdered face and the overall effect. "Shall I be kind or truthful?"

She wrinkled her nose. "I've never known you to say anything but the truth. Not that I always care for it."

I touched her gloved hand. "You look lovely. But that mouche announces to the entire world you want to be kissed. Personally, I'd move it up a bit."

"I should have known not to listen to Julia." Celeste drew out her younger sister's name as she peeled off the mouche. "I don't recall what all the placements signify. Not that a kiss wouldn't be nice." She raised an eyebrow. "Especially from Major André, if he does make an appearance."

I laughed. "Don't be ridiculous. You don't even know the man, and you're giving too much thought to what others say about him. Regardless, you're beautiful, and this isn't Paris. You don't need a mouche."

I couldn't blame her for being curious regarding the famous John André. All reports claimed he was a gentleman's gentleman and the most handsome man this side of the Atlantic. The more the rumors spread, the more sensational they became. Yet I would be lying to say I wasn't a bit curious myself.

Celeste lifted her chin. "You have suitors, Betty. You have your soldier, Christopher Martin, even if he is a traitor. And Jacob. I'm only—"

"They are *not* suitors. As soon as Lieutenant Martin is released, he will find his way home to Connecticut." I saw no need to tell her of his request to correspond. "And Jacob—we were playmates, for mercy's sake. We simply enjoy each other's company. And now, each other's letters. He's lonely at Fort Michilimackinac. There's little to do while guarding the Great Lakes."

Marcus guided the horses to a stop as we reached our destination. A candle burned in each tall window of the two-story brick mansion. The wide entry doors were open and flanked by uniformed servants. Music and laughter spilled from within as guests made their way toward the steps and the ornamental railings.

"At least Jacob is safe, away from the fighting," Celeste said. "Perhaps he'll be transferred to a more agreeable place, such as New York. And you can become reacquainted."

I shook my head. "You are insufferable."

With assistance from Marcus, we descended the carriage steps as gracefully as we could manage, then made our way to the entrance behind a middle-aged officer and his wife, both impeccably dressed and wearing heavily powdered wigs.

Celeste leaned close to my ear. "If you won't permit me a mouche, promise me you'll never wear a wig. Your fair hair and skin will be the envy of every lady here."

I patted the back of my head to ensure the dozens of pins were still in place. "Yes, but we both could have saved ourselves a great deal of trouble today if we had wigs."

We entered the house and handed our gloves to one of the servants. A large banner bearing King George III's coat of arms hung over the foyer. As more guests arrived, we were swept along into an ornate drawing room that opened out to a wide porch overlooking the Hudson. The room's furniture had been set against the walls to make room for dancing.

Amid the ladies decked in a rainbow of silks, laces, and satins were a sizable number of British officers in their smart red coats and white breeches and dozens of Hessian officers in dark green. A most fashionable party, and thankfully, no Crankshaw in sight.

At least half the men wore wigs. A smattering of the older ones had attempted to hide their syphilitic facial marks with white powder. Many ladies wore wigs as well, powdered to match their gowns. Others had their own hair pinned in a high roll, embellished with feathers, flowers, or ribbons. I hoped my attempt to duplicate the elaborate style wouldn't fall flat.

The contrast between New York's high society and most people on Long Island often amazed me. Here, the wealthy put great importance on the latest fashions, where even those who might afford it on Long Island dressed more practically, with less fuss. I'd heard that was generally the custom throughout the colonies, yet New Yorkers took their cue from the courts of France and England, with an unquenchable desire for the finest, the most formal, and the most ostentatious.

We opened our fans, and Celeste beamed with joy. "Do you suppose General Clinton is here? But no matter. I feel as though we're in the king's court."

She bobbed a quick curtsy to a lanky man with a large nose as he worked his way past us holding two glasses of champagne.

A string quintet sat to our left, while two lines formed on the dance floor, women in one and men in the other. Apparently, we had missed the opening minuet.

Celeste pulled me by the arm. "They're about to do a contradance. Let's watch the steps in case we're asked to join in."

Beyond the dance floor near the open doors stood a long buffet table and refreshment stand. "Shall we move for a better view?" I asked. "I see some familiar faces."

We wove through groups gathered in lively conversation. At the buffet, we stowed our fans in our pockets and helped ourselves to tiny sandwiches from ornate silver platters. Two ladies we'd met at a recent party nodded to us. No sooner did Celeste take the last bite of her sandwich when she was whisked away by Lieutenant Parker, a chatty redhead whom she'd danced with on previous occasions.

I accepted a cup of strawberry punch from a servant, then watched the dancers as the violinists and cellist played the first notes. The two lines soon became a merry blur of swirling pastels and red with gold braiding. Before long, I was swaying to the music and copying the dance steps.

In an odd way, learning to dance had helped free me of the habit of always trying to keep my left hand out of view. When not dancing, I still tucked it out of sight when I could. Or I flaunted it on occasion if I was daring enough. But once I learned to dance, and accepted the fact that hands play a part in most dances, I was able to set my uneasiness aside. Unfortunately, there would always be an ignorant Crankshaw-type to put a damper on it.

The dancing grew livelier to keep pace with the music. Onlookers squeezed in around me, and a stocky Hessian to my left, holding a plate full of sandwiches, attempted to push through. I took a step back to allow him room to pass but bumped someone behind me.

I swung around to apologize. Instead, my entire cup of punch splashed onto the white lace cravat worn by a most handsome officer. The guests encircling him all stepped back in alarm.

"Oh, mercy. Forgive me." I grabbed a linen napkin from the buffet and handed it to him.

His gaze lingered as he accepted the napkin from my left hand. I pulled it away, sensing curious looks from every direction.

He daubed at the strawberry-tinted stain. "Quite all right, Miss. I'm afraid I startled you. Please accept my apologies."

His dark hair, tied low in a ribbon, stood out in the room full of so many powdered wigs. The contrast was striking.

I recovered my composure. "I am not a sparrow, sir. I was not *startled*."

He wiped his cravat, now the identical shade of my rose-colored gown. "Ah, surprised then. I apologize for the *surprise*." He seemed to enjoy his little rhyme. "Yet I daresay it was you who initiated the surprise by knocking into me."

A quick glance around the festive room revealed ladies of all ages looking our way, undoubtedly questioning how I'd managed to gain the attention of this handsome man.

"I beg your pardon," I said. "But I'm afraid it was unavoidable."

He gestured toward the dancers as they turned in unison in the center of the floor. "I suppose you are correct. Between your enthusiasm for the music, and the popularity of the sandwiches, a collision was bound to happen eventually."

I followed his gaze to a plump couple maneuvering through the crowd with plates piled high. "Are you inferring it was my error?"

His smile revealed perfect white teeth. "Not at all. I can only say I'm pleased it happened, although I received a good dousing." With a flourish, he waved his hand over his cravat.

This is like a game of shuttlecock. Very well—I'll play along. "I would venture to say you took the risk by standing too close, sir."

"Again, you are correct." He handed the napkin to a servant. "And if this discussion runs any longer without an introduction, you will accuse me of not being a gentleman." He bowed quickly yet ever so dignified. "John André, at your service."

Words failed. *Major André?* My gown, his cravat, and now my face was a bright rose—I felt certain of it.

The music ended. I set my empty cup down to applaud the dancers, hoping he wouldn't notice my shaking hands. Celeste's partner escorted her toward the refreshments, their cheeks flushed. Her eyes widened as she spotted me and the man beside me with the rose-colored cravat.

One of the violinists announced the next dance—the Allemande. My favorite, even with the repetitive handholds. This meeting was off to an awkward start, yet I wasn't about to let the opportunity pass.

"I'm Betty Floyd." I bent my knee in the briefest curtsy. "But you cannot be Major André."

He straightened his broad shoulders. "And why not, pray tell?"

As gentlemen chose their partners, I raised my chin. "Because I believe *he* would have already requested a dance."

He tipped his head back and laughed, then bowed low. "Miss

Floyd, may I have the honor?"

I moved my right foot behind my left and took my time with a proper curtsy, catching a glimpse of his polished silver shoe buckles. Then I rose and looked him in the eye.

"Please be aware, Major, that in the case of the Allemande, staying in step with me may be a challenge."

He presented his hand, warm and strong. "I suspect that may be the case with more than a mere dance."

The music began, and off we went. Five years earlier, Jacob and I had won second prize dancing the Allemande in a Long Island competition. But it was not something the average man would undertake with me, for obvious reasons.

Immediately, Major André proved to be an excellent dancer. He not only knew the steps exactly, but demonstrated such grace yet the confident strength befitting an officer of the king.

We exchanged smiles as heads turned in our direction. When it came time to extend my left hand, he slowly clasped it as if it were the finest treasure.

Then, without warning, he stopped dancing and acknowledged someone in the throng behind me. I stumbled, caught myself, and managed to move aside just in time as the couple closest to us danced into our path.

Major André hurried me off the dance floor, made an excuse that I couldn't quite hear, and hastened toward three officers at the far wall. Two were near his age, perhaps in their late twenties. The other, gray-haired and wearing a red coat heavily trimmed in gold braiding, looked as if he never waited for anyone. I had never seen General Clinton, yet he fit the description of him in the *Royal Gazette*.

I stood embarrassed, not knowing what to think. If the eyes in the room could have burned holes through my skin, I would be a pile of ash.

Two hours later, Celeste and I climbed into our waiting carriage. As much as my stays allowed, I slouched against the leather cushion and groaned.

She removed a satin shoe to rub her foot. "Betty, everyone there wanted his attention. You were fortunate to have any time with him at all. And you danced—beautifully, I might add. It wasn't his fault General Clinton interrupted." She pointed the toe of her shoe at me. "Why would he have left you there if it wasn't absolutely necessary?"

As Marcus directed the horses to pull the carriage away, I turned to watch the departing guests as they milled about in front of the mansion. I was still perturbed at how a perfect dance with an incredible partner could end so abruptly. It reminded me of that odd meeting with Crankshaw. Was there something about me that made a man think it was acceptable to not finish a dance?

"We'd barely begun. I thought he'd return, but no—not once, not even to apologize."

"Perhaps he needed to leave the party," Celeste said. "Quit brooding. 'Tis so unlike you. It was not as if you didn't dance with anyone afterward."

I pulled a loose hairpin from my lopsided high roll and exhaled. I'd come to dance, not to meet Major André. "That's all quite true. He's clearly a busy officer, too occupied with his new position to be concerned with me or any of the ladies fawning over him."

A smirk crossed her face. "He likely became quite accustomed to such attention in Philadelphia."

As Marcus drove the carriage toward my home, I tried to put the incident in perspective. "We had a brief encounter all because of my clumsiness. I suppose he was merely being polite. I doubt I'll see him again."

That would suit me perfectly.

Four

As Mother and I prepared for our walk to Rhinelander's four days later, I brushed my hair, pinned it neatly under my cap, and checked that my simple "prison undress" was spot-free. A mist of rose water was the final touch.

If Christopher hadn't been discharged, he would indeed be feeling stronger. Yet that would depend on whether he could maintain a semblance of health and avoid the constant spread of disease that prevailed throughout the prison.

The cakes I'd baked would give him energy. And perhaps we might discuss more than his illness and the war. What would he think if I told him I met General Clinton's new Director of Intelligence? Would he be angry? Jealous?

I reprimanded myself. Engaging in petty games was so unlike me. Plus, Major André and anyone else in the British military was Christopher's sworn enemy. It was best not to say anything.

Mother stood in the hall near the door, tucking a clean cloth around the contents of our market basket. She looked up at me at the top of the stairs. "Do we have everything?"

I smoothed my apron as I descended the stairs. "There's bread, cheese, the cakes, and the sentry's sausage. And I added a bit of our leftover stew. It's cold—I had it sitting in the Dicksons' icehouse—but I doubt the men will mind. By the way, the cakes are well hidden, so perhaps the guards won't notice them."

"Very well." Mother handed me the basket. "Shall we?"

Joe followed me downstairs, his pounding footsteps rocking the small portraits that hung along the hall. "May I come to the prison?"

"Heavens, no," Mother said. "It's no place for a boy. And you have chores to finish."

I hefted the basket. "Be a gentleman and hold the door for us, dear brother."

He leapt from the last step to the rug and pulled open our entry door. "Cousin Robert needs help with another shipment anyway." He caught Mother's eye. "I'll go after my chores."

She gave him last-minute instructions, and he closed the door behind us. As we headed down the front steps, the air already felt like a wet rag. Mother took one handle of the basket, and we balanced it between us as we walked.

"At least the sugar house remains cool most days," she said. "But we must make certain the men have enough water to drink. You'll help me with that, won't you?"

"I'll try. None of the guards are very dependable at fetching water."

She adjusted her hold on the basket. "Perhaps we can offer one of them a cake or two?"

I groaned. "The cakes are for the prisoners." *For Christopher.* "Not for bribes."

"I hope it won't come to that. I know how much effort you put into your baking. The entire house smelled of cinnamon yesterday."

"Alice insisted I add a small packet of raisins she's been saving, so I chopped them into pieces and stirred them in. We had to sample them. They're delicious."

We reached the corner and stopped to fan ourselves. Two officers walked past, conversing with two older men, most likely merchants. Beads of sweat rolled down their faces as they all tipped their hats. I recognized the officer with the dark curly hair—he'd danced a reel at a tavern party earlier in the summer.

We lifted the basket and resumed our walk. "There is one prisoner that I enjoy visiting," I said. "Lieutenant Martin, the man that was so ill with dysentery. He's showing marked improvement and expects to be released."

"Thanks to the good Lord," Mother said. "And your diligence. Yet you must try not to show any favoritism."

"He asked to . . . Well, he's simply a good man that I've come to know." My face felt hot, not entirely due to the air temperature. Perhaps he would never write to me at all.

As we neared the prison, two of the guards approached us. One was Mr. Jones, the sentry. He spoke briefly to his companion and held up a hand when he saw us.

I shielded my eyes with my free hand. "Why is he stopping us?"

"Perhaps they're conducting an inspection," Mother said. "Long overdue, if you ask me."

As we drew close enough to hear, the sentry spoke. "Ladies, I'm afraid we must ask you not to visit today."

I looked past him. The dead cart stood beside the sugar house, while two men in dirty shirts and breeches tossed a lifeless body on top of the heap already on the cart.

"We'll take the sausage now, if you have it," he continued. "Yet it would be wise if you return another day."

"No sausage until you allow us entry," Mother said. "And why haven't those bodies been sewn into blankets? The diseases—"

I took a few steps closer for a better look at the vile cart. Despite the heat of the day, a chill rushed down my spine. Beneath the stiff arms, legs, and torsos, a limp red neckerchief hung over the edge.

A scream rose in my chest. I fell to my hands and knees, unable to take my eyes from the hideous empty faces on the cart. And Christopher—the side of his bloody head, with his tribute to General Washington like a noose around his neck.

Everything blurred. I was led to the shade, and someone called for a carriage. Clutching my mother's hands, my teeth chattered as we rode the distance we had just walked. I had no words except to ask what had become of our food basket. If she replied, I failed to hear.

Once at home, I pushed past Joe and found my way up what felt like a hundred stairs. I threw my outer clothing to the floor and fell across my bed. Tears would not come. I could only stare out the window at the fluttering leaves on the elm and listen to my breathing.

I tried to grasp the fact that Christopher Martin was dead—the man I'd held, washed, and fed for weeks. How odd it was, how incomprehensible, that the entire world kept moving, the sun remained in the sky, and the birds continued to sing. No one had informed them of what had taken place in a hell not far away.

Mother sat with me, neither of us speaking a word. Alice brought tea and a sandwich, which I left untouched. By evening, my building grief and anger gave way to deep uncontrollable sobbing. When all strength had left me, I willed myself to sleep and prayed never to wake.

In the morning, Mother forced herself to go to the prison and make inquiries. She sat beside me on my bed later that afternoon.

"I was only told their conditions worsened and they died. But when I questioned two of the prisoners, they said men were chosen at random yesterday morning to remove debris behind the building and were led outside. Not long afterward, they heard shots."

She took a long breath before continuing. "They overheard the guards saying more space was needed. One heard the words 'necessary wartime procedures.'"

Horror and disbelief crept through me. I clutched the sheet to my chest. "How could such a thing be allowed?"

Mother's eyes darkened with anger. "I asked who was responsible, but no one could give me a definite answer. The army is in full charge. They're the law." She held her cheeks. "Those poor men. Perhaps if we'd gone earlier—"

"What of Crankshaw? Did you see him?"

She grimaced. "I searched until I found him in their excuse of a pantry. I asked what he knew, but he only said I had no business inquiring into such matters."

I ground my fists into the quilt. "How dare he say such a thing. You've done more for those men than anyone."

Her shoulders drooped as she toiled with the handkin in her lap.

"Christopher didn't die a natural death." I trembled at the memory. "I saw the blood. They all were murdered."

Her voice strained as she held my shoulders. "Elizabeth, saying any more won't do those soldiers still living or either of us any good. We must keep it to ourselves."

Over the next few days, I had no appetite. Alice tried coaxing me to eat by making my favorite chicken soup and serving me tea in my room with toast and preserves. I barely managed to consume anything.

"I hear there's trouble every day at the other prisons," she said one day. "Bridewell's the worst o' them all. And the Provost Jail in the Common. People say the man who run it—Cunningham—he's the devil hi'self."

"I hope I never meet him," I said. "Frankly, I don't want to see another prison or prison official as long as I live."

Mother sympathized, yet she said that perhaps I could help at a prison other than Rhinelander's when I felt ready. That was inconceivable. I had no interest in becoming acquainted with more rebel soldiers and finding them dead the next day at the whim of their captors.

I wrote to Celeste informing her I would be unable to accompany her to any social events for the foreseeable future and asked Joe to deliver the letter. I would explain more at a later date.

How was I to continue living in a city overtaken by such evildoers? During the next two weeks, I refused to leave our house. Instead, I filled my time with dozens of routine tasks, throwing myself into them as if they mattered more than life.

I continued tutoring Joe and assigned him extra pages of Latin and French and world history, accepting nothing from him less than perfection. I helped Alice prepare our meals, packed biscuits and ham for her to distribute at the river, and worked alongside her doing the weekly washing behind the house.

In the evenings, I busied myself long past sunset, mending tears in our never-ending pile of clothing or household linens until the candles burned to tiny nubs. Sleep, when it came, was marked with nightmares involving our farm, Papa, and Christopher. Always Christopher.

My full days and restless nights were interrupted when Mother, Joe, and I spent a languid afternoon at a neighborhood gathering on the Dicksons' front lawn. I was grateful that none of our street's billeted soldiers or their wives participated.

I still lacked the energy for socializing. Instead, I served food and held fussy babies so their mothers could eat. Elizabeth Burgin, a widow whom Joe occasionally assisted with various chores, attended with her three children. She joined the conversation as it turned to war and politics, but I excused myself to help replenish the food platters.

That evening, as I washed away the day in preparation for bed, a thread or two of grief unraveled. Still, confusion and anger festered. I had no idea how to emerge from their grip.

If only I knew a way to return to ignoring the war and simply live my life. Yet I suspected those days were over.

William Floyd, delegate to the Continental Congress and signer of the Declaration of Independence.

Five

Joe and I huddled over his French lesson in the parlor, at the table we used for study. Mother entered, waving the pages of a letter. "I've written to your Aunt Hannah. Would either of you wish to add a note to your cousins?"

"*Oui.*" Joe reached for the letter. "Nicoll will want news of all the ships in the harbor."

I tousled his blond hair. "You're only looking for a way to escape these French verbs."

He glanced at me over the top of the letter. "*C'est exact.*"

Mother adjusted her straw hat over her cap. "I'm leaving to help Mrs. Dickson with her quilt. See to it that one of you takes the letter to Cousin Robert when you're finished. We have no idea when it may reach Philadelphia." She turned and left.

"Isn't Aunt Hannah still in Connecticut?" Joe asked.

"No, she and our cousins were able to join Uncle William in Philadelphia, but we don't know for how long."

Joe tapped his pen on his book. "Was Uncle William truly guilty of treason?"

I grabbed his pen and held on to it. "Don't ever mention that word or Uncle William in the same sentence. Remember, we're never to tell anyone about him. In the eyes of the British, all the signers of the Declaration still are guilty. That's why Aunt Hannah and our cousins had to go into hiding in Connecticut. Now that the British have left Philadelphia, they may be somewhat safer there."

His chin trembled. "I don't want trouble for them. I'll never say anything." He smoothed the pages of Mother's letter and began his note to our Floyd cousins: Nicoll, Mary, and Kitty.

Strong, confident Uncle William had helped us keep the farm in production after my father's death. Then he lost his entire property in Mastic during the occupation. How did he manage to remain a bold voice in Congress and care for his family amid all the danger and uncertainty?

When I was Joe's age and Papa would take us to visit Uncle William's enormous farm, my uncle and I would play a sort of guessing game no one else understood. He would make up a simple story, but with the main characters or events altered. I would then try to guess the true story and what parts of it were false.

The memory of it gave me an idea.

"I believe I'll write my own letter," I said. "But to Uncle William. I'll tuck it in with yours when you're finished."

"But won't the British be watching letters to Aunt Hannah as well, looking for information about him?"

"That's entirely possible. Or they may not know who Uncle William is, so we mustn't reveal anything. Don't mention his name to the cousins."

Joe scratched his ear. "Betty? I'm worried for Mrs. Burgin and her family."

I stood to look for a sheet of writing paper. "And why is that?"

"I went to her house yesterday to move wood to the kitchen, but everyone was gone."

I turned to look at him. "The children as well? Gone where?"

"The lady at the neighboring house said she left in haste. Her children are with another neighbor. I think those men are gone also."

"What men?"

He shifted in his chair. "I . . . I wasn't supposed to say anything, but—"

It was unlike him to keep secrets from me. "Joe?"

He was quiet for a moment, then stretched an arm toward the window. "Men she saved from one of the prison ships—the *Jersey*. Someone with a boat got the men off and they stayed in her cellar until they could get away safely."

"How do you know this?"

"I . . . saw them. Always different ones." He turned to look down at the letter again. "She gave them food and told me to keep quiet about it. But now I'm worried something went wrong."

I barely knew her, but Mrs. Burgin hadn't struck me as someone who would ever leave her children, regardless of the emergency. Yet, if she was involved with rescuing prisoners from the *Jersey*, anything was possible. I needed to put Joe at ease, in case he was tempted to mention her disappearance or the men she'd kept in hiding to the wrong person.

"Perhaps she had to visit a family member who is ill," I said. "She'll return, of course. But keep the fact that you saw anyone else in the house to yourself. No need to bring attention to it now."

Joe resumed writing his letter. I wished I could learn more of Mrs. Burgin's whereabouts, if only I knew whom it would be safe to ask.

For now, I put the matter out of my mind. I pulled a sheet of paper and a quill pen from the drawer in the writing desk and took a seat. The ink well held plenty of ink. How would I communicate what I wished to Uncle William?

We'd learned that most letters passing in and out of the city were opened by the military, seeking anything that might incriminate the sender or the receiver. Cousin Robert's correspondence, however, hadn't aroused much suspicion. A Quaker's orders and receipts for groceries and common supplies apparently didn't interest the British and usually passed through unchecked.

Hence, when he'd offered to conceal our letters among his paperwork, Mother had agreed. The plan worked for mail sent to us as well. That might change at any time, however. We could never take anything for granted.

How could I reveal to my uncle what occurred at the prison without raising the hairs of suspicion on the military's necks? If I said too much, we might both be in danger.

Dearest Uncle,

We are comfortable at my grandmother's home now. I would like nothing more than to regale you with all that I have been doing but suffice it to say I have been quite occupied.

New York is a fascinating city, and I am growing accustomed to its bustling streets. With His Majesty's army stationed here, it can be a bit crowded at times. Even the stray dog population has multiplied. Only last week, the authorities decided that so many dogs are a hazard. They ordered those wandering loose to be rounded up and removed from the city.

In the process, one harmless dog I saw often and grew fond of was needlessly killed. I fear others like him may meet the same fate.

As you will recall, since the days of playing games on your farm, Papa wished for me to find happiness one day. For now, I strive to remain open to all opportunities in order that I may serve others, as you have always done.

I trust we will all be together again in the near future, as your business permits.

> *With affection,*
> *Betty*

That would have to do. I replaced the pen in its holder and fanned the paper to dry the ink. My story was partly true; New York did have a good share of dogs, but most were pampered pets belonging to billeted officers or Loyalists.

Would Uncle William remember our game and be able to interpret my story? I didn't expect him to have the ability to affect any change. However, I hoped he might realize that I was referring to the military's prisoners of war. And I yearned for the day when I could describe it to him plainly.

I creased the letter. If only there was someone, other than my family and Alice, whom I might speak with face-to-face regarding Christopher.

Should I go to Celeste? She would be horrified at my having to witness such a scene at the prison, but I doubted she would understand my outrage. After all, she and her parents were Loyalists to their bones, completely behind whatever the British thought best.

I would try to explain it to her soon, but I needed someone who could grasp the magnitude and senselessness of it—someone who had also experienced great loss.

I sealed the letter and told Joe I would deliver it myself to Cousin Robert. "I want you to practice your verbs while I'm gone," I instructed him.

Resignation in his eyes, he lifted his French book. "When Alice returns, I'll ask if she wants to *parle français*."

"Don't be surprised if she ties an apron on you and puts you to work in the kitchen."

I hurried to my room for my reticule, cap, and a short letter I had written to Jacob. It was time to speak to my cousin and tell him the story of Lieutenant Christopher Martin.

The only known likeness of Robert Townsend, sketched by his nephew, when Robert was sixty years old.

Six

During our nearly three years of residing in New York City, I rarely had occasion to walk unaccompanied when venturing toward the waterfront or finding my way around the lively business district. Celeste and I often visited the shops together, and many of the parties we attended were in the vicinity. Whenever Joe outgrew his breeches, I took him to see Mr. Mulligan, the tailor. And if I embarked on any errands, Mother was often with me. From time to time, we stopped at Mr. Rivington's coffeehouse or his nearby shop, purchased a newspaper at the *Gazette* office, or called on Robert.

Today was different. To speak with my cousin of the carnage at Rhinelander's, I wished to do so alone. Robert was not given to sympathy—far from it—yet he'd suffered greatly at the hands of the British. Perhaps he might share some insight. Regardless, I felt he should know what had transpired.

As I walked to Hanover Square in the direction of the waterfront, the activity—even the unpleasant smells—appealed to me more than the city's narrower residential streets and alleyways. I wouldn't describe it as a dangerous area, as long as one minded one's own business and ignored the occasional drunken sailor or vagrant. I found the variety of sights and sounds interesting and the sense that across the wide river lay my home, even though it was many miles beyond. But what became of our farm, or whether I would see it again, were questions that would undoubtedly be left unanswered for some time.

I crossed the Square, to where Oakham and Townsend could be seen at Smith Street. As I entered the shop, Robert glanced up from behind the counter and moved his spectacles higher on his long nose.

"Come in, cousin. I shall be with you in a moment."

I waved. "I'm in no hurry."

A Hessian officer approached the counter with two bulky packages of dried beef. While Robert wrote up the sale, I browsed the tables and shelves containing everything from buttons to brooms and anything else a person might require. The store smelled of tobacco and sausages, the latter strung in neat rows high above the counter.

If Mother's great-aunt hadn't married a Quaker years ago, I would never have known the large and loud Townsend family or their soft-spoken fourth son. His somber, reserved attitude could be infuriating, and I imagined most women might find him a trifle too somber for marriage.

"I beg your pardon, sir," Robert asked the officer. "Are you stocking up for the arrival of reinforcements? Perhaps a sack or two of Southern pecans would be welcome. Fresh from today's shipment."

The man replied in broken English and added one sack of pecans to his order. Robert totaled the items, and the officer told him where to send the bill. As he left, his scuffed black boots thumped across the roughened floor, rattling the jars of nails on the counter.

I crossed the room and kissed Robert on the cheek. "You never miss an opportunity to increase your sales."

He straightened items on the counter that the Hessian had bumped. "Unfortunately, that is a necessary facet of a competitive business."

Such a forlorn-looking man. Perhaps I shouldn't bother him. I handed him our letters. "It appears you're doing quite well. I'm pleased."

A faint look of satisfaction crossed Robert's thin face as he wiped his hands against his leather apron. "You have not been in recently. Are you still attending the social engagements?"

"Yes, although I . . . may not go for a while." I ran my hand along the gouged edge of the thick oak counter.

He placed the letters inside a cloth sack that was half-filled with more letters and materials. "Joseph might have brought in your letters. Do you have need of anything?"

I took a deep breath and checked the door, hoping no one entered. "Something has happened. I hoped you would not be occupied with customers."

"For the moment, I am not." Robert walked around the counter, led me to a chair next to a small desk, and motioned for me to sit.

He took the seat behind the desk and rested his elbows atop a ledger. That intense gaze of his was so unnerving.

I had better explain before we were interrupted. "You may recall that I've been helping Mother at Rhinelander's—the prison. At least, I was."

Robert said nothing, and I plunged ahead. "I became acquainted with a soldier there, a lieutenant. He was one of several prisoners transported from Connecticut in June."

My emotions fought their way to the surface, and I struggled to explain the facts and not allow my voice to crack.

"He was ill with dysentery when he arrived. I've never seen anyone so weakened." My mind filled with the memory of the miserable state Christopher had been in and his constant apologies for what was not his fault.

"Continue."

I sat up taller and swallowed the lump in my throat. "He did recover, and we thought he might be paroled. 'Tis what I've heard they do when the prisons become overcrowded."

"Yes, on occasion." Robert glanced around the shop as if a better explanation might appear. "It depends on the circumstances. At times, paroled prisoners are exchanged."

"He was not paroled, Robert." I swallowed again. "They shot him."

His facial expression went unchanged. I became aware of the clock ticking on the counter.

As if on cue, the door burst open and three red-coated soldiers entered, all snickering like disobedient schoolboys.

Robert took his time rising from his chair. I jumped to my feet and went to the far wall of shelves, pretending to examine bolts of cloth while sneaking glances at the men. None of them looked familiar.

"Good day, gentlemen." Robert's voice lacked any hint of enthusiasm. "May I be of service?"

One of them removed his hat. "We're in need of supplies for the barracks, Townsend. The usual that and this."

I watched as Robert and the soldiers discussed their requirements. If any of them noticed me, they said nothing.

"Do you expect to be stationed long in the city?" Robert asked. "I will make an effort to adjust my supply orders, if necessary."

The men gave vague replies, saying they didn't know when or if they'd be sent elsewhere. Robert wrote up the sale for buckets, brushes, candles, and other sundries. "I shall send the bill to headquarters. Thank you, gentlemen."

They made a great deal of commotion as they gathered their purchases and left. When the door banged shut, Robert approached me. "Would you care to sit again?"

"No, thank you." Folding my arms, I summarized for him exactly what Mother and I knew of what happened to Christopher.

I slumped against the wall. "Except for helping at the prison, I haven't cared too much about the war, one way or the other. I've managed to ignore it, for the most part, and I attend their functions merely for something to do." I cast a glance at the doorway. "Yet I hate them all now. And I feel so helpless. Mother insists we not mention what took place to anyone. She believes it would only lead to trouble for us or the other prisoners."

He'd barely spoken a word. He simply stood listening to me carry on, his thin frame hardly filling his plain dark shirt and breeches.

I clenched my fists. "How can you remain neutral? And so . . . *passive*? How are you able to wait on them and be pleasant to them when they're murdering sick, innocent men?"

He looked me in the eye. "Have you forgotten what they did to my own family? Our home?"

"Of course not. That's why I wanted to talk with you."

Robert had traveled to Oyster Bay to see his father and younger siblings the previous year, only to find them confined to a few rooms of the house and the entire property brutally taken over by the British.

He faced the door, staring out the narrow window at the passersby. "I have heard of shootings at the prisons. Hangings, beatings, starvation. Rampant filth and disease." He extended an arm in the direction of the harbor. "And the prison ships—the *Jersey* and others—hell on earth, it is reported. But I have not remained as passive as you think." He turned to face me. "I was a commissary in the Queens County militia for a time before returning to New York."

A commissary? I tried not to laugh. "I'm sorry, but that doesn't exactly equate to taking up arms against the invaders." Until then, I had never considered using the term for the British military that was thrown about on Long Island. Now it certainly suited them.

"Friends do not take up arms, Betty, as you well know. I did not serve long past the Battle of Brooklyn. You may have heard what happened then."

I took a step toward him, placing my hand on his arm. "Mother told me you and your father were forced to take a vow of loyalty to the Crown. You had no choice. No one would fault you for it."

He turned away, letting my hand drop. "Please understand. I am quite familiar with how it feels to be angry. I despise all their violent deeds, and I know the difficulty of pretending as if you are not affected."

I released a loud breath. "I don't know how you manage to keep quiet about it."

Facing me again, he started to speak, then took a step back, as if a stage curtain had fallen in front of him.

Just as well. I thanked him for his time and left.

Outside the shop, I gazed beyond Hanover Square to where the British flag waved above Fort George and the cadence of drums rose and fell. In the harbor, dozens of Britain's ships lay at anchor, their masts glinting in the sun. Alice said the *Jersey* was in Wallabout Bay, making it impossible to see from where I stood. I shuddered, thinking of Robert's words concerning the prison ships: *hell on earth.*

Perhaps he understood my anguish, and I felt a release in sharing it with him. He and his family had suffered much at the whims of the British. And yet, he chose to remain in New York, in the center of the world they now occupied.

But I was nothing like Robert Townsend. How could I go on feigning acceptance of such evil? And what was I to do next?

James Rivington

Seven

The following afternoon, a delivery boy brought a note from Celeste, asking me to accompany her two days hence to a play at Theatre Royal and the reception following.

> *Major André has a part in the play, so you simply must come. I'll send Marcus with the carriage at seven o'clock. It will be such fun!*

Celeste hadn't let any time pass since my message to her saying I wished to postpone attending any upcoming events. Of course, she had no way of knowing my reasons.

I would need to write to her. No, call on her. After tea that day would be an appropriate time. Any earlier and Mrs. Walker would insist I stay, and I would not want to bring up the subject of a rebel soldier in her presence. It was imperative that I speak to Celeste alone.

Under normal circumstances, a play would be great fun. But to see Major André again, or anyone connected to those responsible at Rhinelander's, felt completely wrong. I wasn't ready to continue socializing with Britain's military yet, if ever, and seeing Robert only made me more uncertain of where I stood concerning this entire war. I hoped Celeste would understand my state of mind.

Joe entered the back door as Alice and I prepared things for tea. "Look what I found behind the kitchen."

Alice's eyes widened. "What on earth you got there, Master Joe?"

He clutched a black ball of fur in his arms, smaller than my winter muff. Two tiny ears poked above his shirt, followed by shining black eyes and a rosy nose. "It's a kitten. He was all alone. And look, he can't walk."

As he held the kitten aloft, letting its limbs dangle, I couldn't help but gasp. "It only has three legs."

"No wonder it was by itself." Alice rubbed the kitten under its chin. "The mother done left it."

Joe cuddled it close to his chest. "I'm keeping him. He needs me."

"What good is a lame cat?" I said to Alice. "He can't catch mice."

"But he's hungry," Joe said.

The kitten pawed Alice's hand and mewed. "Poor thing must be starvin'. We got some milk out in the icebox."

While Joe nuzzled the kitten, Alice went to the cupboard and rummaged through her collection of old cups and saucers.

I looked at her in disbelief. "We can't keep it. Mother would never agree to that."

"Can't let it go and starve, Miss Betty."

The front door opened, and Mother's humming traveled down the hall.

"I almost forgot," Joe said, glancing at me. "Cousin Robert asks that you come and see him as soon as you're able."

How odd, considering I didn't visit him that often. "Why? I was there only yesterday."

Joe accepted a chipped saucer from Alice. "It must be important."

"What's important?" Mother appeared in the doorway. "Good heavens. Is that a cat?"

An ominous bank of clouds shrouded the city the next morning. Would a thunderstorm materialize? Thunder always produced bad memories of the incident that took place so long ago, yet I was curious as to why Cousin Robert wished to see me. Clutching my umbrella, I forced myself out the door.

The still, moist air bore the scent of kitchen fires as I passed house after house. A door opened, and a young mother ordered her children playing on the front steps to come in before it rained.

What could be Robert's purpose in summoning me again so soon? Perhaps he had information on the killings at Rhinelander prison. What if he had news of our farm on Long Island? Or an important letter he didn't trust Joe to deliver? Whatever it was, it had better merit a long walk in threatening weather.

Celeste had listened patiently when I called on her the previous day and explained what happened to Christopher and all that took place at the prison. But rather than share my shock and disgust at what happened, she seemed resigned to it.

"Those are the unfortunate occurrences that go with war," she'd said. "The rebels have no business standing up to the Crown. And what do we really know for certain? Perhaps your handsome lieutenant truly died a natural death, as your mother was told."

I pleaded with her. "Celeste, why do you refuse to see how evil they are?"

"I'm truly sorry, but I disagree," she'd said, rubbing my arm. "You'll fare better if you leave the military to make their decisions."

I was too dumbfounded to respond. She had made up her mind about the war and the way things ought to be. Her father and his thoroughly Tory patrons had clearly influenced her thinking.

Part of me could see her point. Yes, Christopher's death was tragic, but I couldn't bring him back or expect to make any changes. However, I also couldn't imagine pretending as if nothing happened. That was where we differed, and I didn't know what to do about it.

She pressed me to join her for the play. "I simply insist that you come to the theatre. My father wouldn't hear of me attending alone, and you're the only friend who genuinely appreciates a good play."

Eventually, she wore me down. "I'll go, but don't expect me to be at my best. Please, let's make an early night of it."

She'd given me a warm embrace. "Thank you, dear Betty. It will be good for you to take your mind off that disagreeable prison. Perhaps you'll have an opportunity to talk with the major."

He was the last person I cared to see. "You must understand, he means nothing to me, and I mean nothing to him, and that isn't apt to change."

Celeste tilted her head. " 'The lady doth protest too much.' "

It was no use. She could continue thinking whatever she cared to think. I had much more on my mind than John André.

As I neared Oakham and Townsend, four soldiers stepped directly in front of a horse pulling a creaking wagon. The driver managed to turn the frightened horse before it ran them down. The horse threw back its head and neighed; the soldiers laughed and entered Rivington's coffeehouse at the corner. I wished the horse had given them all a good stomping.

Drops of rain hit my gown and face as I was about to reach the shop, making me wish I hadn't come. Then the door opened and Celeste's mother and two youngest sisters exited.

"Betty, how lovely to see you, my dear," Mrs. Walker said.

"Good morning, Mrs. Walker. Hello, girls."

Susan, age eight, and Rebecca, nearly five, put forth shy smiles. Both were missing baby teeth.

Their mother frowned at the sky as she opened her umbrella. "I'm afraid we must make haste before we're all quite wet. I regret I was out yesterday when you called on Celeste. Do come for tea soon, won't you? Your mother too. It's been too long since we've seen each other."

"Yes, we shall. Thank you." I opened the door as they hurried off.

Inside, Robert turned from the far wall, holding a small pile of men's shirts. He adjusted his spectacles. "Cousin Betty."

I wiped raindrops from my face. "Joe said you wished to see me again."

He set the shirts on the counter and showed me to the desk where we'd sat two days before. "There is a matter of immense importance I believe we should discuss."

I perched on the chair's edge. "Very well. What is this matter of *immense* importance? It's beginning to rain, and I shouldn't stay long."

Robert blinked several times and licked his lips before he spoke.

"When you were here, I told you that I am not as neutral in regard to the war as you may think."

This is important?

He continued. "It is more than true. I have read and reread Thomas Paine—I expect you are familiar with him—and I embrace his reasoning. Plus, all that happened to my father and our farm has opened my eyes to the wrongs done by the British and the absolute need for complete independence from England."

He paused, appearing to assess my reaction. He'd hardly ever spoken that many words to me at one time.

I remained still. "I'm listening."

"For a month or so, I . . . I have undertaken the task of providing what intelligence I can regarding the British here in the city, hoping to be of assistance," he said. "Of course, no one must ever know."

"Providing intelligence." I stretched the words as I said them, imagining their full meaning. "Do you mean you're . . . passing information to . . . to whom?"

"If the information is useful, it is ultimately sent to Washington."

General Washington? I worked the nubs on my left hand. "What are you saying?"

He stared at me, as if the answer were obvious. "I am saying I obtain information that may aid the Continental army in defeating the British."

Shadows moved across the floor as individuals hurried past the shop. The clock ticked while I tried to absorb his words.

"They frequent my store," he said, "making purchases for their barracks or the ships. Or I meet them at the wharves. I am working at the *Gazette* now as well, as a reporter of sorts, and I have a share in Rivington's coffeehouse. It affords me an opportunity to ask questions or hear conversations, and anything I believe is useful, I send along via verbal or written reports."

No wonder he was uncharacteristically friendly with the customers the day before. Had he only been prodding them for information?

"That could be dangerous, could it not?" I asked. "If anyone discovered . . . But why are you relating this to me? Does Joe know anything?"

"Joseph has no inkling, I am certain." He licked his lips again. "No one knows."

The theatrics were becoming annoying. "Again, why are you telling me?"

Robert's eyes narrowed. "You have connections unlike anyone else with the officers stationed in New York, due to your frequent attendance at their parties and such. You have met them, danced with them, earned their trust to a degree, I imagine. You are surely able to engage them in conversations regarding their duties that I myself cannot."

This was becoming more confusing by the minute. In what way did my social life have any bearing on his activities? Nevertheless, I tried to answer truthfully.

"I don't know anyone well. I only attend with my friend, Celeste Walker. Her mother and sisters were leaving as I came in."

"But you do have opportunities to talk with the officers, do you not?"

Thunder rumbled, accompanied by raindrops hitting the front window. I tried to ignore it and instead follow this confusing conversation.

"Of course, although . . ." I was sorry to disappoint him. "I danced with the new Intelligence Director recently, but we talked only of silly things, nothing of his duties. And he deserted me on the dance floor."

Robert was silent for a few seconds. "Major André."

"Yes, but Robert, I'm afraid I don't understand what you're trying to say."

He leaned forward. "Cousin, you could be a valuable link in the chain, unlike any other."

A link in what chain? The clock ticked on. Thunder shook the building.

'Tis only thunder—
Then I bolted upright, suddenly realizing what he meant.

"You want me to spy?"

I held out my hands, wishing to put a halt to this insane idea. "I am not participating in your *chain* or whatever it is. Absolutely not." I gathered my reticule and umbrella and stood to go.

Robert jumped from his seat and caught my arm. The look in his eyes—I'd never seen him so earnest.

"The king is a tyrant. You know firsthand what his armies did to Long Island, to your father's farm, to those prisoners . . . all of us. And the taxes imposed on the colonies by Parliament are ruining the lives of good men and women, not to mention the American economy as a whole. If this war is the only way to rid our land of such oppression, then so be it."

He relaxed his hold. "And you, with your access to those in authority, could learn what no one else can. It may well affect the outcome of the war."

I eased my arm free and took a deep breath. I wished Robert would do the same.

He continued. "General Washington calls it a ring, not a chain. The Culper Ring."

"Culper Ring?" I laughed a little at the name. Was this my simple, law-abiding, bookish cousin I used to know? "No, thank you. It's entirely too dangerous. Out of the question."

I crossed to the door, then turned back to face him. "But you needn't worry. I won't mention any of this or your involvement to anyone."

Robert hurried ahead of me to the door and stood with his back against it, blocking my way. "You have always been trustworthy. That is the primary reason I asked you."

He eased his stance, lowering his voice again. "We have spoken long enough. Should you, by chance, reconsider, have Joe bring me one of your spice cakes. I will inform you when it is safe to meet."

He moved aside. Rain pounded against the door. I never wished to be home more than at that moment, yet perhaps I should delay my exit.

I turned around. "Are you the only person involved in this scheme?"

Robert ran his hands across his apron. "There is a mutual acquaintance."

I almost pressed for the name, but frankly, I'd had enough, thunderstorm or not.

I opened my umbrella. "Do be careful, cousin."

Rain pelted the brick pavement as I left the shop. A fierce wind gusted off the harbor, blowing straw around from the stables next to Rivington's. Newspapers twisted down the street and landed in mud puddles. Down the street toward Fraunces Tavern, a coachman pulled his horse-drawn carriage to a stop as the wind whipped the tricorn from his bald head. I kept a firm hold on my umbrella as I started for home.

It was enough of a shock to think of Robert doing anything remotely against the law; quite another to imagine him at the center of a clandestine spy operation. *And he thinks I should participate because I happen to socialize on occasion with the military?*

Conversations with them usually concerned trivial matters—dance steps, the canapés, or the weather. The play and reception the following night with Celeste would be more of the same.

How foolish of him to think I could contribute anything worthwhile to the Patriots—even if I had the desire to do so. Yes, my doubts had grown substantially regarding the rights of the British to remain in America, and yes, I hated the men who killed Christopher, but how could I consider becoming a *spy*? And what mutual acquaintance was involved? Questions hit me like the driving rain.

All I knew was that Robert had best take care. The last I heard, the penalty for someone caught spying was death by hanging.

A jagged bolt of lightning sliced the black clouds churning over New York. I bit back a scream. I needed an escape. I looked left, right . . . where was I to go?

Ahead was the apothecary's shop. Breathless, I hurried over slippery stones and threw myself against the door, but found it locked. I huddled in the doorway under the awning, shaking. Thankfully, no one heard my cries.

You're not worthy.

I took deep breaths to still the voice, yet the storm raged on.

Peggy Shippen, drawn by John André while in Philadelphia.

Eight

The next evening, Celeste and I walked beneath the long entryway canopy to the red wooden doors of Theatre Royal. Despite the excitement of seeing a new play, it simply felt too soon to be out among all those pompous elites who knew nothing of Christopher. If only I hadn't allowed her to coerce me into attending. Perhaps I would feign illness and leave early.

Two placards announced the evening's attraction.

Theatre Royal presents

a play in two acts

for Ladies and Gentlemen

"The Recruiting Officer"

featuring Adjutant General Major John André

Celeste let out a tiny gasp. "The major has a featured role. Now, don't say you're sorry you came."

It made no difference to me what his role was in the play. He was one of *them*. "For a newcomer to British headquarters, he's wasting no time in making a name for himself."

The storm from the previous day had washed away the stifling air and delivered a cool breeze off the water. But rather than calming my troubled thoughts of Robert and his new venture, I could think of little else. He'd always used prudence, yet I worried for him. And I still wanted no part of it.

Once we were inside the theatre, an usher led us to our seats in a stuffy upper box. Below on the main floor, dark velvet draperies covered the large stage. Hundreds of voices buzzed as men and women milled about and found their seats.

I wore my favorite gown, white satin with a pale blue sash. Mother had made over the gown after I discovered it in Grandmother's old trunk, letting out the bodice, shortening the puffed sleeves, and adding a front panel of leftover lace. Alice had given it a good soak in lemon water and dried it in the sun, returning it to its original, snow-white glory.

Fanning my neck and laying aside my thoughts of Robert, I admired the décor and watched the assemblage. I turned to Celeste. "It's unfortunate that Long Islanders frown upon live theatre. We've seen excellent plays here in New York."

"So true," she said. "Did you know this was previously called the John Street Theatre until the British took the city?"

They couldn't even leave a theatre alone. "The military renamed it?"

"No need to sound so incensed, Betty. It does belong to the king now."

I couldn't fathom how the king could simply claim ownership of the theatre any more than when his army took possession of our farm. "Do they think they have the right to everything?"

Ignoring my question, Celeste pointed out officers we knew as they moved up and down the aisles. "I'm not familiar with this play," she said. "What sort of character do you suppose the major will portray?"

"I cannot imagine. Regardless, he must have prior acting experience to be given a lead role."

A woman seated behind us leaned forward. "Oh, Major André is quite the actor. I was told he painted all the backdrops as well. He's exceptionally talented. You should hear what they say of him in Philadelphia."

Before either of us could respond, the lamps were dimmed, voices hushed, and the stage curtains opened.

Set in an English town called Shrewsbury, the play commenced with two recruiting officers: Captain Plume, played by Major André, and Captain Brazen, enlisting townsfolk for the army. From there, the story became a convoluted mix of characters masquerading as other characters for assorted reasons.

The audience roared with laughter at all the humorous lines. I managed to follow along, yet it struck me how fitting it was for the military, with all their self-righteous pretense, to stage a play with that as the theme. No wonder they were enjoying themselves.

The witty plot moved quickly, and it took all my concentration to keep track of which characters were pretending to be someone else and which ones were themselves. I had to admit "Captain Plume" clearly outshined the other actors with his performance. The play ended happily with all the disguised characters revealing their true identities, and the cast took their bows to plenty of huzzahs and bravos.

Celeste insisted we attend the reception. I was hungry, so I consented. We followed the other theatregoers across John Street to a private home and entered a lamp-lit, richly carpeted salon. Tables festooned in billowy white silk were laden with fine food and beverages on gilded trays. Red and yellow roses in silver vases accented the tables.

I spoke quietly to Celeste. "It always amazes me how the military, not to mention the wealthiest citizens of New York, manage to acquire the very best for these events amid all the shortages."

"Yes, it is interesting, isn't it? My father received the order for the wines with little notice, and he was able to oblige, thanks to the privateers. He claims virtually anything can be purchased by those willing to pay."

"And what of those who are simply unable to pay?"

Celeste gave me a blank stare. "I suppose it's another effect of the war."

Her laissez-faire attitude was disconcerting to say the least. The war was disrupting lives in ways most of us could hardly fathom. Mother and I had tried to help a few prisoners while Alice took food to the hungry in Canvas Town, but how much of an impact did our measly efforts truly make?

As the room filled with guests, the play's director introduced the cast members one by one. Each was greeted with enthusiastic applause.

"And last but not least," the man said, "playing Captain Plume, our one and only, highly esteemed Major John André!"

The celebrity of the evening made a grand entrance as his

admirers applauded and cheered. He bowed to the room before circulating among the guests.

"Ah," Celeste beamed. "It appears I'm finally about to meet him, and you're going to meet him again."

I started to turn away. "No, that won't be necessary. I really—"

She pulled me by the hand. "We must move closer."

"Celeste . . ."

She wove us between guests until we stood immediately behind him. With his back to us, Major André chatted with three wide-eyed ladies who were clearly awestruck to find themselves in his presence.

Celeste moved to his right, waited for an opening, and curtsied. "I'm so pleased to finally meet you, Major."

He turned. "A pleasure, Miss—"

"Walker," Celeste tugged my sleeve. "And I believe you know—"

The major's dark eyes shone as he reached for my hand. "Miss Floyd, how delightful to see you again."

"Good evening, Major." At least he still remembered me. My heart raced, but I had no intention of curtsying. Instead, I gazed at his cravat to determine if it still held a rose tint.

His expression turned mischievous. "I am relieved to see you aren't holding a cup of punch."

Does he find it entertaining to embarrass me? "Sir, you said yourself you were pleased it happened."

"I did say that." He licked his lips, as if considering his next line.

The other guests pushed closer, eager to speak with him.

"You mustn't let us keep you," I said. "Congratulations on your performance."

Celeste curtsied again. "You were wonderful, Major."

"My thanks, ladies," he replied. "We shall see if my portrayal of Captain Plume is worthy of a good review from Mr. Rivington."

He acknowledged a group engaged in conversation near us. The *Gazette* publisher raised a glass to the major. If the two men only knew that my own cousin was using his position as Rivington's reporter to spy on half the men in the room.

Celeste excused herself to speak with friends. I gave her a how-dare-you-abandon-me look before she swished away.

A uniformed servant approached with a tray of tall champagne flutes. Major André took two and handed one to me. "I believe this is English champagne and not French."

"Let us hope so, Major. Although French champagne is often superior." *Perhaps I shouldn't have said that, yet 'tis true.* "Pity the French are coming to the aid of the Americans." *I definitely shouldn't have said that.*

His eyebrows lifted. "So, you have heard the rumors. No cause for concern." He took a quick glance around the room. "I regret there doesn't appear to be any plans for dancing."

I couldn't resist. "That is unfortunate. Yet perhaps you won't be suddenly called away, either."

He lowered his voice. "You must forgive me for my sudden desertion the night of our meeting. General Clinton—"

I held up my hand, the left one, then hid it away in my gown's folds. "No need to apologize. I am aware that you are a busy man with a job to do."

He looked toward the ceiling. "The war goes on, even as we dance, like it or not."

"Who could possibly like war?" I took a long, slow drink from my glass, swallowing the boldness it provided. "Unless it's you officers here in New York, who rarely see battle and are paid to . . . What precisely do you do, Major?"

"My position is Director of Intelligence."

"I'm aware of your position. But what is it you *do*?"

I could almost hear my mother: *Elizabeth, what has gotten into you?*

"A number of things, actually." He raised his glass and squinted at it. "All related to gathering information about the Continental army and its plans." His gaze swept the room as he took another drink.

Prodding him was rather fun. *Sorry, Mother.* "And your acting? Is that part of it?"

"Merely something I enjoy. Although, there are times in my profession when one must be a good actor as well."

Robert and his Culper Ring should have been having this conversation with him, not me. I raised my glass and touched it to his. "Indeed."

Just when I thought he was ready to end the conversation, he guided me away from the growing number of guests anxious to talk with him. "Tell me, Miss Floyd, have you always lived in New York City?"

I tried not to show my surprise. "I was raised on Long Island. My father died of influenza, then my family and I came to New York not long after the . . . when the rebels departed the city. Right after the fire."

I hoped he wouldn't ask for more details. I wasn't exactly in the frame of mind to discuss my history.

"And do you and your family find the city to be a pleasant place to now call home, after idyllic Long Island?"

I took another swallow of champagne, thankful for something to do while thinking of the best way to reply. "My mother inherited her mother's house, so I suppose that has made it feel something like home. I don't know if I would call Long Island idyllic. Perhaps it was, at one time. However, I do miss our farm."

"And what became of your farm?"

So, he did want more details. I looked him in the eye. "I haven't the faintest idea. It was billeted. Even our beehives became a British colony."

"Of course." He lowered his gaze momentarily. "I am sorry."

He downed the rest of his champagne, and I fully expected him to excuse himself. Instead, he stepped closer. "Do you enjoy the city's social events, Miss Floyd?"

I eased myself back a half-step. "When I am able to attend. There's always much to do in helping to run the household, and I tutor my younger brother." I nearly stopped there. Why didn't I? "And my mother and I . . . my mother visits . . ."

I caught myself before racing ahead with tales of my trips to Rhinelander's to care for Patriot soldiers. "Our housekeeper takes food to those living in the tents at the river. I help her prepare it."

What did any of that have to do with whether I enjoyed New York's social life? Thanks to the bravado that comes with drinking champagne too quickly.

If he noticed my discomfort, he didn't reveal it. "You tutor your brother?"

I was relieved to change the subject. "Yes, Joseph. He's twelve, and quite a sponge when it comes to books. I'm teaching him the little French I know, along with the usual subjects. Mother wants to enroll him in King's College when he's old enough."

"*Parlez-vous français?*"

"*Oui, je parle un peu.*"

"*Merveilleux.* And does Joseph share your mother's enthusiasm for college?"

"Yes, although he's a bit of an adventurer. There are times when I would not be surprised if he ran away on a privateer boat."

We were interrupted by another young officer and his pretty wife. After brief introductions, I excused myself when it was clear they wished only to speak with the major.

It could not have come at a better time. Those champagne bubbles threatened to make me belch. I drained the last drop from my glass and set it down on a bookshelf, then nodded to a man leaning on a cane and giving me a haughty stare.

Once I found Celeste, she grabbed my hand. "I thought you'd never stop talking." Her eyes were wide. "Tell me everything."

I steered her to the generous buffet. Food would help clear my head. "He asks far too many questions. We discussed his work. And my brother."

A servant handed us each a gold-trimmed plate. I used the table to steady myself.

Celeste frowned. "Are you ill?"

"'Tis the champagne." I reached for a napkin to pat my forehead.

"You must eat." She helped herself to a thin slice of cold ham. "I learned what took place in Philadelphia."

I filled my plate with tiny sandwiches and cheeses, waiting for whatever Celeste had heard of the major's conquests prior to his arrival in New York.

"He gave an elaborate celebration—the largest ever seen anywhere, they claim—with costumes, a jousting tournament, absolutely no expense spared. And word has it that he had an affair or two. *And* a wealthy woman named Peggy Shippen stole his heart, but then she married one of Washington's top generals, a Mr. Arnold. Can you imagine?"

I studied the crudités platter and pretended to be disinterested in the news. "You managed to gather a great deal of gossip in a few minutes."

She gave me a knowing look as she chose a pickle. "One of the ladies I spoke with attended that party—they called it the Meschianza." Celeste laughed and waved her pickle toward the ceiling. "An acquaintance of hers knows this Miss Shippen quite well."

If it were true about Miss Shippen, Major André was undoubtedly still reeling from a broken heart. Doubly broken, I would think, from her choosing an American over him.

What would have attracted her to General Arnold? He couldn't possibly be better looking than the major. Perhaps he had money, although Celeste said Miss Shippen was already wealthy.

A servant placed a heaping tray of sweets on the buffet. I helped myself to a stuffed date from the top.

I shouldn't have been giving it so much thought. "None of that is any of our business, you know. He's no different than the rest of the officers. All self-absorbed and certain they are right about everything."

I bit into my date and considered my assessment. In truth, Major André gave the impression of being more considerate than the majority. Or perhaps he was simply a good actor—a most intriguing actor.

Celeste giggled. "Betty, what does it matter? He's a gentleman, extremely handsome, and a man of many talents."

I tended to agree with her. "I suppose it doesn't. Let's enjoy the party."

Across the room, I caught a glimpse of Major André laughing hysterically as a woman I knew, Mary Shepherd, whispered something in his ear. At her side, her sister Dorah joined in their amusement.

No, he was no different than the majority. Nothing but a cad, flattering me with attention one minute and someone else the next. Perhaps he wasn't nursing a broken heart after all. Would he bother to seek me out before the evening ended? And why was I even wondering?

After we ate, Celeste and I joined a group we'd met at a party earlier that summer. We made the rounds of reintroductions and accepted more champagne. I held the glass but made a point of not sipping from it, all the while fighting the urge to establish the major's whereabouts and see which woman he was laughing with now.

An announcement was then made that he would be reciting a portion of his lines from the play. Chattering with anticipation, the guests fanned out to the sides of the room as the major moved to the center, dressed once again as the indomitable Captain Plume.

Even though I was hoping to remain near the far wall with our friends, the crowd moved in until I was gradually pushed from behind and standing on the inside edge of the circle. He'd probably think it was deliberate, yet I was trapped.

He began with lines from a scene in Act I, gradually turning so that everyone could hear.

"'I'm resolved never to bind myself to a woman for my whole life, 'til I know whether I shall like her company for half an hour . . . if people would but try one another's constitutions before they engaged, it would prevent all these elopements, divorces, and the devil knows what.'"

His rapt audience chuckled. As on the theatre stage, it was impossible not to be mesmerized, such was his command of the role. Finally, he faced me, rested his gaze, and recited the final monologue of the now reformed Captain Plume:

"'But the recruiting trade, with all its train
Of lasting plague, fatigue, and endless pain,
I gladly quit, with my fair spouse to stay,
And raise recruits the matrimonial way.'"

The room erupted in applause. "Huzzah! Huzzah!" Women blushed and attempted to hide their amusement behind their fans. As Major André removed his Captain Plume hat and took a deep bow, my arms and face warmed until I was certain they matched the roses on the tables.

What was the matter with me? He'd charmed every female in the room, and he knew it full well. The man was a complete rake.

On Sunday, Alice knocked on my door and entered with a pot of tea and a plate bearing a thick biscuit slathered in honey.

"Your mother and Master Joe are goin' to church, and it's time for you to go with 'em. Might bring you some peace."

I answered from my bed. "No, 'tis too soon. I don't want to see anyone."

Alice pulled open the doors of my wardrobe. "I'm not askin', I'm tellin'. You saw plenty o' folk at that play and it done you no harm. Here, wear this." She pulled my green gown from the shelf, one of two I saved for church.

Before I could protest, Mother hurried in, tying on her petticoat. "Alice is right. It will be good for you to go, Elizabeth. If it will help, we'll leave the moment the last song is sung."

By the look on her face and Alice's, there was no use in arguing.

Joe rapped on my door. "Are you coming or not?"

I'd been ambushed.

All the Floyd family had been members of the Congregationalist church for years. But when the British took New York, any church not turned into an army barracks or prison was closed or forced to use the Anglican order of service. So, for the time being, most New Yorkers became Anglicans, as did we.

The Quakers were the exception. Their official position favored the Crown but not the war. That is, until Thomas Paine's *Common Sense* caused an uproar among his fellow Friends, inciting some members to take the Patriots' side, as Cousin Robert had secretly done. Traditional Quakers, however, stuck to their convictions as advocates of British rule, and their meeting house had been allowed to remain open. Robert attended faithfully, yet their Loyalist viewpoint must have irked him to no end.

The closest church to our house, St. Paul's Chapel on Broadway, happened to be the largest and most beautiful church in the city. It belonged to Wall Street's Trinity Church and was built to accommodate worshippers from the more northern neighborhoods, but when the great fire consumed Trinity, the number of individuals attending St. Paul's grew overnight.

On the path, Mother turned around to urge Joe to hurry. "Let's hasten, son. We mustn't be late."

He sauntered behind us, craning his head for a better look across the road at the area known as Holy Ground. Mother hated that it was practically next door to St. Paul's and that her letters of protest to the rector had gone unanswered.

A conglomeration of small alleys filled with ramshackle lean-tos, Holy Ground had sprung up after the fire. According to certain hushed conversations I'd heard at parties, all sorts of despicable sins could be indulged within its brothels and other houses of ill repute. With thousands of British military members now in New York, it was a well-known fact that business there was thriving.

The church's ornate spire rose ahead of us. We entered through the double doors facing the river, and Mother led us to a back pew on the right side of the main aisle. The army was well-represented; their smug faces and white wigs dotted the pews. Accompanying them were their wives and children—or, as I knew in some cases, their mistresses.

People continued to file in and took seats in the main sanctuary or in the balconies, where most of the pews had been paid for and were reserved by well-to-do members. I recognized several faces from previous Sundays. Yet I was relieved that Major André was not present. He was too much of a distraction. If I happened to see him again at the occasional social gathering, that would be more than enough.

We opened our hymnals and stood for the first hymn, led by Reverend Inglis. Originally stationed at Trinity, he'd moved to St. Paul's after the fire. His wig reminded me of a newly shorn ewe.

Once we were seated, he delivered a flaming sermon on the sovereignty of God and His blessed servant King George III. God had always been on Great Britain's side, he thundered from the pulpit. Therefore, its mighty army would prevail over George Washington and his rebellious band of misfits.

Most in attendance nodded in agreement. The faces of the officers seated around the church looked about to burst with pride. Any minute, I half expected them to give themselves a standing ovation and shout their huzzahs. All that was missing was the royal fife and drum corps marching up the aisle and playing a hearty rendition of "God Save the King."

Not that long ago, all their showiness wouldn't have bothered me. Before the outbreak of hostilities, loyalty to England came naturally to most, despite the complaints that circulated through the farms and towns of Long Island. Then, even with all the changes the war had brought to my family, we still had identified with the mother country even if we saw the Patriots' reasoning, and I took the war in stride. But that was before the murder of Christopher Martin.

Now that I despised her army and their treatment of military prisoners, now that Robert was secretly doing his part to assist General Washington, I questioned everything. Where did I truly stand? And what was the prize should Britain win this war—the right to do as she wished with her subjects and the vast land this side of the Atlantic?

Like an unwelcome gust of wind, Major André entered my mind again. Was he aware of the prison atrocities? Perhaps I should have been more daring at the reception and described the dead cart at Rhinelander's, heaped with the bloody bodies of men younger than him. Would he have cared or simply waved his manicured actor's hand and ascribed it to the evils of war, as Celeste had done? *"War goes on, even as we dance."*

Beside me, Mother let out a heavy breath. She had to feel the same conflict as I did, yet she wouldn't dare speak of it to anyone. We were living not only in Tory country but in the heart of Britain's war headquarters in America. It was no place for argument from two farm women.

She gave me a warning look. *Keep it to yourself, Elizabeth.*

Rubbing absently at the nubs on my left hand, I said a fervent prayer for wisdom.

Nine

August 1779

Sitting on the bottom step outside our kitchen, I broke off the ends from the string beans heaped in a bowl at my feet. If they weren't ready for the pot by the time Alice needed them, she'd have my head.

When we gave two loaves of fresh bread to our neighbors, Mr. and Mrs. Richards, they had reciprocated with a half bushel of beans from their garden. We would preserve the majority for winter by stringing them up in the attic and, if I could work fast enough, eat the rest with our midday meal. By the looks of things, however, we'd be eating beans for the next several days.

Joe and his three-legged new friend played near the kitchen's brick wall.

"Please stop pestering that pitiful creature and come help me," I said.

Joe tickled the cat under its chin. "I'm teaching him to pounce so he can catch mice. And he has a name."

I repeated the appellation he'd settled on that morning. "Do you still wish to call him Triple?"

"*Oui*. Three is a lucky number. He's a *chat chanceux*."

I grabbed more beans and corrected his pronunciation. Triple *was* one lucky cat. If Joe hadn't rescued him, he would likely have starved, or some animal in possession of the proper number of legs would have devoured him by now.

"He's lucky that Mother allowed you to keep him. But I still don't see him being of much use."

Joe raised the cat to his chest. "We'll show her, won't we, Triple?"

Mother appeared at the back door to the house. "Everything going well here?"

"I'm buried in beans," I replied, kicking the bowl with my toe. "Did Robert have anything for us?"

She waved a letter and a small package. "A letter from Aunt

Hannah, and something from W. F. addressed to you. Did you write to Uncle William?"

She wouldn't have wanted me to bother him, even with something as serious as the murder of an innocent prisoner. "We haven't seen him in such a long time. I thought it would cheer him."

Apparently, our mail had made it through the military checkpoints once again, although I couldn't imagine why he would send me a package of any sort.

Alice poked her head out of the kitchen door behind me. "How them beans comin'? Meat's half done."

Mother crossed the tiny yard on the path. "We will finish the beans, Alice. And tend to the meat. You should go in and rest."

Alice stepped around me. "It does get mighty warm by the fire this time o' year." She patted her face with the hem of her apron. "I won't be long. Jus' need somethin' to drink."

Mother made Joe come and help with the beans, then she and I took them into the kitchen to add them to the pot of beef and potatoes boiling over the fire. Alice returned and I was dismissed long enough to change out of my work apron and see what the package from Uncle William contained.

The string around it appeared to have been undone and hastily retied, probably by some inspector as it entered New York. Inside the brown paper lay a small, worn volume of poetry by an obscure English poet. An odd gift. I had never expressed a fondness for poetry to Uncle William or anyone else.

Then as I flipped the pages, a folded piece of paper fell to the floor—a letter, in my uncle's elegant handwriting.

> *Dearest Niece,*
>
> *What a delight to receive your letter, as I have been quite preoccupied with this business. It reminds me of the best reason for the work I strive to do, the love and devotion of family and a hopeful future for us all.*
>
> *I remember well the games you and I played when you were small, the guessing games in particular.*
>
> *It pleases me to know that you and your family have*

settled in New York City and that you are enjoying its benefits. However, I understand your dismay regarding the dogs. It is very unfortunate to hear of their plight, especially the one you befriended. Please know that your concerns have reached those who may affect change in that area. We must all remain vigilant and prayerful.

My dear, I will venture to say you remind me of a young love of mine. She, too, is willing to stand for truth and longs for the freedom to be all Providence desires for her. During these changing times, I pray you will take courage and not allow fear to hinder you from wherever the Almighty may lead. I trust you will find your way.

Your devoted uncle,
W. F.

I read the letter again, not wanting to miss the hidden meaning behind his words.

"A young love of mine . . ."

The William Floyd I knew couldn't possibly love anyone more than he loved Aunt Hannah. Yet his intense conviction to risk his life by signing the Declaration of Independence meant only one thing. That young love could be none other than this country—a free nation, the dream of which had captured the hearts of the signers, Christopher Martin, Cousin Robert, and countless others.

I slept in fits and starts that night, my mind creating twisted snippets of Papa, Robert, Major André, Uncle William, and Joe's cat. They each made an appearance, doing the mundane and the extraordinary. Then I was caught in a thunderstorm, much like the night in the barn so long ago. . . . Finally, I dreamed of Christopher in his red neckerchief, smiling from his prison cot.

When I awoke for the fourth time and sleep failed to return, I went to the window, pulled aside the curtains, and turned the iron crank, letting in a warm breeze. Crickets chirped somewhere in the grass below, and a full moon shone between the branches of the elm.

'Twas no wonder I couldn't sleep. Uncle William's letter that day had prompted a barrel of disconnected thoughts. I dumped them out to consider them, one by one.

There was no use denying or dismissing it any longer—I hated the British. Perhaps not every last Tory, but certainly the military. And King George III, most definitely.

What they had done to our farm, to the Townsends, and most of the farms on Long Island was inexcusable. And I shuddered to think of all the brutalities committed along the way, of which I probably only had an inkling.

According to the *Gazette* and other papers, a host of violent deeds were also attributed to the Patriots, namely, to the Sons of Liberty. It was true—they and many others had done their share of instilling fear across the colonies. Riots, tarring and feathering, and murders had spread, all in the name of their desire for self-government.

I'd also recalled hearing that there had been numerous attempts by colonial representatives to compromise or appease the Crown on various matters, ever since the ridiculous Stamp Act, only to be met with more taxes, more restrictions, and finally with force. The Patriots' anger and the actions that grew from it came in defense of freedom and the right to govern the way they chose. America was their home, and they had every right and an absolute duty to defend it from anyone who would deny them that right.

Yet what did I fully know? Britain and America had been fighting in one way or another ever since I could remember. I breathed a long sigh, fluttering the curtains.

I had my own reasons to be angry. Ever since we'd moved to my grandmother's, I'd endeavored to ignore this horrible war. I thought I could enjoy New York's social activities and keep the war from affecting me. Then I'd met the noble, freedom-loving Christopher Martin. His death was the tipping point for me—the last straw, as Papa might have named it. I couldn't ignore the war any longer. Now I wanted revenge for all that my family and I had suffered and for Christopher's needless death.

But what could I do? I couldn't take up arms or destroy the ships in the harbor or poison General Clinton at the next party. And if I were to accomplish such an act, I'd surely be caught and hanged and another man equally as evil would step in to take his place.

The elm's leaves waved in the moon's soft glow as I recalled Uncle William's words.

I pray you will take courage and not allow fear to hinder you.

If only I could go to him for his advice now. What would he say of this desire inside me to retaliate for what the British had done? Would he tell me to be quiet and wait?

I trust you will find your way.

He had found his way by serving in Congress.

Apparently, Mrs. Burgin's way was in helping men escape the prison ships.

Cousin Robert had found a way, through the gleaning of information. And he somehow believed I possessed a unique advantage to do the same.

That voice back in the barn crept into my head. *You're not worthy.*

I covered my ears. I would not listen.

If I were to join Robert and the Culper Ring with the goal of seeking facts and plans of the military's making, could it be used against them? Perhaps their schemes could be stalled or thwarted, and lives could be spared. Or—dare I imagine? Could a bit of information gleaned by me and passed through the appropriate channels affect the course of the war?

Most likely not. Yet, it was a worthwhile desire. And often, small tasks done well lead to big differences.

. . . take courage . . . do not allow fear to hinder you.

Was I willing to take the risk, even if it meant obtaining information from Major André? Along with his obvious gentlemanly talents, I assumed he could be as cunning as a fox. However, I hadn't grown up on a farm without learning the fox's ways. Perhaps I could be just as cunning, if the need arose.

As another breeze swept through the elm and cooled my face, I imagined employing all my charms in beating Britain's Director of Intelligence at his own game.

In the morning, I wore my dressing gown over my shift to the cheerful yellow dining room, where the sun was already casting patterns on the walls through the partially open shutters. A platter of spoon bread lay in the center of the table with a bit of beef left from the previous day.

Alice entered with a steaming tea kettle. "Mornin', Miss Betty," Alice said. "Was you readin' late again?"

I stifled a yawn. "I wasn't reading. But I didn't sleep well."

"That's a shame," Mother said from her chair. "I hope it won't interfere with all we have to do today."

I prepared a cup of strong tea. "As soon as I drink this, I'll be as good as new. I haven't forgotten to make the biscuits." *And something else, if there's still enough nutmeg in the pantry.*

"Good," Mother responded. "Mr. and Mrs. Richards have been so generous to us—I'm glad we can host them for a meal."

"Mr. Richards owns half the privateer boats on the Sound," Joe said. "Isn't that why he can get fresh foods?"

Mother laid her napkin beside her plate. "Now, Joseph, that may be true, but he has a privateering license from Governor Tryon. And I'll have you know that all those beans they gave us came straight out of their garden."

Joe hung his head. "Yes, ma'am."

Her eyes shone. "Alice, I'll help you truss the chickens for roasting. And we'll use my mother's dishes." She rose from her chair. "I must cut some flowers from the garden. The zinnias are blooming nicely, although I wish I could say the same for the daylilies."

I had to laugh. "You're in your element, Mother."

She'd always loved to entertain on the farm, whether for family or acquaintances, reveling in the extra work and thinking of special touches to make guests feel welcome. I had more on my mind than company for dinner, but at least I could rely on Mrs. Richards and Mother to carry most of the conversation.

Mother turned to Joe before she left the room. "I need you to carry the smaller rugs outdoors and beat them. Then run to the grocer for a few items. I'll sweep the floors after I cut the flowers."

She was still chattering about the day's tasks as she headed toward the hall. Alice went to fetch the chickens from the Dicksons' icehouse. After changing into my work clothing, I scraped the breakfast dishes. Joe and I carried them outside to the kitchen.

He dropped his load on the worktable. "Whew. It's hot in here."

"No hotter than usual," I said. "You may go and start on the rugs. I'll wash these dishes, and then I want to bake something for Cousin Robert for you to deliver when you go to the grocer."

"I thought you were going to make biscuits."

"I'll have time, and the oven's exactly right for both. Get going, please."

As soon as I returned all the clean dishes to their places in the pantry, I inspected our flour crock and the nutmeg jar. Yes, there was plenty.

Two hours later, Joe sniffed the basket I handed him. "What am I taking?"

I turned him toward our front door. "A spy cake. Take it straight to Robert before stopping at the grocer."

"What did you say?"

Mercy . . .

"A spice cake, Joe. Spice." I opened the door and gave him a slight shove. "Go, for heaven's sake." I closed the door after him and leaned against it.

The last spice cakes I made were for Christopher and his fellow prisoners, and they had probably wound up in the bellies of the Rhinelander guards. I shut my eyes, remembering that day—the day that led me to this day, this decision.

Very soon, Robert would have my answer to his proposal to join George Washington's ring of spies.

I lifted my apron to wipe my brow. I had now committed to whatever lay ahead.

Persons Names		Alphabet		Directions for the Alphabet
Gen. Howe	718	a	e	
North, Lord	719	b	f	
Germain Ld	720	c	g	
B. Allen John	721	d	h	
Culper Senr	722	e	i	
Culper Junr	723	f	k	
Austin Roe	724	h	b	
C. Brewster	725	i	c	
Rivington	726	j	d	
Places		k	o	
		l	m	
		m	n	
New York	727	n	p	
Long Island	728	o	q	
Setauket	729	p	r	
Kingsbridge	730	q	l	
Bergen	731	r	u	
Staten Island	732	s	v	
Boston	733	t	s	
Rhode Island	734	u	t	
Connecticut	735	v	w	
New Jersey	736	w	x	
Pensylvania	737	x	y	
Maryland	738	y		
Virginia	739	z		
North Carolina	740			
South Carolina	741			
Georgia	742			
Quebeck	743			
Halifax	744			
England	745			
London	746			
Portsmouth	747			
Plymouth	748			
Ireland	749			
Cork	750			
Scotland	751			
West Indies	752			
East Indies	753			
Gibralter	754			
France	755			
Spain	756			
Holland	757			
Portugal	758			
Denmark	759			

Page from the Culper Ring code showing some of the members and their code numbers.

Ten

Robert kept me waiting for three entire days before informing Joe "the article" had arrived and I "may claim it at the store." Fortunately, Joe said nothing about it to Mother nor pressed me for details. I told her I was to meet friends for tea and set out.

The sun shone and the streets bustled with life. Horse-drawn wagons and carriages competed for the road, while the usual number of soldiers, sailors, merchants, and townsfolk crisscrossed Hanover Square and the surrounding walkways. A breeze off the water added the smell of fish and wet wood to the ever-present aroma of horse manure. Flies buzzed over the piles. I shielded my eyes from the blazing sun and watched where I stepped as I neared Oakham and Townsend.

As I reached the shop door, it flew open. A man emerged wearing a cocked felt hat. He barely glanced at me, then turned and hastened toward the waterfront, disappearing around the corner near the *Gazette* office.

Something about him felt familiar. Had I seen him at the theatre or perhaps the reception? Or was he a soldier I'd met another time, out of uniform today? I brushed it off as I entered the shop.

Robert looked up from behind the counter, his expression even more serious than usual. "Come in, cousin."

I crossed the floor and checked for any customers. We were alone.

"The cake was most appreciated." He came around to my side of the counter. "Your brother ate a large portion."

I removed my gloves. "I must say, I wondered if I made a mistake when I didn't hear a word from you, or if you forgot that you asked for the cake and assumed I sent it simply because I'm so fond of you."

Without the smallest reaction to my comment, he opened the door and turned the OPEN sign hanging on the outside to CLOSED, then bolted the door.

"You're locking me in?"

He motioned for me to follow him to the desk where we'd sat a few weeks before. "We cannot be too careful. I waited to summon you until I knew Mr. Oakham would be away. Also, I had other business requiring my consideration."

I took a seat in the chair across from the desk. "Fair enough. Still, three days—"

Robert leaned forward. Sweat beaded on his nose. "I trust you've made the decision to join us?"

"I believe so. But pray, who is *us*?"

He removed his spectacles and pulled a handkin from beneath his apron to wipe his face. "You have given this careful thought?"

I rubbed my left hand, then held it tightly with my right. "As much as possible, without a full understanding of what I must do. I don't know how much help I may be, but I'm willing."

Robert's brow furrowed, his intent stare making me uncomfortable. I took an interest in the objects on the desk: a few old quills, a ledger, a tidy stack of papers and receipts, an open box of nails.

Finally, I leaned back against the chair. "What would you have me do, specifically?"

"Observe. Watch and listen. Eavesdrop, as you are able. Ask questions and get them to talk."

"The officers? Yes, yes, of course. But—in regard to what?" I looked up at the shelves behind him. "How will I know what's useful? I doubt you want me to approach Major André, flutter my fan and say, Sir, I find this entire war incredibly fascinating. Do tell me *everything*."

Rather than lightening his countenance as I intended, his expression darkened. "This is not a game, Betty."

He stood and paced from the desk to the shelves and back. "I may ask you to seek certain information from time to time. However, in general, we are instructed to relay anything we hear in the way of current strategies, movements on land or water, pains taken to secure transports, any adjustments in troops into or out of the city. Above all, no one must know your motivation whatsoever."

"It all sounds a bit dull, to be perfectly honest."

He ignored my comment and further explained General Washington's specific intelligence needs.

Rising from my seat, I wondered if I could retain it all. "So, if I'm understanding correctly, I won't be a spy, per se. More of a reporter." That was the solution—perhaps I would take notes.

Robert stopped pacing and turned. "But there is a significant difference, cousin. A reporter need not keep his identity a secret."

I aimed to reassure him. "I thought you trusted me to do so."

"Yes, yes." He ran his hands over his apron. "But please, you must use discernment. They must never know you are anyone other than the most charming and loyal of all Loyalists."

"You needn't worry." I held my arm toward the door. "Most of them love nothing more than repeating tales of themselves to any woman who will listen. They make a sport of bragging of the power and reach of the king's armies."

"That is what we are counting on. And on you—to make the most of it." He tapped his forehead. "And remember it."

He returned to the desk. I followed, settling once again in the chair.

Robert straightened the pile of receipts. "Report to me, and I shall add it to what I learn myself. But you must be discreet. As soon as possible, come here in the guise of making a purchase or bringing letters to post. If anyone is here, walk by and return later. On occasion, you may come in and browse, but there must be no other exchanges until we are completely alone."

I was a bit mystified at the fuss he was making. "All these precautions—are you certain they're necessary?"

He slapped his hands down on the desk. "Yes, and you must commit everything to memory—nothing written unless I say otherwise. I cannot adequately stress how dangerous that might be for you."

Nothing written. How would I remember the details of what I gathered?

"Are you trying to frighten me, Robert? I appreciate your concern, but you worry far too much. I'm a grown woman and capable of taking care of myself."

He exhaled and spoke in a gentler tone. "If anything should happen to you—"

I raised my hand. "Please, I must ask you again—who were you referring to when you used the word *us*? And by the way, who was the man that left as I came in? I believe I've seen him before."

He stared, taking a moment before answering. "Abraham Woodhull."

Woodhull?

"From Setauket," Robert said. "His father and yours may have done business together. I have known him since my youth."

Setauket wasn't far from our farm on the north side of Long Island, but a good day's ride from Oyster Bay, home of Robert's family.

I remembered now. "Yes, he and my father met on occasion, as I recall. We're distantly related in some way. His family sat near us at church when I was growing up. He never could sit still."

"That would be him. His older cousin was General Nathaniel Woodhull. You must know the name."

I now recalled hearing of General Woodhull's mortal wounds a few years ago as he tried to prevent the British from seizing a large herd of Long Island cattle.

"Ah, I believe Mother said he'd married my father's older sister, Ruth Floyd. But I'm not certain I ever met either of them."

I pondered the family connection. It wasn't unusual for Long Islanders to discover their ancestors had married each other a hundred years ago or more.

"Mother and I saw Mary Woodhull here in New York recently. Isn't she his sister?"

"That is correct. She is now Mrs. Amos Underhill and they run a boarding house. When Abraham is in the city, he boards with them on Queen Street. I rent a room there, as well."

He lowered his voice until I could barely hear him. "Abraham is the leader, if you will, of the Culper Ring. His code name is Samuel Culper Senior."

So, that fidgety boy in church was now in charge of the Ring? I hoped General Washington knew what he was doing.

"Seriously, Robert? Code names?"

He glanced toward the door, as if it would burst open and everything he shared would be spilled out onto the streets of New York.

"This is most serious." He didn't hide how miffed he was. "Everything, especially our true names, must remain a secret."

I shifted in my chair. "I didn't expect anything quite so . . . covert. Do you have a code name?"

He coughed. "Samuel Culper Junior."

"Junior? I would think you'd want something more imaginative."

"Washington's idea." He shrugged. "I suppose the reason is that Culper Senior and I are the main intelligence gatherers."

Now I had a host of questions. "Who else is involved? Does Woodhull know that I've agreed to this? Will I have a code name?"

Robert held up his hands. "There is no need for you to know the identities of any others at this time." He glanced down, then back at me. "Perhaps there is one you should know—Benjamin Tallmadge. He is serving as chief intelligence officer to Washington."

I jerked in surprise. "Reverend Tallmadge's son? I didn't know he entered the military. Before we left Long Island, Mother heard that he graduated from Yale College and went to teach in Connecticut."

"Quite true. He left there to enlist after hostilities erupted. He receives communications from Woodhull and delivers them directly to the general. And, as of today, Woodhull knows your role."

I let out a long breath and considered this fact. "I wonder if he recognized me as he was departing your shop. If so, why would he not at least give a greeting? We were practically neighbors—"

"He most likely knew it was you. I informed him you might come in. He is extremely cautious, however. And quite nervous regarding this entire endeavor."

"Nervous?" I had to laugh. "More than you, Robert?"

He narrowed his eyes, clearly not amused. "I doubt you will have any contact. I have absolutely forbidden him from revealing your name to anyone while he has breath. He knows of your uncle's work, but of course, it is essential that neither your uncle's name nor his ever be mentioned in any connection to you or your work in the

Ring."

A mixture of confusion and doubt swirled through my head. "Why has he undertaken this task if he is so cautious? He strikes me as a man who would avoid conflict at all cost."

"He has good reason. As do I." Robert lowered his gaze. "John Simcoe, the despicable officer who took over my father's house and burned our orchard, brutally beat his father when he went looking for Abraham."

I gasped, trying to imagine his anger. "It's personal then."

"Most definitely. It is also the right thing to do."

I have my own personal reasons.

He continued. "I told him of your connections and your acquaintance with Major André. He is of the opinion, as am I, that you can be most helpful. No code name for you was mentioned, however."

"And why not, if I am to be of service?"

"It is for your protection. Not every member of the Ring has a code name. Nevertheless, each is given a number as part of the communication cipher that Ben Tallmadge has drawn up."

A cipher? What next?

His expression tightened. "We have ascertained the British already know there is at least one spy in New York, due to certain letters being intercepted. Therefore—"

"They know?" The skin on my arms prickled. "But how?"

Robert waved a hand, dismissing my question. "Therefore, the code will enable us to still pass intelligence to the proper channels. In case any of our communications are discovered en route, the code will prevent the enemy from knowing the particulars of what is being sent and from whom. Should they see any of our communications, they will not make any sense of them."

"Do the British employ a code as well?"

"They do, at times, yet ours is superior."

The more we talked, the more I determined what I didn't know. "What sort of code do we use?"

"In essence, it consists of three-digit numbers that correspond to names, places, and so forth. I will explain it in detail, should you need to use it, yet that is highly unlikely."

"Very well." I attempted to sound confident, as if such things were everyday occurrences. "And what is my code number?"

He glanced to the door again before fixing his eyes on mine. "You will be known only as 355. It is the same number in the code for the word 'lady.'"

Lady. *My new identity.*

Suddenly, this was all becoming quite real. "I suppose 'tis better that it be simple."

The clock ticked. My stomach tightened as I slowly whispered my new number/name—the only name I would be known as within George Washington's Culper Ring.

"Three. Five. Five."

Eleven

I sat at Grandmother's worn pine dressing table in Mother's room, facing the small mirror. Alice steadied my shoulder from behind. "Stop your fidgetin'. Your hair's all knotted and it needs a good brushin' if you want me to do anythin' with it."

I planned to wear my hair plaited and pinned a certain way, and Alice was more adept at braids than Mother. And she had more fingers than I did.

"Please hurry," I said. "Celeste agreed to meet me at the ball, and I would hate to keep her waiting."

From her chair beneath the window, Mother did her needlework and supervised the creation of my new hairstyle. "That reminds me. Celeste's mother sent us both an invitation to tea for Thursday next. Shall I accept?"

"Yes, we should go. She mentioned it when I saw her recently."

"Good. Your grandmother would be so delighted that you've been wearing her gown. You did a superb job with whitening it, Alice."

I ran my hand across the gown's blue sash. "It suited the theatre, but I'm not certain it's fine enough for a ball." I focused on Alice in the mirror. "Hopefully my hair will compensate for it."

Alice began dividing and clipping my hair into sections. "I see what I can do. With all them high rolls and wigs they wear, somethin' different be good. Now, be still and let me work."

Since my visit with Robert, I'd practiced being the dutiful daughter and helpful sister, filling my days with endless chores and everyday conversations. But I was eager to try out my new role as 355. After all, how difficult could it be?

Now I would have that chance tonight at the ball given by Mr. and Mrs. Rodney at their home on Wall Street. Celeste's parents had received the invitation weeks ago, but Mr. Walker took ill with a cough, so Mrs. Walker asked the hosts if Celeste and I could attend in their place. Little did Mr. Walker know, and could never know, what good timing his illness might prove to be.

I had my marching orders from Culper Junior, along with his admonishments to not give anyone the slightest reason for suspicion. He'd warned me repeatedly that not a soul could be trusted, not my family, Celeste, or even Joe's cat. A number of high-ranking officers were expected at the ball, including Major André. My main concern would be finding ways to garner useful information, and perhaps something of the military's "movements by land or water," per Robert's request.

As I handed hairpins to Alice, she finished braiding my hair, then wound and looped the braids as I instructed her. She added five white rose buds in the back, claiming she'd "borrowed" them from a neighbor's rosebush. Finally, she pulled loose a few shorter curls at my temples and forehead.

She scrutinized my hair in the mirror. "It should stay put no matter how much dancin' you do."

My thoughts were not on dancing. Yet, what did one expect to do at a ball? I studied my reflection. Unique, sophisticated, not too pretentious—just the impression I hoped to convey.

Joe knocked at the open door, holding his cat. "Messieurs Zhoseph and Triple Floyd, at your service."

"You, sir, may escort me to the ball." I rose from the bench. "But no cat."

Alice reached for Triple. "What did I say, Master Joe? This cat belong outside."

Mother pointed a finger. "Come straight home, young man."

Five minutes later, my brother and I headed toward Wall Street. I tugged his arm to slow him down. "I don't wish to arrive breathless. Has Triple caught any mice yet?"

He paused, letting me set the pace. "No, but he will. He doesn't even know he's missing a leg." He kicked a stone off the path. "Why are you and Miss Celeste invited to so many parties?"

"Because we enjoy dancing, I imagine. And the unmarried men wish to meet unmarried ladies." In truth, some of the married men wished the same, but that was better left unsaid.

"Isn't that the reason for Holy Ground?"

I hoped no one heard him from their open windows. "There is a great difference."

He laughed. "Sorry."

"I suspect you'll enjoy dances and parties when you're older."

"Don't assume you're going to teach me to dance."

It was great fun to tease him. "If not I, perhaps Mother shall."

Minutes later, we neared the Rodney mansion. Music floated into the street through the open double doors.

We spotted Celeste at the same time. "There she is," Joe said. "May I go?"

Other than hoping to steal a glimpse of General Clinton, my brother had no interest in giving anyone the impression he might be attending the ball, especially with his sister.

"Yes, you needn't linger a minute more."

"Don't step on any toes." He gave me a wave before hurrying off.

Celeste approached me wearing a dark blue brocade gown with matching lace petticoat and lace sleeves. I wasn't surprised—her father could afford all the latest fashions for his wife and daughters. In contrast, she wore her hair in a simple style—a much lower version of the high roll.

She gave my arm a squeeze and admired my hair. "Is it Alice's handiwork? You'll be the talk of the ball."

"Oh, I hope not. But thank you."

On second thought, if my hairstyle attracted the right kind of attention from those with the right kind of information, so much the better.

"How fares your father?" I asked.

"The cough makes him ornerier than ever. Mother went to the apothecary and purchased a new remedy. And he's drinking cup after cup of tea with your bees' honey. More honey than tea, I suspect."

"Ah, 'tis good he isn't often ill. You look beautiful, by the way. I'm glad you've taken my advice and no longer wear a mouche."

She laughed as we reached the steps to the house. "Shall we?"

Inside, we greeted our hosts and chatted with Mary and Dorah Shepherd, who both complimented me on my hair. I was tempted to mention seeing them at the theatre reception laughing with Major André, although I wouldn't want to appear as if I cared. My main objective, if he indeed came to the ball, was to learn anything of importance to give to Robert.

The musicians played soft melodies as guests continued arriving in an endless show of finery. I followed Celeste into the expansive, lamp-lit ballroom, and watched New York's most well-known Tories and General Clinton's finest officers parade in, greeting and admiring one another—another wasteful, snobbish event, that they might forget they were at war.

The extremely wealthy and overweight Major-General Oliver DeLancey and his wife entered, along with another couple I didn't recognize. Behind them came Mr. Archibald Kennedy. Where did he reside now that his mansion at Number One Broadway had been commandeered by Clinton, and by George Washington before that? I'd heard his second wife was somehow related to the DeLancey family. Perhaps she owned a house or two where they could live out the war.

Everyone appeared to be wearing their very best, from the ladies' loveliest silks with matching shoes to the officers' laciest cravats and gentlemen's detailed coats. I began to regret my choice of gown.

The Shepherd sisters excused themselves, and I turned to speak in Celeste's ear. "Perhaps I should have worn my rose gown again."

"Nonsense," she said. "You are beautiful from head to toe. Stand straight and look fascinated."

My stays could straighten a ram's horn. "How is it possible to stand any other way?"

The minuet was announced. Mr. and Mrs. Rodney took the floor, signaling the official start of the ball. Then two young officers approached us, whom we knew—the very tall and slender Captain Higgins, and the ever-present Lieutenant Parker, who had eyes only for Celeste. The men bowed and invited us to dance.

I was soon occupied with the gentle movements of the minuet, followed by two more livelier dances. Our partners were quite decent dancers. When the music stopped, the four of us were more than ready to catch our breath.

Celeste and I pulled our fans from our pockets as we made our way to the refreshments table. Crystal goblets waited at one end, silver trays of petit fours at the other. Two uniformed servants poured cups of bubbly champagne punch for us. I restrained myself not to swallow the sweet fizz in one gulp.

Captain Higgins was nearly two heads taller than me, although I was considered tall. I had to back up to see his eyes, which were shaded by dark eyebrows resembling two kissing caterpillars.

"Tell me, Captain," I said, "are you and your men finding New York to your satisfaction?"

He slurped his punch. "Indeed we are, Miss Floyd. New York is a fine city. Nearly as fine as London."

He covered his mouth in a furtive attempt to hide a belch. We all pretended not to notice.

"I should like to see London one day," Celeste said. "As soon as the war is over, and we all return to our normal lives."

Lieutenant Parker had more freckles than any man I'd ever seen. "It cannot come soon enough," he said. "Although I plan to stay in America. Commissioned officers are to receive two hundred acres of land after two years' service, and I've given that already."

"What an excellent plan," I said.

Unless, of course, Britain loses.

How could I ask a more pertinent question? I gave it a try. "If I may ask, gentlemen, exactly how does Britain expect to finish this war?"

The officers exchanged glances. Higgins spoke first. "Miss Floyd, your question is akin to asking the Almighty how He will make it rain. It shall not be a problem, I assure you."

Lieutenant Parker and Celeste chuckled. I took another sip of punch.

Higgins stood even taller. "We're the most powerful army on earth. Our generals far exceed Washington in experience and ability, and our men are better trained and disciplined than his sorry lot of rebels. We also greatly outnumber them."

"Then why haven't you finished them off by now?" I asked. "Please forgive me if I'm mistaken, but wasn't the war expected to be over in '76?"

Captain Higgins looked down at me as if I were a small child. "It won't be long now. The rebels are running low on men, supplies, and I daresay, any new strategies."

"Most colonists want to remain part of the empire, you know," Lieutenant Parker added. "As it should be."

"Enough about the war," Celeste said, setting her cup down. "Let's enjoy the ball, Betty."

I doubted if all they believed was true. And if they held to their attitude, they might be surprised at the Continental army's resolve. Regardless, trying to learn any substantial facts from them seemed futile.

A commotion broke out near the entrance, indicating the arrival of some prominent officer or citizen.

"Ah, if it isn't the governor," Captain Higgins said.

A pudgy-cheeked man wearing a silk frock coat stood in the entrance and was immediately surrounded by a half-dozen men, all competing for the chance to talk with him first.

Celeste stared. "Governor Tryon? How exciting!"

I bristled. So, this was William Tryon, the Royal Governor of New York. Word of him had spread to Long Island well before we'd left the farm. After being named governor, he'd escaped with his life and tried to govern from aboard a sloop offshore when the Continentals took the city.

I'd lost track of what became of him after the British takeover until Christopher Martin told me that Tryon had been the man who'd led the attack on New Haven and captured him. Now, another man shielded his mouth as he spoke in his ear, and Tryon shook with laughter.

As far as I knew, Tryon was to do Parliament's bidding and institute taxes on New York's residents. I wasn't certain if he would be privy to current military strategies, despite his New Haven conquest. I didn't trust myself to stay silent about Christopher should I meet the man now. I held back the urge to walk over and slap his fat face.

Lieutenant Parker asked Celeste, "Care to dance again?"

"Yes, I'd be delighted." She glanced my way, as did Captain Higgins.

I simply wasn't in the mood to dance now. Here was an entire ballroom filled with British officers, and I didn't want to miss the opportunity to discover what they knew.

"Please, go ahead and enjoy yourselves," I said. "Would you excuse me, Captain?"

Higgins frowned, then swirled the punch around in his cup. "Perhaps you'll wish to dance a bit later?"

I didn't want to promise. Ignoring his question, I turned to Celeste. "I'll find you afterwards. There's someone with whom I must speak."

I weaved my way to the opposite corner of the ballroom, out of Celeste's view. How would I continue to attend these occasions with her yet keep from raising her suspicions if I wished to gain any valuable information?

I scanned the room to see who else may have entered. What could be keeping Major André? Robert had said the British suspected there was a spy in New York. It was apparent that he and Abraham Woodhull took great care to work in complete secrecy, and I hadn't even begun yet. But could the major's absence have something to do with the Culper Ring or locating that spy?

Then, there he was, to my right. "Miss Floyd, how delighted I am to see you." Major André was in full uniform with a gentleman dressed in fine civilian clothing at his side.

I felt my cheeks warm. "Good evening, Major. I didn't realize you were here."

He turned to the middle-aged, white-wigged man beside him. "Allow me to introduce Miss Betty Floyd. Mr. William Franklin."

Mr. Franklin offered his hand and spoke with a deep voice. "A pleasure, Miss Floyd."

"My pleasure as well, sir," I said. "Are you possibly related to Mr. Benjamin Franklin?"

His face and neck tensed ever so slightly. "You are referring to my father."

The major blinked, facing me. "Do you know Ben Franklin?"

"Not personally," I replied, "although everyone has heard of him. My grandmother owned several copies of *Poor Richard's Almanack*. I must say, he's certainly improved the mail delivery." I smiled sweetly. "Mr. Franklin, are you a rebel like your father, here to disrupt our delightful city?"

His eyes narrowed and he glanced at Major André before replying. "On the contrary. He and I happen to disagree on many subjects, and in particular, England's sovereign right to the colonies."

Until now, I hadn't noticed that several of his teeth appeared to be missing. He excused himself and went to speak with another man.

"Oh, I'm afraid I upset him."

"No need for concern." The major waved off my comment. "Remarkable fellow. He spent well over a year in prison at the hands of the rebels. And you may be interested to know I lived in his father's home while I was stationed in Philadelphia."

"Did you?" *I doubt Dr. Franklin had any say in that.*

"Now if I may say so, your hair looks quite lovely. Very becoming."

"I'm pleased you like it, Major." I winced, embarrassed at how flirtatious I sounded.

He laughed. "And I am afraid I have a confession to make. I hope you won't be offended."

What would he have to confess? I had a feeling I wasn't going to like it.

He touched his fingertips together. "I inquired a bit about you after we met at the post-theatre reception."

"I beg your pardon?"

"Forgive me if that sounds inappropriate. Rest assured, I have only the highest regard for you."

I struggled to keep from showing my irritation to any observers. "Why would you inquire about me? Simply because you're a spy for the military doesn't give you the right—"

He held up his hand. "Ah, but the Director of Intelligence is not a spy."

I was indignant. "If you're not a spy, then what are you?"

A couple near us turned around. The major chuckled as his ears darkened.

"Forgive my rudeness." I softened my tone. "But please enlighten me as to what this is about."

"If I may explain." He touched his brow. "I kept thinking of you and our one dance, which unfortunately ended too soon."

"That doesn't explain why you made inquiries."

He spoke into my ear. "I wished to know more about you."

How often had he said those words to eager young women? "You could have simply asked me. With whom did you speak? And what did you learn?"

"I only spoke with these ladies." He indicated Mary and Dorah Shepherd as they danced by with their officer partners. "They didn't reveal much more than what you told me yourself that evening. They stated you attended school on Long Island, that your mother inherited your grandmother's home in New York, et cetera."

I wasn't happy knowing I'd been the subject of a conversation without my knowledge, yet it was gratifying that Mary and Dorah hadn't said more. I tried to recall just what I may have told them at our various meetings. And why hadn't they thought to tell me he'd questioned them?

He shifted his feet. "I did learn something new, however. Apparently, you have been caring for rebel prisoners for some time."

My chin started to quiver. Not knowing how to respond, I could only stare dumbfounded at those penetrating dark eyes.

"Don't be alarmed. Is this correct? I'm merely curious."

I forced my voice not to shake. "My mother. . . . She heard of the conditions at the prisons, the overcrowding and such, and wanted to assist however she could. Rhinelander's Sugar House—it's now a prison—isn't far from our home. I accompanied her when she asked me, but . . . I no longer go with her."

The music ended and couples left the floor as the musicians set down their instruments.

I needed to put an end to his curiosity. "I'm sorry to disappoint you, Major, but I'm afraid there's nothing more to know."

He laughed. "On the contrary, I find you quite interesting, Miss

Floyd. In fact, I have a proposition for you. Would you consider returning with your mother to the prison, or even another prison, for the purpose of gathering intelligence for the Crown? As you come to know the prisoners, you could inquire as to their regiment's numbers, plans, and so forth. It could prove quite beneficial to us."

If I wasn't taken off-guard already, I was now. "You want me to spy? For you?"

He glanced sideways. "Well, in a manner of speaking—"

I held up both hands as if to push him away. "Absolutely not. How appalling!" This was much too similar to the time when Robert invited me to join the Ring. I took a deep but shaky breath.

"Forgive me . . . I asked only in the event you might consider it."

I could sense several pairs of eyes directed my way. "I don't wish to discuss it, Major."

He rested a tender hand against my waist. "Very well. Shall we dance when the music resumes?"

My stomach was in more knots than my hair had been that afternoon. If he thought I was capable of dancing now, he was grossly mistaken. Yet I couldn't simply walk away, tempted as I was. I'd been given a task and I was determined to carry it out.

I said the first thing that came to mind. "Perhaps some punch is in order first."

"Ah, excellent idea." He glanced toward the refreshments table. "Please excuse me while I locate the beverages."

The evening was *not* going as I'd planned, to say the least. I'd come eager to play the carefree Loyalist while gathering useful news for General Washington. Yet thus far, I had not only learned next to nothing but had been confronted with my own previous assistance to Washington's soldiers—a potentially treasonous offense. Plus, the Director of Intelligence asked me to spy for their side, also a treasonous offense in the eyes of the United States Congress.

What would Robert think now? He'd likely regret assuming I could keep my personal life a secret or make any contribution to the Culper Ring.

And what of Major André? Did he only find me interesting because he wanted me to spy for the British? And would he be satisfied with my refusal? What did he think of my account of the prison visits? Would he accept my mother's and my desire to be charitable and make no more of it?

Or would he dance with me, then have us arrested in the morning?

I drank two full cups of punch and enjoyed three dances in a row with Major André, including, finally, a lively Allemande from beginning to end. He said no more about his "proposition." My anxiety eased, at least temporarily.

I now had a decision to make—either let this evening pass and wait for another chance to learn the military's plans or make the most of what was left of it. I chose the latter.

Champagne punch or not, I needed to remain sharp. As the musicians stepped away for another break, I leaned as close to Major André as I dared. "If I may ask, do you expect to stay in New York City now, or will you be transferred?"

"I don't foresee a transfer, as long as I can be of use to the general." He bent closer. "Does this please you, Miss Floyd?"

If he planned to have me arrested the next day, he had an odd way of showing it. Then again, he was the consummate actor.

"I will admit, I'm pleased." Flirting came easily, thanks to the punch. "Does that apply to only you or to all the men currently stationed here?"

He frowned. "I cannot speak for what General Clinton may have in mind. I'm not always privy to his plans. We are to hold New York, however."

A cluster of officers stood chatting near us. When their heads turned our way, Major André raised his glass to them.

I tossed my head, careful not to shake loose a braid. "There are those here who still wish to spend some time with you. Perhaps it would be best if you oblige them." I lowered my gaze. "Or there could be rumors."

"Very well. Do not leave before allowing me to bid you goodnight." He took my hand and kissed it.

And perhaps you'll consider visiting me in prison.

He walked toward the officers, taking long but relaxed strides, giving him a rather distinctive gait.

A tap on my shoulder made me jump.

"Someone has been occupying your attention." Celeste raised her brows.

I ignored her remark. "Are you enjoying yourself?"

"Not as much as you, I imagine, although I did meet a very nice gentleman. He rescued me from that silly Lieutenant Parker." She glanced over to the musicians returning to their seats. "I promised him a dance." She hurried away, swinging the skirts of her gown.

The tall mahogany clock near the entrance began chiming the midnight hour. Most of the older guests had already left. Others had moved off to adjoining sitting rooms for cordials and desserts, while the dancing continued in the ballroom. As Celeste and her handsome partner joined a half-dozen other dancers on the floor, I pondered what to do next.

"Beg your pardon, miss." An officer in a tightly curled white wig sauntered over with his arms behind his back. The rum on his breath preceded his words. "I'm Capan . . . Charles Willington. I have been hoping for a chance to sp-speak with you."

Twelve

R obert banged his hand down on the counter. "Why did you ever, *ever* mention your prison visits to anyone? I told you they already suspect a spy in the city."

He slammed both fists, making the jars of nails on the counter jump.

I stood in the center of the shop, heat rising in my cheeks. "You're being ridiculous. How would I have any idea my friends would reveal that I visited prisoners? And it was weeks ago—long before you ever so much as hinted you were in this Ring, and before I met Major André. Regardless, he could have arrested me by now if he wished. I'm certain I defused it." *Mostly certain.*

I went on, riled now. "You know full well there are people who bring food to the prisons from time to time. My mother wouldn't have done so if she had a concern. We paid the sentry; he allowed us in. Simple as that."

"You cannot be certain—"

"Would you please calm down? I've never seen a Quaker become so agitated."

His body went rigid. "Do not bring my religion into this."

I inhaled, wishing to move on to another subject. "There's more I wish to say. I might as well relate everyth—"

The door to the shop opened. We both flinched. I went to examine the display of copper pots, my hands shaking. If only he'd locked the door this time.

A graying, disheveled-looking man and a young Negro boy entered the shop. "Townsend, my good fellow." The man spoke with a heavy Dutch accent. "I trust I'm not interrupting anything."

"Not at all." Robert's tone was carefree. "How may I assist you, Mr. Claassen?"

The man grunted. "Some miserable thieves broke into my house last evening while we were calling on friends. They took money from a drawer and all my rum."

"A terrible shame," Robert said. "Unfortunately, it is a common occurrence."

"Aye, it's the third robbery in our vicinity this month," Claassen said. "We're near the dock at the foot of Broad Street. Those dirty sailors, no doubt. Scavengers, all of 'em, worse than the rats aboard their ships."

He raised his voice, as if he didn't have our attention already. "And with only martial law in place, it's our word against the army's. There's a patrol of sorts to keep the peace, but they cannot be everywhere. It's not enough."

I folded my arms. I may have tapped my foot. Was he ever going to stop talking?

Robert glanced my way. "Perhaps if you place an advertisement in the *Gazette* requesting the apprehension of the criminals, it will help bring it to the military's attention."

"I suppose a notice of some sort may be useful," Claassen replied. "People do advertise everything—"

Robert came around the front of the counter. "I suggest you stop there on your way home. What do you need for your repairs?"

While he and Mr. Claassen discussed how to fix a broken door frame and selected the proper glue and two lengths of trim wood, the boy waited patiently by the door. I caught his eye and nodded, but he dropped his gaze to the floor. They left at last, the boy carrying the wood over his shoulder.

Robert adjusted his spectacles with both hands. "Where were we?"

"I asked you to calm down. Have you?"

"Yes, I suppose." He returned to the counter and wiped it with a rag. "I trust you have something to report other than news of your near arrest."

I moved toward the chair beside the desk. "And I have questions. But first, may we sit down?"

He went to the door to turn the sign and the lock. "We dare not be interrupted again."

As he took his usual chair, I hoped I would not upset him further. "I must first inform you that Major André made a request related to my visits to the prison." I paused without looking at Robert. "He asked if I would consider resuming them in the guise of gathering intelligence from the rebel prisoners. I refused, of course. Adamantly."

Robert let out a soft groan.

"I was completely taken aback," I said. "I made sure he knew I was insulted."

"Do not expect him to take your refusal as your final answer," Robert said. "The man is devious."

"He seemed satisfied, however. We then danced and had a lovely time."

Robert shook his head, pursing his lips. "You must always remember who you are dealing with and the mission you have undertaken. Is that clear?"

For the sake of time, I chose not to argue. "Quite clear."

He sat forward. "You may continue with your report."

I recited the names of all those I remembered who had been present at the ball. I informed him of who I met, who I already knew, and the topics of the conversations.

Robert straightened his papers as he listened, then straightened them again. "That was a good number of words with very little substance."

"I beg your pardon, but I'm new to this." It was my turn to calm down. "Between all the talking and dancing, I was quite fatigued by the time they shot off the fireworks and Celeste and I left."

"Anything else from André, other than his discovery of your deceptive activities and his invitation to spy on prisoners?"

I gave him a cold stare.

The pleasant back-and-forth banter with the major repeated in my head, including our brief but sweet farewell in the presence of various inebriated redcoats. There wasn't much that might interest my cousin, but I wanted to show him I'd given it my best effort.

"He expects to remain in New York for now. He claims he conducts quite a bit of correspondence, but he wouldn't elaborate. . . ." I studied the low ceiling beams as I remembered more. "He lived in Ben Franklin's home in Philadelphia."

Robert exhaled loudly. "Only because the military laid claim to it."

I had no news, after all. "You're disappointed. I did try, but—"

"Perhaps you tried too hard. You must learn to employ a more subtle approach and not appear to be overly inquisitive."

I didn't care to be criticized for my attempts at something so foreign to me. This was all much harder than I'd imagined.

His chair's legs scraped the floor as he adjusted it. "You said you have questions."

Where to start . . .? Ah, here's a question. Why did I consent to this?

I looked down at my hands to think. "First of all, I don't know enough about the war or politics to know what to ask. I fear I have already exhausted my knowledge of it. For example, how do I inquire about 'movement on land or water,' as you requested? Would you be willing to help me?"

"I can give you a clearer understanding. Yet truly, in your lack of it, no one will suspect you of anything. Too much and you could raise suspicions. Does that make sense?"

I groaned. "It does. However, I don't like it."

He opened the top drawer of his desk. "Next question."

"If I do obtain detailed information, how am I to remember all of it if I am not to write anything? You said there's a written code. Can you explain it to me? May I use it? And how do you pass information to Woodhull? Do you wait until he comes to New York?"

As I talked, he withdrew a sheet of paper from the drawer and a quill pen. Then he pulled a ring of keys from his apron pocket, unlocked a lower drawer, and retrieved a small bottle.

"Perhaps I will show you the code, but there is no reason at this point for you to put anything in writing. Your memory is your best asset." He tapped his temple with the end of his pen.

"As for passing on information," he said, "there is a courier we employ when Culper Senior is not in New York. He sees that any correspondence is personally delivered to him."

So, another member of the Ring. "Can he be trusted? Is he fast?"

"Yes, and he is. Repeat the names of those at the ball, please."

He dipped the quill tip in the bottle and began writing, but nothing appeared on the paper.

I reached for the bottle. "Something's wrong with your ink."

He pulled it away. "Do not touch. It must be used sparingly."

I stared at the dark bottle in his hand, and the blank sheet of paper. "What exactly is it?"

"A special ink, developed for the purpose of passing on information undetected. Invisible ink."

I stared at the paper and the wet markings he'd made. "But how—"

"The recipient, who in most cases is General Washington, is in possession of a reagent that, when applied, reveals what is written." Robert lowered his eyes to the paper. "Repeat the names, please."

I went through the names again while Robert wrote them with the strange ink. "William Franklin. Governor Tryon. His aide, Captain Willington, who was quite drunk and annoying, by the way. Archibald Kennedy. Rivington was there, as always. The DeLanceys . . . Oh, I heard someone behind me mention the name Cunningham."

Robert looked up. "The Provost at Bridewell?"

"I assume it was him. I didn't want to look, but I detected an Irish accent. Alice says he's the devil."

"She may be correct." He tapped the quill against the bottle. "I am troubled by the relationship between Major André and William Franklin. What did you make of it?"

I recalled the meeting. "I'm not certain if they're well acquainted. However, the major informed me that Franklin was in an American prison for a year. He and his father are apparently at odds over the war. It was clear he didn't like to hear his father's name mentioned."

Robert scratched his chin. "It could be nothing, but if you see or hear any more of Franklin, I want to know. And what of General Clinton?"

"He was absent. Everyone wanted to speak with Tryon, however."

"Tryon is a ruthless bastard. Pardon me for saying so, but there is no better term. He was part of a plot to kill General Washington in '76."

I shivered at the thought of the evil minds that had merrily danced and sipped champagne alongside Celeste and me, with their gentlemanly manners and polite words.

"I met others, but I did not hear the names," I said. "Captain Higgins and I danced. He's rather dull. Celeste danced with Lieutenant Parker. He's so confident of victory that he's ready to claim his gift of American land from the king."

Robert snorted. "An incentive for service in the army. Instead, he and the rest of the opportunists will be on the first brig back to England."

I delighted in the prospect. "Now may I please see the code?"

He replaced the stopper in the bottle of invisible ink. "Very well, if you have nothing else to add to this dismal report."

He was getting on my last nerve, and I sensed he knew it. "I'm afraid not. I thought I might learn more as the night progressed, but by the time Captain Willington approached me, I decided it was no use."

I waved a hand in front of my nose, recalling the man's breath in my face. "He said he enjoyed watching me dance, although he certainly was in no condition to dance himself. I had difficulty getting away from him to be quite honest."

"He should never have been so forward. I know the man—he is a customer and most fond of the navy grog we carry. What did he have to say?"

I recalled our brief conversation, if one could call it that. "He was slurring his words. He claimed he'd recently been in a few skirmishes with the rebels."

Wagging my finger the way Willington had, I repeated his garbled chatter. "'Paul Sook is a sitting duck.' He made little sense. I finally was able to excuse myself."

Robert frowned. "Paul Sook?"

"I'm certain that was the name. Do you know the man?"

He whispered it. "Paul Sook." Then his eyes widened, and he jumped from the chair. "Why did you not disclose this until now? It may be important. I must inform John Bolton."

"John Bolton? Who is—"

He pulled me to my feet. "Tallmadge's code name. Thank you, cousin. That is all for today." He ushered me toward the door.

"But I . . . You haven't—"

The doorknob rattled. Robert peered through the window. "It is your brother."

"What is he doing here?"

Robert turned the lock and opened the door. "Come in. I need you to run an urgent errand."

Joe entered. "Why was it locked? Betty, what are you doing here?"

"Your sister is about to leave," Robert said. "How quickly can you find Mr. Roe and bring him here?"

"I'll go straightaway," Joe answered. "But—"

Robert gave me a gentle push across the threshold. "Have a pleasant day, cousin."

I turned around. "What about the—"

Before I uttered the word *code*, Culper Junior had shut the door.

Benedict Arnold

Thirteen

I trudged home in the unrelenting August heat, questioning what I was thinking when I'd said yes to the Culper Ring. What exactly did Robert expect of me? And why all the fuss about this fellow, Paul Sook?

Mother called from the back of the house. "Is that you, Elizabeth?"

"Yes, 'tis I." I stopped in our entryway to remove my shoes and cap, then considered climbing the stairs, peeling off my clothing, and collapsing on my bed. Instead, I trudged toward the pantry.

Alice and Mother sat at the worktable by the open door, cutting potatoes and onions into wedges. Alice wiped her forehead against her sleeve. "Where you been, Miss Betty? Thought you said you wouldn't be long."

"Only at Cousin Robert's shop. He was quite busy with customers today." *Blast it.* I'd promised to buy her a new packet of sewing needles. "He was out of needles, however. He expects them on the next supply ship, any day."

"Any sign of your brother?" Mother asked.

"Yes, he came in as I was about to leave." I took a pewter mug from one of the cupboard hooks and poured some cider from the pitcher on the table. "Robert sent him on an errand."

"You goin' to change and help with supper?" Alice asked. "I still gotta hear 'bout that ball."

A sharp knock made the three of us look in the direction of the front door.

Wonderful. André had me followed, and now I'm under arrest. Mother too.

I pulled my cap over my limp hair. "Are we expecting anyone?"

Then came another, louder knock. I wiped my sleeve across my perspiring face and went to the door. If soldiers were there to take me away, I hoped they didn't expect me to walk.

A boy in his teens stood on the porch's top step. He held a folded note in his hand. "Message for Miss Betty Floyd."

Was this a warning? "I'm Miss Floyd." I reached for the note with my left hand.

The boy stared, but I was too tired to care. As I moved to close the door, he said, "Miss, Major André said I am to wait for your reply."

Major André? "Very well. You may step in."

I opened the note as the boy stood inside on the rug.

The honor of your presence is requested

at a dinner given by General Sir Henry Clinton

Saturday, 21 August 1779, At 6:00 p.m.

One Broadway, New York

Another sentence below the invitation read:

I shall have a carriage call for you at 5:45 p.m.
Yours truly,
John André

I read the note again. And again.

"Miss?"

Mother called from the pantry. "Elizabeth? Is everything well?"

I said to the boy, "Please inform Major André that I accept the invitation." I gave him a small tip from the coins we kept near the stairs and closed the door after him.

I was not under arrest, nor would I be. On the contrary. But why had the major asked me, out of all the women who would have traded anything, including their virtue, to attend a dinner with him and General Clinton?

And how did he know where I lived? I supposed he was not the Director of Intelligence for nothing.

Of course, the most important question was: *What on earth shall I wear?*

I considered not speaking of the invitation to Robert until after the dinner took place, in the event that I failed to learn anything or tried too hard, as he'd put it. But a lesson regarding the war and who was in charge of what might be helpful, should conversations turn in that direction.

Clinton was the leader of the British forces, so I assumed they would. The most natural thing would be to brag of his accomplishments, while everyone lavished their praises. My nervousness grew daily at the thought of it, yet I had to prepare.

Oakham and Townsend hummed with customers the next morning. A large shipment of goods had arrived on a transport and stood stacked against one wall, awaiting Joe's help later in the day.

While I lingered, Mr. Oakham stopped in, a rare sight indeed. But rather than stay and assist, he only had enough time for Robert to introduce me before he was off again.

Robert rubbed the back of his neck. "This is not the best time. Might you return in an hour?"

Three sailors barged through the door, in dire need of baths.

"I quite understand," I said. "I'll do that."

What would be the best use of my time? I took a chance and set out for the Walker home, hoping to find Celeste.

The tall pines framing the house soon came into view. Their young servant, Willa, opened the door and led me to the small library, where Celeste had been reading.

Celeste rose from the settee to embrace me. "Come and sit, Betty. Willa, would you please bring us tea?"

I was grateful for the chance to rest my feet. "I can't stay long but I have a bit of news. And I need your advice."

I proceeded to tell Celeste of the invitation from the major to General Clinton's dinner.

She grabbed my arm. "Oh, heavens! I'm so excited for you, Betty. What an honor."

As Willa brought in the tea, I asked Celeste what she thought I ought to wear, given my limited wardrobe of formal gowns.

"That shall not be a problem." Celeste's face lit up. "I have just the gown for such an occasion."

We took a few minutes over tea to discuss the particulars, then I walked back to Oakham and Townsend, which was now empty of customers.

"Things have quieted, for the time being," Robert said. He led me to my chair at the desk. "I have given some thought to what you may wish to know for your future encounters."

"Good, and while I'm thinking of it, Alice needs a packet of sewing needles. And Major André has invited me to a dinner given by General Clinton."

Robert's eyebrows rose above his spectacles. "Well then, you will keep your eyes and ears open, will you not?"

"Are you seriously thinking I wouldn't?"

The receipts on the desk fluttered under his long sigh. He rose quickly and pulled a small box on the floor toward him and opened the lid. He handed me a packet of needles from the box.

"No charge." He pulled his chair forward. "First of all, you should be aware that Britain will only accept complete submission from the colonies. The king will not compromise."

I recalled the grand statements made by Captain Higgins and Lieutenant Parker. "And the colonists? How many are on the side of Britain?"

"Remember, the colonies have chosen to declare independence. We are states now—the United States of America, despite our differences. There are plenty who still do not agree and hope that Britain will prevail. However, Congress and its supporters want no proposals or compromises. Britain must totally withdraw its troops and accept our independence."

"Then we are truly at an impasse. I often hear talk as if Washington is about to give in."

"We shall not give in," Robert said. "The Declaration of Independence states our belief that, 'we are endowed by our Creator' with unalienable rights, meaning that God gives us freedom, and it is government that must protect that freedom."

I shook my head, thinking of Christopher Martin. "The Crown certainly doesn't see it that way."

He nodded. "Therefore, the war rages on, and it will likely

become only bloodier before it is done. However, with much prayer and a great deal of effort, the Patriots will see victory."

The ticking clock marked the seconds as I considered how much longer the war might continue. Outside the shop, soldiers marched, the sound of their boots pounding the street in unison.

To the best of his knowledge, Robert summarized where the war currently stood. Names of various British and American commanders, along with their recent battles, were more than a bit overwhelming. I doubted I would ever be able to keep them straight. One name stood out, however—Benedict Arnold.

"Celeste was told he married a Loyalist from Philadelphia by the name of Peggy Shippen, an acquaintance of Major André."

Robert adjusted his spectacles. "I am not aware of anyone's marriages or romantic entanglements. Washington trusts him—that is all I know."

"I didn't say there was a romantic entanglement." *And I don't care. I shouldn't care.*

Robert was silent for as long as it took him to push his spectacles higher on his nose. "Is that sufficient, or do you have any specific questions?"

At least one came to mind. "When I was here last, what was the to-do about Paul Sook and your need to notify Ben Tallmadge immediately?"

"When you mentioned that Willington said Paul Sook was a sitting duck, I surmised he meant Paulus Hook, a British-held fortification in New Jersey." Robert's voice became more emphatic. "If something has changed, making it vulnerable to attack, General Washington would want to know."

"Paulus Hook." How little I knew of local geography. "I didn't even think it was relevant."

He unlocked the bottom desk drawer where he'd kept the invisible ink. "These may be of some use to you as well and give you a true perspective on the war." He handed me two newspapers. First, a rival to Rivington's *Royal Gazette*—the *New York Journal*. The other, the *Connecticut Courant*.

"Also, you promised to show me the code."

"I did not promise. However . . ." He unlocked another drawer and pulled out several loose papers. He pushed them slowly across the desk toward me. Columns of names and words with corresponding three-digit numbers filled the pages—hundreds of numbers representing words.

I leafed through them, amazed. "Ben Tallmadge put a great deal of effort into this."

General Washington's name was followed by the number 711. Beside Tallmadge's name was his Culper name, John Bolton, and the number 721. Samuel Culper, or Culper Senior, was 722. Culper Junior, 723. Austin Roe . . .

"Is he the Austin Roe you sent Joe to find when I told you about Paul Sook?"

"Yes, he is another Long Islander and one of our couriers."

More names followed. C. Brewster, 725; Rivington, 726.

James Rivington? I pointed to the name and looked at my cousin.

He nodded. "The least likely of anyone."

I looked further for my number, 355. As Robert had said, across from it was simply the word *lady*. Not impressive in the least, yet that was the intention. Written this way, with no name beside it, made it impossible to connect me to anything having to do with the Culper Code or the Ring. Even so, seeing the number 355 there on paper, I felt more joined to the Ring and its purpose.

Culper Junior clasped his hands and laid them atop the code pages. "Be cautious, I beg of you. You are stepping further into the lions' den, and André is just as bloodthirsty as the rest of the pride. He did not achieve his position without earning it."

I laughed then at his scowling face. "Dear cousin, the Major André I know and the word *bloodthirsty* simply have no relation to each other."

He was undeterred. "I am warning you, Betty. Do not be fooled by his charms."

My tolerance limit for Robert Townsend had run out. "You are the most negative, overbearing, overprotective—"

The shop door opened. Neither of us could have jumped more if a cannon had shot through it. How had the King of Caution forgotten again to lock the blessed door?

He was on his feet. "Good . . . good afternoon, madam. May I assist you?"

I felt him watching me as I quickly gathered up the newspapers and shoved the code pages under the pile of receipts.

An elderly woman using a cane stepped in. She wore a pale gray gown and feather-trimmed straw hat. Behind her came two girls around Joe's age, their unruly hair tied back in wide ribbons. The woman walked straight to the fabric selections, and the girls followed.

"You're Mr. Townsend, I trust?" the woman said. "I require some decent linen for gowns for my granddaughters, preferably dark colors. Ordering clothing from London takes much too long, prices are rising daily, and I have a seamstress who can do the work herself. And your lightest weight cotton for shifts."

The girls exchanged looks and giggled.

Robert motioned for me to go as he pulled out his keys and hurried to the desk to lock away the Culper code. "Of course, madam. I shall be with you momentarily."

I had what I needed, and I'd overstayed my welcome. "Good day, cousin," I called on my way out.

Brilliant sunshine filled Hanover Square, teeming with pedestrians, horses, carriages, and wagons. I crossed Smith Street and dodged a trotting horse and rider on my left. But I didn't see the two young boys running toward me from the right. Apparently, they didn't see me either.

I collided with one of them and fell, losing my hold on the newspapers and just missing a pile of manure.

The boy ran off. "Beg pardon, Miss."

"Watch where you're going, young man." A scowling officer called after him as he moved to help me to my feet. "Are you hurt, Miss?"

With my eye on the newspapers four feet away, I took his hand and attempted to stand gracefully. "Not at all. I—"

"Ah, it's fortunate these weren't trampled." He scooped the

newspapers off the road. A corner of one of the code pages protruded between them. How had it escaped Robert's watchful eye?

I reached for them. "Yes, thank you, sir."

He clung to the papers and took a better look at me. "Ah, Miss Floyd. We met at the ball." He removed his hat and bowed. "Captain Charles Willington."

Fig. 1.

THE JERSEY PRISON SHIP,

As MOORED AT THE WALLABOUT NEAR LONG ISLAND, IN THE YEAR 1782.

HMS *Jersey*, British prison ship

Fourteen

A week later, a polished open carriage arrived at our home, pulled by four coffee-colored horses. I was on my way to One Broadway for the second time in my life.

With her forehead tensed in concern, Mother watched from our porch. My anger at the British hadn't wavered, so she was somewhat mystified when it came to my acceptance of an invitation to General Clinton's dinner and all the attention from Major André. I merely said he was a gentleman and a fine dancer, and who would pass up such an invitation?

She'd warned me repeatedly to be prudent. Of course, she had no knowledge of the Culper Ring or my role in it—a role with few rules other than Do Not Get Caught. I needed to keep her suspicions to a minimum. Therefore, the less I said, the better. She prayed for an end to the bloodshed, while I continued to pray for wisdom.

As the carriage rolled forward, I took a deep breath, wishing I could let all my anxieties out with it. Poor Robert—after my last visit, he'd practically fainted when I returned to his shop holding a page from the Culper code. I decided that was enough excitement for him and chose not to include my impromptu meeting with Captain Willington or that he insisted on taking me to tea at the coffeehouse or that he had so much to say that he never once bothered to open those newspapers to see what I was reading.

I toyed with the pearl-trimmed petticoat on Celeste's scarlet gown, which she'd insisted on loaning to me. Thanks to Alice, my hair was perfectly curled and held back with Mother's pearl combs, with several ringlets draped over my left shoulder. This was one of the rare times when I was thankful for no breeze and a slow driver. My primary focus for the evening would be to play the role I'd been assigned and remember anything that might be worthwhile to share with Culper Junior.

Nearing my destination, I willed my heart to slow its beating as I donned my long white gloves. I had modified all my gloves to fit my left hand properly. They usually proved to be less of a shock to others than seeing my bare hands.

The carriage pulled to a stop, and the driver stepped down to assist me to the street. At the mansion's top step, two young privates stood at attention on either side of the wide entrance. Unlike the night of the party when I met the major, the tall doors were closed.

One of the privates tapped on the door as I approached, and it opened from the inside. A white-wigged servant wearing a black satin waistcoat, high-collared white shirt, dark green breeches and white gloves silently beckoned me to enter and follow him. Now I knew how Cinderella felt as she first stepped foot in the castle.

The king's banner still hung over the foyer, with its bright red, blue, and yellow coat of arms, claiming the house for the Crown. How long would it remain?

With my footsteps echoing off the ceiling, I followed the servant across the foyer and turned left, passing the main ballroom where I'd first met Major André, now darkened and empty but for two large carpets.

Voices grew louder as we approached a doorway leading to a long, magnificent dining room. The servant stood to the side and gestured for me to enter.

Into the lions' den I go . . .

I stepped inside the room, taking in its beauty. The walls, covered in pale blue damask silk, were decorated with several pastoral paintings. Two high arched windows, draped in sweeps of ivory linen, overlooked an enormously long table set for a formal dinner. Flowers, silver, crystal . . . Not one detail had been spared.

Several guests stood among the officers near the far window. Every lady wore their hair in the high roll style. Not one wore red, and my decision to stand out turned to instant regret.

Then a hush spread through the room as one guest after another turned their head toward the room's entrance. I checked to see who or what had caught their attention. Was it *me*?

My arms and neck warmed as my hands perspired inside my gloves. Rather than Cinderella, I now felt a bit like a harlot. Yet it was too late now. I pulled off my gloves and swallowed hard. I had been given a noble task, and it was time for me to draw on my own acting abilities, such as they were.

Major André stepped from the back of the group and hurried across the room to meet me. "Miss Floyd, what a pleasure to see you."

And you. May we please leave? "Good evening, Major. Thank you for the kind invitation."

He extended his arm. "I'm quite pleased that you could join us. You look much lovelier in red than the rest of us." His dark eyes shone in the waning light. "I shall introduce you to the general and those who have arrived. Others should be here momentarily."

General Henry Clinton, larger than life, stood with another officer slightly away from the guests. Clinton wore his full-dress uniform, with more gold braiding and polished buttons than any officer in the room. As we approached, he appeared just as intimidating and bothered as he did the first time I saw him. He reminded me of Old Red, our oversized rooster on the farm—self-important and perpetually angry.

"General," Major André said, "may I introduce Miss Floyd?"

Clinton gave me a cold stare. "Miss Floyd."

I curtsied politely. "General."

The man beside Clinton wore a dark blue and gold uniform. "This is Sir George Collier, commander of the navy in the colonies," the major said.

"Though not for much longer," Collier replied. He bowed half-heartedly, perhaps fatigued already.

We quickly moved on to meet the other guests. "Is the general always so friendly?" I asked the major.

He showed off those perfect teeth. "He happens to be in good spirits tonight."

"I would never have guessed. And why is that?"

"Because one of the great pleasures in life, especially in a time of war, is a fine meal with excellent company, including charming and beautiful ladies." He lifted my right hand to bestow a kiss.

"Major, my mother often quotes this saying: 'Sweet words are like honey; a little may refresh, but too much gluts the stomach.'"

"I shall keep that in mind; however, it won't change the heart from whence they come."

I couldn't help but chuckle. He certainly knew how to deliver a line.

A servant approached with a tray of crystal flutes, filled to their rims with bubbly champagne. The major handed me a glass and took one himself. I held the glass with my left hand in order to shake hands with my right. He introduced me to Mr. and Mrs. Rivington, neither of whom I'd officially met before, then to two officers and their wives whom I had met briefly at the ball, then to Mr. and Mrs. DeLancey.

It didn't take the DeLanceys long to notice my left hand. Their looks of surprise dissolved into disapproval. If they'd wondered at all why the major hadn't invited a more prominent member of New York society for the evening, now they surely deliberated his choice of company. I switched my glass to my right hand.

Only Mr. and Mrs. Rivington seemed more impressed that I'd grown up on a farm than how I held my champagne glass. I couldn't fathom how Mr. Rivington became part of the Culper Ring. The Sons of Liberty had attacked the *Gazette* more than once before Britain occupied New York, and Rivington himself had been jailed, yet everything he printed in his paper always sided with the king.

If Rivington was aiding the Patriots, he had the perfect disguise. It was somewhat comforting to know that a fellow Ring member was present, even though he had no idea I was one of them. Or did he?

At a break between conversations, I turned to the major. "If I may ask, why did you choose to invite me? Everyone here is well-connected to the military or a city leader, yet I'm neither of those. I feel quite out of place."

His gaze softened. "I invited you because there's no one else I'd rather ask. You belong here as much as anyone. And you happen to be more intelligent and pleasant than most. *D'accord?*"

"*Oui, merci.*" I tried not to blush—I already wore enough red.

"I do have another question," I said. "I wondered . . . will Governor Tryon be attending?"

"Tryon? Heavens, no. The general and the governor are not friends, to put it delicately."

A stocky gentleman in a dark green uniform strode toward us. The major gestured toward him. "Here is someone I wish you to meet."

He shook the man's hand. "Good of you to come, John. May I introduce Miss Betty Floyd? This is my good friend, Lieutenant-Colonel John Simcoe of the Queen's Rangers."

Simcoe! The very man who'd attacked Abraham Woodhull's father, quartered himself in the Townsend home, and terrorized Long Island. *They're friends?*

Even as a chill ran down my back, I forced my face to reflect the calm boredom of a New York Loyalist. "Good evening, sir."

"A pleasure," he said, bowing slightly. "Floyd, is it? Are you perhaps related to the Floyds of Long Island?"

Now my heart pounded in my ears. "Oh . . . I was born on Long Island, but Floyd is quite a common name. The Floyds settled there over a hundred years ago—"

"Miss Floyd has told me she has relations she has never met," the major said.

How kind. But what is this evil man thinking?

Simcoe's gray eyes darkened. He folded his arms and tapped his cheek with his index finger. "I may have recently heard the name William Floyd bandied about as a member of the rebels' Congress, and as a signer of their Declaration of Independence. Does the name ring a bell?"

My heart thumped with new vigor. I glanced at Major André, whose demeanor I couldn't read. What would an actor do? Or Captain Plume, for that matter?

"No, sir," I said, lifting my chin. "William Floyd is also a common name. I don't know anyone connected with their Congress. My father fully supported the king all his life and wished for the colonies to remain under the Crown. It's shameful . . . outrageous . . . to desire anything less."

Simcoe raised an eyebrow. "Well, then. Let us toast to that, shall we, André?" He lifted a glass of champagne from the passing servant's tray.

The major held his glass high. "To the colonies. May they ever remain so."

We hadn't even sat down to eat yet, and I was already being tested. I touched my glass to theirs and took a good swallow.

How can I warn Uncle William that John Simcoe may be on his trail? Robert was right. This is surely a den of lions—hungry ones.

As soon as more guests arrived, the servants opened the windows and lit the tall candles on the dining table. The major again offered his arm and led me to the table. General Clinton took a seat at the head of the table on the left, and the major pulled out the second chair for me and claimed the first, immediately to Clinton's right.

When all were seated, the general rose from his chair and tapped a spoon against his champagne glass.

"Good evening and welcome. I am most pleased to act as your host tonight in our fine headquarters. I wish to propose a toast before we begin our dinner."

We all stood and raised our glasses together.

"To victory, to Britain, and to King George," he said.

Shouts of, "Hear, hear," and "to King George," rang out as glasses clinked.

Mr. Rivington, on my right, raised his glass to his wife's. On my left, Major André tipped his toward mine. "To victory."

Once we were seated again, the major remained standing. "Let us bow our heads for the blessing."

"Almighty Father," he began, "we ask thy blessing upon our country, its leaders, and our king. Grant us wisdom, protection, and victory, and bless the food we are about to receive, in Christ's name. Amen."

Wisdom, yes. Grant me wisdom.

"And now, ladies and gentlemen," he continued, "in the spirit of the Continentals and their fondness for calling us Lobsterbacks, I hope you'll enjoy this outstanding lobster dinner."

Laughter and applause followed as he took his seat. One of the officers farther down the table shouted, "Thank God we aren't having to eat frog legs."

As the guests howled with laughter, Mr. Rivington leaned forward. "The French jokes will never end, Major."

"Indeed, they will not." Major André chuckled.

"Mr. Rivington," I said, "I happened to read an article about the French in the *Gazette* regarding their own difficulties. Yet isn't it true that England is under threat now from France and from Spain?"

Thanks to Robert and the other newspapers he gave me to read, it was gratifying to show I gave more thought than most New Yorkers to the contents of the *Lying Gazette*, as it was known by some.

Rivington had mischief in his eyes. "You must have read the latter in another paper, Miss Floyd."

If Major André appreciated my knowledge, he didn't reveal it. "Let us not concern ourselves with such stories tonight. Have you noticed any of my drawings that our esteemed publisher has so kindly printed?"

Obviously, he didn't wish to discuss France. In truth, I'd been hoping for a way to bring up the subject of his drawings. "Why yes, Major. I happened to see one you drew of Miss Peggy Shippen."

His ears reddened. "Miss Shippen was a friend from Philadelphia."

"Always happy to print your work, Major," Mr. Rivington said. "Keep it coming."

"She's no longer a friend?" The moment I said it, I hoped I wasn't treading where I shouldn't. "I . . . thought your drawing was lovely."

General Clinton leaned over and interrupted him. I still found it perplexing that a wealthy Philadelphia Loyalist had left the major for a Patriot general.

As the servants brought the soup course, I counted seven pieces of silverware at each place setting. Which spoon was meant for soup? Discreetly, I watched Mr. Rivington choose the spoon above his dinner plate.

Simcoe sat directly across from me, and I was grateful that the table was wide enough to prevent any more probing questions from him. Mrs. DeLancey sat to his right and proceeded to deliver her opinions on everything from the war to the weather.

Another servant leaned in and filled my champagne glass, which I appreciated. It was going to be a long meal.

"Tell me, Miss Floyd," Mr. Rivington said, "what brought you to New York City?"

I began relaying my story, until I heard General Clinton say the words *Paulus Hook* to the major.

"Miss Floyd? You were saying?"

I held up an index finger and reached for my glass, hoping to stall long enough to hear what Clinton was saying. I pretended to take a long, slow drink of champagne.

". . . middle of the night during low tide, for God's sake. Their Major Lee and his blasted dragoons attacked . . ."

"Miss Floyd, perhaps you shouldn't—"

Major André rested his spoon in his soup bowl. "What was the outcome?"

I set down my glass. "I beg your pardon, Mr. Rivington, but I believe my soup . . ."

"Of course," he said. "You mustn't let it get cold."

". . . intelligence from local militia," Clinton said, "or it would not have been the success that it was. They took more than one hundred prisoners but hardly lost any men themselves."

"Quite disappointing," the major said. "How they acquire their information is baffling at times."

You can thank your Captain Willington. Also, I may have had something to do with it.

"Just when we crack one of their ciphers, they create another," Major André continued. "We still believe they have their spies in New York. Our codes appear to be secure, however."

I ventured a glance at General Clinton. Red-faced, he tugged at his cravat. He hadn't touched his soup.

Major André brushed against my sleeve as he turned toward me. "I must apologize. Please don't think I'm ignoring you."

"Not at all!" I gave him a reassuring smile. "I know you must talk with the general. I truly don't mind."

The conversation at the table turned to the weather, and someone asked how the men in the barracks and tent camps around the city managed to keep cool. I was sorry to learn they were not averse to stripping off their clothing and jumping into the river, then swimming along the shores and frightening unsuspecting young ladies cooling their feet. Judging by a few whispers, I gathered they often did more than merely frighten them.

When our soup bowls were replaced with small plates of greens and strawberries, I filled in Mr. Rivington regarding my family's journey to New York.

Simcoe looked our way. How much had he heard? Was he still contemplating a connection between Uncle William and me?

Mrs. DeLancey spoke up. "I'm curious, General. What do you plan to do regarding the prison ships in Wallabout Bay, with so many other ships in the harbor? From what I could see on our last outing to the racecourse, the waters are becoming quite crowded."

Clinton drove a fork into his salad. "Madam, the prison ships are serving their purpose. I regret the crowding in the harbor, yet I assure you, everything possible is being done to alleviate it."

"By the way, sir," Simcoe said to the general, "I received a report regarding a woman from New York who was assisting prisoners off the *Jersey*." He stopped and took a swallow from his glass, then caught my eye across the table. "We sent troops to her home to detain her; however, she has disappeared."

Mrs. Burgin. My arms tingled.

Mr. DeLancey spoke up, on Simcoe's left, "Perhaps the woman was simply doing her part to alleviate the crowded conditions."

Clinton and Simcoe exchanged glances, as everyone laughed but Mrs. DeLancey. Apparently, the fact that men were starving and dying aboard those ships was irrelevant compared to the unsightliness of a congested harbor.

The servants carried in the main course with great fanfare: lobster tails accompanied by tiny cups of melted butter, alongside a sweet carrot pudding topped with toasted breadcrumbs. The relish trays and bread baskets were replenished as the wine was poured.

"I'm not accustomed to eating such a large meal," I said to the major.

"I plan to do it justice," he said. *"Bon appétit."*

We toasted the luscious meal. With wine on top of the champagne, I had better be able to stand when it came time to do so.

Mr. Rivington dipped his fork into the tender lobster. "I must say, it's much easier to eat just the tail and not wrestle with the whole creature."

"If mine were whole, sir," I said, "you could be in danger. The one time I struggled to crack open a lobster, most of it landed on my brother's lap."

He and Major André laughed, and Mr. Rivington said, "You have a delightful sense of humor, Miss Floyd. Poking fun at oneself is a sign of intelligence, I always say."

"I agree, Rivington," the major said. "And based on what you allow in your paper regarding yourself, you're one of the most intelligent gentlemen in New York."

While I chatted with Major André about his family in England and the next play at Theatre Royal, General Clinton and Simcoe discussed this or that regiment or leader or skirmish with the enemy. I kept one ear on their conversation, but a good deal was beyond my understanding. So far, however, I heard nothing of any future plans.

Mrs. DeLancey excused herself from the table, most likely to find the necessary. I wanted to wait, in the event something important was said. Considering the rate at which the wine flowed and the men consumed it, they would soon either be divulging crucial strategies or dashing off for the nearest shrubbery.

Clinton's voice grew louder as he drank, making it easier to hear his words. He set down his empty wine glass. "Their taking of Stony Point in July was bad for us, regardless of their abandonment of it, a setback to our plans and bad for morale. Then the Paulus Hook business . . ."

He signaled a servant to bring more wine. "I have called for more troops, which we must have if we are to take West Point. And it is imperative we have additional men for Charleston."

Simcoe sat taller and held aloft his own glass for a refill. "General, the Queen's Rangers are at your disposal, wherever you shall require them."

"We shall have West Point, sir, one way or the other," Major André said.

The general raised his full glass. "The road to victory runs through West Point."

The major replied. "That it does, sir."

Fifteen

H e did it. Betty, he did it!"
Was Joe pounding on my head or my door?

"Aren't you awake? Triple caught a mouse. He brought it to Alice in the kitchen."

I let that register as I realized Joe stood just inside my half-opened door. Then I remembered I'd promised Mother I would attend church with her today.

"What time is it?" I asked him.

"Eight o'clock. Better hurry."

Too much wine and too little sleep makes for a rough start on a Sunday morning. Yet I'd promised, and there was no denying I had much to pray about. I rose, throbbing head and all.

"How was your evening?" Mother asked as the three of us left the house. "I didn't hear you come home."

"It was"—I settled for a vague, all-encompassing word—"wonderful. It was a bit past midnight when I came in."

"And did Major André see you home?" The trepidation in her voice came through.

"He wanted to remain with the general, but he made certain I was safely in the carriage, and the driver was most courteous."

"I can't believe you had dinner with General Clinton," Joe said. "Was Triple in his box on the porch when you came in?"

"No, I don't believe so. He must have been out hunting."

I wished I could inform Joe and Mother that Simcoe spoke of Mrs. Burgin. Yet I didn't know if in fact Simcoe meant *her*, and I didn't wish to worry them. Still, I would need to warn my brother once more to keep quiet about what he knew.

Mother asked for more dinner details, including who was present and what foods were on the menu. By the time I'd described it to her satisfaction, we reached the doors leading into the chapel.

The building was already stifling, though it was only nine o'clock. My headache returned as I dropped into my seat. A quick glance around proved none of the dinner guests had ventured to church, probably due to their overindulging. While waiting for the service to begin, I pulled out my fan and closed my tired eyes, letting my mind drift.

After the lengthy and eventful evening, I'd found it impossible to fall asleep afterward. Instead, I made a long list of notes for Robert while my memory was fresh. I also wrote a short message to Uncle William, informing him he may be in danger, without saying so outright:

> *Dearest Uncle,*
>
> *It has come to my attention that your name is among those chosen to receive an award for the work you are conducting. It may soon be presented to you in person, perhaps by a representative of the king whom you may know.*
>
> *Your affectionate niece,*
> *Betty*

He'd understood my letter about the dogs of New York, and I assumed he would determine my meaning now and take whatever precautions he saw fit. If only we had a code such as the Culpers employed.

As an extra safeguard, I tucked the note inside the poetry book he'd sent to me, on the same page where his letter had been. I would post it on Monday when I visited Culper Junior.

Sleep still eluded me. Gathering intelligence for the Patriots, portraying the socialite with Britain's military leaders, and flirting with Major John André to keep the channels open—the dinner convinced me I was clearly in over my head. How long could I fight to keep myself above water?

If I were honest with myself, half of the problem lay in the fact that I was growing attracted to the very man who happened to be bent on seeking and destroying American spies. I would need to keep the relationship in its place and remember my role as 355, or I would be courting danger.

The other half was that I truly doubted my capabilities. However,

I took on this task because of what happened to Christopher and others like him, and I would see it through.

No wonder I'm unable to sleep. Perhaps a nap later . . .

Joe elbowed me, pulling me out of my stupor. After the first hymn, Reverend Inglis began his sermon, based on the story of Esther, a young Jewish woman whom the king of Persia had chosen as his queen. He droned on with an impressive but dry history lesson of how Esther's uncle, Mordecai, encouraged her to go to the king and beg him not to annihilate her people.

Mordecai's words caught my attention.

"For if thou altogether holdest thy peace at this time . . . thou and thy father's house shall be destroyed: and who knoweth whether thou art come to the kingdom for such a time as this?"

As before, Reverend Inglis had a way of relating the Bible story to current events as he viewed them. "I ask you, has Almighty God raised up our beloved mother country to preserve the colonies for such a time as this?"

Not in my eyes, nor those of thousands of citizens spread across this land. On the contrary, perhaps God was raising up America to be a free nation, as declared by Congress in '76, one that would rule itself with no interference from any other.

How much of a part did I have in His plan? I only wanted to make some kind of contribution.

It's going to get worse. Who do you think you are?

The next day at the noon hour, I walked to Oakham and Townsend with the notes for Robert and package for Uncle William tucked deep in my pocket. As luck would have it, Mrs. Walker and Mother had settled on this date for us to come for an early tea. I'd explained to Mother I had a personal errand and would meet her there afterward.

Heavy rain overnight had washed the dusty streets, yet it left large puddles, luring bare-legged boys and their dogs to run and splash in them. The air carried the burnt smell from the big fire once again, as if it had just been extinguished and water had been dumped on the ashes. On the bright side, the temperature had fallen, bringing welcome relief to us overheated and weary city dwellers.

Mr. Oakham greeted me with a scowl from behind the counter. "I'm afraid Mr. Townsend is working at the coffeehouse today. He should be here, however, as we have more orders to go out with the mail than one person can deal with while waiting on customers."

"I am sorry," I said. "However, I have something to post, if you don't mind."

He grunted, taking the package. I paid him for the postage and left before he could resume his complaints.

Robert had advised me to only meet him at the shop when I had information for him, yet I felt I mustn't wait. He would surely understand if I dropped into Rivington's, given the urgency of my report and that I wished to be at the Walkers' home on time. If there were no customers in the coffeehouse, we could speak privately. If there were, I might wait for a bit. I did not wish to return after tea.

At the coffeehouse door, three officers tipped their hats and hurried off toward Fort George and the Battery. Inside, the room was empty but for Robert. He stood over one of the small tables, loading a tray with used cups and saucers. He wore a cloth apron rather than the leather one he always wore at his shop.

"Hello, cousin."

He whirled around. "Why are you here?"

"I'm pleased to see you, as well. Don't you wish to know—"

Frowning, he set the tray on the counter. "Keep your voice down. There is someone in the storeroom. I thought I told you—"

"Mr. Oakham said I would find you here and I must hurry to meet my mother. I have information." I pulled out my notes. "And what is so wrong with meeting my cousin in a coffeehouse?"

His eyes grew wide at the sight of the paper in my hand. "What have you written?"

"Only a list to help me recall everything of importance." I smoothed the paper. "May we sit down?"

He spat out the words. "You are never to—" He glanced out the small window and went to the storeroom doorway. "That will be all for now, Elijah. Please see if Mr. Oakham needs help and say I will be there when Mr. Rivington can relieve me here."

A young voice replied. A minute later, a door shut that must have led to the alley.

Red-faced, Robert turned from the doorway. "I thought I made it clear that you are never to write anything. It is too dangerous."

"We're wasting time, Mr. Culper." I moved to the farthest table and chairs. "I'll destroy this as soon as we're finished."

He looked as if I'd struck him. "You must never use that name."

"Please sit down." I took a seat in one of the chairs. "If anyone enters, say the truth—I'm your cousin. Unless you'd rather speak with 726. He sat beside me at the dinner."

Robert gazed at the ceiling. "Rivington—"

I laid a hand on the other chair. "I have much to communicate."

Robert went to the sideboard and poured cider into two small tankards. "You can at least appear as if you have come in for a refreshment." He set the tankards on the table, took the other chair, and glared at me.

I dropped the page of notes and took up the tankard. "The dinner was incredible."

He pointed to my notes. "Please get on with it."

After a good swallow of cider, which contained more spirits than ours at home, I went through the vital details, point by point—who attended the dinner and what was disclosed. The news of Paulus Hook seemed to gratify him.

"Washington will know, of course," he said. "He may have had other intelligence before ours, yet hearing from us no doubt aided the attack."

I waited, thinking he may wish to thank me. Instead, he drank his cider.

"I met your friend Simcoe."

Robert lowered his eyes and set down his tankard.

I recalled for him the bits and pieces of Simcoe's conversation with General Clinton during dinner. In the interest of time, I left out Simcoe's curiosity regarding my last name and his questions about Uncle William. It would only raise Robert's fears. He had enough to contend with already, and I didn't want to veer off the subject.

"You made no mention of me or the Townsend home, I trust?"

"Robert, you disappoint me." I shook my head. "Of course not."

He held up both hands. "This business has put me under a great deal of strain."

"That is obvious. Have you discussed it with Culper Senior?"

Upon hearing the name, he cringed. "He does not care to hear it, considering the danger he himself faces." He glanced back at the door. "Someone may walk in any minute."

I summarized my last few points, including what Clinton had said of the Stony Point attack, his need for more troops, and the comments Major André made to the general.

"The major said something interesting: 'We shall have West Point, one way or the other.'"

Robert stared at the table. "Not surprising, I suppose. West Point is an important fort in a strategic area. We must heed anything we hear of it and notify Washington."

"Clinton wants it more than anything. I'll never forget his emphatic tone—'The road to victory runs through West Point.' And Charleston. He wants more troops before attacking Charleston."

Robert moved to push back his chair. "I will convey what you have said."

That appeared to be all the thanks I was to receive. The only sounds now came from the street—horses snorting, wagon wheels crunching over stones, men shouting. Robert tipped back his tankard to finish his cider. I handed mine to him, and we stood.

"I must go." I held out my page of notes. "Would this be of help as you write your report?"

The door opened, and Mr. Rivington stepped in. "Hello, Townsend. Miss Floyd, what brings you in on this fine day?"

Breathless, I arrived at the Walkers' residence just as Marcus pulled the carriage to a stop at the front stone walkway. Mother emerged from the carriage, wearing her straw hat and her best pale yellow gown. She carried the gown Celeste had loaned me for the dinner.

"Hello, Mother." I reached for the gown. "Thank you for bringing this with you."

"I had a most pleasant ride. I don't often see this part of the city," she said, stepping down. "Thank you, Marcus."

He tipped his tricorn to us, then urged the horse forward with a jiggle on the reins.

"Did you have sufficient time for your errand?" she asked as we walked to the door.

"Barely. I was . . . detained. By an acquaintance."

Mr. Rivington's arrival at the coffeehouse had led to a lengthy conversation on the problems faced by the press. He was quite surprised to learn Robert had a cousin in the city, let alone one that happened to have sat beside him at the Clinton dinner. Robert had been clearly relieved when I explained I had to leave for an appointment.

As soon as Willa welcomed us into the foyer, Celeste and her mother weren't far behind.

"Dear Margaret and Betty." Mrs. Walker kissed our cheeks. "I'm so pleased you've come."

Celeste gave us each a quick embrace, then took her gown and handed it to Willa. "I must hear all about the dinner, Betty. Was the gown sufficient? Did you talk with the general?"

Her mother laughed. "Celeste, let's make our guests comfortable before you start with your questions."

"That's quite all right, Constance," Mother said. "I certainly won't mind hearing more of it. But first, I must thank you for providing the carriage today. It was much appreciated."

Mrs. Walker led us to the lovely blue and white drawing room, where a table for four was set with an embroidered tablecloth and silver tea service.

From the hall came the sound of footsteps and giggling. Julia, Susan, and Rebecca entered, their eyes dancing. Each girl wore a large white bow in her hair.

Mrs. Walker bid them come closer. "Girls, would you like to say hello?"

Julia, the oldest at age thirteen, rested her hands on the younger ones' shoulders. "Hello, Mrs. Floyd. Hello, Miss Betty."

Susan and Rebecca shyly echoed their big sister. Then Susan said to me, "We're making paper dolls. Willa is helping us. May we show you after tea?"

"I'd love to see them." I looked to Celeste for clarification. "Paper dolls?"

"They're cutting out shapes of people from heavy paper Father brought home," Celeste said. "The mistress of someone Willa knows saw them in Paris and taught her and Willa. They make clothing from more paper and then paint it, or they use fabric scraps."

Mother beamed at the girls. "How creative."

"Let's have our tea," Mrs. Walker said. "Julia, would you take them back now?"

As the three girls headed down the hall again, Mrs. Walker poured us cups of English tea from the shining silver teapot and passed a platter of chicken and ham sandwiches.

"As you may have surmised, Betty," she said, "Celeste is eager to hear of your dinner at the general's, as am I."

While we enjoyed our tea and sandwiches, I relayed the other side of the dinner story that Robert had no interest in hearing—the one replete with the colors, conversations, aromas, and jokes—at least the ones that our mothers wouldn't find offensive.

"Your gown was perfect for the occasion," I said to Celeste, "and the major complimented me on it. And yes, General Clinton and I spoke briefly, but he isn't the most pleasant person."

Mrs. Walker poured more tea in Mother's cup. "I have no doubt of it, given the immensity of his duties. 'Tis a wonder that man has time to sit for a meal, let alone do any sort of entertaining."

"Whenever I've seen him, he always appears to be a grump," Celeste said. "I pity Major André, having to work closely with him."

"They appear to get along well together," I said. "From the little I've seen."

"But the major is friendly and jovial, not at all like the general," she said. "And much more handsome, of course."

Mother cleared her throat. "Betty said dessert was served at the table to everyone at once, and the men remained, rather than moving to another room by themselves."

"That is certainly a departure from the usual custom," Mrs. Walker said. "Gentlemen normally like to leave and go drink their brandies together or whatever it is they do."

"They had brandy brought to the table," I said, "and everyone simply continued talking." *Although some could hardly sit up at that point.* "We ladies were served cherry cordials."

Celeste's eyes widened. "Champagne, as well?"

"Plenty," I said. "My glass never ran out."

"When is the next dinner?"

"Now, Celeste," her mother said. "That is a bit rude." Mother and I laughed.

When we finished, Mrs. Walker invited us to see the flower garden. Celeste pulled me aside as our mothers walked through the rear door to the path leading to the garden.

"Did he kiss you?"

I couldn't help but laugh. "Of course not. It was a very formal, official occasion. We weren't alone for a minute. Even so, I'm not—"

She leaned against the wall. "Perhaps the next time?"

"I—I don't expect that to happen, truly. Please stop intimating things you know nothing about. All *I* wish to see is your mother's garden. And the paper dolls."

With a smirk, she turned toward the door. "Very well."

It wasn't as though a kiss from him hadn't crossed my mind. Any woman could hardly look at him without imagining such. Yet if he sent me more invitations or if we saw each other elsewhere, I would converse and dance and flirt with him for one purpose only—to gather intelligence for General Washington.

It would not be simple, however. Of that I was certain.

Sixteen

September 1779

Savory aromas of chicken pies and mutton stew filled the Navy Coffeehouse as Celeste and I entered through the open door. A fiddler in the far corner played a spirited tune as folks at the small, rustic tables shouted to each other or clapped along.

Celeste led the way to a group of tables against the back wall where our friends laughed and talked, tankards and mugs in their hands. I almost didn't recognize Captain Higgins and Lieutenant Parker, both out of uniform and dressed in simple, dark clothing, like everyday merchants or artisans. They and two other gentlemen rose from their seats as we approached.

Mary Shepherd greeted us. "Welcome, ladies. I'm pleased you could join us." She sat at the far end of the table with her sister Dorah and their older cousin Sophia.

Captain Higgins made the introductions. One of the gentlemen, Henry Fellowes, had danced with Celeste at the ball and was acquainted with Mary Shepherd. The other, Lieutenant Logan MacCallan, a burly man with kind eyes, knew Lieutenant Parker.

I was given a chair with Celeste on my left and Lieutenant MacCallan on my right. Thanks to the Shepherd sisters, Major André knew of my visits to the prison and I'd received a stern reprimand from Robert. Given they were several chairs away, I was grateful not to have to converse with them.

Captain Higgins asked what Celeste and I would care to drink, and we both requested ciders. He stopped one of the beleaguered servers, who affirmed the order and hurried off.

Lieutenant MacCallan spoke just loud enough for me to hear him above the noise. "We've already placed a food order—platters we all can share."

He and I were soon discussing the food served at the city's taverns and coffeehouses, which ones provided the best entertainment and other options for passing the time during the summer and autumn. His Scottish accent took some getting used to, but his friendly, relaxed manner was refreshing.

"I'm told this place is also known for its food," I said. "And these Friday parties."

"Aye, that fellow over there is Mr. Grant, the owner." He indicated a tall man wearing a dark shirt and breeches who was seating a party of four young officers. "Seems he's well-liked."

"Wise of him to open an establishment in the Battery," I said, "and so near the fort."

"There's a great lot of us, that's for certain."

It would be lovely if Major André knew of the party, but I couldn't expect him to attend every social event. Still, I hadn't seen him since we parted after the Clinton dinner. Perhaps he was simply busy with other engagements. Such a prospect made me uneasy, especially if it might involve another woman, although that was always a possibility. Regardless, I couldn't help but speculate as to his whereabouts.

At least the lieutenant was interesting and pleasant enough. He might even be willing to share what he knew of military plans.

Two servers brought heaping platters of handheld chicken and meat pies to our table, a basket of assorted hot breads, and a large bowl of corn pudding. They passed a stack of pewter plates, forks, and knives, and refilled our tankards and mugs with cider, grog, or ale.

"What do you think?" Celeste leaned close. "I know it isn't the Kennedy mansion. And no Major André—"

I hated to shout, yet it was the only way to be heard. "'Tis much more relaxing. And everything smells incredible."

The food tasted as delicious as the aromas promised, and before we'd eaten our fill, another platter of pies arrived. Us ladies moaned, but all the men were as gleeful as pigs in a pumpkin patch.

"Lieutenant, what are the plans for your company?" I asked. "Do you expect to be long in New York?"

"We'll be quartered here for some time, I expect. We're building another barracks not far from here, and we drill most days." He smiled at his plate the way Joe did when I caught him staring at girls. "Why do you ask?"

"What of other companies or regiments? Will they all remain in New York for the time being?" I grew a little bolder. "Are there plans to engage the enemy soon?"

The servers began moving empty tables away from the center floor as the man playing the fiddle was joined by a second fiddler and a guitarist.

The lieutenant answered my questions with vague replies. He either didn't know or wasn't about to divulge it to me. He wiped his mouth with a napkin and placed it beside his plate.

I decided to drop the subject. "Are you a dancer, Lieutenant?"

"Depends on the dance, I have to say. Country dances, aye. Minuets and such, no."

I laughed. "Perfectly understandable."

Sophia Shepherd traded seats with Captain Higgins, who had struck up a conversation with her cousin Mary. Mr. Fellowes, who'd been talking with Celeste across the table, took the vacant seat beside her when Lieutenant Parker excused himself. I could sense her relief and excitement. Hopefully, he would ask her to dance before Parker returned.

The musicians invited dancers to the floor for a reel. Chairs scraped the rough floorboards as gentlemen bowed and ladies stood and accepted their hands.

Lieutenant MacCallan turned to me. "If it's a Scottish reel, then I should know it. Would you do me the honor, Miss Floyd?"

"I'd be delighted."

We moved to the center floor, where five other couples gathered, including Celeste and Mr. Fellowes. I didn't think the Lieutenant had noticed my left hand yet.

Some sort of scuffle at the entrance caused heads to turn. A group of men stood inside the doorway with arms draped around three or four young women, looking for available seats.

Mr. Grant directed them to a far corner. I didn't get a good look at the men, but by their unkempt and rather vulgar appearance, I guessed the women had come from the Holy Ground area a short distance away. As they paraded past, they stared longingly at the plates of food on the tables.

The cheerful music soon had us hopping and circling, as the seated patrons clapped in time. The lieutenant was lighter on his feet than I expected. When we briefly clasped hands and formed a circle with the other dancers, we were on to the next part before my deformity was noticed.

A simpler dance followed the reel, although neither of us knew the steps and we stumbled a bit until we caught on. When the tune ended, we followed Celeste and Mr. Fellowes back to our table. We all held our stomachs, out of breath.

The lieutenant laughed. "In Scotland we say, 'I'm fair puckled.'"

A hard tap on my shoulder made me stop and whirl around.

I noticed the rum on his breath before I saw the hideous black mark beneath his eye. He sneered, raising a tankard. He wore civilian clothing, but with the buckskin hat of the Loyalist militia, complete with a black feather.

"If it isn't the prisoners' favorite nurse."

I took a step back. I hadn't seen Crankshaw since my last day inside Rhinelander's. Of all people—the man I was certain knew more of Christopher Martin's death than he'd shared with my mother.

The skin on the back of my neck pricked. I'd drank just enough cider. "If it isn't the prisoners' favorite fool."

I sensed several pairs of eyes on me, including those at my table, but I didn't care who heard me.

He sneered. "I work for Mr. Cunningham now, by the way."

"Ha! Such a promotion. You're the perfect bootlicker for that evil man."

I cringed as the words left my lips, however true. One of the Shepherd ladies gasped.

Crankshaw backed away, waving two fingers at me. "Have a pleasant evening."

Mother stepped into the parlor a few days later to bid goodbye to Joe and me. "I'm leaving for the sugar house. Ask Alice how you might assist when she returns from the market."

"We will," I said. "Please take care, Mother."

She'd resumed her visits with the prisoners at Rhinelander's a few weeks earlier and chose to call it the sugar house now. Perhaps using the building's original name eased the reality of all she faced there.

When I told her of my encounter with Crankshaw at the party, she inquired at Rhinelander's, where they confirmed that he indeed had been sent to guard the Provost Jail. With him no longer present, she had invited me to accompany her, but I refused.

Reminders of Christopher and his death, as she believed, weren't my only reasons not to go; any link to sympathizing with Patriots had best be avoided, according to Culper Junior. Culper Senior had agreed with him when the subject came up during one of their meetings. However, it relieved me to hear that they thought Mother could do as she saw fit.

The front door clicked shut as she left. I signed my letter to Jacob, in which I described the Clinton dinner and all the parts he would find humorous, excluding the mention of military actions, past, present, and future. He would love to hear of them, no doubt. But such things couldn't be written in a letter, especially one meant for an enlisted man, in the event it fell into the wrong hands.

I didn't tell Jacob from whom I'd received the dinner invitation either. In any case, Major André was either caught up in his duties or had lost interest in our friendship, because I still had yet to hear from him since the dinner, now more than three weeks ago.

In some respects, I was growing less enthusiastic regarding my Culper Ring activities. The work was dangerous and could prove fatal. Furthermore, I had to commit everything to memory because Robert had refused to provide me any invisible ink or allow me to use the code.

Regardless, no valuable intelligence had come my way since the Clinton dinner. That, coupled with the uncertainty of my relationship with the major (if there indeed was one) brought all my doubts and misgivings regarding the Ring to the surface. Truly, I had no idea how to proceed.

My brother shut his Latin book and dropped his head back. "I'm falling asleep."

I couldn't blame him. It occurred to me that the next time my worries kept me awake, I should try improving my Latin.

"Perhaps some air will help." I folded the letter to Jacob. "Let's take a short walk."

Joe hopped to his feet. "As long as we can speak English."

On the porch under the parlor window, Triple observed us from his box with eyes half-closed. He opened his mouth in a wide yawn, stretched his entire body down to the toes of his three legs, then stood, rearranged himself, and shut his eyes.

"I think he was out all night again," Joe said.

"He seems capable of taking care of himself." I had to admit that my respect for the cat had grown. He hadn't let his disfigurement stop him—something we had in common.

Joe snickered. "I can tell you like him now."

I suppressed a smile as we crossed the porch and descended the steps. Warm sunshine bathed our lawn and the leaves on the elm, which were slowly transforming from deep green to a golden orange.

The cooler nights of late, another sign of autumn's approach, made sleeping more pleasant than the summer months when my sheets and hair often stuck to my skin. My favorite season would forever be autumn, yet I dreaded the confinement of winter that would follow. It always arrived too soon and stayed well past its welcome.

We turned left out of habit, the way that led to the business district and waterfront. Mrs. Richards waved to us from her porch. A baby's cries carried from an upper window at another house. A portly man making a delivery stopped his horse and two-wheeled trap at another.

"Have you any news of Mrs. Burgin?" I asked Joe.

He stuffed his hands in the pockets of his breeches, which were beginning to look a bit too short again. "Nothing. I went by her house, but it's deserted."

When I'd asked Robert, he said he didn't know of Elizabeth Burgin, yet he was aware that a small number of prisoners aboard the *Jersey* had managed to escape. However, most starved or died of disease and were then thrown overboard, their bodies often washing up on shore not far from the ship. I shuddered to think of it, and

Robert shared my disgust when I relayed to him General Clinton's apparent indifference.

"Perhaps we'll hear something soon," I said to Joe. "But again, you mustn't speak of those men she helped to anyone. It simply isn't safe for you or her children."

He mumbled an agreement as we reached the alley and turned around. All I could do was make my brother aware and pray he and the Burgin family stayed safe.

I placed my hand on his shoulder. "What if you thought of Latin as a code, and your assignment is to decipher it?"

One of us might as well make use of a code. It was unlikely *I* ever would.

Alice came up the walk from the opposite direction holding a sack in each arm. Joe hurried to help her.

"Jus' the man I want to see." She handed him the sacks.

After we put away the millet and oats and I took the eggs to the Dicksons' icehouse and returned with a small piece of our beef to cook, Alice poured three mugs of cider. Joe took his mug back to the parlor to renew his battle with Latin, while she and I took ours outside to the back steps.

"Good thing we made plenty o' candles this summer," Alice said. "Won't be long and we won't be sittin' out here like ladies o' leisure." She laughed. "We be holdin' tight to our shawls, bringin' in wood."

"I don't mind that so much," I said. "It's what comes afterward that I can do without."

She took a long, slow drink from her mug. "It don't sound like they makin' much progress in the war. So, I'm guessin' they'll be havin' plenty o' parties and balls all winter."

"I think you're probably right on both counts, Alice."

"Worst part's findin' food and firewood, 'specially for the poor." She gazed at the worn patch of grass by the bottom step. "I know the soldiers all gotta eat and stay warm, but the city can't keep feeding 'em and take care of its own."

I nearly shivered at the thought. "Last winter was dreadful when people started chopping up church pews for firewood and so many starved to death." What would happen by the time the icy winter winds swooped in over New York City once again?

"Your mama and me, we been putting up extra food so's we can help if it come to that."

"I'll knit more stockings to give away again this year."

What would the coming winter bring for the Culpers? The usual hazards of travel could be far worse in winter. If both armies took their usual recess until the spring thaw, would there be a decrease in intelligence to forward to General Washington? And if there was anything to communicate, how would Abraham Woodhull accomplish it? The difficulties and delays that came with frozen channels and roads buried in snow could make it impossible for correspondence to reach Washington in a timely way.

And what if Clinton took his men and attacked Charleston? If he were successful, would he continue through the south? Was the south prepared?

Of course, there was no stopping my thoughts of Major André. What would his duties be during winter? Would he remain in New York to continue with his acting? What if I were to take part in a theatre production and tell Robert and the Ring goodbye?

Alice put a hand on my knee, bringing me back to the present. She pushed herself to her feet. "I best see to the fire and get the meat goin'. You stayin' home, or you and Miss Celeste got somethin' to do?"

I rose and followed her across the yard to the kitchen. "I'm not going anywhere."

In the kitchen, Alice went to the fireplace and poked the embers until they flamed. We added small pieces of wood to raise the heat to the right temperature for boiling the beef, then prepared a spider pan to make spoon bread.

She bent over the hot coals. "How be that nice Major André?"

I hoisted the heavy pot from the worktable onto the lug pole. "That nice Major André is a busy man, assisting General Clinton."

"Mmm-hmm."

Sensing her eyes on me, I adjusted the pot's height so it would heat properly. We then filled it with water from two large pitchers we kept near the hearth.

Alice spoke up. "I s'pect he not that busy. He'll come 'round, you watch."

I laughed. "I thought you said that I don't need to be getting caught up with a soldier."

"I still say so. But—"

I led the way back to the house. "I'd rather not talk of him, Alice."

Joe met us in the pantry. "Special delivery for Miss Betty Floyd."

He handed me a small, sealed note. Alice gave me a furtive glance as she pulled a wooden ladle from a drawer.

I recognized the major's elegant handwriting.

"Your cheeks are turning red." Joe said. "The fellow is waiting on the porch for a reply."

"It's the kitchen . . . 'tis warm." I turned my back to him.

The wax seal bore the Crown of King George III. I broke it, unfolded the message, and read it aloud.

Dear Miss Floyd,

I request that you join me for a visit to Vauxhall Gardens on Saturday next, followed by dinner at City Tavern. If this is agreeable to you, I shall look forward to arriving by carriage at your home at three o'clock.

Yours truly,
John André

"Well, how 'bout that?" Alice slapped the ladle against her apron.

Joe held out his hands. "So, is it agreeable?"

I pocketed the note. "Tell him I accept."

Joe went to the door, and I bit back a grin as I pulled out the salt crock to rub the beef. Alice rummaged in the cupboards, humming a haphazard tune.

This would be one event I wouldn't discuss in advance with anyone outside of my family. Certainly not Celeste, as she would only pry me for details afterward.

And I didn't need any more admonishments or warnings from Culper Junior. As 355, if I learned anything of importance, I would make certain to speak to him.

Aside from that, what I did as Cousin Betty was none of his concern.

Seventeen

At one minute before three o'clock on Saturday, I peeked between the draperies in the parlor for the twelfth time. At last, a black carriage approached. In the driver's seat, a pleasant-looking man wearing a tricorn and white shirt pulled the horses to a gentle stop.

I called to Mother, who had been pacing in the hall. "He's here."

I smoothed my rose gown and patted my hair again. Rather than a more formal style, I'd twisted and pinned it up rather simply.

There would be no thought of the Culper Ring today. Betty Floyd was to spend the day with Major John André, and 355 would not be making an appearance. She could wait for another day—I only wished to enjoy myself and this remarkable man, and perhaps ignore the war again, just for a day.

The carriage's passenger door opened, and the major emerged. Seeing him out of uniform, wearing a dark blue frockcoat, matching waistcoat, white shirt, and tan breeches made my hands start to shake. One of the most popular men in America was at *my* house to call on *me*.

"He's punctual, I'll give him that." Mother patted her hair and adjusted her cap. "Wait for his knock, Elizabeth."

I listened for his step on the porch. With whom was he speaking? Then came the knock, and I opened the door.

He wore a tentative smile and held a small bouquet of yellow and white flowers. "Good afternoon, Miss Floyd."

I opened the door wider and invited him in. "Were you speaking with someone?" My words shook, despite all effort to sound calm.

He removed his tricorn. "A most wary cat. I explained to him I mean no harm. Is he yours?"

Mother entered the foyer from the parlor. "Welcome, sir." She curtsied. "The cat belongs to my son, Joseph."

I took a deep breath. "Major, may I introduce my mother, Margaret Floyd?"

"I'm delighted to meet you, Mrs. Floyd." He handed her the bouquet. "These are for you."

She reached for the flowers, clearly impressed. "Thank you, they are lovely."

"Shall we?" I grabbed my reticule and gloves from the table by the stairs. On impulse, I left my straw hat on the step.

"Again, it was a pleasure," he said to Mother. "We shall return sometime following dinner." He bowed—the respectful and proper officer. She curtsied again, her cheeks in full blush.

I hurried ahead of him down the porch steps and out to the carriage. He introduced me to Peter Laune, his valet. I resisted the urge to see if Mother was watching from the window or on the porch, waving my hat. As soon as we were settled and the carriage pulled away, I relaxed against the smooth leather seat and exhaled.

He laughed. "Is something wrong?"

"Not at all. I . . . Forgive me, I've never had an actual gentleman caller before."

He raised a brow in apparent surprise. "I'm delighted to know I'm the first. And now I see where your beauty comes from. Your mother is a stunning woman."

I couldn't stop the warmth rising to my cheeks. "Thank you, although I inherited my father's height. My brother has as well. By the way, Joe was quite disappointed that he couldn't be at home to meet you. He works for our cousin at his shop on Saturdays."

"We shall meet another time," he said. "What is your cousin's name?"

Robert would disapprove of him knowing our connection, of course. Yet I couldn't very well withhold his name. "Robert Townsend. He's part owner in Oakham and Townsend, the dry goods store—"

"Townsend's your cousin? Good man. I see him at Rivington's on occasion. And when John Simcoe was quartered at the Townsend home in Oyster Bay, I happened to visit when your cousin came."

I smiled at the coincidence. "I used to think no one would know my family here in the city." At least Simcoe didn't hear of my relationship to the Townsends at the Clinton dinner.

He apologized for not corresponding sooner, claiming his duties had taken him out of New York. I tried not to concern myself with it while we chatted about mutual acquaintances and his upcoming theatre rehearsals.

I would have been content to remain in the carriage and ride in circles the entire afternoon, but all too soon Mr. Laune pulled the carriage around the last waterfront warehouse and up the hill on Greenwich Road to Vauxhall Gardens.

Before he jumped out to assist me down the steps, the major pulled a notebook from the door pocket. "My sketchpad," he said.

He paid our entry fee and held the iron gate open for me. Four large square gardens were divided by sunny gravel paths for strolling, with a fountain in the very center. Trees in bright autumn colors provided shade.

"How lovely." I shielded my eyes. "And we could not have asked for a better day."

A string quartet played from an outdoor stage. We strolled the paths alongside other couples and families, admiring the variety of flowers and the marble statues among them. He impressed me with his knowledge of floral names, and I explained what we'd grown on the farm—lavender for the bees, peonies and dahlias because they were Mother's favorites, and several grain crops for feeding livestock.

"Do you know what became of your farm workers when you left?"

"All but two were slaves. Some ran when the military moved in, and Mother released the rest. Perhaps they stayed on."

He gazed across the gardens. "I'm afraid slavery is something that's hard for me to grasp."

How could I explain what had become commonplace in some of the colonies? "Owning slaves is quite customary, especially on farms. It's how things have been done for years, although I'm aware there are good arguments for change."

Even the Declaration of Independence opposed it, although I thought better than to let him know I had read it. "Since I've been in New York," I said, "I have a better sense of how abusive it can be. On our farm, though, it was simply our way of life."

"Are you aware that the military is promising safety to any runaway slave who cares to enlist?"

"Yes, however, it doesn't apply to those already living in New York, which is confounding. My father . . . Well, I will just say he had his faults. But he treated his slaves decently, compared to some."

Refraining from comment, he kept his eyes on the path.

"I'm sorry, I don't wish to sound as though I'm justifying it. I'm not proud of the fact we owned slaves."

"Regardless, you had no say in the matter." He cleared his throat. "Tell me, were you educated at home?"

"Yes, at my mother's insistence. She taught me some, then I had a tutor who also took on Joe when he was old enough."

He shook his head. "'Tis quite different in England—except for the very wealthy, young ladies are seldom taught more than the basics. And now you've assumed the role of his tutor."

"Yes, although I worry that he won't be prepared for college."

We turned down another path and passed the musicians. A barn-like structure stood just off the path. A man pushing a wheelbarrow filled with soil exited the wide-open doors.

My throat tightened at the sight of the barn. I took Major André's arm. "May we turn around, please?"

He looked momentarily puzzled but made the turn with me. "I find it fascinating that you and your family had a large farm, so much land, and much to care for every day. And you dealt with the loss of your father and your property, and now you have a new life in the city, yet you've managed to embrace it quite well."

My throat relaxed a bit. "It has not been easy, by any means, Major."

"Yes, I would imagine it has taken a great deal of courage."

He led me to a shady oak and squeezed my gloved hands. "Would you feel it appropriate if I call you Betty? And for you to call me John?"

We'd known each other longer than I knew Christopher Martin, yet he could not have surprised me more. Onlookers passed, and I felt their questioning eyes. "Why, yes. That . . . I would like that very much."

He lifted my hands and kissed them. "Betty it is."

What did this mean to him? Probably nothing. I couldn't make much of it.

At the path's end, we stopped at a lemonade stand and took our glasses to a small table and chairs overlooking the river and the coves of Long Island beyond. All sorts of ships moved through the water. Others were anchored not far offshore.

The wind off the river loosened some of my hair from its pins. "If there weren't all the warships with their cannons, it would be a lovely scene indeed."

"The reminders of war." His eyes turned forlorn. "It must be difficult to look across to where you grew up, so near, yet so far. I often yearn for England."

He always gave the appearance of complete self-assurance. His longing for his home was a side of him I hadn't seen. I considered reaching over to touch his arm in comfort, yet—

"I once loved someone there," he said suddenly. "Someone I didn't deserve."

His unprompted divulging of a serious relationship, even if long ago, took me by surprise. I waited for him to continue, unsure how to respond.

Then as if nothing happened, his cheerful countenance returned. "Forgive me. I didn't mean to turn our conversation into a melancholy one." He rose and reached for my hand. "Let's find a place out of the sun."

We headed away from the path toward a grove of trees. "May I ask you something, John?" It would take practice not to address him as Major.

"*Que voulez-vous savoir?*"

"What can you tell me of your time in Philadelphia . . . and of Miss Shippen?"

He drew back, ever so slightly. "I promise to answer all of your questions if I may draw your portrait."

I laughed. "If you must."

We selected a bench under a canopy of honeysuckle vine. He instructed me to sit with my back toward the sun and remove my gloves. Then he turned my head and arranged my arms at my sides with my hands resting on the seat, until he was satisfied.

I moved my hands to my lap, but he moved them back again.

"Trust zee artiste, *Mademoiselle*."

He perched himself on a tree stump beside the bench and opened his sketchpad. "Look here, *s'il vous plait*." From his coat pocket, he pulled two long pieces of graphite wrapped in cloth and a small rag.

"I feel ridiculous." I laughed. "I should have re-pinned my hair. How long will this take?"

"Your hair is perfect. Now, you shall hear my Philadelphia story."

While he worked, glancing back and forth from me to his sketch, he related how he'd entered the military in England and came to Quebec, then to Philadelphia, then to New York. And in 1775, he spent a year as an American prisoner.

"When I learned of your assistance to the rebel prisoners," he said, "I naturally thought of that time. I can imagine how much your presence must have meant to them, and I trust you and your mother acted in good faith. After all, we're called to love our enemies."

"I was certain you were going to have us arrested."

His downturned mouth showed his disappointment. "I would never do such a thing."

He was a unique and complex man, to be sure, especially for one in his position.

I stretched my arms, then rested them on the bench again. "You promised to tell me more of Philadelphia."

"Hold still, please. I acted as interpreter, planned events for the officers, and assisted General Howe. You may have heard of the Meschianza, an enormous party I organized for him before he returned to England. Rather ostentatious, but quite wonderful."

Are you going to explain about Miss Shippen or not?

He dusted off the page where he'd been drawing and closed the sketchpad.

I dropped my pose. "Is it finished? May I see it?"

"In a moment." He came to sit beside me on the bench. "There were numerous wealthy residents in Philadelphia, and many parties. I took part in several theatrical productions and was introduced to Miss Shippen at a party following one of those plays. She and I became well-acquainted, yet when we abandoned Philadelphia, we never saw each other again."

His eyes were a mixture of frustration and sadness. "It wasn't long before she met the man she was to marry."

How could she have treated this kind, handsome man in such a manner? Yet I could not help but hope he no longer had feelings for her, or the lady in England.

"Did it surprise you that Miss Shippen married an American general?" I asked.

He ran his hand over the sketchpad. "I imagine she saw his power and position as a means to continue her wealthy lifestyle and maintain a certain position of her own in society. That mattered to her a great deal. But let's talk of it no more—she is Mrs. Arnold now."

He opened the sketchpad to where he'd drawn my portrait. There on paper sat a girl on a bench, relaxed and happy, wisps of hair blowing gently away from her face.

I took in the light breaking through the honeysuckle, the curve of lace along her gown's neckline, the calm way her hands lay open at her sides. What I was accustomed to seeing in my grandmother's dark, wavy mirror was nothing like it.

"Is this me? No one has ever done my portrait before."

He reached for a lock of my hair and twirled it between his fingers. "It's entirely you. I hope this conveys, at least in part, the beauty I see. Inside and out."

When we arrived at City Tavern, several customers occupied the tables. Some played whist; others ate and drank. Many of them called or waved to the major, staring at me with curiosity.

He led me to the far corner, to a rough-hewn table lit by a small oil lamp. A waiter greeted him, and the major ordered a full bottle of their finest wine.

"Please don't expect me to have more than one glass," I said. "I'm determined to keep my wits about me."

A grin teased the corners of his eyes. "Have whatever amount you wish."

Our conversation in the carriage ride to the tavern had somehow turned to the state of the war, despite my wish to avoid it. When the wine came, it surprised me when he kept to the subject. Perhaps if anything valuable to the Culpers surfaced, I had best pay attention.

"The rebels have outsmarted us several times," he said, "which never fails to frustrate General Clinton. Then we hear of their smaller numbers, desertions, lack of uniforms, et cetera, yet we cannot be certain what's true. The need for proper intelligence never ceases."

If he only knew how Robert would agree on that point. At least the major hadn't asked me to spy for the Crown again.

"Forgive me, Betty. You're always a gracious listener, and I'm afraid I take advantage."

"No need to apologize, John. You have a way of explaining things in a straightforward manner, and I appreciate it." I leaned a bit closer and assumed a look of wide-eyed innocence. "I wonder, could what's true for one regiment or one area of the country be different in another? For example, dwindling numbers in one part, and heavier enlistments elsewhere?"

"Ah, that is a very interesting question." He moved his chair closer to mine. "Yes, it is entirely possible. Recently, we received quite the surprise at Lloyd's Neck on Long Island. Are you familiar with the area, by chance?"

Now we may have something. "I've heard of it—I believe it wasn't too far from our farm. There are many narrow coves and landings in that area, some with similar names."

The waiter arrived with a plate of rolls and described the food choices available. We decided on two dinners of roast chicken, Indian pudding, and baked apples.

When the waiter left with our orders, Major André filled his wine glass from the half-empty bottle. "Fort Franklin was constructed at Lloyd's Neck in order to serve as a base for raids into Connecticut," he said. "The fort was named for William Franklin, whom you met at the ball. Earlier this month, our encampments near the fort were attacked, taking the men completely by surprise."

I tried to visualize such a feat. "That's quite remarkable in such a remote area."

"They landed and made their approach without a sound. The charge was led by a Long Islander, Major Tallmadge. Do you know the name?"

I feigned a cough, hoping to hide my shock. *Of course.* Ben Tallmadge would know the complicated inlets and be able to obtain locals in undertaking the attack. Not only did he manage Washington's spy ring, but I was gratified to learn he was a warrior as well.

I regained my composure. "Tallmadge? No, I don't believe so."

The major drew a breath and released it. "They were unsuccessful in taking the fort, yet they did a great deal of damage and took prisoners. It's a blow to our morale. . . . Truly, this war should have been over long ago." He tipped back his wine glass and emptied it. "But we may have a breakthrough coming."

More customers had arrived, and the noise level compared to that of the Navy Coffeehouse. I chose a roll from the plate and took my time tearing it apart, hoping to appear only mildly curious. "What sort of breakthrough?"

He set down his glass. "You've let me go on again. I find your interest in the war refreshing, but I don't wish to bore you with it."

I reached for his arm. "You couldn't possibly bore me in any way, and I mean that sincerely." It was an honest statement. I genuinely enjoyed our conversations, no matter the subject.

Perhaps I would learn of the breakthrough at another time. I felt it best to change the subject. "Tell me, how would you compare yourself to Captain Plume?"

His eyes widened. "Ah. Plume, the Recruiting Officer . . . I will say we both enjoy poetry, the military, life in general, and people in particular. But I differ from Plume. Primarily, I'm not cut out for deception and disguises."

I tilted my head, scrutinizing him. "Do not spies use deception and disguises in their work?"

He relaxed against his chair, clearly amused. "I may direct others, yet I expressed to you before that I do not see myself as a spy. I'm not duplicitous enough."

Neither am I. At least, I don't believe I am.

I sipped my wine, considering what information would be useful to General Washington, although I couldn't help feeling a tinge of disloyalty to John André. On the other hand, *he* may not think himself a spy, yet the goal of his superior, General Clinton, was to find Washington's spies in New York.

To find *me*.

The waiter served our piping hot dinners. Between bites, we engaged in lighter topics of conversation. Soon we were laughing over how my brother had adopted a three-legged cat that had become as good of a mouser as any we'd kept on the farm.

A trio of violinists set up their stools and prepared their instruments. The dance floor consisted of a space the size of our pantry, but it would suffice.

The major poured the last of the wine into his glass. "Are you interested in dancing?"

I smiled. "Do you believe you need to ask?"

After two dances, we both felt ready to leave. The proprietor, Mr. Roubalet, saw us to the door and bid us "*Bon Nuit.*"

The sky had grown dark and a steady rain fell. While I pulled on my gloves, the major removed his frockcoat and wrapped it around my shoulders. Laughing, we stepped over a few puddles and found Peter Laune waiting with the carriage not far up Broadway. The compartment was warm and dry, but I kept the major's coat around me as we set off.

"I truly enjoyed this day," I said. "*Merci.*"

"I did as well." He pointed his thumb at the window as we turned a corner. "I'm quartered this way, in a house that was vacated. Would you care to see it?"

"At a more appropriate time, perhaps." I brushed my wet hair off my face. "With others present."

He reached for his sketchpad in the side pocket. "You mustn't forget this."

I laid it in my lap. "Thank you. I'll remove the page with the drawing and return the rest."

He rubbed my hands through my gloves. "I hope you won't mind if I state something rather personal."

"What is it?"

He caressed my left hand, lifting it slightly. "You've always been quite straightforward about this, which I admire a great deal, because I can imagine how some are taken aback by it and have been unkind."

"There are those who tend to make it more of an issue than necessary." I extracted my hand from his. "But . . . I don't want or need your admiration."

"It's an admiration of your bravery, Betty. Your forthrightness, in coping with all you've been through. Yet 'tis only a small part of who you are, as I discover each time I am with you. My sentiments go far beyond admiration."

I stared at the tiny rivers of rain cascading down the carriage window. How was I to reconcile my growing feelings for him and my commitment to the Culper Ring—the very group of Patriots he and Clinton were determined to catch?

Who do you think you are? You're not worthy of him or the Ring.

"I'm not . . ."

He ran a finger over my cheek until that thought was forgotten.

The rain beat against the carriage hood as the horses clip-clopped over the stones toward my home. Then John André took my face in his warm hands and softly kissed my waiting lips.

Eighteen

October 1779

Four lines of soldiers, five abreast, crossed ahead of me in their march toward the waterfront. I was not in a hurry. Robert had sent for me two days prior, informing Joe he had a package I must claim—his way, I assumed, of alerting me of business to discuss. He was undoubtedly hoping I had intelligence to relate as well.

He could wait. Perhaps new information had come in through his various channels, but mine were stagnant. I'd already reported to him what I learned on my Vauxhall Gardens outing with John André, but nothing significant had surfaced since then.

I suppose I still desired to help, and I still wanted revenge for Christopher's death. Yet I wavered daily regarding my role in the Ring and whether I could, or should, continue the whole charade.

Attempting to cover up my secret made it necessary to constantly think twice before I spoke. I hated misleading my family, Celeste, Major André, and nearly everyone I met, one way or another. And I would be lying to Robert as well if I continued to keep him from knowing the extent of my relationship with the major, although I wasn't certain I could define it.

After our first kiss, I told myself I didn't want or need a romantic relationship. I blamed the Ring, the war, the major's prominent position in the army, which I still hated, and my duties at home. Certainly, I had no business trying to balance spying on the enemy and falling in love with him. No, I would not. *Could not.*

However, none of that stopped me from accepting his invitations.

Small parties and a concert were the more public events where we were surrounded by his usual admirers. Then one afternoon, I took Joe to Mr. Mulligan's for new woolen breeches and the major came in for a uniform fitting. The three of us went to tea at Rivington's, where he entertained my brother with tall tales of pirates, which only fueled Joe's desire to run away to sea.

After I'd sent my brother home, we went for a quiet fireside dinner at Montague's Tavern, then a walk in the Common. Near the road stood the Provost Jail, a dark, foreboding building, lair of the evil William Cunningham and now Mr. Crankshaw. A dim lamp lit the lowest windows.

I'd taken little notice of the cold, only the swirling leaves along the footpaths and the diamond-studded sky. When the major pulled me into an embrace in the shadow of a great oak, the warm glow I felt inside melted away the dread of the approaching winter.

When Mother questioned where things stood, it was difficult to answer. "We are not courting, if that is what you're thinking. There's a war on, you know."

I doubted that did much to reassure her. Yet there was little else to say.

At one of the parties I attended with the major, Celeste had come with Mr. Fellowes. According to her, they'd seen each other often since the evening at the Navy Coffeehouse. She invited me to another party when Mr. Fellowes was unavailable, but I'd had to send my regrets, due to plans with the major. I hoped she didn't think our friendship had taken a lower priority. I would need to visit her soon or arrange to meet her for tea.

As I made my way to Oakham and Townsend, the scent of chimney smoke lined the air as a robust wind off the harbor fought to push me backward and tore the multicolored leaves from the trees. I pulled my heavy shawl tighter and kept going.

At Hanover Square, three soldiers with muskets slung over their shoulders watched me from the street corner until I reached the door to the shop. What, or whom, were they awaiting?

Inside, Robert helped a young soldier at the counter. He barely raised his eyes as I entered. "I will be with you momentarily."

From the window, I could see the corner where the soldiers stood watching the door. Robert's customer soon departed with a hammer and three sausages protruding from his sack.

Robert turned the sign, locked the door, and motioned for me to take my usual seat at the desk. His expression drooped into a scowl.

"Perhaps you should leave it open," I said. "Soldiers watched me enter, although they may have been waiting for those sausages."

He checked the street from the window. "They are crossing near the coffeehouse now. Although we cannot be too careful. They have increased their surveillance across the city." He went to his chair. "Where have you been? I did not think I would need to ask your brother—"

"I haven't been anywhere." I lifted my shoulders. "As far as I know, there isn't any unusual activity. I only heard that some troops are preparing for a move south, but—"

He seized the edge of the desk. "You should have reported this sooner."

"Why are you raising your voice? I didn't think it important."

"It is not your place to decide what is important. We report everything we hear and let John Bolton and 711 determine what is important."

I attempted to break the tension and show some effort. "Do you think they're preparing to attack Charleston? Yet if they are, they're not in much of a hurry."

Robert leaned forward, disturbing the neat stacks of receipts on the desk. "You do not see what I see here at the waterfront. The fact that they are moving the troops at all is significant. The transports have been extremely active. Charleston may well be the destination at some point, but it is believed that many men are currently bound for Georgia.

"In addition, a large French fleet was seen leaving the West Indies, and apparently Clinton expects them to possibly join our forces in an attack on New York. He has sent a number of troops to points on Long Island as a preventive measure. As you might imagine, this is causing Culper Senior far more anxiety than usual."

It was a great deal to absorb—so much taking place beyond the garrison of New York City. How had I not noticed? Was I so preoccupied with my nonrelationship with John André that I'd missed it?

I let out a breath that blew receipts off the desk. "I had no idea."

"That is quite clear." He raised his slender, hardworking hands as if in surrender.

He didn't need to say it: in his eyes, I'd failed again. Rather than actively seeking information from sources other than Major André, I'd wrongly assumed there was nothing new to learn. And clearly, my mind had been more on *him* than anything else.

Robert retrieved his receipts from the floor. "I will add your abysmal report of the troop transports to mine. Did you hear it from Major André?"

I chose to ignore the way he spit out the name. "I believe it was a conversation I overheard at a party, and at the time, I sensed that it was not a matter of urgency."

Before he could admonish me again, I continued. "I don't believe I mentioned to you that the major told me of an attack on Lloyd's Neck in September and that Ben Tallmadge was the leader."

He pulled out his keys and opened the drawer where he kept the Culper code pages. "Yes, nothing we did not know." He drew a breath, relaxing the furrows between his eyes. "It was well executed, although they did not accomplish all they anticipated. He conspired with another member of the Ring—Caleb Brewster—the man who usually delivers our correspondence across the Sound to Connecticut."

I had seen Brewster among the code names. "They're quite brave to take such risks."

"Have you any new information in regard to West Point?"

I lowered my eyes, barely shaking my head. I hadn't given a thought to it since the day I saw Robert after the Clinton dinner.

"John Bolton and the general wish to be informed immediately if there is *any* further mention of it."

"Of course, Robert." From his emphasis, there was to be no misinterpretation.

"There is a matter to bring to your attention, although it does not currently affect you. General Washington requests that future correspondence be not only written in the invisible ink but also enclosed inside of a small book or register, as an additional disguise. I only have a limited number of such books I no longer use, but I am seeking to obtain more."

"Perhaps Mr. Rivington would have that sort of thing around the *Gazette* office. He always has pamphlets to give away."

He cocked his head. "That is possible."

I still wished to know the manner in which Mr. Rivington furthered the work of the Ring, yet I sensed it was not the proper time to raise that question.

"There is another, graver issue." Robert pressed his fingers against the edge of the desk. "Culper Senior informs me there has been a surge in the questioning of individuals at various checkpoints, the inspection of their belongings, and the like. If, by chance, I am ever detained or imprisoned, you must continue the business with him the best that you can, unless the general says otherwise."

Imagining such a scenario gave me chills. "Even if you were stopped, what would lead them to have you imprisoned? You've been impeccably secretive."

"They might use anything, or nothing. I am only saying we must be prepared. Therefore, should that occur, and should you have vital intelligence to pass on, I have made a copy of the Culper code for your use. Mind you, it is against my better judgment."

He withdrew two sheets of paper from the drawer on which he'd neatly transcribed all the code words, names, and numbers. "I cannot stress enough the sensitivity of this document, or the absolute necessity that you protect its whereabouts at all times. I am unable to give you any of the ink, however. I hardly have enough for my own correspondence."

I ran my hand over the top page, shocked that he was now willing to trust me with it, given his frustration with me. "I will guard it with my life—you needn't worry. And I hope the need for it won't arise."

"If it does," he said, "Culper Senior and I have agreed you will either signal him that you must meet or that you are dropping correspondence in a particular location."

He waited as I let his words take hold and the seriousness of what they entailed.

"How will I signal him?"

"At the stables next to Rivington's, there is an old iron boot scrape near the left outside wall where hay is piled. It is rarely used.

Tie a small red cloth to it. That will indicate you will call on his sister, Mary Underhill, at the boarding house that evening before sunset. He will meet you there, or she will know how you may find him."

I hated having to plan for the worst, but it was better than not knowing what to do if the worst came. "What if I want to leave a note for him? Could I not simply insert it in a small book and give it to his sister?"

Uncle William's book of poems came to mind. I had yet to hear from him since returning the book and alerting him to the possibility of danger at the hands of Lieutenant-Colonel Simcoe. If he sent it to me again, perhaps one day he would enjoy hearing how his little poetry book was used to forward valuable secrets to the Commander-in-Chief.

Robert shook his head. "Too much risk. Someone may see it. Regardless, you must follow Culper's direction and not deviate.

"To leave correspondence, there is a broken pot with a false bottom in the alley behind Fraunces Tavern. Wrap a letter in an old rag and place it inside. Then tie a blue cloth instead of a red one to the boot scrape at the stables. Of course, you must always ensure you are not followed."

I envisioned carrying out such a deed. "Suppose I am followed. Or otherwise prevented from going to tie the cloth or make the drop. Or I'm not even able to come here. What then?"

Robert's eyes scanned the ceiling. "If I am still here and you cannot come, send a spice cake with Joseph, and I will have Mr. Roe come to you. Should it happen that I am gone, Joseph will likely tell you. If you need to deliver correspondence and cannot carry out Culper's plan as I have given you, send a cake to Mr. Roe. I will explain this to him."

He removed his spectacles and wiped his sleeve across his brow. "Is that all quite clear?"

"Completely clear." This was the most convoluted scheme I'd ever heard.

But the strain of his efforts and covering every possibility was clearly taking its toll on my cousin. I covered his hand with mine.

"I apologize for not being as attentive to our work as I should be, Robert. Thank you for still trusting me, nevertheless."

We stood. I folded the Culper code pages and wrapped them tightly inside my shawl. I longed to be on my way, commit his instructions to memory, and secure the pages in my room where they would never see the light of day again.

Robert hesitated, arms folded against his apron. Was he about to scold me further?

"This business is a great weight on Culper Senior, hence on myself," he said. "The general presses us for more timely dispatches, yet we are in a heightened state of alert. So, with that, I do not mean to ridicule. I know it is difficult."

He couldn't begin to know how difficult. My eyes suddenly filled with tears. I turned aside and willed them to stop.

"I wish to encourage you," he continued, "to not back away from it, as you are serving a vital role in this endeavor. We must all remain fully engaged and set aside our personal interests for the sake of the country. This war is long and ugly, yet we are driven to pursue the prize."

I faced him again, wiping my tears away with the back of my hand.

He spoke in a softer tone. "However, if at any point you feel the need to quit, then you must say so and be clear about it."

No soldiers stood watching as I left the shop, and with the wind at my back, the walk home would be swift. Yet ever since I agreed to this outlandish role as a Culper agent, my walks following a meeting with my cousin were always troubling. This was one of the worst.

Could I continue to juggle my relationship with Major André and seek the timely intelligence General Washington demanded? Did I still wish to do so? If not, I would need to resign, simple as that. But the decision wasn't simple with so much at stake.

My mind was in turmoil. British troops on the move . . . rising tensions . . . new fears of discovery . . . orders from Abraham Woodhull should Robert be arrested. And now, here was the Culper spy code in my very hands. Should it be discovered, I would hang by sundown.

I traversed Hanover Square, dodging fresh horse droppings. A company of soldiers heading toward Fort George crossed the road up ahead. Carts loaded with tools, kegs, and barrels rattled along while merchants went about their business on foot, holding their hats against the wind.

Three officers rounded the corner. "Good day, Miss," one said. "A bit brisk, eh?"

Please don't be someone I know. I kept my eyes down and clung tighter to my shawl and the secret wrapped within.

Firm steps. No eye contact.

Their steps slowed, and for a moment I felt certain they were about to question me. Yet they brushed past.

I quickened my pace until I turned the corner and hurried to my own street, grateful to see familiar homes and neighbors scurrying in and out. In minutes, I would be across the porch, in the house, and up the stairs. While I changed into my work clothing, I would stash the code pages under my mattress.

And think. I must think.

Alice opened the door before I reached the porch. She clutched the front of her apron. "I been watchin' for you. We got trouble."

I ran inside. "What's happened? Is Joe hurt?"

Mother descended the stairs, her face tight with concern. "He's well. I asked him to carry some blankets to the spare bedroom." She waved a hand at the foot of the stairs.

A large black trunk with brown leather straps and a smaller knapsack leaned against the steps.

"Where did those come from?"

Alice shut the door. "They was delivered. Seems somebody's gonna be quartered here. Never thought I'd see it."

I stared at the invader's luggage. "After all this time? Whose are they?"

Alice rested her fists at her waist and frowned. "They don't say, jus' that he comin' soon."

Mother reached the last step. "If only there was some way to prevent it. But I won't allow—"

Joe called from above stairs. "Is he here yet?"

The sounds of horse hooves and carriage wheels drifted in from the street. I went to the parlor and pulled back the draperies.

A polished black boot emerged from the carriage door first, then the red uniform, then the white wig.

Of all people. An officer I'd planned to avoid for the rest of the war climbed down from the carriage and grabbed a tricorn from inside.

There was no time to think now. I removed my shawl and wrapped it around the Culper code pages. Where could I hide it before Alice or Mother noticed?

I jammed it behind the writing desk, then, out of habit, I smoothed my hair and returned to the foyer.

"Elizabeth, what did you do with your shawl?"

I brushed past Mother and Alice and let out a heavy sigh. "I've met this man before. I'll show him in."

I opened the door just as Captain Willington removed his hat.

"Good afternoon, Miss Floyd." He looked about to burst. "I assume you've heard the news. Uncanny luck, wouldn't you say?"

Nineteen

The first day and evening with our unwelcome tenant passed quickly, if not awkwardly. The blustery wind rattled the windows, and a drop in temperature required a joint effort to haul in enough wood for heating all the bedrooms for the long night. Captain Willington helped us with the wood, then we ate a modest dinner together of spoon bread and reheated vegetables.

He answered Mother's questions regarding his background, his work in the military, and how our home had somehow been selected when the homeowners where he'd been quartered returned to New York and demanded that he leave.

"Elizabeth tells me you've met before," Mother said to him.

He glanced my way. "We met at one of the summer balls, Mrs. Floyd."

It was a wonder he remembered, given his inebriated state that night. I speculated if he'd heard what became of "Paul Sook."

"Then a second time," he said. "As Miss Floyd attempted to cross Smith Street and was nearly run over. We were so near Rivington's that I invited her for a cup of tea."

The tea I only consented to so you wouldn't see what I carried. I glanced toward the parlor. If he only knew what was in my possession then and now.

My brother had mixed feelings regarding an officer living with us. His sentiments were still with Washington and the Patriots, yet it gave him someone to pepper with war questions, not to mention a reason to brag to his friends the next day.

Willington had risen to the occasion and obliged him with stories that were likely exaggerated, but Joe was in his glory. As long as he remembered to make no mention of Uncle William, I sensed we were reasonably safe.

To Mother, Alice, and me, however, Willington's arrival was an invasion of privacy, a great disruption to our routines, and would no doubt add to our already never-ending list of chores.

At last, after everyone had supposedly retired for the night, I tiptoed downstairs for my shawl and what it held. Halfway down, the flicker of a candle in the parlor made me jump.

"Is someone there?" Captain Willington called from the parlor.

Mercy! With my own candle, I hurried down the rest of the stairs.

"Captain!" He stood beside the writing desk. Had he looked behind it? I whispered loudly. "Why are you in the parlor?"

"I beg your pardon, Miss Floyd." He held the candlestick higher. "I've misplaced something, and I thought I might have left it in here when Joe showed me the parlor."

I glanced around at the shadows. "And have you found it?"

"I'm afraid not."

I backed toward the hall, wanting him to leave. "Perhaps you will find it in the morning."

"Yes, of course." Then he moved his candle to illuminate the desk. "This is an exquisite piece. My grandmother had a similar one."

I cleared my throat and fought for calm. "We will see you tomorrow, Captain."

"Yes. I'm terribly sorry for disturbing you, Miss Floyd. Goodnight."

I stood aside and waited for him to get the hint. Finally, he walked past me and ascended the stairs.

When his door clicked shut, I wasted no time in going to the desk and reaching behind it. My shawl lay undisturbed. I wrapped it tighter around the contents and crept up the stairs, holding my breath. After soundlessly closing my door, I tucked the code pages safely under my mattress. Then I plopped on the bed and exhaled.

What just happened? Was Captain Willington simply an overly talkative, somewhat nosy and annoying sort? Or could he be a spy, deliberately sent to live in our home by Major André himself? I never would have thought so but for the strange encounter in the parlor.

Regardless, Robert was certain to despise the idea of an officer quartering with us and would caution me to be particularly on my guard. I would assure him that the Culper code was well hidden. He didn't need to know of the close call that evening.

Preparing for bed, I tried to look at the situation objectively. A British officer under our roof, spy or not, created greater risk and gave me an excellent reason to quit the Ring. Yet what if Willington was not a spy at all, and I remained in my position? He was always eager to talk. If I was careful and we were to get better acquainted, it could prove useful.

I burrowed beneath my quilt and watched the crackling fire. On my windowsill rested two paper dolls I'd made to represent the Major and myself—he in a dark blue coat and breeches, me in a rose gown—just as we were dressed at Vauxhall Gardens. It didn't matter to me if it was somewhat childish. Beside them stood the sketch he drew of me.

How well did the major know Captain Willington? If he didn't assign him to our house for the purpose of spying, what would he think of him quartering with us?

I rolled onto my back and stared at the dancing shadows on the ceiling. All my fears and failures of the past three months as 355 marched through my head. Again, I prayed for wisdom regarding what to do, yet no clear answer came.

As the sun rose the next morning, Captain Willington joined us in the dining room for breakfast. Thankfully, he didn't mention our unnerving meeting in the parlor.

When it was time for Joe to leave for work at Robert's shop, Alice cleared the dishes, and Mother asked the Captain if she might have a word with him. By the tone of her voice, it was evident he was about to learn the Floyd House Rules.

With a slightly trembling hand, he passed his cup and saucer to Alice.

"Sir," Mother began, "while you are in our home, there are rules that I must insist you follow. First and foremost, no ale, rum, or other such beverage will be tolerated. And if any one of us even suspects you of drunkenness, you and your belongings will be in the street immediately. Is that clear?"

She speaks the truth. I gave him my best glare.

"Yes, quite clear," he said. "You needn't be concerned, ma'am. I—"

"Excellent." My mother raised her chin. "Secondly, you are to maintain good hygiene at all times. You will obtain your own water for washing, you will wash your own clothing, you will maintain your own fire, and you will empty and clean your own chamber pot daily."

My face burned. But if Mother didn't verbalize the rules in detail, who knew what he might expect?

"Ma'am," he said, "if I may interrupt, 'tis customary for the ladies of the house to see to the quartered officer's laundry, at the very least."

Mother briefly closed her eyes as if summoning her composure. "And sir, 'tis customary for me, as the lady of *this* house, to have no interest in what takes place in any home but my own. Is that understood?"

"Understood." He started to push back his chair.

"I'm not finished, Captain." Mother held up a hand. "Under no circumstances are you allowed in any bedchamber other than the one we have assigned to you. None of our possessions are any of your business at any time. You may join us for our meals if you are here, otherwise, there will be no other cooking or eating."

For once, words failed him. I would love to have read his mind.

Mother then sat as tall as she could and pointed a finger at him. "Finally, if Miss Alice or I suspect you of so much as glancing at my daughter with ill intent, I give you my solemn promise you will forever regret the day you walked in that door. I own a musket and I am not afraid to use it."

I squirmed. When I chanced a look at him, his ears were crimson.

He rose from his seat, perhaps contemplating a run for the hills. "Mrs. Floyd, I would never consider anything of the sort. You have my solemn word as a gentleman and an officer of the king."

Mother stood to her feet, satisfaction lighting her face. "Good. Then we shall all get along as well as can be expected, given the fact that you are an uninvited guest. A pleasant day to you, Captain."

With a curt bow to Mother, then to me, he turned to go. He stopped short just as Alice came around the corner, then hurried for the stairs.

"You told 'im, Miz Margaret." Alice beamed. "Jus' like we talked about."

I took a deep breath. "I hope he takes it seriously."

Mother turned to Alice. "In case he doesn't, we better lock up the sherry."

Two days later, Marcus brought Celeste by carriage so she might deliver three of her gowns to me that she no longer wished to wear. Captain Willington had left for the day, and I told Celeste about our new boarder as we carried the gowns to my bedroom.

"Oh, I'm envious, Betty." She laughed. "We have no room whatsoever for quartering anyone. Captain Willington sounds like a decent man."

"Let us hope so. We're . . . adjusting. It's all we can do."

"Does the major know?"

"I'm not certain. I haven't seen him. He's quite involved with the play rehearsals."

As busy as the major was with his duties and the next theatre production, he'd sent a bushel of fresh-picked apples to our house, delighting us all.

"I would think he knows," she said. "I doubt if much escapes him."

I moved my knitting from the bed—thick stockings for Jacob, which I wanted to complete soon before the winter winds ravaged Fort Michilimackinac. We spread out the gowns, including the deep blue brocade she'd worn to the ball. I ran my hands over the exquisite fabric and delicate needlework.

"This is so generous," I said. "I cannot thank you enough."

She patted my arm. "I know you have parties and events ahead, and I've ordered two new gowns for myself, so I'll no longer need these. Just have your mother or Alice see what requires altering."

My windowsill decorations caught her eye. "What are those?"

She admired the sketch, and I explained the paper dolls. "Your sisters gave me the idea. I know it's silly, but—"

"Not at all. They're very sweet." She lifted the paper Major André. "Shouldn't he have a red coat?"

Now I wished I'd hidden them in my wardrobe. I took the cutout from her and set it back on the sill. "He shall have one when I find a scrap of red cloth." It reminded me that I also needed red cloth if I ever had to signal Culper Senior.

Celeste had asked that I help her shop for a few accessories, followed by a stop at a coffeehouse. We donned our cloaks and stepped out into the autumn sunshine, where Marcus waited with the carriage.

As we rode toward Broadway, Celeste tugged on her gloves. "Henry and I are looking forward to the major's play on Friday. We'll come for you at half past seven, if that suits you."

I had to tease her. "Oh, is it Henry now? No more Mr. Fellowes?"

"Only around my family." Celeste gazed at a young mother on the path who was pushing a baby carriage. "I'm not convinced I'm in love, but he's a good man, and we do enjoy each other's company."

"I'm happy for you." I meant it sincerely. "Perhaps love will come in time. I believe you're a good match for each other."

That made her eyes sparkle. "Thank you, Betty."

Celeste asked Marcus to stop at the confectionary, where she purchased a small box of tiny, decorated candies for her sisters. She then told him he could return to the house and we would walk. At a ladies' shop in Hanover Square, Celeste bought an intricate lace tippet and a new winter muff. I purchased three plain linen handkins—for Mother, Alice, and myself.

More than the usual number of pedestrians traversed the footpaths and streets. I owed it to the clear blue sky and warm autumn sun. Soldiers and officers of every rank wished us a good day or tipped their hats. Elderly ladies strolled arm in arm, and children skipped and called to each other.

"I should stop at Robert's for our mail," I said. "And we could do with more ink."

"Go ahead, then." Celeste glanced down the street. "I'll walk to City Tavern and order our tea and sandwiches."

Hoping to meet her shortly, it would save me time if Robert was away. I could inform him of Captain Willington's arrival the next time I saw him.

Mr. Oakham was sweeping the floors as I walked in, and in more agreeable spirits than the last occasion. My cousin was at the wharves, he claimed, gathering news for the *Gazette*.

And for Culper Senior.

He handed me two letters for Mother and one from Jacob to me. I purchased the ink, tucked the letters in my pocket, and headed for City Tavern.

Across from Rivington's, two armed soldiers stopped a ragged young man carrying a small bundle. The man argued with them until one seized the sack and threw it to the ground. A small crowd gathered, and I slipped into the shade of a maple tree where I wouldn't be noticed. The other soldier shoved the man against the closest storefront, holding him fast while his partner tore open the sack. It contained what appeared to be several papers. Amid the man's foul protests, the soldiers grabbed the papers and led the man by the arms down the alley.

My heart pounded. Was this what Robert meant by an increase in arrests? Who was the man, and what did his papers contain?

Twenty

The wine and champagne were already flowing on Friday when Celeste, Mr. Fellowes, and I reached the post-performance theatre reception. The Shakespearean play *As You Like It* was another momentous success for Theatre Royal. I may have been partial, yet in my opinion, John André outperformed the rest of the cast in his role as the melancholy Jacques.

We followed the guests to the beverage station, and as soon as everyone had a glass in hand, the cast was introduced. Each actor was given a rousing welcome, with Major André arriving last, wearing his theatrical face makeup and seventeenth-century costume.

His devotees shouted their huzzas and raised their glasses. I caught his eye, and he hurried over to kiss my cheeks, much to the delight of some guests and shock to others.

"Please, sir," I said, "I was expecting an officer with a more realistic complexion."

Mr. Fellowes clapped him on the back. "An excellent performance, sir."

Celeste curtsied. "Yes, you were splendid, Major."

"You're most kind. Thank you for coming." He turned his cheek to me. "I didn't have time to remove it. What do you think? Should I keep it?"

I stood back, narrowing my eyes and pretending to assess the whole effect. "Not unless you wish to appear quite ill."

The major and Mr. Fellowes roared with laughter. Celeste sipped her champagne and tugged Mr. Fellowes's arm. They quickly excused themselves and went to greet the other cast members.

"Was my joke that bad?"

The major chuckled. "Celeste has been a good friend to you, yet on occasion I notice that she dislikes not being the center of attention."

"Oh, I disagree. We're different, yet she does have a thoughtful heart."

He helped himself to a glass of champagne from the buffet. "I understand there's now a captain at the Floyd helm—none other than Watermouth Willington."

"Wha—I beg your pardon?"

"Not to worry, though. Willington's an honest man, does his work, although he tends to drink too much. He became Tryon's aide when the governor took a liking to him. We call him Watermouth."

Heads turned at my loud laugh. "Because his words keep on flowing?"

"Precisely."

My gaze swept the coffered ceiling. "It suits him. Although he's been rather quiet since my mother laid down the law. *She* won't give up the helm, no matter what."

"Quite admirable," he said. "You come from good stock, Elizabeth Floyd."

So far, it sounded as if Willington could be anything but a spy. I took a tiny fruit cake from the tiered server. "Can you shed any light on why our home was billeted now, after so long?"

"I know certain shifting is taking place among the billeted homes, with troops and their commanders being directed south and elsewhere. Some homes have been vacated, while others, such as yours, are now quartered for the first time. But it's not my area of concern, so I'm unfamiliar with the particulars."

A rather long answer—perhaps he truly had nothing to do with Willington's new domicile. I brushed crumbs from my lips, making a mental note to inform Robert of his statement.

He perused the sandwiches. "The tensions in New York have risen in the last few weeks, as you may have noticed."

I drew closer. "Why is that? I watched soldiers arrest a man near Rivington's recently. Could he have been a spy?"

He frowned. "Possibly. We are conducting more arrests, looking for suspicious-looking documents, et cetera."

I suddenly lost my appetite. We were interrupted by Mr. DeLancey.

"Good evening, Miss Floyd," he said. "An outstanding performance, Major. I was just informed by the theatre director that proceeds from tonight's performance will be donated to benefit the city's poor."

"I do hope it's put to good use," I said. "Perhaps for fuel or food."

"Yes, absolutely," the major said. "I'll make certain."

Mr. DeLancey bowed. "Forgive me, but I must go and offer my greetings. Have a pleasant evening."

I turned to the major. "Alice heard that the woodcutters have been raising their prices. The poor can't possibly pay them. My mother isn't sure how we will manage either. And now with Captain Willington, we must heat another bedroom."

He took my elbow. "You needn't worry." He spoke low, ensuring no one was listening. "There's plenty of wood should your family require it."

"But . . . how is there plenty?"

"We have *plenty*. For the army, through the winter. Now, shall we enjoy the party?"

With the colder October air, every spider in New York was attracted to the dark corners of my grandmother's house. However, I would not allow it to be a spider sanctuary if I could help it.

I'd been keeping an eye on the captain, looking for any sign of him being too inquisitive, yet he was nothing but polite toward all of us ever since Mother had issued her orders. He told us he would be attending the dog races later in the day but was available for the afternoon if needed, so I put him and Joe to work in the parlor. They moved the furniture away from the walls so I could wipe everything down with vinegar, a spider deterrent.

Mother entered as they carried the writing desk onto the center rug. "Thank you for your help, Captain. Betty, I'm needed across the street. Mrs. Green took a bad fall and her husband sent their little daughter to ask for my help."

The captain lowered his end of the desk. "May I have a word, Mrs. Floyd?"

Mother buttoned her wool cloak. "Yes, what is it?"

"Your son claims he has some difficulty with his Latin lessons. I happen to know Latin quite well. In fact, I earned excellent marks when I was a boy in all my studies. So, if you approve, I shall be more than happy to give him some assistance."

Joe set down the desk's other end. "May he, please, Mother?"

This was a surprise to me, although a bit of a relief. I chided him. "Why is it you're never so excited to study with me?"

Mother's expression was a mix of surprise and surrender. "Oh, very well. If it helps him, I would be grateful. Joseph, pay good attention to the captain. And don't let him miss the dog races . . . poor things."

As she left, I asked Joe to check if Alice had enough wood for the kitchen fire before he went to find his Latin book. My sentiments on remaining in the Ring were yet undecided, but I couldn't let an opportunity go to waste. Perhaps there was some useful intelligence that I could draw out from Watermouth Willington.

I clasped my hands. "Thank you for your help, Captain . . . with the furniture and with Joe."

"Oh, I'm glad to lend a hand. Joe is a fine young man and eager to learn."

I moved a bit closer. "I'm certain it isn't easy to move into a home filled with strangers. Is there anything you require?"

He looked surprised at my question. "No, I have all I need. But thank you for inquiring."

"How would you say the war is progressing?" I employed a moderately flirting gaze. "In your professional opinion?"

He stood taller and puffed out his chest the way Reverend Inglis did from the pulpit. "I believe it's progressing quite well, aside from occasional losses. My men are in good health and good spirits, which is my main concern until we receive further orders."

"That's wonderful to hear, Captain." I ran a finger along the wingback chair. "Do you think it will end soon? Perhaps by spring?"

He glanced out the window, a wistful look in his eyes. Triple crouched on the outside ledge, scowling at the invader.

"I wish I knew the answer to your question, Miss Floyd. I'm not part of General Clinton's inner circle of confidants, as is Major André."

How much did he know of the major and me?

"However," he said, "I did happen to overhear a conversation recently between a few officers at the Navy Coffeehouse. One of them remarked that if we don't destroy their army, we will do so to their currency."

I pretended to be only mildly curious. "Their currency? How would that be done?"

"I wanted to ask what the devil—I beg your pardon—what they meant. I thought it interesting because counterfeiters have been forging the rebel dollars with some success for a few years and distributing them throughout the colonies. They're practically worthless, and so now I wonder if there's a new tactic in the works."

Captain Watermouth clearly gave no thought to the possibility that he should keep the currency conversation quiet, unless he was purposely giving me misinformation. Regardless, I was absorbing every word.

He ran a hand over his chin. "I'm not certain it's a matter for my superiors, or they may be already aware of it. But destroying their currency—can you imagine? That could hasten the war's end, could it not?"

"I'm ready, Captain." Joe returned to the parlor, raising his Latin book aloft. "Destroy whose currency?"

Twenty-One

I arrived at three conclusions that night.

First, Robert needed to know of the plentiful wood supply for Britain's New York troops and that America's currency may be in danger. Also, I wasn't about to leave the Ring until I had a chance to use the Culper code.

A cold, lashing rain came in before dawn, and Mother and I agreed the weather was too nasty to attend church services. We chose instead to help Alice stoke the fires and prepare a larger and later than usual breakfast of ham, baked eggs, skillet potatoes, and apple cobbler.

Captain Willington, however, chose to sleep through it all.

"Did any of you hear him come in?" Mother asked at the table.

"I heard him," I said. "I'm not certain what time."

Joe stirred his eggs and potatoes together. "Before he left for the races yesterday, he showed me a way to remember Latin verbs."

Alice poured more tea. "Fine with me if he sleeps. That man can talk more'n any woman I know."

When we'd all gone about our Sunday tasks and the rain eased, the Captain rose, dressed, and announced he was going out for the day. None of us asked where, although he would no doubt have told us.

In my room, I closed the door and retrieved the code pages from under my mattress. I planned to write Robert a coded note regarding the wood and the currency, then deliver it myself. Why not practice rather than wait for an emergency? I would also tell him about Willington's arrival.

After a few false starts, I was convinced writing the message in Latin would have been simpler. How did Robert and Abraham Woodhull manage to write long, detailed letters to Major Tallmadge and General Washington?

Finally, I had what I wanted, minus the news of our new boarder. I could save that for a face-to-face visit.

723,

280.249 learned jlqn aqqh uqwlgiu 626.630 is "rmipvs of yqqh" jql 625 gqncpa ycpvil nqpvbu for 712.635. Emuq, qjjcgilu were ligipvms bielh to ues, "Cj yi hqpv hiuvlqs their elns, yi ycmm hq uq vq their gwllipgs." 284 is 379 bqri vbcu cpjqlnevcqp rlqxiu bimrjwm.

355

How could the British ever crack such gibberish? It still wasn't perfect, but if translated, the note read:

Culper Junior,

I have learned from reliable sources that there is "plenty of wood" for the coming winter months for Clinton's troops. Also, officers were recently heard to say, "If we don't destroy their army we will do so to their currency." It is my hope this information proves helpful.

Lady

While I still had the writing paraphernalia on my desk, I penned another note.

Dear Jacob,

Thank you for your recent letter. I am glad to learn your regiment is involved in moving your garrison to Mackinac Island and building a new fort there, although it must be extremely difficult in the cold. It saddens me to learn that you have had to resort to stuffing your boots with my letters for warmth. Please know that I am knitting a pair of thick stockings for you and that I will send them the moment I complete them. Until then, I pray you will stay well and that you will still experience some warm autumn days ahead.

Yours truly,
Betty

I folded each letter inside another sheet of paper for security, and addressed Jacob's to *J. Drummond, Private. Fort Mackinac, Mackinac Island.*

I would post it the following day when I delivered my coded message to Culper Junior. In the event Jacob was forced to again use my letter to pad his boots, I'd better finish knitting those stockings I promised him.

I awoke in the dark with my hair stuck to my neck and forehead. The fire burned low. Why was I so warm?

Sitting up, pain shot through my head. I pulled back the quilt and reached for the cup of water I kept nearby, then lay back and closed my eyes, wincing at the pressure in my temples. I was hardly ever ill. Why now? I dozed until morning, but the headache and fever remained. I alternated shivering under the covers or throwing them off entirely.

In the morning, Mother knocked on my door when I failed to appear below-stairs. She took one look at me and hurried to my bedside to feel my forehead with the back of her hand. "Elizabeth, you're ill! You're burning up."

She wet the small towel from my washstand, squeezed it out, and positioned it on my forehead. "You should eat and drink. I'll return in a few minutes with something."

After a cup of tea and a few nibbles of bread and honey, I felt a bit better. But I was in no condition to dress or leave my room, let alone leave the house.

"Is Joe going to Robert's today?" I asked Mother.

"He is. Shall I ask him to stop at the apothecary?"

"No, I won't need anything, just some sleep. But would you ask him to post a letter?" I waved my hand at the desk. "There are two; one is blank and the other is addressed to Jacob. I'll deliver the blank one when I'm able."

Mother went to the desk and took the addressed letter. "Try to rest, my dear. I'll return in a while. Oh, by the way, Captain Willington was about to leave when I brought up your tray. He said to tell you he hopes you feel well again soon."

By evening, the pain in my head had eased. Although the fever held, I hadn't developed a cough or sore throat or other unwelcome symptoms. Alice carried up a bowl of squash soup, and I managed to eat a fair amount. With renewed strength, I washed, wrapped myself in my dressing gown and a wool blanket, and sat in my chair by the fire to knit Jacob's stockings.

Joe came to stoke the fire. "The captain asked me to give you these in case you wanted something to read." He handed me two thin books—one of poetry and the other a commentary on something or other. "He said you won't need to return them."

"That was kind of him. Did you post my letter?"

"I did. Cousin Robert sends his regards, and he had good news. Mrs. Burgin sneaked into New York last week. She fetched the children and took them to Philadelphia."

I sighed with relief. "Thank God she's safe and they've reunited. I cannot imagine what she suffered. How kind of Robert to look into her whereabouts."

Joe placed a log on the embers. "I wish I'd known she was here. I would have asked her what happened."

"Perhaps it's better that you don't know the details."

The log caught fire, and he added extra kindling. "I told Cousin Robert about Captain Willington billeting here. He's concerned but I told him it's going well. . . . Oh, I almost forgot. We hauled a shipment from the wharf today and we saw Major André on Wall Street. He inquired after you, and I told him you're ill."

I almost dropped a stitch. "What was his response?"

Joe stood and reached in his pocket. "He came into the shop later and said to give you this." He handed me a folded sheet of fine white writing paper, now smudged and wrinkled.

I could hardly believe he'd waited to give it to me. "Please don't tell me you read it."

"Nah, why would I?" Joe left, closing the door behind him.

Sparks from the crackling wood fell to the hearth and died out. I pulled the blanket closer and tucked it under my feet.

The major had sketched himself in the Common under bare trees, standing alone with shoulders drooping. Beneath the sketch he'd written, *My dear Betty, I pray you return to good health straightaway. Tu me manques. John.*

I missed him, as well. I laid the note atop the books from Captain Willington. Their subjects didn't interest me, but I appreciated his thoughtfulness, especially that he didn't want them returned. They were the perfect size General Washington had requested for concealing intelligence.

A steady rain fell for two entire days while that stubborn fever hung on, lessened, and spiked again. Alice made me a tea of rosemary and licorice boiled together and sweetened it with honey. I drank pots of it day and night until the fever dissipated at last.

Mother thought I should wait an extra day to return to normal activities and chores. I was still a bit weak and tingly, but when the sun finally pierced the gray skies, I couldn't tolerate one more hour indoors.

I was spurred on by the need to deliver my coded note to Culper Junior. Even if I was still on the fence over my place in the Ring, he had to know of the potential for a currency sabotage, if not the stockpiling of fuel.

After fully dressing for the first time in days, I stuffed the note inside my reticule, picked up Captain Willington's books, donned my cloak, and set out for Hanover Square.

Few things are as refreshing as finally stepping outside after a long rain, no matter the scenery. Piles of wet leaves sat on the lawns and covered the paths and streets where muddy wheels and hooves had trampled them flat. The smoky, putrid odors from New York's waterfront hung over the city, yet the bright sky, geese calling overhead, and squirrels chasing each other through the treetops made for a pleasant walk.

My thoughts of Major André were partly responsible for my good frame of mind. He'd sent a box of chocolates the previous day along with an invitation to a concert the next week to be followed by a small dinner party at his own quarters.

I looked forward to seeing where he lived, even if he was not the homeowner. I also had an ulterior motive, should I choose at that point to remain in the Culper Ring—the evening might prove to yield worthwhile intelligence.

After I saw Robert today, I would stop in to Mr. Mulligan's and ask if he had a bit of red cloth to spare. I could then outfit my paper version of the Major in his uniform colors and save a few strips in case I ever needed to leave a signal for Culper Senior at the stables.

Robert was outside the shop, sweeping wet leaves from the entrance. Seeing him made me second guess my decision to write a message using the Culper code. Once he deciphered it, however, wouldn't he be pleased that I took the initiative? Perhaps he would allow me to use the invisible ink at some point and write my own missive to General Washington.

As I crossed the street, I waved when he saw me. Then his expression darkened with concern. Something was wrong.

Just then, two soldiers approached me from the left, muskets in hand. One wore a soiled red coat and squinted at me with clouded eyes.

"Miss, may we have a word?"

I stopped. "What is it?"

Robert propped his broom against the door and came closer.

"Just a routine inspection. Open your bag."

I clutched my reticule. "I beg your pardon?"

Robert spoke up. "Gentlemen, is this necessary? Detaining a lady in the street for no reason?"

"You 'eard right, Miss." The younger soldier stood a head taller than the other. His blond hair stuck out like straw from under his dark cap. "Open it. And you . . . Townsend, isn't it? This is none o' your business."

"It's fine, Robert." I faced the soldiers, smiling with all the sweetness and courtesy I could put forth while trying to think what to do. "Gentlemen, my name is Elizabeth Floyd, and Mr. Townsend and I are cousins. We grew up together on Long Island, and my younger brother helps him here at his store. So, you see—"

"All fine and lovely, Miss Floyd." The younger one glanced skyward. "Let's 'ave a look at what's in the bag. Hand the books over as well."

Trying to stall, I gave him the books, one at a time. He rifled through them and tossed them at my feet.

Robert stooped to pick them up, but the younger man held his musket against his chest. "Stop right there, Townsend."

The older one was growing impatient. "The bag, miss. Let's 'ave it."

I fumbled with the drawstrings. "If you insist . . . but I believe I only have a few coins and a handkin." As soon as I had my fingers inside, I tried tucking the note against the white lining, hoping they wouldn't notice it.

Pedestrians assembled, likely curious to know what I had done wrong. Women from Holy Ground often wandered this way toward the wharf, seeking customers. Did they think the soldiers stopped me because I was a prostitute?

"Enough stalling. Give it here." The older soldier grabbed my reticule and pulled it wide open. My mouth went dry. He rummaged through and fished out the note.

There was the coded letter, plain as day. I was about to be arrested for aiding the enemy. To some, that amounted to a far graver sin than prostitution. I could barely breathe.

Robert pushed against the musket. "I insist you give my cousin her belongings and leave the area immediately."

The younger man glared at him. "Quiet, Townsend. We're under orders."

I panicked. "Whose orders? Find Major André and bring him here. He knows me. I insist."

What am I saying? Then he'll see the note, have me hanged, and hate me forever.

"No use botherin' Major André," he said, chuckling. "It's 'is orders to stop anyone we see."

The older man tore away the outer blank sheet of paper and unfolded the letter inside.

A chill raced down my spine. "Sir, it's nothing. I was only—"

The soldier made a show of holding the letter at eye level and clearing his throat. "Dear Jacob, thank you for your recent letter . . ."

What? In disbelief, I glanced at Robert. I was at a complete loss. *What have I done? Where is the message to Culper Junior?*

The man read aloud the entire letter in a high voice, much to the onlookers' amusement, then tossed it in the muddy street, along with my reticule. A shilling fell out and rolled away.

"Why all the fuss?" The younger soldier laughed, yanking his musket away from Robert's chest. "Poor chap. Better knit those stockings for 'im soon."

My hands shook as I bent to retrieve the letter.

"Not so fast, Miss." The older man held the letter to the ground with the toe of his boot. "In what army does this Jacob serve? Where's this island?"

I straightened, only managing a whisper. "The British army." I tried again, forcing the words out. "He serves at a new fort at Mackinac Island, in the Great Lakes. And proudly so."

The shaking in Robert's voice was almost undetectable. "There you have it, gentlemen. You have no right in keeping her a moment longer. For the last time, be on your way."

The older soldier muttered under his breath, then jerked his head toward Fort George, letting his accomplice know it was time to leave. They turned and walked through the crowd, waving their muskets. "Return to your business," one said. "All is well, all is well."

Robert grabbed the letter, the books, and my reticule from the street and wiped away the mud on his apron. Then he retrieved my shilling. I took them with shaking hands.

"You are as pale as paste," he said. "Come inside. I have the impression there is something you need to tell me."

Twenty-Two

With head in hand, I sat with my back to Robert. After I explained about the note I'd written to him employing the Culper code and how I'd somehow addressed it to Jacob, he paced back and forth, berating me first, then himself for trusting me with the code dictionary in the first place.

"There is nothing we can do now," he said. "The message is on the way to Fort Mackinac, provided the mail has not been intercepted. Should that happen . . ."

From what I could surmise, the British had negligible interest in letters sent to their own troops. I took a bit of comfort in the fact that Jacob and I had corresponded for months without any trouble. And knowing him, he would disregard my scribbles and use the paper to protect his feet from the cold.

But my arguments would mean nothing to Culper Junior, and I had no will to make them. My mistake had been a severe error and might be my last act as 355.

Robert droned on. ". . . You would likely have been arrested today, however, had you not sent it to your friend. This was a narrow escape."

I sipped the water he'd given me, wishing only to be home in my bed. I would crawl far under the covers until after the war.

"General Washington must be notified of the breach," he said. "But I shall keep your name out of it. With what you learned regarding the currency issue and the stockpiling of wood, plus intelligence I have gathered, it may serve to override this potentially costly blunder."

He certainly had a way of twisting the knife.

I handed him the books. "These are for you to use in your communications. Compliments of Captain Willington. Now, may I go?"

I rose, but the shop tilted on its side and grew dark. I felt myself crumpling.

Then Robert knelt beside me, wiping a musty handkin across my brow. "Betty?"

I blinked, trying to ascertain what happened. "How long—"

"Only seconds. Are you able to sit? I shall call for a carriage to transport you home."

Mother adjusted my pillows and tucked the quilt around me. "You should have listened to me and remained at home today, Elizabeth. Now, please try to rest."

I'd only told her I fainted at the shop—nothing of the incident in the street. I made an effort to do as she asked, yet the frightening events of the day came rushing back in. The soldiers, the onlookers, the moment I thought would mean my arrest, the realization of what I had done, and Robert—how I had let him down.

I covered my face with my cold hands. *You're not worthy.*

I let the voice have its way, accepting it. *You're a failure and not worthy to be part of the Culper Ring. You're a deceiver and not worthy of John André.*

Tears caught in my throat before bubbling up and breaking loose. I wept for all I had done wrong, for Christopher, and for all my unanswered questions.

Finally, I was poured out. A deep, dreamless sleep overtook me. At some point, a gentle knock pulled me back to consciousness. I sat up and pushed hair off my face.

"Come in."

Mother carried a tray with a steaming bowl of potato soup and a generous slice of bread topped with the Dicksons' fresh apple butter. "You look better, my dear. Your color has returned."

Joe knocked on the open door. "Package delivery."

"For me?" I was surprised at how weak my voice sounded. "What is it?"

Mother set the tray by the bed. "Joseph went to ask Robert if he needed help after you arrived home, and Robert gave this to him."

Joe came to the bed and handed me the small package. "I'd say it's from Uncle William."

I glanced at the handwriting and knew it must be my uncle's

poetry book again. This time, the brown paper around it appeared to have cleared the checkpoints unopened.

"That is rather unlike him." Mother peered at the package. "Sending another gift?"

"He thinks I should read more of the great poets." I forced a smile. "I'd like to eat before I open it, though."

After Joe stoked the fire, he and Mother went downstairs to eat with Alice and Captain Willington. I ate most of the soup and all of the bread, then unwrapped the package.

It had been several weeks since I'd written to Uncle William following the Clinton dinner. I'd worried for him and Aunt Hannah, wondering if the devious Simcoe had attempted to locate William Floyd of Long Island.

The same book of poetry opened to a new letter inserted on a different page.

> *Dearest Niece,*
>
> *Your aunt and I wish to thank you for alerting me as to the chance of receiving an award. You may be certain that we shall watch for its arrival. However, these types of awards oftentimes amount to nothing, therefore I shall continue in my current business for now.*
>
> *The times we live in require great patience and faith, as you and your family can attest.*
>
> *Until we are together again, I urge you to remain steadfast in whatever work you undertake. As Scripture states, it may have been given to you "for such a time as this."*
>
> *I have full confidence that you shall succeed in all your endeavors.*
>
> *Your devoted uncle,*
W. F.

I read the letter again, then replaced it inside the book. I clutched it to my chest and closed my eyes.

If only my father had been an encourager like his brother. Yet if Uncle William knew what work I'd undertaken and the muddle it had become, he wouldn't have so much confidence in me. He referenced the same scripture verse from the book of Esther that had heartened me after the Clinton dinner, which I found rather uncanny. Now, however, I'd lost all self-assurance in ever aiding the Culper Ring again, should Robert even wish me to do so.

Any faith I held on to before had been completely shaken. I had no idea what I wanted, what I should do, or what to believe.

Twenty-Three

November 1779

Peter Laune arrived with the carriage to transport me to City Tavern for the chamber concert, where Major André would be waiting. I buttoned my cloak over the blue brocade gown Celeste had given me and bid Mother goodbye. She beamed with approval as she handed me my long gloves and kissed my cheek.

I'd spent the last seven days recovering from the unexplained fever, knitting Jacob's stockings, tutoring Joe, and considering what my true sentiments were regarding the Culper Ring and Major André. And with each day, those sentiments wavered. I was no closer to any sort of decision or commitment. I remained a fence-sitter and a coward.

The major had sent a written apology as soon as he heard of the confrontation with the soldiers. They had no sense of decency, he said, and begged my forgiveness for the suffering they caused me. I didn't blame him for their actions, however. Any respectable Director of Intelligence would want to sift out spies from among the citizenry. Despite their brash and embarrassing way of detaining me and unnecessary treatment of Robert, the soldiers had merely been following orders.

Of course, the major would never know the full extent of my anguish over the incident. It would not have upset me as much if I'd had nothing to hide and it had been a simple search of my reticule. Yet I shuddered to think of what almost happened, which would have been entirely my fault.

However, I set my troubles aside this night. I was determined to enjoy myself and again return to the safety and naivete of ignoring the war.

I'd paid a dear sum to Celeste's hairdresser, who came and styled my hair in a modified high roll, added a hairpiece with cascading ringlets, and topped it off with dark blue feathers. With the addition of my mother's topaz pendant and a bit of pomade to my lips and cheeks, I was prepared for what I hoped would be a pleasant and uneventful evening.

Peter helped me descend the carriage steps at City Tavern. "Enjoy the concert, Miss Floyd. I shall meet you and Major André at its conclusion."

Mr. Roubalet offered to take my cloak and gloves, and a servant showed me to the room reserved for concerts and large parties. Heads turned when I entered. The ladies, of course, wore stunning gowns in myriad colors and most of the officers wore their red uniforms. Many were no longer strangers to me, thanks to the major who had introduced them at previous occasions.

He and I saw each other almost immediately. He flashed his magnetic smile and hurried to welcome me. "My dear, you are more breathtaking each time I see you."

I extended my hands, and he grabbed and kissed them. "I'm so relieved that you've fully recovered and could join me tonight."

"As am I, John." I took his arm. "I'm quite well, at last. Thank you for your kind messages. And the chocolates. We all enjoyed them."

He led me to our seats in the second row facing the musicians. We were soon joined by Celeste, Henry Fellowes, William Franklin, and another officer I hadn't yet met, Major Baxter. Mr. Franklin was as aloof as when we'd first met, although he surprised me by remembering my name.

After introductions and greetings, Celeste pulled me aside to the aisle. "You've never looked more beautiful, Betty. The major can hardly take his eyes off you, nor can any of the gentlemen in the room for that matter. Are you pleased with your hair?"

"Yes, although it took hours. Alice didn't appreciate the fact that I hired someone to do it, until she saw how much work was involved."

She leaned closer. "Dorah Shepherd told me that soldiers detained you last week in front of your cousin's shop."

Not wishing to arouse any suspicions, I attempted to hide my shock. "How did she know?"

"She was there apparently. She claimed a crowd gathered, and something about a letter. I can't imagine anything more humiliating. Why did they question you?"

I flinched at the thought of Dorah seeing me embarrassed in public. Why hadn't she come to my defense or spoken to me?

"'Tis their routine now, so I've heard. Anyone may be stopped for any reason or none at all. I had a letter to Jacob in my reticule. They read the letter, then let me go."

Celeste shook her head in empathy. "Shame on them, as if you weren't on their side."

To my relief, an announcement was made for the audience to be seated. Celeste took her seat beside Mr. Fellowes, and I stepped around them to the chair beside the major.

The chamber orchestra performed a stirring violin concerto by Vivaldi. I so wanted to get lost in the music and forget everything else, yet Celeste had brought the whole ugly incident of my near-arrest to the forefront. Now all I could think of was Dorah and what she must have thought when she watched those two loathsome soldiers make a public spectacle of me.

The major reached over to squeeze my hand.

I'm not who you think I am, John.

By the time we left the Tavern, darkness had fallen and the temperature had plummeted, coupled with strong winds. Peter met us with the carriage, and the major and I departed for his home. The others had arranged for their own carriages and would soon meet us there.

A low, wrought-iron fence enclosed the treeless front lawn of the major's billeted house on Water Street. The red brick exterior and white-columned entrance resembled other homes in the city, except for the ivy climbing past the windows on either side of the door.

Lamps lit each of the first-floor windows. The major led me through the gate and up the steps. "I do hope you're hungry. Amelia, my cook, promises a splendid dinner tonight."

"That sounds wonderful," I replied. "After days of little appetite, I'm famished."

The aroma of roasting beef filled the center hall. He took my cloak and gloves and laid them on a carved armchair. "Come into the parlor, Betty. The others should arrive momentarily."

I followed him into a large room painted a soft green and trimmed with dark carved moldings. A multicolored Persian rug covered the floor.

"What a lovely parlor, John. And so welcoming."

"*Merci*. Although I cannot take any credit. I prefer to think I'm the caretaker until the owners return."

I gazed around the room. "Is there nothing of your own?"

"Only what I have in a small office down the hall. Mostly of the paper variety."

A narrow mantel over the fireplace held several lit candles of various heights. Two settees with thick, dark green cushions sat at right angles to the fireplace and were flanked by ornate chairs with needlepoint seats. Several side tables held more candles, vases of late autumn flowers, and art objects.

He rubbed my arms over my thin satin sleeves. "I apologize for the chill. As soon as Peter comes inside, he'll light the fire. Again, I cannot express how sorry I was to hear the soldiers' report and the mention of your name. Those fellows have been reassigned."

"I'd rather not talk of it if you don't mind. It was unpleasant, yet it's done."

As he inclined his head for a kiss, we heard voices outside the door.

I slid my hands away from his coat. "Your guests, Major."

He wrinkled his nose. "I suppose I should let them in."

Celeste and the three gentlemen all entered at once, exclaiming about the frigid wind. The promise of dinner in the air caught their attention, as well as the major's stately home. Peter had quietly entered to start the fire, and the six of us were soon seated comfortably around it with glasses of fine red wine.

"It's a pleasure to have your company." The major stood, raising his glass. "To Britain."

The other men stood and repeated, "To Britain." Celeste and I raised our glasses in accord.

"Tell me, André," Mr. Franklin said, "how fares the search for the rebel spies?"

Mercy, are we going to start with that? I attempted a look of mild interest rather than fear.

"Thus far, they've eluded us," the major answered. "However, I have every confidence they will be apprehended. We have eyes and ears in more places than you might imagine."

I shivered, and not from the room's low temperature.

"If I may ask," Celeste said, "why would anyone dare to spy in New York? With the military presence here, they would surely be discovered and shot immediately, would they not?"

"Hanged, actually," the major replied. "Or sent to the prison ships. The truth is, we have reason to believe there are several operating here in the city and managing to communicate with others elsewhere."

How do they know?

I fought the shaking in my hands, knowing I must contribute, lest I be thought impolite. "I cannot imagine how difficult that is for you, John."

He raised his glass. "Truth always prevails, my dear. I assure you, they will be discovered."

Celeste continued. "Why are soldiers questioning private citizens on the streets? Is it entirely due to your search for the spies?"

I glared at her, hoping she wouldn't add my own experience to the discussion. Enough people knew of it already.

"Somewhat." The major glanced at me, contrite. "And as the war escalates and more refugees have come to New York from other colonies, we must . . . take all precautions."

I stared at the pattern in the rug. *Here is one spy, Major. On the settee, sipping your wine.*

"They must indeed be close," William Franklin said. "To think they're in this very city . . ."

Major Baxter chuckled. "Right under our noses."

Peter appeared at the parlor threshold. He'd changed from his heavy outdoor clothing into a suit of chestnut brown breeches, matching long coat, and white shirt with ruffled cravat.

"Ladies and gentlemen, dinner is served."

I'd never been so grateful to hear those words. The major led us down the short hall, and we passed what appeared to be his office. I could only see a desk and chair beneath a window in the darkened room.

We entered a dining room with rose-covered vines painted on creamy walls. A long mahogany table was set with fine gold-rimmed charger plates and crystal glassware. A roaring fire provided plenty of warmth, and the light from dozens of candles danced across the walls and ceiling.

"Oh, this is quite beautiful, Major," Celeste said. "You really should entertain more often."

"I do enjoy it," he said, "and I haven't done so to a great extent since arriving in New York." He pointed out the place cards bearing our names at each seat, and pulled my chair out for me, to the right of his at the far end.

When we all were seated, a petite Negro woman entered through a doorway, carrying an enormous tray of steaming plates. She skillfully placed it on the sideboard without a sound.

"Friends, this is Amelia," the major said. Her snow-white hair was perfectly tucked under a neat cap and she wore a simple dark gray gown, covered by a crisp white apron.

"Hello, Amelia," I said. "Thank you for preparing this lovely dinner for us."

She glanced from the major to me with wide eyes. "A pleasure, Miss," she said.

Peter went to the sideboard and served our plates while Amelia left the room. Each plate held a generous slice of roast beef, onions and carrots swimming in hot mushroom gravy, and roasted yellow potatoes. A roll platter was passed, along with fresh butter and preserves. Peter then poured tall glasses of water for everyone.

The major stood to say a short blessing, then replenished the wine. "I trust you all enjoyed the concert?"

"Very much," Major Baxter said. "Excellent music."

Mr. Franklin set down his knife. "Yes, 'twas very well done. However, I would say this beef is cooked to perfection."

Celeste's eyes shone in the candlelight. "Are you planning your next play, Major?"

"The consensus at the theatre is to produce *Much Ado About Nothing* sometime during the winter months," he said. "Though if I am given a part, I should like it to be in the painting of the backdrops rather than on the stage."

"You excel at both," I said, "although painting shouldn't entail as many hours. Or any rehearsals."

"A good plan," Mr. Fellowes said, "in the event General Clinton has need of you elsewhere."

The major took a sip of wine. "That is always a possibility." He gave me a gentle look. "But we won't concern ourselves with that at the moment."

The leisurely dinner ended with Peter and Amelia serving us pumpkin custards and coffee. We moved again to the parlor, where the major distributed snifters of brandy to the men and sweet dessert wine to Celeste and me.

While the gentlemen's conversations turned to political topics, I tuned them out as Celeste and I discussed our families. We were soon laughing over stories of her sisters' latest antics.

It wasn't long before Mr. Fellowes consulted his pocket watch and said the carriage he'd ordered would be arriving. Taking the prompt, Mr. Franklin and Major Baxter rose from their seats. They each had planned to walk to their residences. We all gradually moved to the door and I waited as the major helped the others don their outer apparel.

"A most pleasant evening, Major." Mr. Franklin shook his hand. "We'll be seeing each other soon, undoubtedly."

Mr. Fellowes said to Mr. Franklin, "Let's plan a day at the horse races, shall we?"

As everyone bid goodnight and descended the porch steps, I was glad when the door shut on the bitter night air.

The major turned to me. "Would you like to enjoy the fire a bit longer?"

I rubbed my arms. "You know I would, although I truly should go."

"I'll ask Peter to have the carriage ready in twenty minutes, and I will accompany you. Would that be acceptable?"

I touched his sleeve. "Yes, thank you."

He walked toward the back of the house, and I settled in front of the fire again. I'd thought I wanted a few minutes alone with him, but now I wasn't so certain. I was impossibly, hopelessly conflicted—one minute I wanted information for the Ring and the next minute I simply wanted *him*.

I took a few deep breaths and observed the parlor once again. Who previously lived here, drinking tea or wine and entertaining friends? Where had they fled when the British occupied New York? Did they wonder now what became of their beautiful home?

The major returned, joining me on the settee. "Peter will ready the carriage straightaway. Would you care for anything? More wine?"

"Nothing, thank you." I laced my fingers through his. "Something you said at dinner concerns me a bit—the fact that General Clinton could have you sent elsewhere. I don't wish you to think I'm unaware of the realities, yet—"

He brought my hands to his lips and kissed them. "Truly, I don't foresee it, but we must be prepared at all costs. We are still fully at war until it's over."

I leaned back against the cushion and watched the fire. "What do you plan to do when it finally *is* over?"

"Ah, other than dance and paint and write poetry?" His expression turned serious. "In all honesty, I endeavor not to think too far beyond today's concerns and my current duties. For all intents and purposes, I belong to General Clinton. Therefore, I cannot know until the time comes."

I was silent, not wanting to press him further. After all, I had no more knowledge of the future than he did.

He pulled my hands toward him, his dark eyes drawing me in. "Betty, regardless of what happens, please know that my fondness for you grows the more I'm with you. You are indeed an extraordinary woman and deserving of so much more than you realize."

I was caught off guard. He was such a thoughtful and perceptive man—if only he could know the full extent of the turmoil harboring inside of me and the reasons behind it.

Tears welled in my eyes, and I fought not to blink for fear they would escape. I focused my gaze on our hands.

I whispered. "You are correct in that I don't realize it or believe it. I'm not . . . so deserving."

He released my hands and brought my face close to his. He spoke with conviction. "Perhaps you have chosen to believe what is not true."

He kissed my cheeks as I considered his words.

John André had never once spoken a false or negative word in my presence. And this much I knew: with the exception of his friend John Simcoe, he was a good judge of character, whether it be man or woman, rich or poor, Tory or Patriot.

What if he spoke the truth now and I *was* deserving? And *worthy*? That would mean only one thing.

Papa had lied. And all these years, I had believed him.

Twenty-Four

Freezing rain transformed into snow flurries as Alice and I baked bread in the kitchen. With long pairs of tongs, we took six hot, round loaves of bread from the brick oven, then placed six more dough rounds inside with a slate paddle. We wrapped the fresh-baked loaves in cloth, then draped our shawls over our heads and ran with the bread to the house.

In the snug pantry, we set the bread on the table to cool—two loaves for us, and four destined for the hungry in Canvas Town. Mother would take the six loaves now in the oven to the prisoners at Rhinelander's.

"This snow best not stick," Alice said. "I got too much to do."

I pulled my snow-dampened shawl off my head. My cap came off with it. "'Tis too soon—the leaves haven't all fallen yet. But everything will be accomplished, Alice."

"You been bakin' like we gonna feed the whole British army. Good thing we got plenty o' flour to last us."

I laughed. "The British army can fend for itself."

Cold air whooshed down the hall as the front door opened and Joe stomped his boots on the entry rug. "It's snowing! I ran all the way from the shop. Have you seen Triple?"

I stepped into the hall. "I may have noticed a ball of black fur near the kitchen fire. Could that be him?"

"It better be him." He removed his coat and cap. "Do you think it will snow all night? When's the captain coming? Oh, Cousin Robert said he wishes to see you tomorrow. Something important."

I hadn't been in to see Robert since the day the soldiers stopped me. It was impossible to guess what he might want to discuss. But I was finally off the fence of indecision and was anxious to meet with him. I would go, weather permitting, and post a package to Jacob with the stockings I'd finished.

"It cannot snow all night," I said. "It's only November. As far as the captain coming, do we ever know?"

Joe followed me to the pantry. "Alice, may I have something to eat?"

Alice draped her shawl over a chair. "Master Joe, I believe you startin' to sound like a gentleman. You can eat anythin' 'cept for this bread."

Captain Willington had come and gone for several days with barely a hello. On occasion, I heard him stumble up the stairs after we were all in bed, and I assumed he'd been drinking but I didn't mention it to Mother. By morning, he was always talkative and cheerful, and left as soon as he had his coffee and toast, claiming duties at the fort.

The less he was in the house, the less I assumed he was a spy. Yet I still didn't want to let my guard down or leave anything lying about in my room that might arouse suspicion.

Only my brother minded his absence. I hoped he would take time for Joe soon, especially when helping him with his Latin lessons had been his idea.

The bread now filled the house with its crusty-buttery scent. Mother, Alice, and I always took to baking more bread when the weather cooled, and this year I had volunteered to do the better part of it. It was a good, physical task—bending over the worn worktable, squeezing the coarse dough together and pushing it with the heels of my hands, then lifting and heaving it down in a blizzard of flour. I repeated the process until each batch was smooth and pliable, divided it into rounds, then covered them and left them to rise before baking.

Kneading the dough had been a tonic. I took my time, embracing and working through my fears concerning the Culper Ring, my failures as an effective and prudent agent, and all of Robert's chastisements, which I'd fully deserved.

I'd pounded away at my tangled emotions for John André. We both felt a strong attraction to each other and, I sensed, a deepening affection. But I knew he might be sent anywhere, perhaps at a moment's notice. Even if he remained in New York, and regardless of the war's outcome, there was a distinct possibility that our feelings may not be sufficient to lead to a true and lasting love. Above all else, unbeknownst to him, we served opposite sides in this war. If he were ever to learn of it, how could he forgive my deceit?

Finally, for the first time in my life, I'd torn apart my anger at Papa. I recalled every disgusting thing he'd said and done to ridicule and threaten me, all apparently stemming from my being born with a defective left hand. I let the tears flow freely, confronting the memories of all the ways he caused me to think I'd never be good enough for anyone or do anything of value.

My mother had done her best through the years to compensate for his cruelty, yet was it enough? I faced her shortcomings head-on, as well as my own. And I made myself let them go.

Over ten days' time, I'd kept the oven coals burning, baking loaf after loaf of golden bread until my arms and fingers ached. But with it all came clarity, and what I sensed was the wisdom I'd asked for in prayer throughout the summer.

If Culper Junior was willing to allow me another chance, I knew without a doubt that I wished to continue as 355 and undertake all it entailed. With my distinct opportunities, I believed I could still gather intelligence of great benefit to General Washington and the Cause.

I also fully knew, however my relationship with Major André evolved, that I desired to see it through. He was not bloodthirsty, as Robert had surmised, but an honorable man who held my heart completely. Nevertheless, if I acquired useful intelligence from him related to the war, I had a duty to the Culper Ring and would deliver it as expected.

Another, larger revelation emerged during my labors in the kitchen, one that the major had begun to show me, buried under the layers of lies I'd believed for years: Regardless of my weaknesses, I *was* worthy. And quite possibly, as he had stated, *extraordinary*.

It was about time I proved it.

The snow tapered by morning and the sun shone bright, yet the air remained icy-crisp. I dressed quickly, adding my woolen stockings, quilted petticoat, and tucking a warm kerchief under my stays. Captain Willington came down early to start the dining room fire, and we all hurried through our porridge. As if he'd read my mind the day before, he and Joe went over a page of Latin.

Mother asked me to post a letter along with my package to Jacob. Leaving the house, I headed for Mr. Mulligan's before going to Oakham and Townsend. At Rivington's, I turned the corner and passed the stables and adjoining barn where I spotted the old boot scrape that Robert had described, half-hidden against the wall by overgrown weeds and ice-encrusted leaves.

For years, I avoided buildings that reminded me of our barn and what took place when I was but ten. During my bread baking, I had faced the memory and wrestled with it—or perhaps it wrestled with me. Finally, I came to terms with it. The past was past, and I would no longer accept the lie that a barn was something to fear.

A stable boy led a tall black horse out of the dark stables toward the coffeehouse, just as two mounted officers slowed their horses and turned in. One tipped his hat upon seeing me. If ever I had to signal Culper Senior, I would need to find a quieter time of day.

A few doors beyond the stables, the sign over the doorway, *H. Mulligan, Tailor,* swung in the cold wind. Upon entering, sunlight poured in through two small windows, brightening the tiny shop. Bolts of cloth were piled high on every available surface, surrounded by boxes overflowing with buttons, buckles, and notions. A fire blazed in the fireplace at the back wall where two ladies sat with sewing projects in their laps.

Mr. Mulligan, tall and distinguished, turned from a long cutting table heaped with white linen. "A blessed good morning. Miss Floyd, correct?"

"Yes, sir. Thank you for remembering my name."

"Remembering is my business." His Irish brogue flowed like music. "How may I be of assistance?"

"I'm afraid it's a simple request. Do you happen to have any red fabric to spare? A small piece or two would be sufficient."

He laughed and held his arms out. "Who in all of New York City has more red fabric than the tailor to His Majesty's army?" He turned and walked toward a back room. "We usually have a veritable barrel full of leftover pieces. What is it you wish to fashion?"

"I only require a little for . . . a small item." I called toward the back room. "Whatever you can spare, sir."

Mr. Mulligan emerged a minute later, carrying a small stack of red wool fabric and a few feet of gold braid.

"Here y'are, will this do?" His *r*'s and *i*'s softened and bent all the more with his excitement. "This fine braid is from a coat we just completed for General Clinton. You are welcome to it as well. There is more, Miss Floyd, should you desire it."

I would love to find a use for the braid. "Thank you; that's very generous."

He waved a dismissive hand. "Give me a moment, and I'll wrap it up tidy."

Clutching my packages, I hastened back around the corner and made my way to Oakham and Townsend. A group of perhaps two dozen prisoners shuffled down the center of the street, flanked by three soldiers with muskets. The men were emaciated and pale, unshaven, and wore Patriot militia clothing—filthy, lightweight coats and breeches, a few in caps, none in decent shoes. Many held their arms to their chests and shivered as they walked, staring ahead with vacant eyes.

The soldier farthest from me raised his musket higher. "Move along, you stinkin' bastards."

I knew that voice. Crankshaw's fur cap was pulled low, and his syphilitic mark had spread and darkened. I hid in the wigmaker's doorway until they passed. A bitter breeze off the harbor stung my cheeks, and I tugged my cloak's hood closer to my face. If Crankshaw and the other soldiers were leading the men to one of the prison ships, how would any of them survive?

At Robert's shop, the door opened as our generous neighbor, Mrs. Dickson, was about to leave.

"Good day, Betty," she said as I entered. "We haven't seen you in quite some time. I understand you have a handsome new boarder."

"Oh, that would be Captain Willington." I nodded politely, wondering who had spread the news.

"A captain? How wonderful. I've also been told that Major John André has called on occasion."

It was enough to warm my frozen cheeks. "Yes, although—"

Robert exited the storeroom. "A good day to you, Madam."

She paused, then raised her nose in the air before rushing out. "Good day to you both."

I closed the door after her and removed my gloves. "I don't think she cared for the dismissal, Robert. She can be a bit too inquisitive but she is a good neighbor."

He came to turn the lock. "Joseph claims you are fully recovered and have resumed your usual duties."

"Yes, chores and tutoring, among other things." He didn't need to hear of my visit to Major André's home, at least not yet. I walked to my customary chair, placed the package of fabric on the floor beside it, and laid the smaller one for Jacob on the desk.

"But Robert, just now—I believe they're leading prisoners down to the ships." I rubbed at my left hand's absent fingers, my old habit from childhood that didn't align with my new resolve.

His chair creaked as he took his seat. "I am afraid there have been many such processions over the past several days, especially from Bridewell, if Cunningham does not starve them first. They are why we must persevere in our work. It is vital that we do all we can to bring an end to this war. There is no time for laxity."

Or hesitation. I opened my hands in my lap, rough from their toil in the kitchen, then raised my head. "I came to ask if you still believe I can be of service to the Ring."

He didn't pause a moment. "Yes, most definitely. As does Abraham Woodhull, provided you are diligent and careful. He lives in constant fear of being found out, as we all do. And the risks are greater than ever. None of us dare underestimate that fact."

I'd half-expected him to say no, or at least to interrogate me. With a deep breath I placed my palms on the desk. "I understand the risks, and I'm terribly sorry for my mistakes. I want this very much, Robert. And I won't fail again."

He adjusted his spectacles as if reviewing a customer account. "Then we will proceed."

So, it was settled. He had little idea how seriously I'd erred or how much I'd contemplated quitting "the business." Only the clock's ticking marked the anticlimactic moment.

He took notice of the address on Jacob's package. "You have not heard from your friend, have you?"

"No, but I may not until he receives these stockings."

"At last, the famed stockings." He clutched the package. "I shall dispatch it with today's post."

I shuddered to think that all of New York City had heard the story by now. "'Twas a terrible day. I'd prefer you not mention it again."

He straightened the ledger and receipts, his typical down-to-business response. "I did inform Woodhull. He has been particularly anxious, due to the increase in searches around Long Island and the influx of more Loyalist refugees. It proved to him how vulnerable we are here as well."

I knew that now, firsthand. "Am I ever to meet him?"

"Only if you must. His comings and goings are sporadic, and he does not wish to meet with anyone unnecessarily. The risks are too great."

General Washington himself was undoubtedly easier to see than Culper Senior. "Joe said you have something important to relate."

"Yes, and Woodhull has already notified Tallmadge." He glanced at the door, then lowered his voice. "As you heard, information has come to light in regard to the plan to destroy American currency. Their strategy is to print enough counterfeit bills to make them worthless, thereby bankrupting Congress and the army."

"But it's nothing new. It's no secret that they've made counterfeit currency before. It's brought down the value repeatedly."

"Quite true. The saying 'not worth a continental' is fitting. Yet only this week I was informed that paper specifically made for the printing of money by Congress, as well as the printing plates, has been seized by the British in Philadelphia and brought aboard ships to New York."

Clinton must already know. And John André. "What kind of paper is used for currency?" I asked.

"Paper of the right weight and imbedded with special fibers. If a large quantity is printed here by the British and widely distributed, it would not be long before America is brought to its knees."

Apparently, this is what the men meant that Captain Willington had overheard. I envisioned the anger amid the congressional delegates, including Uncle William, when word of the theft became known.

Such a discovery could be the biggest for the Ring yet. "How were you able to obtain the information, Robert?"

"Mr. Rivington gathered further intelligence at the coffeehouse, substantiating what you heard. Also, I have made acquaintances among a handful of unsuspecting sailors and their superiors at Murray's Wharf. With the right questions, they supported the story."

"I suppose your contacts enjoy bearing news to the uninformed here in the city."

"Precisely," he said. "If they see their names in the *Gazette* now and then, they are more apt to deliver."

"Bribing them with fame, I see. What will happen now?"

"I suspect General Washington will inform Congress, and they will do what they think best."

I couldn't imagine having such patience to assemble the many bits of information into a useful report. "What would you have me do next?"

"Continue to socialize as much as possible, whether with the officers or those they are close with, gaining their trust. Major André in particular if that is still agreeable to you. I do not wish to pry, although I've warned you—"

I held up both hands. " 'Tis still agreeable."

"Very well." He studied me over his spectacles. "General Washington insists on faster communication. He and Culper Senior and Tallmadge are seeking a better route for our transmissions as winter approaches and the army camps in Morristown. Above all, he stresses specificity and details, as much as we can obtain. You report to me verbally and I will relay the information. Do not employ the code unless I am absent *and* it is an absolute emergency."

"I'll seek the details, but other than Captain Willington, the officers aren't always as forthcoming as those sailors at the wharf. The major is occupied with many things, especially finding us. . . . Have you heard any more of their move on Charleston?"

"Preparations continue daily, but a departure date remains unclear."

I grabbed my package from the floor and donned my gloves. "Anything else?"

Culper Junior rose from his chair. "If you catch anything more regarding West Point—"

"I'll inform you, of course." I stood to leave. So much time had passed since the Clinton dinner. Was West Point still on the General's mind? Or anyone's?

He glanced at the package in my hand. "Another parcel to send?"

"No, only some fabric scraps from Mr. Mulligan."

He folded his arms and sighed. "He was a member of the Sons of Liberty, you know. Quite the upstart."

"I also heard he served time in prison. Do you believe he still sympathizes with the Patriots?"

Robert went to unlock the door. "I am confident Hercules Mulligan does more than sympathize. He serves General Washington every day. And like us, he is always listening."

Twenty-Five

December 1779

Bone-chilling winds and a hard freeze ushered in the Yuletide season. Little snow had fallen, yet we knew it was only a matter of time.

How would those in Canvas Town and other areas of squalor survive another brutal winter? St. Paul's and various merchants held collections specified for the poor, although I wasn't certain how much difference they truly made.

We were frugal with wood during the day, only heating the rooms we used. Each night before retiring, we all worked to start our bedroom fires and heat the bed warmers to place under our quilts. And in addition to our continuous kitchen fire, we kept one burning low in the dining room. Anything we didn't want to find frozen in the morning was kept on the mantel, such as ink, paste, eggs, or bread.

I didn't want to bother the major for wood, regardless of his offer to supply it if necessary. Mother paid dearly for the delivery of an extra cord when it became available, although we weren't certain how long we could make it last.

One particularly chilly Friday, the major planned an evening of games and a light meal at his home, inviting me and the same friends who'd attended his dinner party. Celeste, Henry Fellowes, Major Baxter, and I gathered in his parlor to play whist and cribbage by the fire. Mr. Franklin had not yet arrived.

After several games accompanied by hot spiced wine and cider, the laughter grew louder and the competition more intense. Across from me at the small table we shared, the major rose from his seat. "I hate to break up this revelry, but is anyone hungry?"

Just as we all said *aye* and pushed back our chairs, Mr. Franklin let himself in at the front door. He removed his hat and waved a half-hearted greeting from the hall. It was clear something agitated him.

The major went to his friend. "I was beginning to wonder if you were coming."

Mr. Franklin wasted no time. "May I have a word?"

The major turned back to the parlor. "If you'll excuse us, please feel free to help yourselves to the buffet in the dining room." He then showed Mr. Franklin to his office.

What was so urgent that Franklin needed to speak with the major immediately and in private? Might I find out?

Mr. Fellowes, Celeste, and I chatted a bit while Major Baxter excused himself to locate the necessary. On our way to the dining room, we passed the partially open door to the office, where a lamp burned inside. I managed to let Celeste and Mr. Fellowes go ahead of me. The moment they entered the dining room, I slipped close to the office doorway.

I could hear Mr. Franklin's voice. ". . . heading for Morristown to (muffled) Washington."

The major answered in a loud whisper. "Good God. How do you know this?"

"Our informants passed it on to me before I arrived."

"Simcoe then?"

"Betty?" I whirled around.

Celeste beckoned me. "Are you coming?"

"Yes, I . . ." I stepped softly toward her, thinking of what to say. "I'm afraid I'm not feeling well. A bit too much wine, I suppose."

The men left the office and entered the hall. Seeing Celeste and me, the major's darkened expression brightened immediately.

The quintessential actor was also the perfect host. "Ladies, shall we eat?"

Mr. Franklin left before the meal, and I endured another two hours at the major's house. When Mr. Fellowes and Celeste were ready to leave, I asked them to take me home due to a headache, which was close to the truth. The major voiced his disappointment, yet I sensed his thoughts were on Simcoe and the daring plot to somehow harm General Washington.

Too late in the evening to alert Culper Junior, all I could do was wait for the sun to rise and pray I wouldn't be too late.

Before dawn, I hurried to dress. I told Mother and Alice I wished to post a letter early and would begin chores as soon as I returned. Whether or not they believed me, I knew not.

Snow trickled down as I hastened to Oakham and Townsend. The streetlamps had yet to be extinguished and few people were about at that hour. I assumed Robert would be in, however, preparing for the day.

Strangely enough, the "Closed" sign was out and the door locked. Was something wrong?

I knocked. "Robert?"

The lock turned and the door opened a crack. Robert frowned at me over his spectacles, then opened the door wider for me to enter.

I rushed in, brushing snow from my cloak. "I know 'tis early, but I have—"

Across from the desk, a man seated in *my* chair stood and faced me. Abraham Woodhull, in the flesh.

"Miss Floyd."

Although I'd caught a glimpse of him that one day outside the shop and occasionally in Setauket years ago, this was our first official meeting as adults. He was not a tall man or handsome, by any means. Although young, he had the face of many a farmer on Long Island— dark, roughened, and creased from hours in the sun, laboring in the fields. He wore a long, misshapen coat and the dark knit cap of a sailor. What struck me most were his eyes—twitchy and suspicious, scrutinizing me like a cornered animal.

I flipped back my hood and extended my gloved hand. "Mr. Woodhull, at last. What a pleasant surprise."

He gave me a weak handshake, his gaze darting behind me to the door.

Robert coughed. "What is the reason for your visit this early in the day, Cousin?"

"I apologize for interrupting, but I have intelligence to share." I turned to Culper Senior as I removed my gloves. "And 'tis good that you're here."

They exchanged glances, then listened while I repeated the conversation I overheard the previous evening.

Woodhull flinched when I mentioned Simcoe. "André said his name?"

"His words were exactly as I've repeated to you, but I couldn't hear Franklin's reply. I was forced to stay through dinner, otherwise, I would have found a way to come immediately."

I held out my hands and ignored his notice of the left one. "Simcoe and his men could arrive at Morristown any minute. Can you warn Washington?"

Robert turned to the Culper leader. "This also confirms that Franklin is spying for them. John Bolton must be notified."

Abraham brushed past me. "I'll see to it." He opened the door and left, letting it bang against the inside wall.

You're welcome.

"Where will he go from here?" I asked Robert as he closed the door.

"Amos Underhill is serving as courier now." With a glance out the window, he turned the lock. "He will find him at the boarding house and send him off as soon as he writes the correspondence with the ink. I do hope there is enough; it has been in short supply."

Fear of the danger we all were in made me shiver. "It must reach Morristown in time."

Robert took another fleeting look at the street before he faced me. "And you must stay on your guard, especially in Major André's presence."

Twenty-Six

One point agreed on by the military and most city residents was that a holiday in the middle of a war was a most welcome distraction. Therefore, the coming of Christmas meant more parties, dances, and concerts on the calendar. It was great fun for Celeste and me, especially knowing that Mr. Fellowes and the major would likely be invited, and hence, we would be asked to join them.

For weeks, the shop windows had boasted their Yuletide fare. The number of ships arriving from London had decreased due to the weather, but in early autumn the shopkeepers had the foresight to begin stocking all sorts of requirements for elaborate entertaining, from the finest of sweets and brandies to silver, crystal, and furniture.

Enterprising locals contributed fresh items that filled the shops daily, where premium prices were charged. Sugared hams, geese and other fowl, late season fruits and vegetables, and plenty of boxwood wreaths, holly branches, and pine roping were some of the items for sale. For those who could afford it, the city's merchants aimed to provide all one could require or imagine. Even Robert and Mr. Oakham did so, anticipating their customers' every need.

To further add to the frenzy, the *Royal Gazette* printed an announcement stating that the military's long-awaited departure for Charleston would finally take place on 26 December. The customary Twelfth Night celebrations were rescheduled for earlier dates to allow the thousands of troops who would be leaving New York to be given suitable farewells.

I propped an invitation on my frosted windowsill, between paper Betty and paper Major André, who now wore a resplendent red coat, thanks to Mr. Mulligan.

> *Your presence is cordially requested*
> *At a Yuletide Frolic*
> *And sendoff for His Majesty's Troops*
> *Stuyvesant Estate*
> *22 December 1779*
> *Six o'clock*
> *Dancing and Dinner followed by a Show of Fireworks*

There had been no indication from the major, Captain Willington, or anyone else pertaining to Simcoe's mission to harm or capture General Washington. And with no word from Robert, I could only think that the plan had been delayed, canceled due to inclement weather, or foiled as a result of my eavesdropping outside the major's office. Meanwhile, I was forced to bide my time and look forward to the "Frolic."

Celeste was due any minute. I'd invited her to come for tea and to help me decide what to wear to the party. Afterward, I planned to pick up my new shoes at the cobbler on Queen Street, then meet the major for a hot cider at Fraunces Tavern and a stroll around the shops.

Perhaps he might let slip something regarding the results of the plot. And if not, I would use the opportunity to casually inquire about any troop movements prior to the departure for Charleston and whether he'd caught any spies.

I tossed my dressing gown into my wardrobe and tidied the bed pillows, then hurried downstairs to stoke the fire in the dining room. I hadn't heard Celeste's carriage yet, but someone knocked at the front door as I reached the bottom step.

A delivery boy shivered on the porch and handed me a sealed note. "Message for Miss Betty Floyd."

I recognized the major's handwriting, finding it strange that he would correspond on a day we were to meet. I tipped the boy two pence. He thanked me and hopped off the porch to the snow-covered yard.

Ma chère,

I have just received word that J. Simcoe was captured by the rebels during a raid on Morristown. Please understand that I am thus prevented from meeting you today.

Désolé,

John

I leaned on the stair railing and read the note again, pondering the turn of events. Had the message from Culper Senior reached Tallmadge in time and led to Simcoe's capture rather than General Washington's? Robert would be overjoyed when he heard the news if he hadn't already.

Carriage wheels crunched through the snow, announcing Celeste's arrival. Disappointed in the cancellation of plans with the major yet encouraged by the reason he gave, I tucked the note deep into my pocket.

Celeste navigated the ice along the walk and climbed the steps. "Why is it this cold so soon? We hardly enjoyed the autumn."

"Hurry, please—the heat is slipping out the door." I held it until she came inside, then shut it tight.

She shivered out of her cloak. "While I'm thinking of it, Father said he saw you last week, early in the morning after our evening at Major André's. You were pounding on your cousin's shop door in the Square. I thought you had a headache when we brought you home. What was so urgent at that time of day?"

Mr. Walker was now watching the activities at Oakham and Townsend?

I frowned in an attempt to appear forgetful and waved a hand in the direction of Hanover Square. "I was merely—"

The back door squeaked open. Alice hummed a tune as she stomped her boots. "Miss Betty? You here?"

I called down the hall. "Celeste and I are about to have tea, Alice. Would you care to join us?"

Twenty-Seven

Bound for the Yuletide Frolic the following week, Major André and I sat beside each other in his carriage, two heavy woolen blankets across our laps. Peter guided the horses around a snowy curve toward Bowery Lane and the old Stuyvesant estate.

The major handed me a small wooden box tied with a red ribbon. "An early Christmas gift," he said, "and a small token of my affection."

He could still make me warm inside. "Shall I open it now?"

"Yes, absolutely, before we reach the party."

I pulled off my muff to untie the ribbon and open the box. It held two silver shoe buckles, encrusted with tiny sparkling stones. "Oh, John . . . for my new shoes. They're the loveliest I've ever seen."

Perhaps it would be inappropriate for me to accept them. They *were* beautiful buckles, the kind that only the wealthiest ladies wore, and often a customary gift from a well-to-do suitor. The suitor part was unclear, yet I didn't wish to disappoint the major.

He ran a thumb over one of the buckles. "I also must apologize for having to cancel our plans last week. As it turned out, we were able to arrange for a prisoner exchange and obtain Simcoe's release."

My heart sunk with the news, but I kept my expression vacant of emotion. "An exchange?"

"Three of their privates in exchange for Simcoe. 'Tis more than fair, wouldn't you say?"

"I suppose it is." *Three men? Thirty would be better.* "I did wonder, do you know what led to his capture?"

He lowered his head. "Another failed attempt to get Washington. You cannot imagine the times we have tried."

I squeezed his warm hand under the blanket. "At least Simcoe is safe."

He nodded toward the box. "Happy Christmas! Would you like to wear them tonight?"

I laughed. "Yes, although . . ." My shoes were miles away, hidden under the blanket and topped by yards of silk and taffeta. "I can't even see my shoes."

He gave a sly grin. "I shall remedy that, if you would allow me the honor."

We turned onto Bowery Lane, yet it would be a long ride to the estate. I freed one shoe at a time from the warm blanket and moved my cloak just enough. Major André reached down for my right shoe, unbuckled it, laid it in his lap, then removed the other.

In the waning light, our eyes met as he caressed my stockinged feet. He tucked the blanket around them, then changed the old buckles on my shoes to the new ones, sparkling like the faintest stars. Once my shoes were back on my feet, he took my face in his hands.

By the time Peter slowed the horses at the entrance to the estate, the carriage windows were fogged over and the only sounds came from our breathing and the rustle of taffeta.

You don't make this easy, John André.

I braced myself against the sudden gust of wintry air as I took his hand and descended the carriage. We rushed inside to the warmth and light of the grand foyer, already crowded with British and Hessian officers wearing their most formal uniform accoutrements, and guests in the finest party attire.

The major helped me out of my cloak and removed his own, then spoke to Mr. Stuyvesant while waiting to hand them to one of the uniformed servants. I checked my hair in the full-length gilded mirror and smoothed my gown of deep green.

It was one of the three gowns Celeste had given me that I hadn't yet worn, and I couldn't wait for her to see its transformation. Alice had fashioned the sleeves to be worn off the shoulder. Mother hadn't approved at first, yet she changed her mind once all the adjustments were made and she viewed the final results, including the switch of petticoats from Celeste's green one to my own petticoat of tiered white silk. My favorite touch was the gold braided trim, compliments of Mr. Mulligan, which Alice had applied to the waist and along the front opening of the skirt.

She styled my hair much the way I'd worn it for the Clinton

dinner that summer—curled and pulled high and back, with ringlets grazing my bare shoulders.

When the major returned, I twirled around. "Does anything look familiar?"

He took an assessment. "You look quite familiar."

I caught his arm and led him toward the bustling drawing room. "Perhaps later you'll recognize it. For now, *profitons de la fête.*"

The major laughed. "By all means, lead the way."

The enormous room dazzled the senses. Light from two fireplaces and hundreds of lamps and candles danced in the tall, gold mirrors and illuminated the huge garlands of greenery strung along the tops of carved white columns. A quintet of violinists played a lively melody, accompanied by laughter and spirited chatter.

Servants in black frock coats and white gloves hurried back and forth near a buffet that stretched the width of the room. They carried silver platters laden with steaming dishes. I inhaled the welcoming aromas of wild game and Yorkshire pudding, promising a fitting salute to Britain and her venerated officers prior to their journey to Charleston.

"All eyes are on you," the major said. "Shall we locate the wine, then say hello to your admirers?"

"It's you their eyes are on," I said. "As it should be."

I couldn't help beaming with pride in accompanying the gallant Major André—the officer most esteemed, if not envied, by his colleagues, the most respected by Tory gentlemen, and the one dreamed of by ladies of all ages and political leanings.

It would be another night of conflicted feelings regarding my choice to serve his enemies, but there would be no going back. All would fall into place eventually; I needed only to do my duty and remain on my guard. *And be extraordinary.*

Glasses of wine in hand, we made polite conversation with Reverend Inglis, plus various officers and their wives and guests. I looked for Celeste and Mr. Fellowes, but apparently they had yet to arrive.

Someone coughed behind me.

I turned to see Captain Willington. "Hello, Captain. I wasn't sure you would be here."

The major gave him a hearty handshake. "If it isn't the man with the most coveted quarters in New York."

"Hardly," I said. "I'm afraid the captain must cope with three generals and a pestering young private. Not to mention a cat who believes he's lord and master."

The major laughed. "That describes most cats, wouldn't you say?"

Captain Willington turned to me. "In truth, you've all made me feel as if I'm part of the household, and I've quite enjoyed it. However, my men and I just received final orders today." I could tell he was putting effort into sounding enthused. "We're to sail for Charleston."

The major raised his glass. "Congratulations."

Genuine dismay filled me. I'd grown accustomed to having this likable man in our home, not only for the wealth of information he'd unknowingly provided to the Culper Ring. We'd never discussed our strange meeting in the parlor on his first night, yet by now I had given him the benefit of the doubt.

"We shall miss you, Captain." I touched his arm. "Please promise you'll be careful."

"Thank you. I'll inform your mother, and if isn't too much of an imposition, I would enjoy spending Christmas Day with your family before we leave early the following day." He turned to Major André. "Of course, if you wouldn't mind, sir."

The major gestured with his glass. "That is entirely up to the ladies of the house. I'm afraid I'll be dining with the general that day."

"We would be delighted," I said. "And we will pray for your successful and safe journey."

After the captain excused himself, the major said, "Is Watermouth Willington growing on you after all?"

I watched the captain attempt to cut in on a group's conversation. "Perhaps he is. He tries hard to appear brave and prove himself, although I suspect he is somewhat lonely."

"I imagine so," he said. "That shows good instincts on your part. And *I* suspect that some watermouth . . . ah, mouthwatering food awaits us."

With a glance at the ceiling, I shook my head. "You are in top form tonight. Have you seen Celeste, by chance?"

"I have not. However, I do see an item that may interest you." He took my hand, led me to an arched walkway, and pointed above our heads, where a large bunch of mistletoe hung from cascading white ribbons.

He spoke with the utmost gravity. "We must not allow the mistletoe's purpose to go to waste. It would mean terrible luck for both of us."

Before I could comment, he kissed me hard, as though sealing out all possibility of misfortune. Heat crept upwards from my exposed arms and shoulders. Bystanders tittered and cheered.

Recovering, I steered him away. "If that doesn't bring us good luck, I cannot imagine what will."

We weaved our way to the buffet table and squeezed in line behind an ample woman in a fawn-colored silken gown trimmed in mink. We eyed the countless choices, from cheese-stuffed olives and radish roses, to piles of sugared ham and roasted duck, Yorkshire pudding, light-as-air cream puffs, and frosted cakes topped with tiny British flags.

After making our selections, we followed others to a large parlor where several rectangular tables were set with linens and silverware monogrammed with an ornate *S*.

"André!"

At the far side of the room, the one and only John Graves Simcoe, at a table with General Clinton and other officers, lifted a hand in greeting. My throat went dry.

The major carried our plates and headed toward his friend. I could only follow. Mercifully, with the general at the table and every chair taken, it was unlikely we would be asked to join them.

Major André set the plates down nearby and embraced Simcoe. "Welcome back, my friend. What a relief it is to see you. And General, you both remember Miss Floyd?"

Clinton remained seated and nodded to me, not letting go of his forkful of duck. The braid on his red coat was identical to the braid on my gown.

Simcoe's hard gaze made me want to cringe. "How could I forget a good Long Island name?"

I held my head high and ignored their rudeness. "Good evening, General. Lieutenant-Colonel."

"Your dinners will get cold," Simcoe said. "You mustn't let us keep you."

The major touched his plate to his friend's arm. "Let's have a good chat tomorrow, shall we?"

As I led the way to the farthest possible table, I took a deep breath and made mental notes of all I would need to report to Culper Junior.

At the table were two officers and two shy young ladies, clearly surprised to see the legendary Major André joining them.

After we exchanged pleasantries, the major whispered to me. "Is anything wrong?"

I did my best to appear as if nothing was. "May I trouble you for more wine?"

"Of course." He pushed back his chair. "Am I mistaken, or does the braid on your gown match the general's?"

Following dinner, we were directed to another grand room for dancing. Eight musicians gathered on a raised platform, including the violinists from the drawing room. Evergreen trees draped with long strands of colored glass beads surrounded the room's perimeter. The beads shimmered in the candlelight.

"I'm told the trees are called tannenbaums in Germany," the major said. "A tribute to the Hessians."

I had never seen ornamented trees. "They thought of everything."

"And may I have the honor of the first dance, *mademoiselle*?"

"You may, sir. And I happen to have new buckles on my shoes, so I plan to show them off."

"We shall step lively, then," he said. "Perhaps an Allemande is in order."

"Ladies and gentlemen, may I have your kind attention?" Mr. Stuyvesant stood on another platform and raised his hands. "Before we dance, I want to thank each of you for joining us this evening, as we celebrate not only the Christmas season but His Majesty King George III's illustrious army and navy."

The crowd erupted in applause and shouted, "Huzzah! Huzzah!"

"As you are all aware, many of our beloved troops, with the aid of the brave and devoted Hessians, will depart New York on the day after Christmas and sail for Charleston, South Carolina, where they will engage the Continentals and put an end to their unlawful rebellion."

While the guests cheered, their heroes went forward, crowding the platform and surrounding it on all sides. Captain Willington stood on the far-left end, waving to the crowd. I caught a glimpse of the opinionated Lieutenant Parker behind him, his freckles less pronounced than during the summer.

Beside me, Major André applauded his comrades. Mr. Stuyvesant invited Simcoe and General Clinton to take his place in front. Cheers rose as they stepped forward, and the general waited for the room to quiet.

A small commotion made me turn around. Guests moved aside, annoyance on their faces. Muttering apologies, Celeste moved quickly toward me, holding her gold damask gown close, and squeezed in on my left. She had never looked more distraught.

"Thank you, Mr. Stuyvesant," the general said. "Ladies and gentlemen, I am honored by your generous outpouring of support."

I murmured to Celeste. "What has happened?"

The major gave her a momentary look of concern but turned back to listen to his commander.

She stared ahead with angry eyes and spit out the words in a loud whisper. "Henry and I . . . will no longer be seeing each other. Someone else has caught his eye." Her forehead wrinkled. "Dorah Shepherd, if you can believe it."

"Oh, no! I'm so sorry." It *was* hard to fathom—both Henry Fellowes's rejection of Celeste and his choice of Dorah.

". . . endured the utmost cruelty and half-starved." Clinton placed a hand on Simcoe's shoulder, who looked about as starved as a prize cow. "If not for Adjutant-General Major John André and his quick thinking, our Lieutenant-Colonel Simcoe would have been lost."

The major himself had orchestrated the exchange?

Robert warned me that he was more cunning and secretive than he appeared, yet I'd refused to believe it. What else did he keep from me? As several guests turned to shake his hand, I disguised my shock and gazed at him with pride and admiration.

My skin warmed with guilt. *If they only knew. There's the hero who liberated the great Simcoe. Oh, the innocent-looking girl on the hero's arm? She was behind the capture.*

Celeste spoke in a strained whisper. "Regardless, I did not want to miss this party. And now that I'm here, I'm planning to dance until late and do my part in sending our men off to battle." She waved her arm with a flourish, yet her eyes glistened with unshed tears. "Is that my gown you're wearing? It's . . . lovely."

General Clinton beckoned the major to join him. "Let us show Major André our appreciation."

As he went forward amid applause and cheers, I leaned close to Celeste. "You need to calm down."

She glared at me. "Don't tell me what I need to do, Betty."

Poor Celeste—jilted and out for revenge. I'd wanted her honest opinion on the remake of her gown and to show her the gift the major had given me in the carriage. Now I could only hope that she wouldn't do something foolish.

The general carried on with his speech. "Major André will be accompanying us on the expedition, as will Lord Cornwallis and Admiral Arbuthnot, who shall command the naval fleet . . ."

Did he just say—

"The major's going to Charleston?" Celeste asked.

I held out my hands to say I was as surprised as she was.

Clinton continued. "As we make our final preparations to defeat the enemy, I ask for your ongoing support for all of us under the king's command, including the ten thousand men who shall remain in New York in the capable hands of General Knyphausen."

I caught the major's eye. *Why hadn't he informed me?*

He shook his head ever so slightly, as if to say he'd had no voice in the matter. Then he stared ahead as Clinton shook hands with Admiral Arbuthnot.

I shouldn't be surprised. He'd told me this was always a possibility. I would be expected to send him off with proud assurance and endure his absence, as other women did wherever there was war. Yet it hurt that he hadn't uttered a word of this all evening. And as far as my role in the Ring, what would happen now? Could I still contribute with my main source out of reach?

The major replied to something the admiral said. On either side of them, Clinton and Simcoe wore smug expressions, as if victory was guaranteed. Behind them stood the overconfident, uppity officers in all their bright red coats and gold buttons, representing thousands of troops under their charge, each one employed by George III to keep his foot on America's throat and kill anyone who got in the way.

A young man in front hollered, "God save our King and General Clinton."

The crowd took up the cry. "Huzzah! Huzzah! Huzzah!"

As the cheers diminished, Reverend Inglis came forward. He began a prayer for the military's protection and swift victory.

My own prayer became a string of questions, like beads on the tannenbaums. *Will the major return unharmed? What will the year 1780 bring? And which of us in this room tonight will live to see it through?*

Part Two

Twenty-Eight

February 1780

Heavy snows buried New York, accompanied by a steady freeze. The army employed dozens of horses and wagons to remove the snow from the most traveled streets and dump it in the harbor, making it possible for city dwellers to continue with important business. As for me, other than a sleighing party in January, occasional coffee with friends, and a quick visit with Robert, I had stayed close to home.

Mother, Alice, Joe, and I huddled around the dining room table before the crackling fire and asked God to bless our reheated potted meat and bread. I let my tight shoulders relax under my shawl as a measure of warmth reached them.

Mother passed the breadbasket. "At least they've halted the fighting in New York for the winter. That's the only good thing I can say about this horrible weather."

"Everybody's just tryin' to survive," Alice said. "This got to be the worst winter I can recall."

Joe tore his slice of bread in pieces. "The harbor's frozen. My friends have been skating on it."

"And you will do no such thing," Mother said. "It's much too dangerous. If the ice should crack . . ." She waved her hand, dismissing the unthinkable.

Joe silently pleaded with me not to mention that I'd recently seen him returning from the harbor with his friends George Vanderbrook and James Townsend, Robert's second cousin. Joe had made me promise then to keep it our secret.

I changed the subject. "Cousin Robert learned that some of the regiments went to Staten Island before the river froze in the event it's attacked, although I can't imagine anyone bothering in this weather."

"Has there been any word from Charleston?" Mother asked.

"Surely they've arrived." All eyes looked to me, knowing I had been awaiting news of the major.

I stirred my spoon around in my bowl. "No word yet, and it's been well over a month. Mr. Rivington should hear soon. He'll announce it in the *Gazette*, of course."

Most of my days were now consumed with tutoring Joe and keeping the fires burning at home, in every sense. We did receive a wonderful surprise one cold Monday morning—a delivery of aged firewood that the major had ordered prior to his departure.

It took constant effort to balance my feelings for him while remaining alert to any intelligence. Yet any useful news had all but stopped since the arrest and exchange of John Simcoe and the military's departure for Charleston. Now my best sources were absent, the tight grip of winter had put the war on hold, and most forms of commerce had slowed to a crawl.

Other than the occasional party or concert, a lethargic temper prevailed over the city. Mother heard a friend remark that church attendance had dropped, along with business at the brothels. Perhaps it was due to the weather, but that business had plummeted as soon as most of its patrons sailed for Charleston.

I happened to see Peter Laune when I ventured out on an errand for Alice. He'd taken temporary employment as a valet for one of General Knyphausen's aides. We speculated if Theatre Royal's upcoming production of *Much Ado About Nothing* would be well-received or if the absence of Major André, their star performer, might lower the attendance.

For the wealthy, the play title was an appropriate name for life in New York. But for hundreds of unfortunate souls suffering from the lack of fuel and food, not to mention the spread of smallpox and other diseases, Alice was correct; survival had taken precedence.

With the shortages came rampant corruption in the form of rising prices and theft. Anything that would burn was taken and used for fuel, including porch steps, window shutters, church pews, and trees in the Common.

Some of those in Canvas Town, if they were able, had moved on for better living conditions. For those who remained, Mother, Alice, and I spent many an evening knitting stockings and preparing food, and Mother continued to visit the prisoners at Rhinelander's and take them what she could. I didn't think our meager efforts would do much good, yet they were met with sincere gratitude.

Joe passed his empty bowl to me as I collected the dishes. "I miss Captain Willington. Do you think he's well?"

"Certainly." I hoped it was so. "And you're the man of the house once more."

"Never thought I'd say it, but I worry for him," Alice said. "The cap'n and the major, they good men."

Mother agreed. "They've both been honorable and helpful gentlemen. We must keep them in our prayers." She gave me a quick glance, as if to confirm they had been honorable.

Overall, the captain had followed Mother's rules after he moved in. No apparent harm was done when I suspected he'd been drinking prior to his stumbling in late at night. When Alice found his pipe in the rear yard, he said he'd been looking for it ever since the day of his arrival. To me, he claimed it was the item he'd sought that night I discovered him in the parlor. I didn't know what else to think but discarded my theory that he'd been sent to spy on me.

As far as the major's behavior, he liked to push physical boundaries now and then, which I refused to cross. Otherwise, he was more than honorable. All my concern now, however, was for the safe return of both men.

Alice and I loaded a tray from the sideboard with our dishes while Joe topped the fire with another log. I lifted the tray and followed Alice to the pantry. "I'll help you heat the bed warmers. We shall need them tonight."

Celeste had sent a note requesting that I meet her for coffee the next morning at Rivington's, so I started out, bundled against the elements. The frozen air made it difficult to take a deep breath. The normally busy streets were deserted but for a few brave or foolish souls. Slipping along the icy paths, I felt more like the latter.

She and I had seen each other at the sleighing party, yet we hadn't had a chance to speak privately since the night of the Yuletide Frolic. When the major and I sought her out to say goodnight that evening, she was too occupied with the attentions of two inebriated Hessian officers to pay us much notice. By now, I hoped she had accepted the end of her relationship with Henry Fellowes and would be prudent in how she conducted herself.

If Robert was not at the coffeehouse today, I would stop into Oakham and Townsend after seeing Celeste. I had only seen him once since Christmas, to inform him that his shop might be under surveillance by Mr. Walker and to pass on what information I'd gathered at the Frolic. I should at least pay him a visit.

"Ah, Miss Floyd." Mr. Rivington exited the storeroom wearing a white apron over a heavy shirt and drying his hands on a towel. "What brings you out today? Can it possibly get any colder? Although, I asked that yesterday, and it has done just that." The corners of his eyes creased as he laughed.

My teeth chattered. "I'm here to meet a friend, yet I'm a bit early." I nodded to the roaring fire. "What a welcome sight. I believe I shall stay all day."

"Many do, although it's often the political discussions that provide the most heat in this room."

I couldn't help teasing him. "Why, Mr. Rivington, is not every New Yorker a supporter of the king?"

He tossed the towel over his shoulder. "There are yet a handful who loudly disagree from time to time." With a hand on the side of his mouth, he spoke softly. "And some who choose to disagree in secret."

Oh, if only I could discuss with him the Culper Ring's activities, not to mention all he'd witnessed prior to my arrival in New York. Yet I didn't know for certain if he knew *I* knew he was Agent 726. Or if he knew I was 355. Thus, there we were, two spies for the same side, alone in the room where the Sons of Liberty had once plotted a rebellion and now the British brewed their schemes, and we were both too cautious to speak freely.

"Please, sit anywhere you wish," he said. "Your cousin will not be in—he's conducting inventory in his shop while it's quiet. You're my first customer today, although more will arrive before long. Not the boisterous crowd that went to Charleston, however." He laughed, gesturing toward the harbor.

I chose a table beside the fireplace. "Have you any news of Charleston?"

"Alas, I have none." He raised his eyebrows. "If I do hear any specifics regarding Major André, I shall make certain you are informed."

I set my cloak on a chair close to the fire. "Thank you. No one receives the news of the war before you do, Mr. Rivington."

He laughed. "You flatter me, Miss Floyd. Some describe what I print as lies, however—"

The door swung open. "Here is my friend, Miss Walker."

Celeste wiped her boots on the doormat and pushed back the rabbit-lined hood from her cloak, revealing her bright red cheeks.

"Welcome, Miss Walker." Mr. Rivington gestured toward the fire. "Do come and warm yourself. Two coffees?"

"Yes, that would be lovely," Celeste said.

As Mr. Rivington went to the back room, she removed her cloak and draped it beside mine. "I walked from Father's shop. Mother advised him not to open today, as cold as it is, yet he claimed he had stock work to do. Marcus dropped us both there and I said I would walk to meet you." She pulled off her gloves. "I've longed to see you. We haven't talked since that dreadful night."

I rubbed my chilled hands together. "It must have been terrible for you."

She slid into the chair across from mine, frowning and rubbing her arms. "How dare he, Betty?"

Mr. Rivington reappeared with two steaming mugs of coffee and set them on our table. We pulled the mugs close, warming our hands.

Celeste waited until he disappeared behind the storeroom door. "You don't know the entire story. Instead of meeting me face-to-face, Henry sent me a note that afternoon as I was dressing for the evening. He stated he could no longer see me because he was in love with Dorah Shepherd." She sipped her coffee, glancing up for my reaction.

I barely had the words. "What a miserable, spineless—"

"Exactly. My parents both thought highly of him until then. Of course, now they say he didn't deserve me. A week later, my father heard that he left New York. I don't know where he would go, not that I care. It could be dangerous for Loyalists to travel in certain areas, though, and the weather . . ." She shook her shoulders.

"The post riders and messengers get through, so there are ways. But why would he leave?"

Celeste took a long drink of her coffee and set her mug on the table. "My guess is because of what Mary Shepherd wrote to me in a letter."

The coffeehouse door burst open and the wind that followed made me clench my whole body. Four soldiers stomped in, all talking at once. They chose a table by the entrance, with barely a glance at us. Mr. Rivington reappeared to take their orders.

I turned back to Celeste. "Mary wrote to you?"

She lifted her mug and held it. She lowered her voice, although I doubted the men could hear a word over their own chatter. "Only a few days ago. She informed me that Dorah is with child. Their parents are sending her to England to stay with an aunt as soon as the ships can travel."

I couldn't help but gasp in shock. "Oh, Celeste . . ."

"Henry must be the father." She set her mug down hard, splashing coffee over the rim. "According to Mary, Dorah told him the news, and they are certain it's why he left. He didn't say goodbye or make any offer to help. Mary thought I deserved to know, although the family hopes to avoid a scandal and keep this private until Dorah can leave."

I imagined Dorah, expecting a child and abandoned by the man she loved, facing a move across the ocean and possibly never seeing her family again. Yet with Henry's disappearance, she would have no other choice. It was the customary way of handling such matters.

"He was always such a gentleman, Betty. We had a wonderful time together. Why didn't I see it?"

Mr. Rivington returned with a large tray of drinks and bowls of soup for the soldiers. The door opened again, and I braced myself for the wind gust. Three men stepped in, including Mr. Hudson, the apothecary.

I turned back to Celeste. "No one can possibly know everything about a person, I suppose."

She turned her coffee mug in a circle. Her tone took a slight shift then, from self-pity to snappish. "What about you? Do you think you know Major André?"

"I beg your pardon?"

"When you met him, you thought he was a cad. How is he any different from Henry?" She leaned closer. "Or any other man?"

"Major André *is* a gentleman," I said. "He's trustworthy and honorable and—"

She raised her brows, barely hiding the smirk that crossed her face.

"Celeste! Henry may have turned out to be scum, but it doesn't justify these accusations."

She held up a hand. "I'm not accusing, I am only suggesting that you keep your eyes open when he returns from Charleston. You don't know what you don't know. For example, what about Miss Shippen? Yes, yes . . . I know she's Mrs. Arnold now and in Philadelphia." She waved her fingers in the general direction. "But I recently heard that she was in New York only a few months ago, supposedly delivering letters for her Philadelphia friends."

A wariness crept through my chest. "The major assured me they were friends, nothing more."

Her cynical expression conveyed she thought me foolish to take him at his word. "Where does he go between the times when you see him? What if he's sneaking into Philadelphia or meeting her somewhere in New York? Regardless, you can't expect to believe he isn't seeking satisfaction elsewhere." She paused, letting that statement sink in. "I don't suppose you've heard of the Hellfire Club, have you?"

I bristled. I had heard of it—a secret men's club where questionable pastimes were indulged. I had no desire to know if the major ever attended.

The chill in my chest turned to heat rising to my face. "You're speaking out of your own hurt and anger. He's with the army now, doing his duty, so this is all quite irrelevant. But regardless, none of what the major does or doesn't do is any of your business. Or mine, frankly. We aren't engaged or . . ." I glanced at the fire as sparks fell near our table. "Could we please change the subject?"

Celeste sighed, clutching her mug. Finally, she spoke. "Perhaps you should make it your business upon his return. I only wish you to be aware of such things, in case you're so in love with him that you're blinded to the facts."

Apparently, she wasn't about to let it rest. I worked to control my voice. "Celeste, I'm terribly sorry about Henry. But I have no interest in discussing this any further." I stood and grabbed my cloak from the chair and tossed it around my shoulders.

"I suppose you'll go run to your cousin's shop now," she said. "Whatever takes you there so often?"

I couldn't think of what to say. I swallowed my anger. "I'm going home."

Ignoring the inevitable stares from the other customers, I left the coffeehouse for the frosty streets. Celeste could pay for the coffee.

Visiting Robert now was impossible. I hurried to the corner to properly fasten my cloak and ram my hands into my muff. I needed the long, cold walk home to recover from Celeste's verbal blows.

She was clearly jealous, and the ugly business with Henry Fellowes and Dorah added fuel to the flames. But how dare she make such crude insinuations? What kind of a friend does so?

Of course, I could not possibly know all the major did when I wasn't in his presence. He had his work as General Clinton's assistant and the work at the theatre, all of which he enjoyed and took much of his time. He also had various friends in and around the city, and he received constant invitations. Beyond that, I had no way of knowing his whereabouts, and I wasn't about to investigate as though I were a suspicious lover. Plus, as hard as it was, I needed to keep a certain distance due to my allegiance to the Ring.

Yet, I couldn't help wondering—was there truth to what Celeste said? Did he correspond with or see Peggy Shippen Arnold? Or someone else?

Frankly, I couldn't imagine him doing so. He'd said himself he wasn't duplicitous enough to be a spy, and I couldn't see him devoting the time or energy to another woman either.

I groaned and pulled my cloak tighter around me, trying to dismiss the seeds of doubt Celeste had tried to plant.

When Joe arrived home that evening after working at Robert's shop, he had a letter for me from Jacob and one for Mother from Aunt Hannah.

I opened Jacob's letter at the fireside. I had lost track of how long it had been since I'd heard from him.

Dear Betty,

The stockings were most welcome. They help warm my feet in this frozen outpost.

All of us look for the mail delivery and any news of the war. The post comes about once each week, but less often now with the Straits of Mackinac frozen over. We cross it on foot, or by dog sled if the wind isn't too high. It makes me long for those warm summer days on Long Island. I think of our dancing and hope one day we may do so again.

Jacob

I leaned closer to the fire and reread the letter—not a word about the message I wrote using the Culper code and accidentally sent to him back in mid-autumn. Did he receive it? Or was it intercepted by those whose mission was to find Patriot spies and see them hang?

Celeste sent a note of apology later that week, claiming her broken heart made her say what she should have kept to herself. I replied and thanked her, yet I couldn't help sensing that our friendship had been altered.

Nevertheless, I continued to wonder if in some way she was right about the major. As much as I denied it or told myself it was not my concern, I couldn't help mulling over the possibility. And Mrs. Arnold—had she visited him when she was in New York?

Still, his safe return from Charleston mattered most. Perhaps I would discover more, in time.

Twenty-Nine

May 1780

The ice-breathing dragon that would be known as the Hard Winter lashed the city well into spring before making a retreat. New Yorkers could finally venture out of doors again without fighting the weather, and the miracles that marked every May burst forth in triumph. Windows and doors were flung open, kitchen gardens tilled and planted, and heavy quilts and clothing packed away. Alice and I slammed the lids shut on the winter trunks, wishing there would never be a need to open them again.

The military voyage to Charleston that began on 26 December had taken an entire five weeks, owing to the onslaught of the most horrible weather seen in years. By the time word of it reached New York and Mr. Rivington printed the news in the *Gazette*, the British had secured decisive victories in Charleston, apparently due in part to the weak leadership of the Continental navy.

I hoped the reports were exaggerated and endeavored not to put too much stock in them. But for General Washington, the news out of Charleston must have been devastating. What a blow to him and his dwindling forces, following the winter in Morristown where the army struggled to survive, with many deserting the camp just to seek sustenance.

Finally, word spread through the taverns and coffeehouses that General Clinton and all of Britain's heroes were returning. The foolish rebels' war was coming to a close, according to speculations. Rejoicing Loyalists planned a new season of parties and entertainments, while the troops remaining in New York under General Knyphausen prepared to welcome their victorious counterparts.

I went along, of course, hiding my anxieties over the outward turn in the Crown's favor. When I discussed the situation with Robert, the idea of Britain being close to winning the war was unacceptable. We may have taken a horrible beating in Charleston, but we would never consider surrender. Congress had declared independence; indeed, there was no choice but for Washington's army to persevere.

Uppermost in my mind was seeing the major again, although I speculated in regard to our relationship and what new intelligence might surface for the Ring.

At Montague's Tavern one evening, I met Celeste, Mary Shepherd, two gentlemen who were distant cousins of Mary's, and Lieutenant MacCallan, my Scottish dance partner whom I first met at the Navy Coffeehouse. He regretted not having been among those chosen to go to Charleston yet changed his mind when he learned of the wretched sailing conditions the ships had encountered.

Seeing Mary, I felt Dorah's absence. I didn't think it appropriate to mention her, not that I had the opportunity. According to Celeste, however, Dorah arrived safely at their aunt's English countryside home in April. The whereabouts of Henry Fellowes were still unknown.

One of Mary's cousins, James Hart, insisted we raise our glasses to the British army and King George. He flagged down Mr. Rivington as he passed our table.

"Sir, I read in your paper today that, given the southern victories, the war may well be ending soon. Do you honestly believe it could be so?"

"It may be the case, sir," he replied. "However, let us see what happens during the next several weeks, at the very least."

"Nevertheless, we are celebrating." Hart waved his glass toward our jovial group as we all raised ours with enthusiasm. We made enough commotion to cause others in the tavern to join in the fun. *Ah, what an actor I've become.*

When our dinners were served, I turned to Lieutenant MacCallan. "The army must be quite eager to return to New York, wouldn't you agree?"

He set down his tankard of ale. "I imagine so, Miss Floyd, especially the general."

"Oh?" I gave him my rapt attention, urging him to continue. The major had told me of Clinton's dislike for venturing from the city for too long.

He moved his chair closer to mine. "I spoke with a fellow yesterday at the wharves, a privateer. He said there's a sizable French fleet on the way to aid the Continentals. Washington's been expecting 'em for some time. If Clinton has wind of it, he'll be in a hurry to return, that is for certain."

My first thought was for the major's safety. My second—to see Robert and tell him of this conversation. "Could they be planning to engage the French before they reach New York?"

He poked a fork into his beef pie. "The man hadn't heard anything 'bout that."

I inhaled deeply, imagining French ships sailing toward our vast continent. What else did the lieutenant know?

"Forgive me, Miss Floyd. I didn't mean to bore ye."

I touched his arm and leaned close. "Why do men think any talk of war is beyond a woman's understanding? You are not boring me in the least, Lieutenant. What do you suppose will happen?"

He sat taller, looking pleased to be asked. "Well, I'm acquainted with a couple of Knyphausen's assistant officers. They know 'bout the French fleet as well. Their guess is that the ships are bound for Newfoundland or Halifax."

I smoothed the napkin in my lap. "I see. It must be so difficult, not knowing quite where they are. If you were General Clinton and learned that the French were heading this way, what would you do?"

He could not have looked more proud. "I'd prepare to engage 'em."

His contacts had only been guessing as to the destination of the fleet, but the fact that the French were definitely on their way was good news. Perhaps it was nothing Washington didn't already know, yet it might assist with his strategies.

At long last, I might have a bit of intelligence to share with Culper Junior.

The following day, I told Mother I needed to visit a friend and set off for Oakham and Townsend. While customers purchased their needed items, I browsed the newly arrived summer fabric selections from England. As the last gentleman left with his articles, Robert turned his sign, locked the door, and we went to his desk. He wore a more-than-usual sullen expression, and I trusted my information would cheer him.

"I have good reason for visiting you today," I began. "Mr. Rivington will undoubtedly print it soon, yet I only learned last evening that the French fleet is on its way to aid our army. However, the British don't know where to expect them. I was told Knyphausen's assistants are guessing it might be Halifax or Newfoundland."

Robert was silent, his gaze drifting to the window.

I continued. "Clinton will want to stop the French. Therefore, I thought—"

He removed his spectacles and tossed them on the ledger.

"What is it, Robert? Has something happened?"

"Yes, I suppose it has." He finally looked me in the eye. "I have informed Culper Senior that I no longer wish to serve."

That was the last thing I ever expected to hear. "You cannot mean that."

"I do, Cousin. Ben Tallmadge most likely knows by now."

My heart pounded. "But . . . why?"

He again focused on the ledger. "I have given it careful thought and have come to the conclusion that my services are no longer required by General Washington."

"How can that be?" I raised my hands. "I know he's been impatient—understandably so—yet I thought he was pleased with your work overall."

Robert scowled. "Allow me to explain. As you will recall, Washington wished to find a faster method of receiving correspondence in Morristown. To that end, some time ago I enlisted the help of a new courier—my second cousin, James Townsend."

"Joe's friend? He's rather a daredevil from what I gather."

"He is young, but he is brave and a fast rider. I gave him a letter containing sensitive information with strict instructions on how to proceed north and obtain passage across the Hudson and into Morristown. He had a fabricated story as to the reason for his travel, should he be stopped.

"Yet of all places, he requested shelter at the home of a Patriot family, then regaled them with tall tales until they were convinced he was a Tory spy. They had him arrested and taken to Washington's camp."

Joe had seen James recently but hadn't mentioned his friend's adventure. "He must have been terribly frightened. Was your letter still in James's possession?"

"Yes, and it was given to the general. Nevertheless, when Washington applied the stain, the letter was unreadable. He was so displeased with how much time and effort was given to sorting out the whole situation that he complained to Tallmadge, who complained to Woodhull. He and I have argued the matter for the past several days. Finally, I saw no other choice but to resign."

I leaned on the desk. "What of the Ring though? We need you, Robert. How will the general gather intelligence in New York?"

His shoulders drooped, a man defeated. "I do not know. There is Mr. Mulligan and Mr. Rivington. You may be asked to assist them, or perhaps he will find others willing to serve. He has talked of establishing a similar ring on Staten Island."

I groaned. "Staten Island is not New York City. The military is headquartered here. It wouldn't be the same."

I couldn't allow him to quit. I rose from my chair. "Robert, please. I beg you to reconsider. I need your help and guidance, and General Washington needs you. No one else has your particular abilities or is in your position."

Robert stood slowly but made no remark. I was undeterred. "We all need you. For such a time as this."

He almost smiled. "Spoken like a true Patriot."

"I suppose a bit of my Uncle William has rubbed off." I sighed heavily, trying to think. "Regardless, when Clinton returns, there's bound to be an upsurge in intelligence. The parties and balls are already filling the calendar."

I took a step toward the door, not wishing to leave without making my point. "General Washington won't dwell on what happened with James. He will be considering his next strategy and, as you said, he won't let the Charleston losses determine our country's future. The French may help, but he's going to need each of us."

Robert held his palms out. "He has my resignation."

I unlocked the door myself and turned back to face him. "You must retract it then. Because I, for one, refuse to accept it."

The window rattled as I pulled the door shut. What would the Culper Ring be without Culper Junior? There was too much at stake—the future of the country—for the Ring to cease operation. Robert and General Washington had better come to their senses.

Meanwhile, what was I to do? My cousin may have lost the desire to serve at present, as I had at one time. But he'd been the one who persuaded me to climb aboard for this outlandish effort. Despite the obstacles, I was determined to fulfill my duty and I would not jump ship.

In the time it took to cross Hanover Square, I made the decision to pay a visit to Mary Underhill in order to locate her brother. I should have thought to ask Robert if he was still in the city, although he would never approve of me looking for him.

I could not sit idly by while Culper Junior quit the Ring. Someone had to find Culper Senior. It might as well be me.

Robert had told me that he and Abraham lived at the Underhill's boarding house on Queen Street. By now, I assumed that Mrs. Underhill would have a sense of her brother's true reasons for his frequent visits to the city, especially with her husband Amos now acting as a Culper Ring courier.

Had she overheard any whispered conversations between Amos, Abraham, and Robert? Of course, without knowing how much she knew, I could not say one word more than necessary.

Walking up Queen Street, I noticed two homes with small signs posted near their doors advertising rooms for rent. One bore the name "Hastings." The other simply read, "Inquire Within." It had to be the Underhill home.

I knocked and took a step back, slowing my breath, rehearsing my words. Would she remember me? *Mrs. Underhill, I'm Betty—*

The door opened just wide enough for me to see Mary Underhill's relaxed, kind face—so unlike her brother's. Her simple work dress and spattered apron meant I'd interrupted her chores.

"Mrs. Underhill? I'm Betty Floyd. My mother and I saw you at the market not long ago. Forgive me if—"

With a glance over her shoulder, she opened the door wider. "Yes? I'm in the midst of the spring cleaning—"

"I apologize," I said. "I only wish to know if you have seen your brother Abraham today."

Her brow knitted. "Why no, although I suspect he may be here tomorrow. May I assist you instead?"

"Would you simply tell him there is a message waiting for him? He will understand."

She didn't act at all surprised at my request. "Very well. I shall let him know as soon as he arrives."

I thanked her and left, satisfied that she would convey the message. If her overly cautious brother put his trust in her, I would need to trust her as well.

Walking home, I mentally composed the note I would write. Then I questioned the urgency of it. Would it be helpful? Practically anyone in the Continental army had better understanding of the expected arrival of the French. Yet if General Washington was told that the British were guessing as to the destination of the approaching fleet, he might wish to use it to his advantage.

Robert had instructed me what to do if the occasion arose when I needed to reach Culper Senior. The difficulty would lie in securing the note in the correct pot behind Fraunces Tavern, while avoiding detection. It seemed worth a try.

Thirty

I retrieved the Culper Code pages from beneath my mattress that afternoon, wrote the note, and wrapped it in a scrap of the red cloth Mr. Mulligan had given me.

Robert had instructed to tie a blue cloth to the stable's boot scrape if I was to leave a note for Culper Senior at the tavern, but I had neglected to save any blue cloth. Instead, I was counting on Mary Underhill to relay that message to her brother. We were at war—this was not the time to concern myself with details.

I would make the drop that evening, before twilight. The shops would be closed, and the tavern would be sufficiently noisy at that hour to cover any sounds in the alley. Also, Alice and Mother would be at the Dicksons' with several other ladies, finishing the underside of the quilt begun the previous summer.

For protection and the sake of appearances, I asked Joe to come along, saying I had an important errand and needed his companionship. I'd kept secrets for him—now I needed him to do the same for me.

After Alice and Mother left, he waited on the porch as I opened the front door. Triple jumped from his lap as he rose to his feet. "Where are we going?"

"You'll know soon enough. I wish to be home before dark, so let's be off."

He followed me down to the street. "Mother thinks we're staying in and practicing French."

I gave him a sideways glance. "*Très bien.* We shall have *une bonne conversation.*"

"We're doing something secret, aren't we?"

I looked around for any open windows. "Lower your voice. And please try to appear as if nothing is out of the ordinary."

"Ha, it *is* a secret."

His loud whisper would have made me laugh if the situation hadn't been so precarious. "I shall explain, but you mustn't ask any more questions. I need to leave a message for someone in a certain place without being seen. And, Joseph, no one can ever know."

"This must be serious. You haven't called me Joseph since I was five."

We turned the corner, heading toward the business district. It was crucial for him to understand the importance of secrecy. "I've never mentioned to anyone your assisting Mrs. Burgin with the prisoners. And I know things about you *and* your friends that I won't reveal. I expect the same from you. There are times when things must be kept secret, similar to not mentioning Uncle William to anyone."

"Je comprends."

He was quiet the rest of the way. Had he guessed that I might be spying for the Patriots at the same time I was involved with Major André? As intuitive as he often was, that was a distinct possibility. But I needed his help, and I had to trust him.

As we neared Fraunces Tavern, Pearl Street was all but deserted, save for a sailor or two and a few merchants locking their doors. None of them paid us any mind as we walked past.

"Are we close?" Joe asked.

I ignored his question. Even in the waning light, the tavern's yellow bricks and its location at the corner of Pearl and Broad made it easy to find. Now to find the pots behind the building. Was there an alley?

A narrow dirt path ran along one side of the tavern. I led the way until the path ended at an alley leading toward the rear of the building. Litter was strewn about, even a rowboat missing most of its hull. I winced at the smell of rotting garbage.

Joe groaned. "Are you certain—"

I lifted a hand to silence him, although the music and shouting from inside reached the alley, as I had expected. Any noise out the back door would be covered by the revelry.

A number of large pots and barrels lay about, some on their sides. Where was the broken pot with the false bottom Robert had described?

Without warning, the tavern's rear door burst open, scraping against the stone step beneath it. Before anyone appeared in the doorway, Joe grabbed my arm and pulled me down behind two barrels.

Lively music spilled from the open door, preventing me from hearing anything else. Was the person who opened the door now walking in the alley? Did they want one of the very barrels we hid behind? Joe's wide eyes met mine. What would we do should we be caught?

I glanced up to the barrel tops just as a thin gray rat scurried across them and down the side. I bit back a scream. Then something heavy dropped into the alley, followed by the door scraping against the step. The music quieted as the door banged shut.

Joe scrambled to his feet. "That was too close. Whatever you have to do, hurry and do it."

I stood on shaky legs, glancing at the door and the bourbon barrel that someone had just shoved against lumpy burlap sacks. I steeled myself against the fear rising in my chest. "Help me look through the pots. One of them has a false bottom."

We stepped closer to the door to inspect the various pots in the shadows. Each one appeared to be half-filled with dirt or refuse. When two squeaking rats emerged and hurried away, I was ready to change my mind and run.

"What about this one?" Joe pulled a dirty, chipped flour crock out from under a pile of sacks. "I think it's empty."

I went to his side. "Keep watch on the door."

The crock reeked of mold. I stuck my hand inside until my fingers brushed a damp surface more than half-way down. I felt a rough wooden edge and pulled it up. Beneath it lay a space two or three inches high.

Down the other end of the alley where it met the street, someone sang a British drinking ballad. Then footsteps stumbled closer.

Joe whispered, "Someone's coming."

Did I have the correct container? I fumbled in my pocket for the coded note wrapped in red, stuffed it into the old crock, and pulled the false wooden bottom over it. Joe shoved the crock back into place, and we yanked the sacks over the top. We took cover again behind the barrels until the singer's voice grew faint.

Minutes later, heads down, we hurried up Broad Street toward home. My heart raced. All I wished for in the world was a good hand-washing and a cup of tea by the fire.

I had done all I could. Now, if Culper Senior retrieved the message in time, the information might aid the Patriot cause.

Joe clearly could no longer contain himself and spoke too loudly for my comfort. "What sort of person looks for a message hidden in an old pot behind a tavern?"

I scanned our surroundings. But for the lamplighter up ahead, the street was deserted. "That is none of your concern."

"Is it someone you know? Does it have to do with the war?"

"Joe, I—"

A familiar black carriage turned the corner and came toward us. The four brown horses came to a stop. *Oh, no . . .*

"Miss Floyd?" Peter Laune leaned down from the driver's seat. "May I ask what brings you out at this hour?"

Relief and trepidation filled my thoughts—relief, knowing Peter would undoubtedly do anything for me, and trepidation at the possibility of him informing the major. I swallowed, took Joe by the arm, and approached the carriage. "Hello, Peter. I believe you've met my brother, Joe?"

"I have." Peter glanced at Joe. "Are you in need of assistance? I'd be happy to—"

"No, we're on our way home from . . . from a visit with a friend," I said.

"A sick friend," Joe said.

I still held Joe's arm, so I squeezed it. *That'll do . . .*

"I'm heading to Fraunces Tavern," Peter said. "A group of officers hired me for the evening. They've been there for some time. I doubt they'd mind if I took you to your home first."

I envisioned walking into the tavern and surprising the inebriated group, most likely officers I knew. *What a lovely coincidence, gentlemen. I was just at the back door dropping a message for the leader of the Culper Ring.*

"No, we'd prefer to walk," I said. "Thank you just the same."

"As you wish," Peter said. "I trust you'll see your sister home safely, Master Joe."

My brother mumbled, "Yes, sir."

The carriage pulled away, and I steered us toward home once again. Robert would skin me alive if he knew my cover had been the least bit compromised, yet he'd left the Ring. Until I was otherwise instructed, I would do what little I could, with what little I knew, to save my country.

Thirty-One

June 1780

The major raised his glass to mine. "I cannot describe how wonderful it is to see you."

My glass touched his. "As wonderful as standing on solid ground once again?"

The Navy Coffeehouse's waiter set the bottle of champagne on the table as the major gazed out the window at the pouring rain. "Thankfully, our return to New York was nothing compared to being tossed about like toys on the voyage south. I must say, I wasn't entirely certain we would reach our destination. In fact, one of our Hessian transport ships was carried out to sea, and a number of our horses were lost."

I shuddered to think how it might have been so much worse. "All that matters to me is that you survived, you were victorious, and you've returned." I set my glass down. "However, my family and I were quite disappointed to learn that Captain Willington has remained in South Carolina. Joe is devastated."

"He dearly wished to return, but the general chose a few regiments, including his, to stay back and hold the area." He glanced to the window again. "They're with Lieutenant-Colonel Tarleton. Quite a nasty sort. He went on a personal rampage against the rebels."

I thought of Christopher Martin and the atrocities carried out in New York prisons alone. "Captain Willington is nothing like that."

"It might be good for him—I daresay he had it too easy here." He patted his uniform jacket. "I'm finishing a poem for Rivington entitled 'Tarleton in Charleston.'"

I shook my head. "Only you could find the humorous side of the war. I'm so thankful you were unharmed."

"I was in no danger other than what the weather could throw at us. The general asked me to assist him with a number of tasks, yet I remained at a safe distance from the fighting." He reached across the table for my left hand, raised it to his lips, and bestowed a slow kiss.

"Other than I, no one is more pleased to be back in New York than General Clinton, not that he was in much danger either. The man is extremely careful . . . He cannot stand Arbuthnot or Cornwallis. They barely communicated."

I pondered if General Washington knew of those relationships. "That must have been a challenge for you."

He raised a brow. "As I've said before, there are times when a flair for acting is useful. I believe we would have returned sooner, and just as victorious, if another general had been in charge. However, we now must return to the business of war here."

I chewed a forkful of peas before answering, employing the proper amount of polite interest. "Oh? What are the general's plans?"

"Apparently, the French are on their way to Rhode Island." He cut into his steak. "The general is determining what steps to take—whether to engage them, what their next move will be, and so forth. We are preparing, however. Moving cannons northward and such."

Rhode Island then. Not Halifax or Newfoundland?

For the hundredth time, I speculated as to what General Washington had chosen to do after receiving the intelligence I left at Fraunces Tavern. That is, if Culper Senior had delivered it. But it may have all been a waste. Did Washington know that Rhode Island was now the destination of the French ships?

On my latest visit to Robert, aside from the fact that he had not rejoined the Ring, he informed me that he'd spoken with Abraham and learned of my note left in the flour crock. Of course, I received a severe scolding for undertaking such a task, particularly when the "intelligence" was based more on conjecture than any real facts. Then he'd expressed to me that Washington was considering shutting down the Culper Ring.

"Betty? Are you listening?"

I looked up with a start. "Of course, John. Forgive me. I . . . I was only thinking that you could be called to Rhode Island."

He dismissed my comment with a quick shake of his head and reached for the bottle of champagne. "Enough of the war. How I longed for you while I was gone! And New York, the variety we enjoy here, the theatre, even the taverns. The south is sorely lacking in entertainment."

I warmed at the thought of him longing for me. Yet had it driven him to seek out other female companionship? "And how did you find the southern ladies?"

He filled our glasses. "Not that I took much notice, but none were as lovely as you."

I laughed. "I should have known you'd say something ridiculous."

"Ah, but I speak the truth." His expression was that of an innocent child. "There is to be a Summer Soiree in two weeks' time. And I cannot perceive of anything more enjoyable than to escort you."

I bowed my head, feigning coyness. "I shall consider your invitation, Major, but I must consult my engagements calendar."

He grinned and leaned forward. "Now, tell me what I've missed. How fares Celeste?"

How much should I say? "She had some difficulty facing the loss of her relationship with Henry Fellowes, particularly when he left New York. And what appeared to be the cause."

Now I wished I could take my words back. I felt like a gossip.

The major frowned. "He's gone? For what reason?"

"It is quite unfortunate and none of my business. Please keep it to yourself."

"Yes, certainly."

"Dorah Shepherd was the reason. Apparently she . . . she's . . ." I felt the blood rise to my face. "Her father has sent her to England. Because of Henry Fellowes. And what happened."

It took him a moment. "There's only one reason I can fathom for her to be shipped off to England. That is regrettable. Yet it does happen." He took a large swig of his champagne.

I disliked his nonchalant acceptance of the matter. I set down my fork. "How can you be so callous? Henry had no business paying Dorah that kind of attention, let alone . . ."

"Forgive me, I didn't intend to sound callous. I simply meant that I'm not entirely surprised."

I fought to keep my voice low. "It's terribly sad, not only for Dorah and Celeste but for their families. And Henry is still responsible."

"Quite true." I sensed he wished to change the subject. Then he brightened. "Peter tells me he saw you on occasion while I was away."

I pretended to cough. "Did he?"

"He claims *Much Ado* was a success. What did you think of it?"

Had Peter mentioned to him that he saw Joe and me walking that one evening? Try as I might, I couldn't read beyond his dark, questioning eyes.

"You would have been pleased. And your scenery looked wonderful." I touched the napkin to my lips, hoping he didn't notice my hands shaking. "When I saw Peter, he spoke of you and his concern for your well-being."

"He's a good man. I've asked him to plan a small luncheon for Sunday at my home. If the weather cooperates, we shall eat in the garden. I know you'll enjoy it."

I clenched my napkin. "That sounds lovely."

I did enjoy his parties. In addition to the major's hospitality, the mostly pleasant company, and delicious food, his gatherings proved to be a good source of intelligence. With the majority of the army back in the city and Clinton strategizing his next move against Washington, new information was bound to surface.

But how had the British learned the French were bound for Rhode Island? Washington's armies desperately needed the French if there was to be a turn in the course of the war. What would happen if Clinton got to the French first?

By Sunday, the rain had rolled out to sea. Sunshine and gentle breezes off the harbor enticed most New Yorkers to leave their dwellings and partake of the outdoors in some fashion.

As Mother, Joe, and I walked from St. Paul's, the streets and lawns were filled with children romping, couples of all ages out for a stroll, and vendors tempting passersby with spring bouquets or fresh baked goods.

Joe ran ahead to catch up to his friends, while I inhaled the freshly washed air. It triggered a sneeze.

Mother bid me God's blessing. "Indeed, it must be spring. You never sneeze the rest of the year."

"I'd much rather sneeze in spring than freeze in winter." I sneezed again into my handkin.

"Spring certainly gives one hope that this vile war will soon reach an end," she said. "Mr. Rivington—that is, the *Gazette*—states it is possible. He claims a British victory is on the horizon, although I pray he is wrong as to whose victory. Does the major mention anything in that regard, or does he avoid talk of the war in your conversations?"

"We discuss it now and then," I said. "Not specifics, of course."

She shielded her eyes. "I'm sorry to say I read his latest poem in the *Gazette* about Charleston. How does he have the time to write such foolishness? Nevertheless, I should think you have more pleasant subjects to discuss than the war."

"I know what you're thinking." I gave her a sideways glance. "He and I have absolutely no plans. Neither of us wish to consider the future until after the war."

Her mouth drooped as she tucked imaginary hairs under her cap. "Then I shall pray all the more for the war to conclude."

"We mustn't forget, Mother . . . If the British lose, Major André will undoubtedly be driven out of the country."

I hated to think of that possibility, or an even worse fate for him. Yet despite the latest blows at Charleston, Washington and his army—or what was left of it—had no intention of giving in.

And neither did I.

Thirty-Two

For the major's luncheon that afternoon, I dressed in my rose gown, just as when I first doused him with punch the previous summer. In an effort to strike a balance between appearing too formal or too familiar, I wore my hair partially pinned up and the rest curled loosely and cascading down my back, then added Mother's pearl combs.

At my insistence, the major had invited Celeste. I didn't know his other guests, and I wished to have a friend present. Plus, it might do her good to make new acquaintances. She'd accepted and sent me a message, saying she would have Marcus take us together in the carriage.

Major André met us at the door wearing his dark blue waistcoat, white shirt, and gray breeches. He looked handsome as ever, yet a bit hurried, as if something weighed on his mind.

"Welcome, dear ladies." He kissed Celeste's hand and my cheek. "Come in and meet the other guests."

He led us to the parlor, now awash in sunlight rather than firelight, as the last time I entered it. Two gentlemen rose from their chairs while one lady remained seated.

The major introduced us. "Gentlemen and Mrs. Robinson, may I present Miss Betty Floyd and Miss Celeste Walker."

The tallest man stepped forward. He had rather a large nose and a mischievous grin. "Good afternoon, Miss Floyd, Miss Walker. William Stansbury, at your service."

The middle-aged man's eyes were red-rimmed. "Colonel Beverly Robinson." He bowed a bit too quickly, causing his white wig to shift. He straightened it with both hands and gestured to the lady on the settee. "My wife, Mary Robinson."

Following the usual pleasantries, Peter poked his head in and signaled to the major.

"I believe it's time for our luncheon." The major offered me his arm. "Let us enjoy this beautiful day, ladies and gentlemen."

He led the way through the central hall and out to the rear yard, where a long, linen-covered table set for a formal luncheon stood on a brick patio surrounded by tall pots of multicolored flowers. "How lovely, Major," Mrs. Robinson said. "This is perfect."

The rest of us gave our enthusiastic agreements. Flowering pear trees lent their shade to the otherwise sun-filled space. Tidy brick paths led to the kitchen and necessary.

The major showed us to our seats and, as always, held the chair beside his for me. Peter and Amelia again served the meal—a chilled melon soup, followed by a variety of cold meats, breads, cheeses, fruits, and nuts. Sweetened lemonade was served in etched goblets.

I watched Celeste sip her lemonade. I still wondered as to the truth of what she had suggested at the coffeehouse in February and whether or not the major had any contact with Peggy Arnold or other women.

I hoped to have a look at his desk, in the off chance he'd received any female correspondence. Lively conversations ensued as we waited for dessert, although they weren't of the military nature or anything that might concern the Culper Ring. It seemed an appropriate time to undertake a bit of exploring.

I turned to the major. "Would you excuse me? I left my reticule inside."

He rose from his chair. "Allow me. Do you recall where you put it?"

I stood quickly, motioning for him to remain. "No, I don't mind looking. Enjoy your guests. I should only be a minute."

Colonel Robinson and Mr. Stansbury quickly stood, and Peter held open the door to the house for me. I could only hope he and Amelia remained busy with clearing the dishes and serving dessert.

Inside, the tapping of my shoes echoed off the walls as I hurried toward the front of the house. I entered the deserted parlor and grabbed my reticule from the small table where I'd purposely left it.

Laughter filtered in from the rear yard. I listened for a door to open that would signal an end to my plan, but the only sound came from the hall clock, ticking away the seconds. As I slipped across the hall into the major's office, I was satisfied that I was quite alone.

I doubted the major would be so negligent as to leave a letter from Peggy Arnold or any other woman on display. But his desk might give other clues. Regardless, I couldn't resist the opportunity of a brief look.

I scanned the wide desk, where a half-dozen books were stacked beside various papers. A quick riffle through them revealed what appeared to be routine military correspondence—supply orders and receipts, requests for leave, names of a handful of new recruits. Did the Director of Intelligence deal with such mundane matters? Perhaps they might have contained something of value to General Washington, yet that wasn't my purpose at this time.

I shouldn't be snooping. There's nothing here, regardless.

Again, laughter from outside interrupted the near-silence in the house. I would be missed if I didn't return to the gathering. As I backed away from the desk, I caught a glimpse of letter paper, half-hidden under a thin book entitled *L'Art de la Guerre*. The Art of War.

With one finger, I slid the book away.

> *For the delivery of WP, with the addition of plans etc, I shall accept payment in the amount we discussed.*
> > *Your humble servant,*
> > *Mr. Moore.*

What was WP? A woman? No, that didn't make sense—my imagination was reaching too far. A type of wine, perhaps? Wine, wallpaper . . . What required the addition of plans?

I slid the book back in place and made a hasty exit, yet the cryptic message bothered me.

Celeste opened the back door the moment I reached for the handle. "Betty, are you all right? I felt I should look for you."

The guests at the table raised their glasses with Major André as he caught my eye.

I dabbed my handkin under my nose. "I couldn't stop sneezing. 'Tis the trees."

I stepped past her and went to the major's side. He rose to pull out my chair. "Are you ill, my dear? We're waiting to eat our lemon cake."

"Forgive me," I said. "It's only—" My handkin caught a genuine sneeze. The power of suggestion.

"You're not alone, Miss Floyd." Colonel Robinson daubed at his nose, sounding somewhat breathless. "Happens to me as well this time of year."

"Please, everyone," I said. "Don't let me keep you any longer from enjoying your desserts."

I took my seat and lifted my fork to taste the moist yellow confection with raspberry topping on the plate before me.

WP . . . Delivery and plans . . .

Suddenly, the cake became sawdust in my mouth. The major turned to me with a question, but I didn't hear it.

Of course.

West Point.

Thirty-Three

I sat up in bed. Perhaps my imagination was out of control and WP merely meant something benign: Someone's name . . . wall portraits . . . wheat and potatoes?

Cats moaned in the yard, probably seeking Triple. I threw back the covers and went to the window. A crescent moon shone high above the elm, its new summer leaves swaying in the light breeze.

The sketch from Major André remained on my windowsill beside the paper dolls I'd fashioned last summer. If only I knew then that I would still be enmeshed in the Culper Ring *and* a relationship with the major. Just when I thought the battle between 355 and Betty Floyd had been settled, something would light the flames on one side or the other.

Please. I need wisdom . . .

Returning to bed, I pounded and rearranged the pillows. All I'd been seeking the previous afternoon at the major's was some evidence of correspondence with another woman. Instead, I'd uncovered the possibility of a plot that could ultimately decide the war. Or had I?

The major had articulated long before he left for Charleston that there could be a breakthrough. If what I read in the note was connected, to what extent was he involved? Had Mr. Moore sent it to General Clinton, and the major was being ordered to deal with the situation? Or had he been communicating with Mr. Moore directly, even before Charleston?

Robert had ordered me to inform him if I ever heard more of West Point. And now I had, or so I thought. Yet wasn't West Point firmly in the hands of the Americans? How could someone offer it to the major?

Presuming WP indeed stood for West Point, the note could only mean one horrible fact: Someone calling himself Mr. Moore was plotting an attack with the British on the American fort, their stronghold on the Hudson. General Washington must be warned.

With Robert's resignation as Culper Junior and General

Washington apparently debating the necessity of continuing the Ring, my normal methods of operation were useless. Yet I couldn't allow any of that to deter me.

There was only one sure way to warn Washington, short of visiting him myself or trying to locate Ben Tallmadge. I had to find Culper Senior and speak to him personally. Might he be in New York, even though Robert had most likely cut off contact with him?

With no time to waste on leaving signals or hiding coded missives, I would seek him out at first light.

Shortly before dawn, I slipped down the stairs, left a note on the dining room table, and stole out the front door. On the porch, Triple lifted his head and silently questioned my presence at such an hour. I headed down the steps before he could alert anyone.

Butter-yellow haze over the eastern horizon promised a warm day. I would begin at Underhill's boarding house in my search for Abraham. I took a chance that I would find his sister beginning her morning chores.

She stood sweeping the front steps as I approached and paused when she saw me. Was that a look of alarm, distrust, or a bit of both? As on the day I'd asked her to convey to her brother that there was a message waiting for him, I wondered how much she knew.

"Good morning, Mrs. Underhill."

She leaned a hand on her broom and eyed the street each way before speaking. "Are you seeking my brother?"

I peered at the open upper windows, hoping no one could hear. "I know 'tis early, yet we . . . we've been expecting a delivery from him." That might sound plausible to any listening ears that didn't know my voice. However, if Robert's room was located in the front of the house, he better be at his shop.

The corners of her mouth turned up a touch. "You may find him at Rivington's."

My heart soared, learning he was within reach, although this was exactly what I wished to avoid—searching for Abraham Woodhull in public. Yet it was far better than any alternative I could comprehend at the moment.

I thanked her and made my way to the coffeehouse. The temperature had risen in the last half hour, and I regretted bringing my shawl. Shouting and banging of barrels and crates emanated from the wharves as New York began the day. Near Fraunces Tavern, horses, carriages, and pedestrians already filled the streets, raising clouds of dust. Vendors uncovered their carts of wares, calling to each other in various languages, and shopkeepers unlocked their doors.

At Rivington's Corner, the coffeehouse windows glinted in the sun as a handful of officers entered the building. Should Abraham be inside, how could I enter and avoid suspicion? And what of Robert? If he was serving customers, the sight of me would only alarm him and solidify his decision to leave the Ring.

I weaved my way across the street and stood in the shadow of a small butcher shop, behind an abandoned cart loaded high with potatoes. For several minutes, I watched the door to the coffeehouse open and close for customers. I paced, ignoring stares from passersby and debating my few options, none of them good.

The bleary-eyed butcher arrived and opened his shop, mumbling to himself. The shadow at his door shortened. I couldn't remain for long.

Just then, Abraham Woodhull exited the coffeehouse, tricorn in hand. He turned toward Wall Street and quickened his pace.

I had to stop him. What to do? I grabbed a potato off the cart and hurled it his way. Blessedly, it rolled in front of him.

A man shouted. "What's wrong with you, woman?"

I turned to see an elderly man approach wearing a dirty apron and breeches.

"Oh . . . I'm . . ."

Abraham ran toward me, holding the potato. "Beg your pardon, sir. My sister was merely having a bit of fun."

The man grunted as he grabbed the potato from him. "I can't be away five minutes . . ."

Abraham pulled me off the street. "Why are you here?"

I jerked my arm from his grip. "Is this how you treat your sister?"

He glared back and spoke between gritted teeth. "Follow, but at a distance. A good distance."

He donned his hat and turned around to cross Queen Street, stepping in front of a slow-moving ox cart. I bid a good morning to an elderly lady and her female companion, who eyed me with suspicion beneath their umbrellas.

I don't have time for games, Mr. Culper. Neither do you.

He rounded the left side of the *Gazette* beside the stables and disappeared from view. Two long minutes later, I followed.

In the alley behind the building, an open door swung on its hinges. With a quick glance behind me and down the alleyway, I ducked inside.

The dim workroom appeared deserted and all was quiet. Overhead, printed papers hung drying on strings. The huge press filled most of the room, awaiting the next news or opinion on the war. Mr. Rivington must have been working at the coffeehouse on this busy morning.

"You shouldn't be here." Abraham stepped from behind a stack of crates, making me jump. "Did your cousin not teach you anything?"

I gathered my nerves. "I trust we're alone?"

If he possessed any patience whatsoever, it was clearly wearing thin. "Would I have led you here otherwise?"

"I'm well aware of the danger." I willed my heart to relax. "And I would never have looked for you if he hadn't quit . . . and if it wasn't of the utmost urgency."

His hands went to his hips. "What is it?"

As nervous and intolerant as Culper Junior was, he was no match for Senior. No wonder General Washington grew weary of them.

"I saw a letter on Major André's desk." I repeated to him the writing I'd memorized. "Might WP stand for West Point? If so, then—"

"Repeat what you read, word for word."

As I did so, I thought his stare might burn a hole in the floor.

"It may be as you say," he said. "Should you see or hear more of the same, use the boot scrape as a signal, as your cousin described. I'll return to the city in a week's time."

He was about to brush past me until I stopped him. "A week? How will we meet? Are you going to warn 711?"

"Leave that to me." Without so much as a backward glance, he went to the door.

"Pray, one more question," I said. "Did my message at Fraunces Tavern reach the general? Because I—"

Before I could finish, he'd slipped out into the daylight.

I wrung my hands, unsure of when to leave, and by what route, and if I should have undertaken this errand in the first place. Then I straightened my cap and retreated the way I came, eyes down. I'd done my duty, and now it was Culper Senior's responsibility. Whether or not further related intelligence would surface was anyone's guess.

Hurrying across Wall Street again toward home, I wished for a moment of calm to catch my breath. And some breakfast.

At the corner, three or four Loyalist militia surrounded a young man and shouted at him to hand over the papers he carried.

The man clung to them, defiant. "These are private business. You have no right."

Two of the militia grabbed his arms. Another yanked the papers away and spit in the man's face. "No business is private."

As the soldier leafed through the papers, the crooked feather in his buckskin hat pointed straight at me. My blood ran cold.

Crankshaw.

I reversed direction, my heart pounding. It had been months since I'd seen him. I still equated him with Christopher's death. Was that why he still frightened me so?

If I'd left the building any sooner, I might have been the one stopped. He would enjoy nothing more.

Another narrow escape. How many would there be before I had nowhere to run?

Thirty-Four

According to Celeste, coveted invitations to the Summer Soiree at Vauxhall Gardens were dispatched the moment General Clinton and his accomplices returned victorious from Charleston. No one fortunate enough to receive an invitation dared to miss the event, which was hosted by several of New York's most influential families.

The day was already unusually warm. I squeezed the major's hand as Peter drove the carriage to Vauxhall. "I'm afraid I don't remember much of the gardens. I was too nervous to fully enjoy them when we came last year."

He cocked his head. "I was the nervous one. All I wished to do was kiss you, and I kept waiting for the right moment."

"John André, there is not a nervous bone in your body. But I'll have you know, I was beginning to wonder if you ever would."

He leaned closer and kissed my cheek. "And to think I hesitated for nothing."

Peter slowed the horses as we reached the gates, and the major assisted me down the carriage steps. Flashes of silk pastels emerged from other carriages. Most of the women carried parasols to block the hot sun. They paraded their summer finery, while the men, a mixture of officers and leading New York citizens, were clearly doing their utmost to appear distinguished and in control of the world.

I wore my grandmother's white lace gown once again, but I'd switched the pale blue sash for one Celeste had tired of—a wide pleated band of white cotton, lavishly trimmed in yellow and white silk rosebuds.

Once again, Alice had managed to procure living roses to match, adding them to my hair, where she'd made several thin braids and pinned them tightly to my head in a figure eight. When I questioned her resources, she merely patted my shoulders, then secured more pins. Even if the roses wilted in the humidity, my hairstyle would not.

The gardens were in full bloom, boasting summer's bright colors. We accepted tall flutes of champagne from a white-wigged, perspiring servant and chatted with Mr. and Mrs. DeLancey and other acquaintances. A trio of violinists played light melodies from the center lawn, adding to the carefree ambiance. Each person moved with slow, deliberate grace in the heat. I wished I'd remembered my fan or owned a parasol.

I took the major's arm as we strolled the paths. "I don't see Celeste yet. She's eager for me to meet Captain Hollingsworth. It's a shame more officers weren't invited."

"Yes, although there will soon be plenty of gatherings such as this, especially if we succeed in our endeavor to meet the French in Rhode Island."

I tried not to wince. "May it be as you say, John. I assume you realize by now, however, that I am equally as interested in the military's progress as in dances and dinners."

He grasped my fingers and brought them to his lips. "To me, it's one of your charms."

So, as the major had told me at the Navy Coffeehouse, Clinton did indeed plan to chase down the French and prevent them from coming to America's aid. I could only hope that perhaps the French would arrive at Rhode Island early, or General Washington might have a strategy of his own that might foil Clinton's plans.

The major led me to the shade of a large willow tree. "My dear, I asked you some time ago if you'd consider gathering information during your work with the rebel prisoners—"

"And I vehemently declined."

"Yes, and I do understand—"

No, you truly do not.

"—that you haven't accompanied your mother in some time, however, perhaps you might—"

"Ah, there you are, André."

The major's arm twitched under my hand as William Franklin strode up the path. One of my least favorite people, yet I was thankful for the interruption.

His long dark coat looked out of place in mid-summer. He

seemed pained to look at me. "Miss Floyd."

"Mr. Franklin." I didn't want to waste words on the man the Culper Ring knew was a British spy.

He and the major exchanged civilities, and I had the clear impression from Franklin that I was in the way.

"If you'll excuse me, gentlemen—"

The major touched my elbow. "Try not to be long."

I pretended to recognize someone across the gardens. I followed a path that led around the fountain to a refreshment stand, where I said hello to acquaintances. Then I accepted a lemonade punch and moved toward a small grove of trees, out of the bright sun.

I looked back toward the willow at Major André and Mr. Franklin. Were they arguing? Franklin wagged his finger in the major's face. The major scowled and sliced at the air repeatedly with his right hand. Franklin pulled out a handkin to wipe his face and stomped off. Glancing about, the major bowed politely to a passing couple who paused to speak with him. The lady waved her lace fan and curtsied.

I considered following William Franklin, until Mr. Rivington made his way toward the major. He would undoubtedly engage him long enough to buy me some time.

As I debated how to follow at a discreet distance, another familiar gentleman walked across the grass in the same direction as Franklin. Where had I seen him before? Of course—Colonel Robinson. Was he connected to Franklin and the hunt for spies? Or did either of them have something to do with WP?

I hastened around the outermost paths until I reached the one the men had taken. It wound through some trees and led to a privy, surrounded on three sides by wooden partitions. Two voices came from inside. Taking care not to step on any twigs, I slipped as close as I dared and hid behind a clump of overgrown shrubs.

I recognized William Franklin's deep voice. ". . . wait to hear if he gets the assignment."

Colonel Robinson coughed and sniffed, apparently bothered by the trees in full bloom. "Arnold shall inform us then at once, as a meeting must be arranged."

"Yes, yes. We are on the same side of the matter. I shall see to it."

Someone hurried out. I shrank back as Franklin stalked past me up the path. A cold sweat trickled down my back.

Did the Colonel say Arnold?

An officer approached and dashed into the privy. Then Mr. Robinson strode off, sneezing into his sleeve, and headed in the opposite direction from Franklin. I waited another minute before returning to the gardens, slipping past a foursome engrossed in chatter.

My pulse beat in my ears. I grabbed a linen napkin from the refreshment stand to pat my perspiring forehead.

"Betty?" Wearing a lace-trimmed gown of the palest blue, Celeste approached on the arm of a dark-haired, friendly looking officer. "I saw you come from there." She indicated the path from the woods.

Despite the heat and having just eavesdropped by the privy, I did my best to convey a manner of ladylike tranquility. "Yes, I . . . I took the wrong path."

She tilted her parasol. "Captain Hollingsworth, may I introduce my good friend, Betty Floyd."

The captain bowed. "A pleasure, Miss Floyd. Celeste speaks so highly of you and your friendship."

I bent my knee in the slight automatic curtsy I reserved for British officers. "I'm honored to make your acquaintance, Captain. But I'm afraid I must find Major André, or he will think I've gone for a swim in the river. If you'll excuse me."

Celeste was visibly puzzled at my quick leave-taking, yet I hoped she would not make too much of it.

I attempted to slow my breathing as I neared the major and the publisher/spy. "Mr. Rivington, 'tis a pleasure to see you again."

"Ah! Good afternoon, Miss Floyd. And I must say, the garden's blooms take their cue from you."

The major laughed. "Rivington, you're beginning to sound like a poet."

Whatever had taken place between him and Franklin, he'd either regained his air of cool self-confidence or had extracted it from his bevy of acting talents. After what I just heard, or thought I heard, from Franklin and Robinson, I needed to do the same.

"Speaking of poetry," the publisher said, "when may I expect more of yours, Major? The last one on Tarleton was quite well-received, I will say. However, I'm always seeking material for my readers."

"Is that why you're here today, Mr. Rivington, without your lovely wife?" I gave him my best teasing expression and ignored the knot in my stomach. "To gather the latest gossip?"

Pretending shock, he put a hand to his chest. "I print the *news*, Miss Floyd. And entertainments, such as the major's fine poems. The *Royal Gazette* would never stoop to gossip."

The major glanced skyward. "As you say, Rivington."

"As for Mrs. Rivington," the publisher said, "she incurred a foot injury and I insisted that she rest it."

"Oh, I'm terribly sorry." I meant every word. "Please give her my regards."

With Robert bowing out of the Ring and Abraham Woodhull being difficult if not inaccessible, perhaps Mr. Rivington could be of assistance in reaching General Washington. If only I could alert him that I must speak with him privately. Yet, what would I say, given both of our pledges of secrecy?

His glance drifted to another group. "I believe I must go and annoy one of our fine hosts. Do bring in your next poem at your earliest convenience, Major."

As he walked away, the major's expression lifted. "Shall we say hello to Celeste and the captain, or—"

"I'd rather not, if you don't mind." I led the major toward the shade. "I met Captain Hollingsworth. That is what kept me. He seems quite pleasant." I glanced toward the entrance gate. "Is it time for Peter to return yet?"

"Soon, I believe. Shall we be going?"

I only wish to peel off my clothing, bathe in ice, and decide how to pass on what I heard in the privy. I sighed, yanking at my damp sleeves.

"It is quite warm, isn't it?" He stopped a servant who was carrying a tray of cold ciders and took two.

He handed me a cider, and we headed for the deep shade of a tree closer to the gates.

"Betty, as I started to say earlier, you know from previous conversations that there are rebel spies in the city. We are throwing out a wide net and we're confident we'll catch them. And with your charm and connections, I would like you to reconsider being of service."

As if I didn't have enough to warn the Ring of—or what was left of it. I raised my free hand. "I've already given you my answer. I will not be your spy under any circumstances. And frankly, I'm appalled that you would ask me again to do your dirty work for you."

"Very well." He looked as if he'd lost a friend. "I apologize."

We finished our ciders and walked through the gates with barely a word between us until Peter arrived with the carriage.

On the ride to my home, I patted my handkin over my perspiring neck and forehead. "I hope I haven't upset you."

"Not at all. Thank you for your concern, my dear. Forgive my silence." He turned his gaze to the passing homes. "There are decisions that I must make when the time is right."

If only I might ask what those decisions entailed and who they involved. I considered what I saw and heard at the Soiree. What did the major and William Franklin discuss, and just what was the conversation between Franklin and Robinson about? Were either related to these decisions?

And how much longer could I continue to serve a broken Culper Ring and avoid getting caught in John André's wide net, let alone keep my feelings for him in check?

As Peter slowed the horses near my house, the major jerked his head to his side of the carriage. "Look who's here."

I leaned over to see Cousin Robert on one knee by the porch. He and Joe stood as the carriage rolled to a stop.

"Oh, that broken step," I said. "Mother must have finally asked him to repair it."

The major assisted me down from the carriage and called to Robert. "Good day, Townsend."

Robert brushed off his hands. "Major André."

I thanked the major for the lovely day and bid him goodbye.

With three other pairs of eyes on us, he gave me a quick grin and hopped into the carriage. As Peter pulled the horses away, Joe went in to fetch ciders.

When Joe disappeared into the house, Robert spoke in such a low tone that I had to move closer to hear him over the chirping birds.

"Come in as soon as you can," he said. "Washington is reinstating the Ring and I have resumed my post."

I was at once pleased and afraid. "They're increasing their efforts in seeking spies in New York. The major asked me to assist again. And Clinton is preparing to meet the French in Rhode Island. But Robert—"

His gaze went to the repaired porch step. "We must be on our guard more than ever. Although there is much to be done."

Thirty-Five

July 1780

Of all days . . .

The following morning, I intended to pay a visit to Culper Junior as soon as possible. Then Alice burned her hand on a skillet, the ointment and cloth strips for bandaging went missing, and by the time Mother and I took care of her and salvaged the half-cooked eggs and hotcakes, the noon hour approached.

I offered to do Alice's errands with the plan to stop at Oakham and Townsend. Finally, after giving my usual chores a once-over, I left the house.

Customers filled the shop, so I left to buy a packet of lard at the butcher's. Upon my return, Robert only had opportunity to inform me that Austin Roe was in New York and had been dispatched to the city in place of Abraham Woodhull, with orders to wait for intelligence regarding General Clinton's plans for the arrival of the French in Rhode Island.

"According to Roe," he said, "you and I are to gather whatever relative information we can in relation to those plans."

"Yes, of course, but—"

He raised his voice. "With the French coming, it is vital that—"

"Robert, I must relay a conversation—"

His gaze went to the window. Annoyed customers waited outside the locked door. "You will leave through the back room."

"But—"

He directed me to the tiny stock room and indicated a well-worn door behind several crates of goods.

"Very well," I said. "I must return soon, however—"

He'd already strode back to the front of the shop. I yanked open the crooked door and slipped out into the narrow alley. The door swung shut and locked behind me. To the left, the alley reached a dead end. I turned right, stepped around old boxes and refuse, and followed the sounds of horses in the street until I emerged near Hanover Square.

Three soldiers walked toward me on the street, eyeing me with suspicion. Every soldier in the city had to be under the major's orders by now, seeking New York's rebel spies. I suspected General Clinton had authorized handsome rewards for our arrests.

All I could do was hold my head high and sweep past them, praying they wouldn't hear my pounding heart.

Before dawn the next morning, I began another of my bread-baking forays to sort out and pray over all that I thought I knew. Intelligence was one thing—my own battles were another. As always, there were no simple answers.

My feelings for the major were undeniable. Plus, I continued to wage war with the desire to do something of value for my country versus my general incompetence versus mounting fear that I was one step away from being discovered and hanged from the tallest tree in the Common.

I mixed, folded, stretched, and waited as the bowls of dough puffed and expanded. I baked six golden loaves and two dozen rolls—an exhausting yet satisfying effort. And once again, with confidence that waxed and waned, I resolved to continue my charade as 355 until either God or the British put a stop to it.

Thus, that evening I planned to deliver two fat rounds of fresh bread to the major, along with a bottle of his preferred wine I'd been saving from Mr. Walker's shop. If I directed the conversation, the food and drink could prove a good combination to elicit a choice comment on the chase to engage the French, the hunt for spies, or plans regarding WP.

The importance of uncovering information outweighed the impropriety of entering his home unaccompanied—at least, that is how I justified it. If nothing else, he and I would enjoy a quiet evening together, away from the raucous taverns and ever-watchful eyes.

Not wishing to give the wrong impression, I dressed in an

everyday gown and cap. Joe had gone with Mother and Alice to deliver bread and vegetables to a family in Canvas Town—otherwise, I might have invited him to walk with me and carry my heavy basket.

The major himself responded to my knock. He wore his uniform, minus the red coat, his hair falling loose around his shoulders. My palms turned to wet rags.

"*Ma chère!* What a delightful surprise. Come in, come in."

"I'm glad to find you here." I stepped inside and handed him my basket. "This is for you. I apologize for not sending you any warning." A glance around the foyer and up the stairs satisfied me that we were alone.

"No need. You have rescued me from tedious paperwork." He raised the basket toward his nose. "Mmmm . . . Peter and Amelia are off for the evening, and I was just thinking of foraging for something in the pantry."

As I followed him down the hall, I peeked in his office at the cluttered desk. If only I could have stolen a look at his tedious paperwork.

While I sliced the bread in the pantry, he located some cheese and glasses. We carried everything out to the garden and spread a blanket on the cool grass. He poured the wine and joked that the elderly woman next door was undoubtedly watching us from behind her curtain.

I refrained from checking his neighbor's window. Instead, I chose to gaze at the darkening sky above the green canopy of pear trees. With mid-summer's arrival, the trees had fully leafed out and no longer sent me into sneezing fits.

We toasted the beautiful night, ate the bread and cheese, then lay on our backs to watch the stars appear and listen to the birds sing their evening songs.

"It's one of those moments when the war seems far away, does it not?"

He turned and drew me close. "What is this war of which you speak?"

"Oh, just the never-ending tussle with those pesky rebels." I laughed. "And soon, with the much peskier French."

He refrained from commenting, and I let him kiss my neck before asking my first question. "John, do you ever hear word of Miss Shippen?"

If I hadn't been paying attention, I would never have noticed the slight flinch. What had his relationship with her truly been in Philadelphia? And what was it currently? Would I ever know?

He lay back with one hand beneath his head. "My dear, she is Mrs.—"

"Yes, Mrs. Arnold. I'm sorry, I only wondered because I happened to hear that she's been in New York on occasion."

"Is that so?" He appeared to be genuinely surprised. "That isn't likely, given that she's married to one of their generals."

A squirrel dashed up the nearest tree and scolded us from a middle branch. I weighed my response, deciding which way to take the conversation.

"I suppose. It may have only been hearsay." I twisted toward him. "Is it possible that General Arnold accompanied his wife to New York? Under a flag of truce, of course. Or perhaps in disguise?"

Even in the fading light, I could see I'd caught him off guard. Had I inched too close to the truth, and Benedict Arnold himself traveled to New York? And why had Colonel Robinson mentioned his name to William Franklin?

The major turned toward me again, leaning on his elbow. "You have an uncanny knack for asking quite interesting questions. Now, if I may change the subject . . ."

Moments later, I rested in his arms. "John, do you know when General Clinton will go to meet the French? You said he's moving cannons and such, yet it seems to me that time is of the essence. Otherwise "

He sat up slowly and stretched. "The rebels could gain the advantage with France's help. Yet you needn't worry, my dear. Our ships are preparing to depart at this very hour. General Clinton is already underway."

I gasped, sitting up. "He left? He won't leave us undefended, will he?"

"Not in the least." He fingered a strand of hair that escaped my cap. "Why do you fret so?"

"I'm no more concerned than any New Yorker."

He laughed. "*Donc, Mademoiselle Général,* have we your permission to stop the French, hold New York, and finish this war?"

"Yes, however, I insist that you remain in New York for the foreseeable future." I smiled, patting his arm.

He poured the last of the wine into our glasses. "I assure you, I won't be going anywhere for a while."

For the Ring, only time would tell if it had been a successful evening. For me, the guilt of betraying his trust made my stomach knot. I had again led him down the road of divulging military secrets, although all of New York would soon know that Clinton and his ships had departed for Rhode Island. As for the entire Arnold situation—if one actually existed—I didn't know what to make of it.

The warm night was ideal for a long walk. We held hands as he escorted me home, then kissed on the porch, with Triple and all the stars looking on.

I set out for Oakham and Townsend just before dawn, assuming Mr. Walker was not yet in his shop nearby. Robert had suggested that I vary the hours of my visits going forward, and hopefully reduce any suspicions as to why I was there so often.

Robert opened the door before I had a chance to knock. "It is good you are here at this hour." He locked the door after I entered. "Roe insists on leaving for Long Island this morning. And there is an urgent matter I must explain."

There had been urgent matters before, yet I had rarely seen him this anxious. "What is it, Robert?"

He held his arms tight to his chest. "Mr. Roe informs me that General Washington is planning a deception of his own in order to fool the British into thinking there will be an attack on New York."

"An attack here? But—"

"It will be a complete false alarm. However, if successful, Clinton will have no choice but to abandon his plan to meet the French and American armies in Rhode Island if he wishes to defend this city."

I couldn't imagine such an undertaking. "When will this take place? The major informed me that Clinton has already sailed."

"Yes, and many of his ships. We learned of it at Rivington's and from the sailors at the wharf."

As I'd expected, the word of Clinton's departure was out. "What is General Washington planning?"

"The exact method remains to be seen." He turned and walked to the desk. "However, if and when we hear rumors of an attack, and residents are ordered to stay in their homes or other warnings are given, we must comply as if we know nothing, despite knowing that it is all a ruse."

I slowly sat down across from him, thinking of the panic that might ensue across the city with the warning of an attack by the Continental army.

Taking his seat, Robert studied me over his spectacles. "For now, let us return to present-day issues. Have you anything to report?"

"I do." I waited while he prepared the invisible ink. An order form for sundry items lay on the desk.

Then I relayed all that I'd learned from the major regarding Clinton's plans—nothing he hadn't already gathered. "I'm afraid I don't have any other specifics. . . . Are you planning to write on your order form?"

"Between the lines, yes. Given what I have heard at the wharves, your information supports it. Anything else?"

"I've wanted to report what took place the day you repaired our porch step." I went on to describe the Summer Soiree and the conversation I overheard there between Colonel Robinson and William Franklin.

Robert straightened, holding his pen in midair. "Are you certain you heard the name *Arnold*?"

"Absolutely certain," I said. "Yet why would those men have an interest in General Arnold?"

"I am sure I do not know." Robert lay the pen on the order form. "Perhaps Arnold has some interest in them. Apparently, he has accumulated much debt."

"I recall hearing words along that line at a party some time ago."

I couldn't place when or where. "Officers joked about his tendency toward self-promotion. I thought it odd, however, that British officers would know much about him."

"Regardless, we shall inform the Ring."

"There is more in relation to General Arnold." I explained how I had asked the major about Peggy Shippen and her husband possibly visiting New York. "It was as though I struck a nerve, Robert. I cannot describe it."

"What prompted you to ask such a question?"

I stammered, not wishing to explain my reasons. "I . . . well, I heard rumors of her visiting here. He didn't answer, however."

Robert looked as though it took all he had to respond calmly. "I am afraid that Major André not answering a question regarding General Arnold or that you sensed a nerve was struck does not qualify as intelligence."

I folded my arms and stared at the desk. *You weren't there.*

He lifted the pen once more, then set it down. "Woodhull spoke to me of your contact with him during the time of my withdrawal."

Here comes another reprimand. I held my ground. "I had information. I needed to reach him in the event it might be of use."

"He claimed it was most worthy of being passed along. You did what was right, even if your method was not what we had agreed upon."

"Did he say more?" I leaned forward. "Perhaps if General Washington replied—"

"Nothing of the sort."

I made a face. "You have no idea what I went through to obtain that information. And to find him."

Robert's glance drifted to the door. "Rest assured, however, I plan to remain your sole contact as we proceed. Is that clear? We are in enough danger as it is."

I swallowed, considering whether I should reveal the major's interest in again having me spy for him.

He interrupted my inner debate. "Cousin?"

"There's something else I must tell you."

He frowned over his spectacles. "Out with it."

"Major André pressed me once again to assist in locating rebel spies." I sucked in a breath and kept my eyes on the desk. "I don't believe it will come up anymore."

Robert pulled off his spectacles and dropped them on the desk. "Perhaps you should pull away, tell him—"

"That won't be necessary. I'm perfectly capable of continuing as always. He trusts me, Robert. I feel terrible, yet . . ."

I felt much more than terrible. I felt ashamed. Yet I was not about to quit.

"Yet what?"

I shook away the familiar doubt. "My duty to the Ring and to General Washington will always take precedence. And I would never betray those who trust me." I rose from the chair. "You need to write your correspondence and find Mr. Roe."

He slowly replaced his spectacles on his nose and walked me to the door. "Be most careful, Cousin."

I dismissed his comment with a wave. "You mustn't worry. No one suspects a thing. I know what I'm doing."

Thirty-Six

Waiting for word of the impending invasion, I imagined how Mother and Alice would react. What might I say to calm their fears without divulging that it was all a hoax? Joe and his friends would no doubt be more excited than afraid, then disappointed when the attack failed to materialize.

My days were filled with thoughts of whether or not I should begin a task, prepare a meal, or undertake an errand, in case I was interrupted by the big announcement. When Celeste asked me to come and preview a new gown, I obliged, glad to have a distraction.

She twirled before the tall mirror leaning against her bedroom wall. "What do you think?"

I studied the pale lavender gown and her overall appearance. "I will be completely honest. You look divine."

She truly did. And it wasn't only the gown's fabric, its froth of lace at the neckline, or the wide satin bow accentuating her waist. She seemed more her old self—my optimistic, fun-loving, and loyal friend—not the hard, cynical one from last winter. Now with Captain Hollingsworth in her life, her countenance reflected a woman truly in love.

She beamed, straightening the bow. "I do hope the captain will—"

We both jumped at the knock on her door. Celeste went to open it.

Mrs. Walker stood in the hall, wringing her hands.

"What is it, Mother?"

She stepped in. "Girls, I'm afraid I have terrible news." She glanced at Celeste. "Your father has just arrived home. He claims word is spreading that the rebel army is on the march and preparing to attack the city."

"New York?" Celeste pressed her hands to her neck. Her face, aglow just moments earlier, turned pale.

This is it. Washington is setting them up.

Mrs. Walker's lips trembled. "Yes, so he was told. We must prepare and protect ourselves. Betty, I will ask Marcus to take you home in the carriage. Your family will need you."

If only I was able to speak the truth. "I'm sure there's time. We must stay calm . . . and try not to worry."

Celeste's cheeks were wet with tears as she gave me a gentle push toward the door. "You should go. Perhaps the major will contact you. Oh, I pray he and the captain won't need to fight the rebels."

The streets were already bustling with frantic urgency, likely stemming from the news of an imminent attack. Marcus wove the carriage horses between and around wagons, other carriages fighting for the road, and pedestrians attempting to cross. A large group of soldiers marched four abreast along the side of the road toward Fort George. Young boys cheered while a man driving an oxcart waved his fist and shouted at all of them.

The moment I stepped from the Walkers' carriage, Mother beckoned me from our top step. "Come inside, Elizabeth. There's an emergency."

I did as she said, preparing to cooperate as if the story was true and the attack real.

She pulled me by the arm as I reached the porch. "Quickly, please."

"What's happened? Is Joe hurt? Is Alice—"

She closed the door hard and leaned against it. "Joe should be home soon, and Alice is here, somewhere." She waved a hand toward the pantry. "At the wharf today, she heard there may be an attack on New York. Then Mrs. Dickson came a few minutes ago. Apparently, it's true—Washington's army is going to attack the city, perhaps as soon as tomorrow. We have nowhere to go, even if there was time. We must remain here and prepare the best we can."

If I didn't know better, her urgent tone would have convinced me. I grasped her hands. "Of course. We survived countless battles near the farm. We'll be all right, Mother."

A tear rolled to her cheek. "We must pray for protection."

Seeing her so distraught, I longed to tell her the truth. Yet it would only lead to saying too much and giving away the secrets I'd promised to keep.

Footsteps on the porch were followed by a hard knock at the door. I pulled it open.

"Miss Floyd?" A boy no more than twelve held out a note.

"Yes, one moment." I gave him a coin, took the note, and closed the door.

Mother clutched at her apron. "Who would be sending a message?"

I opened the note. "It's from Major André. To warn me—us."

An attack on NY is believed to be imminent. Please take care to remain in your home with your family until the danger has passed.

Be assured we will defend our city from the rebels. Gen C. returning.

J

My heart went out to the major. If he only realized that I knew the information he'd received was completely fabricated and that 'Gen C. returning' was precisely the goal.

"How good of him to alert you," Mother said. "He must have a great deal to—"

The door flew open as Joe burst in. We both jumped.

"Washington's army is on the way to New York." He headed for the stairs. "There shall be a battle!"

Mother called after him. "Joseph, for mercy's sake, this is not a matter to take lightly. Change your clothes and come help us put things in order."

I marveled at the speed with which the news had spread. Joe must have heard before he left Oakham and Townsend. Robert would say all the proper things, close the shop, and make a point of showing he was taking all precautions necessary.

"No need to worry, Mother. We'll all do our part." I pulled off my cap as I moved toward the stairs. "Joe and I will be down shortly."

She turned to lock the front door. "At least we're all at home, and we have provisions. But we must fetch some water and cider. . . . And check on the neighbors."

As I changed into my work clothing to make ready for a false invasion, I tried to imagine the vast preparations the British army would be undertaking. Such a waste of their time, manpower, and supplies—I almost felt sorry for them.

And General Clinton, racing back from his voyage to Rhode Island to face not the enemy but a frightened city and a bewildered army. How had Washington let false information be dropped so strategically? My only hope was for all of the detailed maneuvering to make a difference in this war.

Thirty-Seven

August 1780

The owners of Hicks Tavern propped open the doors and set tables outside on the grass due to the stifling summer air. Sitting at two tables pushed together, Celeste and I were joined by Mary Shepherd, Mary's cousin Sophia, Captain Hollingsworth, and two of his acquaintances, also officers. Each of us held a tall glass of cold cider.

I expected the major any minute. He had sent me a message shortly before I left the house with Celeste, saying that he would be delayed but no longer than necessary.

Gentlemen leaned against the outside walls of the tavern with their tankards of ale, joking about the attack that never took place. A few speculated that Washington had changed his mind out of fear, while others gave him credit for pulling the wool over the eyes of the British.

Captain Hollingsworth and his friends exchanged glances. Most New Yorkers seemed to share the sentiments printed in the *Gazette*—that of relief the attack hadn't taken place and of concern that it might at any time.

Sitting beside me, Celeste leaned closer. "Thank heavens the rebels stayed away. We would not be sitting here if they had attacked."

From inside the tavern, a fiddler struck up a lively tune. As he stepped outside, customers clapped along to the music. Mary and Sophia joined in, and the captain roared with laughter at a joke one of his friends made. What was keeping the major?

Celeste leaned in again. "I heard a bit of news that may interest you—Peggy Shippen Arnold is expecting a new little addition. *And* General Arnold has been given the command of West Point."

I let that sink in, not wanting to appear too interested, yet my skin prickled at the mention of West Point. "Hmm. I suppose that is good news for the Arnolds."

Did the major perhaps know of the pregnancy? My second thought—Benedict Arnold at West Point might be good for the Patriots, considering General Clinton had his sights on it. Surely Arnold would stop Mr. Moore and his collaborators. Yet why did his name come up in the privy at Vauxhall Gardens?

"It could be detrimental for our side," Celeste said. "Benedict Arnold is reported to be quite vicious. With him in command at West Point, General Clinton won't be too pleased."

It was unlike Celeste to care much for war tactics. Perhaps Captain Hollingsworth had discussed the situation with her.

At the tables next to us, customers played a rowdy game of whist. One young man was taking the game much too seriously, or perhaps he'd had more than his share of ale.

"Do you think Major André knows?" Celeste asked.

"About General Arnold?" I looked around for the major once again. "I suppose he does, but I leave those matters to him."

Captain Hollingsworth interrupted. "Pardon me, ladies. Shall we order our dinners, or would you prefer to wait for the major, Miss Floyd?"

"No, it's quite all right if we order," I said. "Thank you, Captain."

The tavern owner took our requests for shareable platters of fish, potatoes, and another round of ciders.

It was unlike the major to be this late. What was keeping him?

With five minutes left until the customary closing time at Oakham and Townsend, my cousin turned the sign and locked the door. I stood near the desk as a woman attempted to push her way in.

"I am terribly sorry, Madam," Robert said to her. "I am afraid we must close for the day."

The woman pounded on the door as Robert locked it and turned toward me.

"You're more impatient than usual," I said to him. "Am I in trouble again?"

He motioned for me to take a seat. "What have you done now that would cause you to think so?"

I dropped to the chair. "You seem especially anxious, that's all."

He tidied a display of tea canisters on a nearby table before taking his seat. "It has been a long day and I wish to be done with this war."

His desk was strangely uncluttered. I rested my hands in my lap. "Everyone is exhausted, what with the scare of last month's invasion, and the heat . . ."

"Quite true. Washington may undertake a real invasion in the future, now that the French reinforcements arrived safely in Rhode Island. And as weary as we may be, we must not for a minute become complacent—not one of us." He looked me in the eye, making certain I understood he was referring to me.

"Robert, I may have my faults, but complacency isn't one of them."

He narrowed his eyes and appeared to consider the accuracy of that statement, then cleared his throat. "Any new intelligence regarding Mr. Moore? West Point?"

I regarded him with admiration, hoping he'd relax. "Nothing whatsoever of Mr. Moore, or West Point, or WP, if indeed they are the same. However, I understand Benedict Arnold was given command of the Fort."

"That is correct. General Washington appointed him quite recently. Yet, as I have previously stated, Arnold is deep in debt and he pressured Washington for that appointment. There is only one thing he loves more than money, and that is recognition."

"I would imagine he will have it with this appointment."

"And it may be of consequence to the British, should they wish to attack. Arnold has a great deal of experience and a reputation for thoroughness."

"That should be to our advantage. Perhaps Clinton will refrain from a confrontation after all. Much has happened since the dinner at the Kennedy mansion; he may have changed his mind about West Point."

Culper Junior rubbed his neck with both hands. "Let us remember that it is not for us to determine what is on anyone's mind."

I shifted in my chair. "Speaking of what is on someone's mind, we still do not know for certain why I overheard Colonel Robinson mention Arnold's name at the garden party."

"We do not. However, it has been reported. Is that all?"

He could be so infuriating. "Overall, most are back to their routines," I said. "Nothing out of the ordinary."

"There has been a surge in activities along the docks," he said. "I am not able to ascertain the significance, if there is one."

"Ah, Cousin." I wagged a finger at him. "If I may quote, 'It is not for us to determine what is on anyone's mind.'"

He only glared at me.

I continued. "A bit more hearsay for you and I shall be on my way. Apparently, there is a decided effort to press citizens into the Royal Navy. And, as you may know, there have been countless desertions from the Continental army to New York City."

"It is regrettable." Robert's brow tightened with concern. "Much has taken a toll on our men—the lack of success, lack of pay by Congress, the difficult conditions, not to mention all sorts of ailments and disease."

It brought up the memory that still produced a knot in my throat—Christopher Martin and all he'd endured as a prisoner, only to be shot and tossed on a cart like old rubbish.

"Before you go," Robert said, "what has André said of the false invasion?"

"He didn't make much of it, as if it weren't a surprise. Only that the French arrived in Rhode Island after Clinton turned around for New York. I chose not to press him."

The major had sent an apology for not meeting me at Hicks Tavern, claiming he'd been called in late to General Clinton's headquarters. We dined together at Fraunces Tavern a few days later.

"He may be embarrassed," Robert said. "The Chief of British Intelligence fell for a rebel trick that shut down the city for three days. I would think he would feel humiliated. And angry."

In truth, John André had been acting quite distracted as of late. I attributed it to long hours working for the boring and methodical Henry Clinton. The false attack certainly must have enraged Clinton, and the major likely took the brunt of it. In addition, the general may have pressed him more than ever to find the spies operating in New York.

At the same time, I couldn't help wondering if the major was simply growing tired of me and our relationship. Yet, we'd grown close. He trusted me. And I—

Robert leaned in. "Are you listening?"

I tried to reassure him. "I've heard every word. And I shall do my utmost to glean what I can and inform you as soon as humanly possible."

He narrowed his brow again. "The Royal Navy situation could be meaningful, in addition to the other matters. Anything may develop. We must not fail to pay attention. That will be all for today."

I took my time on the walk home due to the moist heat with nary a breeze to cool my skin. Each layer of clothing would be soaked with perspiration by the time I reached my door.

Robert was seldom satisfied with my reports, and today he'd been exceptionally difficult. Did he not realize I was giving it my all? Perhaps it was the pressure he was under—that we all were under.

Crossing the Square, I waved away the swarming flies. How could I learn more of the enemy's plans before they were used against the Patriots?

I shielded my eyes against the sun's assault. What was I missing?

Thirty-Eight

I fanned my face as the major and I walked beneath the shade trees following dinner at the Navy Coffeehouse. "I know 'tis not ladylike to complain about the weather, yet . . ."

He stared at the path ahead, wearing his full uniform despite the heat. "I'm quite confident that autumn will arrive eventually."

He was not himself—more serious than I'd ever seen him. "John, you've been withdrawn all evening, and frankly, for some weeks now. May I ask what is troubling you?"

"Forgive me, Betty." He barely glanced my way. "I usually don't allow anything to distract me when we're together. You should know, however, that I may be traveling north for a few days."

That was unexpected. "Oh? May I ask where?"

"I . . . regret that I'm unable to say. It's simply a business matter."

I sighed with reluctant acceptance as we strolled the path, considering how much to ask.

"Will you travel far?"

He seemed to struggle for the right words—not the John André I knew. "No, not terribly far. And not for long, I should think."

If only we weren't serving opposite sides in this war. I patted his arm. "I understand if this business matter or your uncertain travel plans have made you melancholy."

He clasped my hand. "*Merci, ma chère*. It has been rather concerning."

"Shall I see you before you go?"

"I would think so. As of today, the exact date of my departure is unknown. And I promise you I will take every precaution."

"Will Peter accompany you?"

He hesitated before replying. "No, I won't require his assistance."

We waited for a funeral carriage to pass by on Broad Street, pulled by six identical black horses. The white-haired driver turned and stared at the major. The attached cart, draped in black bunting, bore a pine casket.

I said what I thought he might wish to hear. "If your business there can lead you to root out any spies here in the city, it will be well worth the journey."

"Perhaps it might."

As always, I despised myself for my duplicity. Instead of seeking to learn more of what "business" he had going north, I was encouraging him in his hunt for those with whom I secretly collaborated. What a two-faced wretch I was.

Mother, Alice, and I rose before dawn the next morning to undertake our chores before the heat of the day made them unbearable. I dressed in my lightest clothing and rolled and pinned my hair tightly under my cap.

Joe apparently was unfazed by the air temperature and continued to sleep, until Mother roused him and quoted Ben Franklin.

" 'Tis the working man who is the happy man. It is the idle man who is the miserable man.' I shudder to think what your father would have said . . ."

I deliberated if I should go to Robert and relay my conversation with the major from the previous evening. There hadn't been much substance to his words, other than his plan to travel north, yet Robert might have found it interesting. The major wasn't leaving the city yet, however, and I could see no sense of alarm.

Mother and Alice built up a fire outside the kitchen to boil water for laundry, Joe began sweeping all the floors, inside and out, and I assumed the scrubbing of the pantry. It gave me much-needed time to think.

If John André was going north on business, it meant one of two things—the business was either routine and nothing of consequence to our side, or it was more than that. Was it not my responsibility to report his travel plans? Yet I hated to share information that might amount to nothing.

However, as Robert had said, it was not for me to determine what was important, and, in general, I tried to abide by that directive. I hadn't always conducted business exactly his way, yet some of what I'd gathered, such as the matter at Paulus Hook and the plot to destroy the currency, had been helpful to the Cause.

When they finished with the washing and hung it on the back fence to dry, Mother and Alice lowered themselves to the steps outside the pantry door. I carried the last bucket of dirty water to dump next to the kitchen. "I'm ready to join you, if there's room."

Triple was stretched out on the top step and did not desire company, based on his look of disdain as he slunk away, tail dragging.

With various grunts and groans, we removed our shoes and soaked stockings. Mother and Alice leaned forward, their bare feet in the grass. I propped my back against the threshold and closed my eyes.

Alice broke the silence. "We're 'bout the sorriest lookin' washer women I ever did see."

Low clouds had been clustering all morning, smothering the already overheated city. Now the skies grew darker, and the leaves on the trees showed their undersides.

Joe appeared at the pantry door. "Why are you all sitting there?"

I looked up at him. "We happen to be exhausted. Why aren't you sweeping?"

"I finished. May I go meet my friends?"

"A storm is coming, Joseph," Mother said. "You may go after it passes."

The first sprinkles hit the steps. "Here it come," Alice said. "We best grab everything from the fence."

I rose and stepped inside to speak to him. "When you go, would you please deliver a message to Cousin Robert for me?"

He scratched the back of his neck. "I suppose so."

I hurried back outside to help bring in the wash. While it rained, I assembled a small meal of bread, cheese, sliced ham, and cold tea for us. I ate quickly, then went to change into a clean gown and retrieve the Culper code book from under my mattress.

Against Culper Junior's orders, I wrote out a brief note. It wasn't difficult, now that I had memorized a good portion of the code.

JA going north soon on business. No other details.

Perhaps Robert or someone else in the Ring would have intelligence to corroborate it.

A knock at the door made me jump. "Betty? There's no storm. The rain stopped and I'm going."

"Wait one minute, Joe." I didn't have time to sign *355* or seal the note. I folded it in half, half again, then tucked one end inside the other.

I opened my door and handed the message to my brother. "Please get this to Robert before you find your friends."

Joe stuffed the note in the pocket of his breeches. "Does it have something to do with what you left at Fraunces Tavern that night?"

I pulled him close and whispered. "No, it does not."

Joe tried to pull away, but I held his arm. "Promise me this will remain a secret between us."

He mumbled something and turned to go. I would simply have to trust him.

An hour later, thunder rumbled as I stirred a vegetable stew over the fire in the kitchen. By the time I crossed the yard to the house, an angry wind shook the trees and heavy drops of rain splattered the path. Mother met me at the pantry door. "The storm is upon us now. I hope your brother is safe."

I shook out my damp apron. "I'm sure he will take care of himself."

Mother looked toward the ever-darkening sky. "Let's prop the door open for a bit. The wind may cool the house."

By now, I assumed Joe had delivered my note to Robert. He would be furious that I wrote him any sort of coded message *and* sent my brother to deliver it. As usual, I second-guessed my actions.

As the storm raged, my old anxieties over severe weather attempted to surface. I puttered around the darkened house, rearranging books and straightening the pantry, then made an effort to rest in my bedroom. Eventually the rain ceased, birds chirped, and sunshine lit the house.

Not long afterward, Joe returned. "Hello? I'm home."

I followed Alice to the door. "Your mother was worried 'bout you," she said to him.

Joe wiped his shoes on the entry rug. "I stayed at George Vanderbrook's. Their mare has a new colt. Where's Mother?"

"Probably in her bedroom," I said. "You should let her know you're home."

As Alice went to the pantry, I stopped him before he headed up the stairs. "Did you deliver my note?"

He whispered. "I couldn't. The shop was closed, so I went to the coffee house, but Robert wasn't there. Then it started to thunder, so I went to George's. I left when it stopped raining, but when I checked my pocket, your note was gone."

"What do you mean—gone?"

"Lost. I don't know what happened."

Thirty-Nine

Thunderstorms overpowered New York again that evening and well into the next day, preventing me from going to see Robert myself.

I doubted it would matter if I waited a day or two. Stormy weather generally brought most activity to a standstill in the city, including activity of the clandestine variety. Even if I could alert him to the major's plans, the storms would delay Robert in getting the information to the Ring.

While I helped Joe with his studies and tended the cooking, I considered withholding from Robert the fact that I'd written him a message using the Culper code, given it to Joe to deliver, and the note was nowhere to be found. After all, why ask for more trouble and add to his anxiety?

Then the sun appeared at last and cool breezes blew away the heat of the past weeks. I needed to be honest with Robert, come what may. I would simply go and explain what happened and be done with it.

When would I learn?

"What were you thinking?" Robert pounded the counter. "If that message is now in enemy hands, how soon will they trace it to one of us?"

I took a step back. "I've explained my reasoning. At the time, it seemed the best course of action. And given your absence and the weather that day, there is an excellent chance the note wound up in the mud under a carriage wheel. Even if it was found, no one would understand the code."

My cousin spoke through clenched teeth. "If you must know, it was necessary that I meet with Woodhull outside the city that day. He feels the risk is too great for him to travel here so frequently or rely on Mr. Roe." His eyes were wide behind his spectacles. "You are certain you did not sign it?"

"I only wrote a few words and did not sign or address it."

He turned his back to me and rubbed his neck.

It occurred to me that the fastidious Robert Townsend had again forgotten to lock the door. All I needed was for someone to walk in.

He turned around. "Must I continue to remind you of the dangers we face? You in particular, with your frequent interactions with André. You have successfully infiltrated the enemy's headquarters, and their Chief of Intelligence has taken you into his confidence. Yet you push too far by defying orders. I fear at some point you will push one time too many."

"I had a feeling you would say exactly that, yet I thought it was important enough to bend the *orders*. But apparently, I should have ignored the information and followed protocol and—"

"I did not say—"

Footsteps approached the door, followed by the turning of the knob. Instinctively, I retreated toward the bolts of fabric on display.

"Good day, Mr. Townsend." Peter Laune entered the shop. "I'm in a bit of a rush if you don't mind."

"Certainly, sir." Robert glanced my way, his mouth pinched.

I came forward. "Peter, 'tis a pleasure."

"Miss Floyd!" He removed his tricorn. "Forgive me, I—"

Robert spoke up. "My cousin was about to take her leave, sir."

"Yes, I was . . . I am. I don't wish to keep you." Under different circumstances, I would have stayed long enough to converse with Peter. Instead, I was relieved to have an escape.

"Good day, gentlemen." With a cheerful wave, I left the shop.

Good day and good riddance, Mr. Culper Junior. See if I bring you any further intelligence.

"Betty?"

Celeste. I stifled my vile mood and waved as she crossed the street. *Please don't ask me to do anything.*

Beaming in a pale yellow and blue floral gown and beribboned hat, she leaned in to peck my cheek. "What excellent luck. I'm about to meet Mother at the milliner's. Would you join me? Perhaps Mother won't dither as long if you come. Then we'll go for sandwiches and tea at Fraunces."

I cannot possibly go and peruse hats. I feigned great disappointment. "Oh, I'm afraid I simply cannot."

"Why is that?"

"I'm tutoring Joe and if I don't hurry home, he'll grow impatient and slip out." I laughed, hoping to sound convincing. At least the part about tutoring was true.

Celeste glanced at the door to Oakham and Townsend. "Your cousin's shop again? You visit quite often."

I patted my reticule. "Alice ran out of thread for a tablecloth she's repairing. There always seems to be something we need."

Her eyes narrowed. "Could Alice not go herself?"

"She could, but I offered." I stepped into the street. "And now I'm late. I truly must be going."

She let her arms fall to her sides. "We'll see each other on Monday then, won't we? For the party at City Tavern?"

I'd forgotten about the gathering that some of the city's merchants, including Mr. Walker, had planned for their most valued customers. The major had invited me, yet in his current distracted state, I suspected he may have forgotten as well.

"Let me confirm it with the major. Give my best to your mother." I waved and turned toward home.

On Sunday afternoon, the major and I met for a stroll in the Common. His prediction that autumn would eventually arrive had come to pass, and we enjoyed the crisp chill in the air.

We stopped into Rivington's for coffee, and I was thankful that Mr. Rivington was present and Robert was not.

Once we had our coffees, the major took my hand. "I have a bit of unfortunate news to share. I received word that Captain Willington was severely injured in a skirmish outside of Charleston."

"Oh no, how dreadful! Will he survive? Is he returning to New York?"

"He lost a leg, I'm afraid. Yet he managed to pull through. He's being sent home to England to recover."

The news was hard to grasp. "Joe will be shattered. So will my mother and Alice. We all expected to see him again."

"Yes, of course." His shoulders slumped. "There is something else you must know.

I regret that it won't be possible for me to attend the merchants' party tomorrow evening."

"Oh . . ." I didn't care if my disappointment showed. "May I ask why?"

"A dinner for General Clinton. At a private home near Trinity Church. He insists I attend."

I was not particularly surprised. Clinton received frequent invitations from New York's most affluent. "Is the dinner for officers only?" With a tilt of my head, I fluttered my lashes just a bit.

"I'm afraid it is this time, my dear. You do understand?"

"Certainly, John. Might we see each other the following day for a stroll or—"

He shook his head, a bit too sure. "That won't be possible."

I sipped my coffee and waited for his explanation.

"The journey north I spoke of—I shall leave in the morning following the dinner."

I could tell there was no changing his mind. "Very well."

While he drank his coffee, I gathered my courage to raise what had been troubling me.

"John, you must have a great deal to contend with now. When you return from your journey, would you rather we not see each other as often?"

His gaze was sincere. "I would want nothing of the sort. Again, I must apologize for seeming detached. That is not my intent whatsoever."

I looked down at our entwined hands. "No apology necessary. Yet the last thing I would ever want is for you to have any misgivings. Although I would hope we could remain friends."

His eyes searched mine. "Are we not more than mere friends?"

My heart swelled. "Yes. Yes, of course."

We departed the coffeehouse and walked slowly toward my home. The major stood tall as he lifted his eyes to the changing leaves above our heads. And handsome, to the extreme. How had I managed to hold his interest so long?

"If the stars continue to be favorable to the Crown," he said, "I shall have time to devote to more pleasant pursuits when I return." He lifted my hand to bestow a kiss.

"Along that line," he continued, "I'm to meet with the fellows at Theatre Royal regarding the new season, and I trust there will soon be a full schedule of balls and parties."

I gave his hand a squeeze. "So much has happened since the night we met. I do miss our dances."

It was true. And reassuring—thrilling, to be sure—to hear I was more than a friend to him.

At my door, I summoned the only words I knew to say. "I pray you'll have a safe and successful journey, John André."

We kissed, ignoring the neighbors walking by.

"*Adieu, ma chère.*" He descended the porch steps, and with a wave, he set off.

I donned my brightest, most encouraging smile. Yet there was something puzzling about the situation surrounding these travel plans of his. He seemed determined yet uneasy.

If only I knew why.

The next day, I wrote a short message to Celeste, informing her that I would not be attending the party that evening, due to Major André's requirement to attend a dinner with General Clinton. She would wonder why I didn't simply go with her and Captain Hollingsworth, yet I didn't care to this time. Hopefully, she would not press me on it.

Joe had fallen behind in his French lessons and we'd set aside the morning to delve into them, otherwise I might have asked him to deliver the message to Celeste. How might I send it?

He watched me apply the seal at the parlor writing desk. "Ask

Thomas Clemens, down the street," he said. "He is seeking work."

"Excellent idea. I'll go now and won't be long. Prepare your books and papers."

Ten minutes later, I peeked in the parlor as Joe sat drumming his fingers on his French book in a show of impatience.

"'Twas good timing." I laid my cap and shawl on the stairs. "Thomas was about to leave to inquire at St. Paul's for a position, and the Walkers' home isn't much farther. I paid him and he was most appreciative."

"May we start?" he said. "I have a busy afternoon ahead."

I joined him at our study table. "You sound like Mother."

"It's what you say when you're dressing to see Major André."

"That will do, Joseph William Floyd." I was in no mood to be teased, particularly about the man I was trying not to think about.

"Now you sound like Mother." Joe laughed and held his book in front of his face.

"It's a good thing for you that she and Alice are out." I tapped his book. "Let's begin."

We conversed *en francais* for the next thirty minutes, discussing the weather, the proper way to serve tea, and the difficulties of transocean travel—all useful conversational topics.

Joe managed to hold his own, but I could sense he was losing interest. He wasn't the only one. I switched to something easier. *"Récitez la prière du Seigneur."*

Focusing on the ceiling, he recited the Lord's Prayer flawlessly.

"Amen," I said. *"Bon."*

Biting his lip, he lowered his eyes.

"Is something troubling you?"

He took a few seconds to reply. "I've been thinking about the night at Fraunces Tavern when we hid the note. And your secrets . . ."

I couldn't let him notice my alarm. "There are a few matters that are best kept private, Joe. But you shouldn't let it concern you."

He crossed his arms. "I think it's more than a few matters." His quick glance from me to the floor gave away his nervousness. "I wonder sometimes if you're spying for Major André."

My laugh was genuine, even though I'd been invited more than once to do just that. "You should know me better. What would Uncle William think?"

Joe wiped his hand under his eye. "I wasn't certain. But be careful, Betty. Please?"

I wrapped my arms around him. "There's no need to worry."

Forty

With the major gone on his journey and Joe's tutoring requirements, it made good sense to stay near home for several days. Along with assisting my brother in his studies, I returned to baking bread. Cooler nights and gentler temperatures made it so much easier, pleasurable even. I trusted that the major would also be finding the weather agreeable and soon make his return to New York.

I knew of few gatherings that might yield any new intelligence, only those scheduled for a few weeks hence. Of course, if I desired, I could find reasons to meet Celeste or other friends at Rivington's or the taverns and strike up a conversation with unsuspecting officers. However, I had little interest in visiting Culper Junior or seeking out Culper Senior.

Perhaps I was shirking my duty as 355. Remorse grew until I decided to pay Robert a visit—a simple social call, cousin to cousin.

After church on the Sunday following the major's departure, I helped Alice and Mother pick tomatoes in the garden and lay them out on the pantry worktable.

"I believe I'll take a loaf of bread and a few tomatoes to Robert at the boarding house. Would they be finished at the Quaker meeting house by now?"

Mother passed me an especially large, ripe tomato. "They do tend to go on, but he should be home by the time you arrive."

As I took our market basket from the hook by the door, Alice said, "Be sure and tell Mr. Robert I wish him a blessed Lord's Day."

A group of soldiers stood conversing in the street as I neared the Underhill boarding house. Three more soldiers rushed toward them. Officers I recognized milled about. A few turned and stared when they saw me. What was happening?

Perhaps Robert would know. I reached the house and climbed the steps, calming myself with a deep breath. What would he think of me surprising him at the boarding house? I'd never dared to meet him there, yet surely he'd appreciate my thoughtfulness and welcome the fresh bread and tomatoes.

I expected Mary Underhill to open the door. Instead, Robert himself did so. I held out the basket. "Good Sunday, Robert. I—"

Surprise and worry was etched across his face. "You have not heard."

Did this have to do with the soldiers in the street? "I beg your pardon?"

He silently motioned for me to enter. I stepped inside the small entryway, bare of furnishings but for a small table and lantern.

I searched his face for a clue as to what could be amiss and glanced down the short hall. "Is Mrs. Underhill in? What has happened?"

He closed the door, then took the basket and set it on the table. "We are alone. Yet we must keep our voices low. Someone may come at any moment." He rested his balled fists at his waist. "Major André was caught behind enemy lines yesterday and taken to an American camp."

My stomach clenched. "Caught doing what? Where?"

"I am afraid I do not have the details of his capture. However, I learned at Rivington's late yesterday that he was traveling to West Point to receive documents from Benedict Arnold."

"General Arnold? That doesn't make sense. Why would he be meeting him? Has Arnold taken charge of the fort?"

"It appears so. Please listen." Robert looked down at the floor. "Apparently, André and Benedict Arnold were planning for the transfer—or delivery, as you read in the correspondence on André's desk—of West Point to the British."

I gasped. *For the delivery of WP.* "But . . . How?"

"I have no more accurate information. There is much talk—'tis the only topic of conversation at the coffeehouse, and I was not able to distinguish fact from rumor at this point."

I clutched my stomach. "Robert, the note was signed by a Mr. Moore. Was he part of this?"

Robert stared at the floor again before answering. "That may have been Arnold. Or someone with him."

I leaned against the wall, trying to imagine the major involved in something so underhanded. "All the talk of West Point for months . . . It was a conspiracy to take it, with Arnold's assistance?"

It sounded so farfetched. In my last conversation with the major, he'd been alternately preoccupied and composed. Had he been planning this all along, even at Vauxhall Gardens as he'd spoken with William Franklin and Colonel Robinson, and finalizing the details the day we had coffee at Rivington's?

"As of now, that may be the case." Robert hung his head again. "We saw the signs, yet we did not see the plot." Then he pounded the wall with his fist. "I should have recognized what was transpiring."

I shut my eyes in disgust and disbelief. I'd been the closest of the Culper ring members to John André, and I felt responsible.

Tears burned my cheeks as I looked up at Samuel Culper Junior— the man who'd convinced me I could be of service to the Cause. "What will happen to him? How could he do this? And now they've trapped him."

We stood for a minute, wrapped in our own thoughts. From a back room, a clock chimed.

Finally, Robert straightened. "Come in tomorrow. I shall endeavor to learn more by then."

I wiped my eyes. "The Ring—will they know?"

"They will undoubtedly hear of it, as will the world."

Sleep would not come that night, as I battled in fear for the major. Then I slipped into a confusing dream of us dancing, interrupted by soldiers leading him away. I woke late, tangled in damp sheets. If only I knew his whereabouts and could help him.

When I returned from seeing Robert the previous day, I told my family of the major's capture. Joe asked a dozen questions that I couldn't answer. Mother and Alice had been equally frantic and anxious to know what happened. I explained that Robert was making inquiries, which was so kind of him, they said.

I planned to dress and hurry out of the house early, but Mother waited at the bottom of the stairs, wearing her shawl and hat.

"I'm coming with you, Elizabeth." She donned her gloves. "There's no use in arguing. If Cousin Robert has any information about Major André, I want to hear it as well. And if not, we'll find Mr. Rivington. He may know something."

Mother had made up her mind, and frankly, her support was comforting. What frame of mind we would find Robert in, and what he might feel able to say in Mother's presence, remained to be seen. Above all, I only longed to hear of the major's release and safe return.

I could not get to Oakham and Townsend fast enough, yet Mother kept pace with me. Three officers exited as we approached. The moment we recognized one another, they tipped their hats, solemn expressions in their eyes. I longed to ask if they had any news of the major, then thought it better to wait until we spoke with Robert.

"It seems you're well-known, Elizabeth," Mother said as they passed.

"They know the major," I replied. "I'm sure they're as concerned for him as we are."

As we entered, Robert gave us a cursory glance while he tended to a customer at the counter. I paced to the nearest wall and back. The man soon mumbled a goodbye and stumbled out the door.

Mother stepped to the counter. "Dear Robert, it is good to see you."

If my cousin was at all annoyed by her presence, he didn't reveal it. "A good morning, Aunt Margaret, Cousin Betty."

Mother waved a hand in my direction. "Betty has explained that our Major André has been arrested. Have you any word today of the situation?"

I could not stand still. "We came as quickly as we could. What can you tell us?"

Robert's face darkened. He folded his arms, looking as though he might be determining what my mother could hear and what he needed me to know.

"Please, Robert," I said.

He stepped from behind the counter. "Two days ago, the major was traveling alone on horseback, returning to the city, having obtained papers of some sort from General Benedict Arnold of the Continental Army at West Point. He was stopped and questioned by three militia men. When they discovered the papers, they took him to the army's camp at North Castle, despite him having a pass from General Arnold."

"Arnold gave him a pass?" I asked. "Shouldn't they have allowed him to continue on his way?"

"Yes, that is customary," he said. "I am afraid I was not given the reason they held him, if indeed there was one."

Mother huffed. "Well, that is ridiculous, capturing a distinguished British officer because of a few papers. And what of the major now?"

"As far as we know, the commander at North Castle, Colonel Jameson, sent him back to West Point, per his request, in order that General Arnold may clear up the misunderstanding."

Relief shown in Mother's eyes. "Then the major may return to New York, as he intended?"

Robert didn't look as confident. "Let us hope that is the case."

"Thank you for that information, Robert. We will keep the major in our prayers." She bit her lip, then glanced at the nearest display table. "Now that I'm here, we're out of molasses. Have you any?"

"One moment." Robert started for the stockroom as Mother turned to look at the sundries opposite the counter. He bid me follow him toward the doorway, out of her hearing.

"Tallmadge knows," he whispered. "He is heading to the area to sort it out. Washington will know soon. It should be settled."

"Elizabeth?" My mother called me from across the shop.

Robert disappeared into the stockroom, and I had no more opportunity to speak with him privately. I could only hope and pray he was correct—that the matter would soon be handled appropriately, the major would return, and Benedict Arnold would pay for his treasonous crimes.

That afternoon, Celeste rushed through our front door and clasped my hands. "I came as soon as I heard. How dreadful for the major. Are you all right, Betty?"

I kissed her cheek. "Yes, I suppose. Would you like to stay? Join me for tea?"

"I'd love to," she said. "Unless I'm interrupting . . ."

"Don't be silly." I led her to the pantry. "Alice just made a fresh pot."

We took our tea and two spice cakes into the dining room and seated ourselves at the bare table. The afternoon sun cast wavy designs along the wall.

"Where is everyone?" Celeste asked.

I passed the honey. "Mother took Joe to the cobbler, and I believe Alice is out in the kitchen. We are all doing our best to keep busy."

Celeste gave me a look of sympathy as she let the honey stream off the dipper into her cup. "I simply don't understand what happened to the major. Have you heard anything?"

"Not the entire story, but it may be all we hear until his return."

I filled her in regarding the basics of his capture. She didn't appear to know of the Benedict Arnold meeting or the papers the major carried. Yet she would hear it all, sooner or later, so I summarized the story without giving away more than necessary.

"He should be cleared of any wrongdoing," I said, "as soon as General Arnold is consulted in the matter." I set down my cup and saucer. "One fact that bothers me is that Arnold was willing to simply hand over West Point like a sack of flour."

Celeste stared at me in surprise. "Why should that bother you? Does it not indicate that the major is an excellent negotiator?"

"Well, yes. I only meant . . . it shows how little it represented to him, I suppose. What sort of general, let alone a husband and father, would do such a thing?"

Celeste cut into her cake with her fork. "That is true. Poor Mrs. Arnold—it had to come as a shock, wouldn't you think? Yet General Clinton must have been pleased to have his cooperation."

Until things fell apart, Clinton had probably been frothing at the mouth. Thinking out loud, I said, "I suppose they will try Arnold for treason."

Celeste was silent. She stared at me briefly, then continued to eat her cake.

I sipped my tea and imagined what effect Arnold's betrayal might have on General Washington. Yet before Arnold's fate was decided, according to Robert, Ben Tallmadge would meet John André. What would be the outcome? Both were good, decent men, each the Director of Intelligence on opposing sides in a war that may have just taken another unexpected turn.

I longed to saddle a horse and ride north myself.

Life moved forward by inches at home. Each in our own way, we did what was required of us, not speaking of the major yet anxiously awaiting news.

At night, I would wake and go to the window to pray. I would touch my paper dolls and the portrait he'd sketched of me. I recalled our conversations, our dinners and dances and walks. Our kisses. When would he return? And how would I proceed, now that he'd participated in such a deceitful plan with an American general?

Joe had finished his morning lessons and sat on the back doorstep where Triple lay curled in his lap. Mother opened the door to remind him that it was time to leave for Mr. Mulligan's to order new breeches for winter.

He groaned from his seat. "Must we go today?"

"May I take him, Mother?" I glanced at Joe. "We might stop at the coffeehouse for sandwiches afterward."

I'd been too worried to keep up with intelligence gathering of any sort. To be frank, I'd lost my hunger for it. That changed now with the major's arrest. Perhaps I would inquire at Rivington's, depending on who was available, and see where the conversation led.

Joe looked to Mother with eyes full of hope.

"As you wish," she said. "Be patient when you're measured. You're growing too fast, young man. Elizabeth, ask Mr. Mulligan to give the breeches a bit of extra length."

Joe and I were soon off to the tailor. A group of ten or twelve redcoats marched ahead on Smith Street, led by an officer shouting directions. There had been an increase in the street drills recently, perhaps due to the major's arrest. Were the British planning to retaliate before a settlement could be reached?

As soon as Mr. Mulligan had all of Joe's measurements and my instructions, we headed back up the street toward Rivington's. We both spoke of our hunger, and the cooking aromas as we neared the corner enticed us to hurry.

Without warning, two soldiers in well-worn uniforms stepped out of a doorway near the stables and blocked our path, muskets held tightly across their chests. At least three more appeared from nowhere and surrounded us.

We nearly collided with them. "Gentlemen!" My heart pounded. "I beg your pardon."

The soldier directly ahead of me stepped closer. I almost didn't recognize him without his feathered hat.

"We meet again, Miss Floyd."

Joe started to speak until I held my finger to my lips. "So, 'tis Cunningham's lowest henchman. To what do I owe the pleasure, Mr. Crankshaw?"

He came nearer, his vile breath escaping through rotted teeth. "Miss Betty Floyd, you are accused of spying for the enemy and are hereby under arrest."

Now? It can't be . . .

The other soldiers closed in just as Joe took a step back. Two of them grabbed my arms.

I twisted around, facing Joe. "Run!"

My brother's eyes widened in fear as I implored him again. "Run, Joe."

"Let 'im go," Crankshaw said. "She's the one we want."

I caught a last glimpse of my brother as he darted past Rivington's Corner and into the street. I struggled against the men's tight hold. "Want me—for what purpose? I've done nothing wrong. I'm a close friend of Major André's, as you should be well aware. He will see you hang for this."

Crankshaw pointed his index finger at me. "More'n just a friend, I reckon." He sneered, drawing out the words. "Givin' him whatever he wanted, only to learn the military's secrets." He wagged his finger. "Naughty naughty."

"No! You're wrong!"

Where were all the officers now that I saw so often? Why wouldn't they come to my aid?

The guards exchanged vulgar comments. Without thinking twice, I reared back and spit at Crankshaw's syphilitic lesions, now multiplied across his face.

He wiped a sleeve over his cheek and raised his voice. "He's where you wanted 'im all along now, isn't he?"

I gritted my teeth. "I had nothing whatsoever to do with his capture."

A small crowd gathered. I sensed their eyes on me, heard their whispers. The men holding me shoved me forward as Crankshaw led the way.

My heart raced. "What are you doing? Wh—where are you taking me?"

The guard holding my left arm tightened his grip and laughed. "You'll soon see."

We turned toward Fraunces Tavern, then passed a handful of ramshackle buildings, until the wharves remained the only possibility. Sailors stepped out of our way, stretching their necks to see who'd been arrested. Knowing looks passed among them.

The guards steered me toward a small dock where eight or ten rowboats rocked against worn pilings.

"No!" I struggled to free my arms and dig in my heels.

Crankshaw turned to face me, then cast a glance at the gray East River. He held up a hand and wiggled his fingers.

"Enjoy the dancin' on the *Jersey*, Miss Floyd."

Part Three

Forty-One

Before my shoes touched the muddy deck of the HMS *Jersey*, the worst stench imaginable emanated from the ship known as Hell Afloat. Five minutes later, as a guard pulled me off the rope ladder I'd been forced to climb, I was convinced the name didn't do it justice.

Men wearing little more than dirty rags crowded the open deck, leaning or sitting in every available space. Few looked my way. Their drawn, vacant expressions and emaciated bodies showed little of any former vitality. Some appeared to be mere days from death.

Another guard shoved me toward the rear deck. "Women over there until ya' go below."

My shoe caught the hem of my gown and I stumbled over a pile of filthy ropes. About ten feet away, a group of five or six ladies huddled together on a bench. One, her gray hair loose and blowing about her grimy face, beckoned me with a shaking hand.

As I neared, she pulled a ragged length of wool from beneath the bench. "Someone left a blanket. Take it now, or there may not be any tonight."

I wasn't sure how to accept it, or if I wished to do so. Where was my shawl I'd worn as I left Mr. Mulligan's? Probably crushed in the street by now, and my reticule emptied of its contents by Crankshaw or one of his detestable cohorts. I took the blanket and awkwardly perched beside her.

"I am Mrs. Murphy." Her voice shook as much as her hands.

"I . . . I'm Betty Floyd. Please call me Betty."

Two ladies sitting beside her regarded me with half-hearted interest. One turned away, revealing a deep purple bruise on her cheek. The other tucked a limp strand of dark hair under her dingy cap.

I leaned toward them. "Hello."

Mrs. Murphy touched the arm of the dark-haired girl, but she didn't respond. "Mary's had a grim time of it," she said to me. "We all have."

A scuffle broke out across the deck. A guard moved in, shouting obscenities, and raised a club over his head. I gasped and hid my eyes as the club met its mark. A man screamed.

"Such scenes occur all day," Mrs. Murphy said. "At night as well. You will grow somewhat accustomed to it. And to much more, I'm afraid."

I looked again at the man, now slumped on the deck, moaning in pain. Men near him cowered as the guard stood over them. How could I possibly become accustomed to such treatment?

Mrs. Murphy seemed to have a calming effect on her little band of ladies in this sea of forlorn, emaciated men and their—our—brutal captors. I already found myself looking to her for strength. Why was she a prisoner, or any of the women for that matter? What had they done?

Perhaps she wondered the same as she sneaked a glance at me. My unremarkable blue gown stood out among their limp and dirty ones. They were missing strips of fabric around the hems that appeared to have been torn away. I wondered as to the reason.

Absently, I patted my hair. Sometime between my arrest, the journey by boat, and the jostling and shoving, I'd lost my cap and several hairpins. Perhaps I was only a day or two from blending in with the others.

What could have possibly led to my arrest? I sorted through my whereabouts the last few days. I'd kept out of public view, going about my duties, waiting for word of the major. It felt so long ago now, as I perched on the *Jersey's* cold bench, surrounded by despair.

Oh, where was the major, and when would he return to the city? Surely, he would learn of my predicament and come to my rescue. There would be hell to pay then. Or would he discover that I had deliberately lured him into my confidence as I passed along details of our conversations? How clearly I could still hear him—*Truth always prevails, my dear.* How could he not learn the truth now, despite my supposed protection within the Ring. Would he still care to rescue me, or would he order me thrown overboard?

I assumed Joe had run home. He would immediately describe to Mother and Alice what happened, yet could I trust him to refrain from revealing my secrets? They would surely be in shock and afraid for my life. Would they all be in danger as well, once word spread of their relationship to an alleged rebel spy?

I forced these thoughts from my mind, turning again to Mrs. Murphy. "May I ask what brought you here?"

She raised her eyes to the sky without speaking. I began to think she hadn't heard me.

"I assisted someone," she said at last. "A woman who helped a handful of men escape this very ship. Ironic, is it not?"

Could it be? "Are you speaking of Mrs. Burgin?"

Her chapped lips lifted at the corners. "Did you know her?"

"Her home was not far from ours. I was told that she left New York some time ago. How did anyone know you were—"

She lifted her hand, bidding me to move closer. "When she and the young lads brought the men from the ship back to her home, I took food to them. I made stews and baked bread, even cakes and puddings—more than Mrs. Burgin and her children could have possibly eaten." Her smile revealed brown teeth. "Someone was surely watching. After she learned she was in danger of arrest and left the city, I took food to Canvas Town. By then, my association with her made me a suspect, and I was arrested for aiding the enemy."

Clearly, Joe could have been arrested as well, had he been seen helping at Mrs. Burgin's home.

"You were only feeding the poor," I said.

"People often believe what they wish to believe, and don't consider the facts."

I pondered that truth. "Especially in this war."

"And you, Miss Betty? What brings you to the *Jersey*?"

I could only say what I knew to be true at the moment. "I do not fully know. Mistaken identity, perhaps."

I remained with the women the rest of the day. We were given no water or food, and by the time large iron pots were set up in various places around the deck, I ached for whatever they contained. I couldn't imagine where it came from—I only hoped it was edible.

As we stood together in a long, ragged line, Mary spoke to me for the first time, keeping her eyes downcast. "Take what you're given. Don't say a word or let them see any expression of disgust."

I tried to make light of it. "This doesn't sound promising."

She lifted her gaze, her eyes imploring me to heed her words. "You must eat. Do the best you can."

As we neared the table where a thin, bearded prisoner stood with a ladle to dip in the pot, Mrs. Murphy handed me a small earthen bowl and spoon from a stack beneath the table. The bowl appeared clean, the spoon less so. Mimicking Mary, I held out my bowl when I approached the man. He splashed half a ladle full of brown liquid with a few lumps of what might pass for meat into my bowl.

"Thank you," I said.

He glanced up and snorted.

Mary led the way back to the bench, but it was now occupied by men bent over their bowls. We meandered toward the stern, finding enough space to sit down on the deck. The other women followed.

While they began eating, I sniffed my bowl. The smell made me cringe, yet hunger won, and I took a taste of the mixture. I could barely swallow it, then regretted doing so.

Mrs. Murphy leaned over. "Try to eat the meat. You must keep up your strength however possible."

I searched for the meat with my spoon. "This . . . liquid, though. I don't think—"

"It may rain tonight," Mary said. "Leave your bowl here and collect the rain for drinking."

When all the women were finished, we quickly poured out our bowls over the side and set them together behind a pile of wooden crates. There would be no way to know which bowl was mine, yet it likely mattered little.

"Where do we sleep?" I asked Mary.

She looked at me as if I were daft. "Below, of course."

A guard passed by and scowled at us, then turned to spit over the side.

I dreaded going below deck and couldn't imagine what awaited me there. "Is it . . . Are we . . . safe?"

Mary glanced at the bristly guard as he moved out of sight. "It's safe enough if we stay together. Don't take chances by venturing anywhere alone." She nodded toward the young woman with the bruised cheek. "Edith learned that lesson."

As the sky darkened, the women patiently showed me how to use the bucket near the crates, surrounding me and turning their backs. Each took their turn, then the last two women dumped the contents over the side. I longed to wash my hands, yet there were no such luxuries.

The guards herded us to a hatch at center deck leading to the ship's hold, and the women waited until the men had descended the ladder. My attempts to see into the dark cavern were futile.

Behind me, Mrs. Murphy spoke. "Take your time. There are eight rungs, each about a foot apart."

It reminded me of our root cellar on the farm. I'd always dreaded having to go down there, even when I carried a lantern with me. Of course, no one would provide a lantern here.

With the blanket over my shoulder, I lowered myself to the deck and found the first rung with my foot. I climbed down, hands shaking, counting the rungs.

From below, Mary patted my shoe. "You're halfway down."

She steered me toward her as I reached the floor, then we helped Mrs. Murphy. My eyes gradually adjusted, but not before the dreadful odor of urine and death closed in—similar to that of Rhinelander's Sugar House yet multiplied tenfold. And instead of nursing the prisoners, I was now one of them.

With Mary in the lead, we weaved our way between the shapes of men sitting or lying down. Some mumbled obscenities, others moaned or wept aloud. I stumbled against a large crate and barely avoided sprawling across someone's lap. Slivers speared my palms.

We settled behind a rough partition. I spread out the blanket and sat upon it, inches away from other women who had befriended me and one another out of necessity. With no other comforts, their presence provided a small sense of safety. I couldn't imagine being without them in this hellhole stuffed with dying men.

The hatch was dropped into place with a clang, erasing the last of the shadows. Total darkness merged with the nauseating odors. I removed the sash at my waist and tied it over my nose and mouth, its lingering smell allowing me a brief memory of taking hot bread from our kitchen oven.

As the women arranged themselves, they whispered prayers for strength and God's intervention. I was too frightened and stunned by the situation to think beyond the moment. Did God hear prayers in such a place?

Unable to see, I was on high alert, trying to decipher each strange sound. Weeping lessened, and moans turned to snores. Then came scratching and scurrying along the wall to my right, too loud to be a mouse. *A rat?* There was nothing to do but tuck my skirts around my legs.

Again, I pondered what may have led me there. Robert had admonished me countless times to be careful, especially as the hunt for enemy spies increased. And I did take precautions, or so I thought. Now with Benedict Arnold changing sides, he might set his sights on every secret Patriot in New York. That is, if he managed to escape trial and sentencing by George Washington.

There was a point in my favor—should he or anyone in league with him discover the Culper Code, they had no way of knowing that *lady* or *355* was a specific person. Plus, wouldn't my association with Major André shield me from suspicion? Yet I feared for Robert, Abraham Woodhull, Mr. Rivington, and the other Ring members.

I shuddered to think what my arrest would do to Robert. I blinked back tears as I pictured myself nonchalantly entering Oakham and Townsend one day, if I should be so fortunate. There would be no end to the scolding I'd receive.

I could only imagine Mother's anguish at that moment, in our home not so far away. She would seek help from Robert first, then Mr. Rivington, then the major if she could.

Surely, General Washington would free John André. I needed to see him, to know he was safe, and hear his account of what took place on his travels. As for how we might discuss Benedict Arnold, West Point, and my arrest—that could wait. If only I might have the chance.

Had Celeste heard yet? She would be frantic, poor girl. Perhaps her father or Captain Hollingsworth would send word to General Clinton's office on my behalf.

Finally, I dried my tears with my sash and tightened it across my nose. I had endured adversity before—my father's abuses, my disability, leaving our beloved farm in the midst of war, and starting over in New York, surrounded by the invaders.

But as I listened to the breathing of a thousand desperate souls in the belly of the *Jersey*, hard reality threatened to suffocate me. This was nothing close to anything I could even imagine—a living nightmare that only a very few had survived.

I whispered a brief yet fervent prayer. *Help me.*

Forty-Two

*P*apa shoved me against the hay wagon. "Who do you think you are? You're not worthy of—"

Hearing my screams over the thunderstorm, Samuel, one of the slaves, ran into the barn through the open door . . .

The sound of metal scraping metal startled me awake, and I was back in the belly of the hell ship.

A wide shaft of dim light shone into the hold as the hatch was pulled away. Men grumbled, stirring. Mary pushed herself to a sitting position near my feet.

Someone shouted down from the deck. "Turn out yer dead."

Mary gathered her skirts. "Let's make haste."

I tied the blanket around my waist and followed her, as did the other women, through the maze of prisoners and up the ladder. A guard reached for my elbow and lifted me roughly, boosting me to the deck. I pulled away, averting my eyes from his certain leer.

A handful of guards and deck workers sauntered about under the dreary October sky. I pulled the sash down off my nose and hurried out of the way of those climbing up behind me. Had anyone indeed succumbed during the night?

Mrs. Murphy was the last woman up the ladder, grimacing in pain as she pulled herself to the deck. The guard looked on with bored disinterest.

I went to her and helped her climb past the last rung. As she clung to my arm, sweat beaded her pale forehead. She had seemed stronger the previous day, but that meant little on a packed ship where sickness and death flourished.

An overnight rain had left muddy puddles along the deck. I led her to the stern, to our little area of crates and whatnot. She collapsed to a bench, holding her stomach. Edith brought a bowl full of rainwater, careful not to spill a drop, and helped her drink.

Before we finished our morning business with the bucket, loud splashes came from somewhere nearer the bow. A guard standing amid several prisoners appeared to be writing in a ledger.

"Is that—" I started to ask Mary.

"Don't pay attention," she said. "Come, let's drink what the sky has delivered."

Our bowls overflowed. The women had hidden the strips of fabric they had torn from their gowns nearby and used them now to wipe their faces with rainwater.

I took care to raise my bowl to my lips, then chose to save half of its precious contents for later. As I took a seat beside Mrs. Murphy, I set the bowl between my feet and wrapped myself in the blanket.

With that, we settled down to wait out the day until the evening meal. My stomach growled with hunger, and I couldn't imagine how I would last until then, let alone whatever number of days lay ahead.

Just today. Make it through today.

Another loud splash made me tremble. This was truly hell on earth.

"It is for the best, Miss Betty," Mrs. Murphy said. The pain in her expression had eased, yet she continued to rub her middle. "Those men no longer suffer. May they be with God now."

"Is . . . is that what they do, whenever—"

"No, not always. At times, the bodies are loaded onto a boat and buried onshore. That is how Mrs. Burgin helped those men escape."

I envisioned what may have taken place. "They pretended as if they were dead?"

She looked toward the railing where I'd been hoisted aboard. "That may have been how it was done, yet I wasn't part of the rescue, so I'm not certain. I only fed them afterward." She brightened. "The lads that she employed had some daring escapades over here, so I heard."

"They were paid?"

"Only a bit when she could afford it, which wasn't often. They were too young to take up arms, but it was their way of fighting the British."

She regarded the distant shore. "They cannot take everything from us, you know. Our right to think for ourselves, to pray, to love, to discern right from wrong—they cannot take that unless we let them." She turned to face me. "Do not let them take that from you, Miss Betty."

As the day wore on, the clouds remained, yet the temperature rose. Soon, a warm wind blew across the deck. I turned into the wind, removed a few hairpins, and let my hair blow around a bit. The younger women did the same. With my eyes closed, I recalled sitting for my portrait with the major at Vauxhall Gardens and running free through our farm's sunlit fields.

I gazed across the deck at hundreds of ghostlike men wasting away at the hands of their captors. What were their crimes? Most had belonged to the Continental Army, fighting for freedom, the freedom to live in a country where individuals could choose their own leaders and dream their own dreams. And us women, guilty of acting in various capacities to further the cause of that freedom— one that each of us believed in down to our bones.

We made room for Mrs. Murphy to lie down on the bench, yet she was restless. Her brow tensed. "What I wouldn't give for a good cup of hot tea."

Mary perked up. "Ah! Fine English tea in a fine English teacup."

That inspired Edith to speak at last. "From a fine English teapot, with fresh cream."

Mrs. Murphy spoke in a faint voice. "Tea is all the English are good for."

We all laughed softly, a sweet sound in the gloom.

None of the guards or other prisoners bothered us, as long as we remained in our unofficially designated area. When I tired of sitting, I walked about the best I could. I found I could pace ten steps one way and back again without getting too close to the male prisoners.

After one of these excursions, I returned to the bench. "How are you feeling, Mrs. Murphy?"

"You should conserve your strength." She rubbed her stomach. "I am no worse. But I'm worried I won't make it down the ladder tonight. Or that I will be unable to climb out in the morning, and I can't bear to think of staying below all day. It's . . . only for the very weak. And then if—"

I placed my arm around her shoulders. "What would you think if I stayed with you on deck tonight?"

I had already decided not to sleep below deck if I could possibly help it. Between the terrible odors, the darkness, and having no way of escape, spending the night on deck might be preferable.

She raised her brows. "Could we?"

"We must think it through. I'll let the others know to cover for us. Perhaps I could arrange a reasonable shelter with the crates and such." I hoped I sounded more confident than I felt.

"You would be taking a risk, my dear. However"—she grimaced, inhaling—"I cannot tell you how much I would appreciate it."

Our meal that evening consisted of a similar mixture as the previous night's fare, plus a hunk of stale bread. I checked it for worms after the women warned me. I picked them out and ate the bread. This was not the time to be squeamish.

As evening came and we prepared to end the day, I gradually moved some crates closer to the rail and made a shelter of sorts next to our bowls. Mary stood guard, although no one seemed to pay much attention. I arranged my blanket like a tent over the crates and helped Mrs. Murphy to lie down. We were only partially protected from the elements, but it would have to do.

"What if it rains?" Mary asked me.

I couldn't allow that to concern me. "I suppose we'll get wet. And we'll have water to drink in the morning."

I peered between the slats of one of the crates toward the bow. The women lingered around us, hiding our shelter with their wide skirts. When the guards ordered all prisoners to go below, Mary and the others began chattering about fictitious friends in New York as they moved in a group toward the hatch. Hopefully, it would be enough of a distraction to keep anyone from noticing two women missing.

The deck gradually quieted as all but a few guards descended the ladder, and the hatch was shut. Mrs. Murphy coughed into her arm, doing her best to muffle it.

I tucked the stoic woman's worn blanket around her shoulders. "Are you all right?"

"I believe so," she whispered. "And this was a good decision. I wouldn't have the strength for that ladder."

If only I could care for her properly, with clean pillows and blankets and a good broth and medicinals. . . . Mint leaves might help her stomach. I racked my brain to think of something I could do for her, yet I had nothing to give.

"'Tis enough, Miss Betty." She patted my hand. "You've done more than enough."

As I said a silent prayer for her, the wind lessened, and a handful of stars appeared between the dark clouds. A strange calm overshadowed my surroundings, if only briefly. I rested my shoulders against a crate until Mrs. Murphy slept.

We held to the same plan for another four days and nights. Our routine varied little, except when a boat would arrive to unload food supplies or more prisoners. We leaned over the rail to watch, while prisoners would ask for news of the war or beg the sailors to deliver messages to family members.

Another boat came once or twice a day, bearing items to sell—rum, soap, candles, or sweets. Only the guards had money to buy anything, and they would wave their purchases in the air to make certain we noticed, then tuck them inside their coats.

Boats arrived to carry away the dead as well. It seemed a bit more dignified than tossing bodies overboard, although I doubted their burials were any more solemn. The boatmen looked nearly as skeletal and broken as the bodies they loaded aboard their boats. I was reminded of the dead cart that bore Christopher Martin away from Rhinelander's—the nightmarish scene that led me to turn on the British and take up the work that brought me here.

Mrs. Murphy's condition gradually worsened. She developed a fever, soaking her gown with perspiration one minute, then shaking with chills the next. We begged an older guard, named Jim, for something to give her to drink. He later brought a tankard of ale, which Mrs. Murphy drank and promptly vomited.

In one of her lucid moments, she grabbed my hand. "Miss Betty, I do not expect to recover. You and the others . . . I fear you'll all take ill because of me."

I had torn a strip from the hem of my own gown, and now dipped it in a puddle and placed it across her forehead. "You mustn't worry. We are looking out for one another."

In truth, I shared her fears. We had next to nothing for sustenance and no way to keep clean. Disease and starvation claimed more prisoners each day. I could only keep my sash tied over my face to ward off odors. At the rail, I inhaled the somewhat fresher air whenever possible.

If the guards noticed that either Mrs. Murphy or I stayed on deck at night, they simply didn't care. I was grateful for that, and for the occasional rain that kept us alive.

On the fifth morning, Edith found a large, discarded piece of canvas from one of the visiting boats. We fashioned it into a better tent over Mrs. Murphy, who had begun to drift in and out of consciousness.

That afternoon, a cold rain fell. It turned heavy after our meal, prompting prisoners to demand that the guards open the hatch early and allow them to go below.

Mary dipped her head under the canvas where I sat with Mrs. Murphy. "I'll stay with her tonight," she said. "I know you hate the hold, but you should at least get out of the rain for one night and try to sleep."

"No, thank you," I said. "There's no need for you to stay."

She trailed after the others as they hurried toward the open hatch, shivering under their wet blankets. I certainly didn't blame them for wanting a reprieve from the rain. Then she turned around, rushed back, and dove beneath the canvas. Her hair had escaped her cap and was plastered to her wet cheeks and forehead. "I may regret this, but I simply couldn't leave you out here tonight."

My teeth chattered as I shifted position, making room for her. Mrs. Murphy stared at Mary as if she didn't recognize her, mumbled a few words, and closed her eyes.

Icy rain stabbed at the canvas over our heads. We huddled close to this lovely and courageous woman, rubbing her arms and singing lullabies and hymns. I sensed we would find her gone in the morning, and I was grateful that I wouldn't be alone.

What had this kind slip of a girl done to anyone that caused her to be sentenced to the *Jersey*?

"Mary, what led you here?"

She flinched, as though I'd touched an open wound, then let out a resigned sigh as she thought better of it. "You might as well know." She pushed the wet hair out of her eyes. "I was paid by someone for information. I never knew his name."

I studied her face in the near-dark. "Information from the military?"

She nodded. "My customers."

Most likely, there was only one type of service she'd provided— one always in demand among the redcoats in New York City.

"At Holy Ground?"

She sniffed. "My house was nowhere near there. Yet for the most part, I went to them. I was sent a gown, shoes, all the trimmings. I would have my hair styled. We'd drink champagne, eat a splendid dinner . . ."

"And you persuaded them to talk."

Mary chuckled. "If they drank enough. And I would pass along what they told me. Then one of them became suspicious and threatened me at knifepoint until I confessed. I'm sure it was him who had me followed and arrested." She stared into the distance. "I didn't know his name either."

How dreadful, coercing women to obtain intelligence in such a way. Under normal circumstances, Mary and I would never have met. But here, where we were treated like animals and forced to spend every moment side by side, we were equals, relying on each other for survival.

She and I were not that different. We both had attempted to glean intelligence from the enemy by using our charms to gain their trust. Indeed, we had uttered lie upon lie. I hadn't sold myself to anyone, yet I was never proud of leading the major into thinking I was simply an interested Loyalist enjoying his attentions. And then I'd fallen in love with him. I hung my head—an exhausted, starving, conniving wretch.

"Something tells me you aren't as innocent as you want us to believe," Mary said.

"My story is complicated." In my weakened state, I longed to divulge the truth. Indeed, what harm would there be in it, in this place where secrets no longer mattered?

But I'd made a promise and I would die before I broke it. "I'm sorry, I cannot go into detail."

Without comment, Mary shifted her body to face the railing.

Mrs. Murphy's words came to mind: *They cannot take everything from us, you know. Our right to think for ourselves, to pray, to love, to discern right from wrong—they cannot take that unless we let them.*

I vowed to never let them, no matter the cost. Would this new country realize the value in those ideals and forever protect them?

The freezing rain adhered to the deck, creating an icy coat. I shivered and tucked the end of the damp blanket tightly around my shoulder.

Once again, Mrs. Murphy muttered incoherently.

Mary turned around and bent close until her ear was inches from our friend's lips. "Say it again, dear."

Mrs. Murphy mumbled softly once more.

"Are you able to understand her?" I asked.

Mary sat up. "She said, 'The lads are coming.'"

Forty-Three

When the sky lightened from coal to greenish gray, the freezing rain ceased. Mrs. Murphy was still with us, yet her breathing had turned shallow and sporadic, and she no longer opened her eyes or reacted to sound.

We did what we could to keep her warm. I placed a small chunk of ice on her tongue, but it melted and dripped down her chin.

When the hatch was opened and those below began climbing to the deck, Mary and I crawled out from beneath the canvas. A group of men near us had set out their privy bucket the night before to catch the icy rain. As they fought to drink from it, Edith came, took my arm, and led me to our bowls. They overflowed with fresh, ice-cold water. I drank deeply and saved a bit to refresh my face and fingertips. One full bowl was left untouched, in the hope that Mrs. Murphy could take a drink.

Then two days passed with no rain. To survive, we drank water the guards provided, straining it through one of the women's underskirts to filter out pests and dirt.

We were slowly starving. In our weakness, the smallest task took a great deal of effort. It was a constant struggle not to succumb to self-pity. As for any hope of rescue, I laid it aside. I had not the strength for it.

Perhaps it was the third morning, after a quiet night of no rain or wind, I woke early to a creamy orange sky. Mary sat on her blanket near the railing, staring at the expanse over Brooklyn. "Isn't it beautiful?"

I pulled back our canvas roof to get a better look. "I haven't seen a sunrise like this in a long time."

Even Mrs. Murphy's eyes were open. Yet she didn't see the sun. As much as I'd known to expect it, I stared for a moment in disbelief. "Mary? She's left us."

Mary turned her head in surprise, then rose and came to kneel beside me. We gazed down at this woman who'd only wanted to feed people and been punished for it, then befriended us when we thought we had lost everything.

I closed her eyes, and Mary pulled the blanket over her face. We informed Edith and the other women as they came up from below. None of us cried—we had no tears. Instead, we gathered around and sang the hymn, "Rejoice, the Lord Is King."

The daily call rang out. "Turn out yer dead!"

"We cannot let them throw her over," Mary said. "We must see that she's buried."

"How?" Edith asked. "Will a boat come today?"

We had become confused as to what day it was, although it seemed the boats that took away the dead for burial came on random days.

"We can hide her," I said. "And perhaps the boat will come soon."

If we remained largely ignored by the guards and male prisoners, chances were good that Mrs. Murphy's body would go unnoticed. She would not be missed, and we would not be questioned. Any smell would be masked by the pervasive stench over every inch of the ship.

The women agreed, and as the men who had perished during the night were shoved over the side, the women of the HMS *Jersey* went about their business with nary a misstep, acting as if we still cared for one of our own beneath the canvas.

When no boats came and evening approached, Mary and I prepared to remain on deck as always. As the women departed for the hold, she and I took our places beside Mrs. Murphy's body.

"Let's uncover her face, in the event a guard comes," Mary said. "It's dark enough—he won't look closely."

With my eyes shut, I pulled back the blanket.

By morning, I began to think we'd made a mistake. As much as I wanted to give what respect we could to Mrs. Murphy by ensuring she had some sort of burial, how long could we hide her body in all but plain sight?

My anxiety took hold in my stomach. After a swallow of our filtered water, I ran to the railing and vomited.

Mary came and laid her hand on my back. I wiped my sleeve across my mouth and looked toward the New York shoreline. The usual number of small boats moved in and out among the British warships, but none approached the *Jersey*.

"If a boat doesn't come today—"

"But perhaps one will," Mary said.

She and the others quietly wrapped Mrs. Murphy's body in two blankets—her own and a spare one discarded from the body of a man cast into the river that morning. They tied it with strips of cloth we tore from her underskirt and propped the crates around and on top. The canvas was draped over the bench.

As the day progressed, the autumn sun warmed us. I spent a good deal of time at the railing, holding my stomach, retching and perspiring. I came close to fainting multiple times and slid to the deck, drenched and exhausted.

Mary came to me as I crawled to the bench. "You must lie down, Betty. I'll stay with you."

I'd never felt so ill or so weak. I panted between words. "Not . . . on the bench. Here. Under it." I crawled beneath. Mary slid her blanket under my head. Mercifully, I fell asleep.

I lapsed in and out of awareness as small waves of long forgotten moments came and went. These were the sweetest memories—my mother's embrace, Joe's mischievous laughter, chasing fireflies with him on the hill behind our farmhouse. Regardless of what I had accomplished in my life, only my family mattered. In my heart I prayed for their safety.

And I prayed for the major, wherever he was, and that he would sense, in some way, my love for him.

A cold wind blew. Someone called me. "Betty? Betty, wake up."

I forced my eyes open. Dusk approached, and Mary leaned over me.

"A boat is near. The boatmen are quite young. They may be the lads Mrs. Murphy spoke of."

I had no strength to care who manned the boat, yet I summoned the will to speak. "Please see that they take her, Mary." I shut my eyes, wishing to shut out the voices calling to the boat.

She jiggled my shoulder. "Betty, listen to me." A gust of wind blew as she shook me again. I opened my eyes. "Perhaps they are the boys that rescued prisoners from here. They may ask for the dead, and we'll make them take Mrs. Murphy. But you could go as well. You're very weak. Can you act as if you're dead?"

I would have laughed if I hadn't felt so near death already. "Mary . . ."

She leaned closer. "Once you are off this ship, they could take you to your home."

Her words registered and I forced myself to speak. "What if I'm discovered? We all could be shot. And I don't want to leave you. What if—"

Between wind gusts, more shouts came from the railing, indicating the boat must be close.

"Please, Betty. For us."

I was ill enough to not be in my right mind. I handed her my blanket. "Tie me up."

She called to Edith, who seemed to be already aware of the plan. I pulled my sash from around my neck and handed it to Mary, then I held my arms and let them wrap the blanket over my head and tie it at my waist.

One of them patted my shoulder and whispered. "Rest in peace."

I felt the urge to vomit again. Their footsteps retreated, then guards shouted. "Any dead? Let 'em down over here."

I willed my heartbeat to not give me away as I made my arms and legs go limp. If I got off the *Jersey*, how might I be transferred to the small boat—lowered respectfully or tossed like a sack of potatoes?

There was no changing my mind now. Through holes in the blanket, I watched the commotion. Mary brought Jim and one of the prisoners to carry Mrs. Murphy from the deck. Minutes later, they returned for me.

I recognized Jim's rough voice near my feet. "Names?"

Mary answered. "That one was Mrs. Murphy. I never learned her given name."

He grunted. "Won't matter." He kicked my shoe. "This one?"

"This is Betty Floyd."

I flinched, hearing my name. I would forever be recorded among the dead from the *Jersey*.

"Let's go, Betty Floyd."

Raindrops splatted the blanket as the man behind me lifted me under the arms. I let my head fall back. Jim grabbed my ankles at the same time. They carried me forward and through the crowd of hooting prisoners. I felt hands grope me in places they had no business touching. I willed every part of me lifeless.

It means nothing. I am dead.

We passed through what might have been a doorway, then descended a set of steps. With my head still dropped back, I squinted through the holes in the blanket. On my left, a small boat rocked just beyond where my bearers stood. Those aboard were lifting Mrs. Murphy's body toward the rear.

A steady rain fell now. Someone took Jim's place and stepped into the boat, grasping my feet. The man at my head followed, and two seconds later they dropped me on the bottom of the boat in a heap.

Whoever had moved Mrs. Murphy stepped closer, making the boat pitch side to side.

"Let's lift her now," one said.

His voice sounded vaguely familiar. Then he hollered, "What are you waiting for? Tell 'em."

Someone called to the guards that had just carried me. "Sirs, we . . . we have orders to retrieve a prisoner, Miss Betty Floyd, and deliver her to General Clinton."

Joe! *What in God's name . . .*

Jim replied, "And there ye have her. Give the general my regards."

Joe cried out, "No, wait!"

As other guards roared with laughter, thunder rolled. Someone must have given the boat a push and the oars were quickly manned.

Joe whimpered as the rain pelted my blanket and gown. It took all I had to lie still until we were safely away.

I now recognized the familiar voice as belonging to James Townsend. He hollered over the growing storm. "Joe, come and sit with your sister."

The boat rocked as he came closer and crouched where I lay. His sobbing broke me until I could hold back no longer.

"Joe, I'm alive." I pulled at the blanket and twisted toward him. "It's me. I'm alive, Joe."

"Betty?" He tore at the blanket.

The rowers held the oars. Joe and James yanked at the knotted sash with boyish fervor, yelling at each other. I laughed and cried until they finally pulled the blanket away from my face.

Joe gazed at me wide-eyed, breathing hard. Thunder boomed overhead and the clouds fully opened. James Townsend, Joe's friend George Vanderbrook, and our neighbor, Thomas Clemens, all stared, speechless.

I winced. "I must smell horrible."

Joe laughed through tears as waves lifted and rocked the boat. In the pouring rain, George and Thomas manned the oars again and pulled hard to maneuver around one of the British naval ships. Mrs. Murphy's body lay behind James Townsend as he held a lantern and confidently scanned the dark waters. I seemed to be in the hands of quite capable seamen—the *lads* she remembered.

Joe grabbed a loose piece of canvas and held it over our heads. I shivered. "Do you have any idea the danger . . . Does Mother know?"

"Of course not." He looked at me as if I'd lost all common sense. "Not this time or the other times."

The reality of what he was saying became clearer. "You did much more for Mrs. Burgin than you revealed."

He grinned. "You had your secrets. I had mine."

Forty-Four

Tears and shock marked the next days. There were moments where I only vaguely remembered the *Jersey* and my rescue. Others were all too clear.

According to Joe, I was overcome with weakness before our boat reached the city docks, and while I drifted in and out of consciousness, he and his friends transported me home. Mrs. Murphy's body was taken to Canvas Town for a proper burial, honored by the men, women, and children who remembered her.

I don't recall seeing Mother at first. One minute, I was being jostled in a cart over the cobblestones, and the next, I lay against soft pillows on the settee in the parlor, sipping broth as she held the spoon.

She lacked sleep; that was evident. Certainly she had questions, yet she refrained from pressing me, giving me time to heal and regain my strength. But as my stomach calmed and I regained a sense of alertness, my own questions wouldn't wait. When Mother entered the parlor one morning, I asked her to take a seat beside me.

She picked up her mending from the nearby table. "You're looking better, my love. You are remarkably resilient. Is there anything you need?"

"No, thank you for all you've done, Mother. I'm so happy to be home."

Her eyes filled with tears. "Thank the Lord you're safe. I have yet to hear the full story from your brother."

"He'll explain it better than I can. I'm afraid I don't remember a great deal." I took her hand. "I'm more concerned with all that's taken place here. Have you spoken with Celeste or Cousin Robert? Were they aware of my arrest? Do they know I've returned?"

"Oh, I imagine Celeste knows, don't you?" She squeezed my hand. "As for Robert, it must have been the day after it happened. Joseph went to the shop, but Mr. Oakham was there instead."

She took a breath and continued. "According to Mr. Oakham,

Robert had received news that seemed to greatly trouble him, and he left abruptly."

I let go of her hand to wipe my eyes. How did Robert hear of my arrest? Knowing him, he most likely blamed himself and was in fear he would be next. Perhaps he'd gone to try to find Abraham.

"Joseph went from there to the Underhill's and found Robert. He said something strange—he warned Joseph not to divulge to anyone that you were arrested and that he and I should be on our guard. Then he said that he might be leaving the city. Why would he do such a thing?"

I knew, yet I couldn't explain. "I'm certain I don't know. Perhaps he will write to us."

"Yes, he should know we will want to hear from him." Mother's eyes shone. "And then we can give him the wonderful news of your return. Mr. Oakham asked that Joseph continue working at the shop, so perchance he will catch word of Robert's whereabouts."

No longer would my plan of surprising my cousin at Oakham and Townsend come to fruition. Was he safe, wherever he'd gone? And where did that leave the Culper Ring?

Outside the window, timid snowflakes floated and spiraled, the first of the season. One question hung in the air, the one that I'd carried for days before Crankshaw and the others hauled me into that boat.

"Have you any word of the major?"

Mother gazed down at my left hand and ran her thumb across it. "I can't say I have. I've been so worried for you . . ." She pulled away. "Are you comfortable? May I fix you a cup of tea?"

I vaguely recalled Mother and Alice helping me remove my filthy clothing when I'd first arrived home, then sponging off some of the dirt and grime adhering to my body. Now that I had the strength for a better bath, Alice didn't waste a minute setting up the old copper tub in the parlor. She brought soap and towels and a scrub brush, and she and Mother carried in buckets of hot water to fill the tub.

"I hate to say it, Miss Betty, but your hair has got to go," Alice said. "The lice musta been all over that ship."

"There are worse things, Alice. I'll have decent hair again in a year." Cutting my hair—something I never could have imagined—now seemed so unimportant.

"Can't say I won't miss stylin' it for you." Her voice caught as she and Mother left the room so I could bathe. I soaked and scrubbed and shed tears until the water resembled the gray-green East River. Exhausted, I dried off and wrapped myself in a clean sheet.

Alice brought her big sewing scissors to cut my hair and lye to scrub my head. It was painful and difficult, yet it needed to be done. Afterward, she and Mother hauled all the blankets and linens outside to be treated with lye and boiling water and threw my hair into the kitchen fire. The clothing I'd worn ever since Joe and I went to Mr. Mulligan's had disappeared, and I assumed it had been burned as well.

Mother brought me a fresh dressing gown and the quilt from my bed. Wearing a clean cap over my sore head, I consumed a little bread and cider and fell asleep, only I dreamed of rats and Mary and Mrs. Murphy. When I woke, snow fell at a steady clip. How were Mary and Edith and all those aboard the prison ships going to survive the cold and snow?

That afternoon, I felt ready to share a bit about my imprisonment as Mother and Alice came and went. I recounted the basics, skimming over the worst evils. Perhaps one day I would speak of them, but for now, they were better left alone.

As to why I'd been arrested, I repeated the story I had told on the *Jersey*—that it was a mistake. No matter what happened, I would never disclose the full truth to anyone.

Later, when Mother and Alice were tending to the destruction of lice and preparation of supper, Joe entered the parlor with an armload of wood to start a fire.

"I'm glad you're home," I said. "Come and sit when you have it started."

When the wood caught the flames, he plopped onto the chair

beside the settee. He scrutinized my head and cap. "What happened to your hair?"

"Little friends accompanied me from the *Jersey*. Alice went to battle with the scissors."

"You should shave it and wear a wig."

"Absolutely not. My hair grows quickly. And I promised Celeste I'd never wear one."

"I saw her today," Joe said. "She knew of your arrest but hadn't heard you were safe. I told her some friends organized your rescue. She asked if she could call on you tomorrow, and I said yes."

It would be good to see Celeste, and perhaps she'd heard through Captain Hollingsworth something of the major's situation.

I touched my brother's knee. "I never thanked you properly for all you did. And I have a question or two."

A faint smile lit his eyes. "I thought you might."

I listened for any sounds of Alice or Mother entering the house, but all was quiet. "Why didn't you tell me that you and your friends were helping Mrs. Burgin rescue prisoners?"

He laughed, as if the answer was obvious. "You would have told Mother or made me stop. We wanted to do something for the Patriots. Mrs. Burgin knew James and asked him if he could acquire a boat. When she suggested a plan, he didn't hesitate. He recruited me, and before I knew it, the other fellows and I were rowing out to the *Jersey* with him."

My brother had been involved in undercover work far more dangerous than my own. My voice caught. "I'm quite proud of you."

He looked down at the floor. "I think I know what you were doing now, but I'll never say."

"I know you won't. Thank you."

"I went to see Cousin Robert." Joe shrugged. "He said he needed to leave New York."

"Yes, Mother told me." He would miss Robert as much as I would.

Robert Townsend had truly cared for me, the Ring, and this young country. My heart broke for him. As much as I'd resented his criticisms and overprotectiveness, it had all been for my benefit. No doubt, he was second-guessing everything now. I longed to tell him he needn't worry.

Perhaps Joe would know the answer to my other burning question. "Are there any reports of Major André?"

He twisted in his chair and glanced out the window at the snow clinging to the bare trees. "Um, only rumors, that's all." He stood to go. "Sorry, Triple's meowing at the door."

"Joe, I—"

Before I could finish my sentence, he left the room.

I took supper in the dining room. How wonderful to sit at a table again with my family and enjoy a hot meal! The potato and leek soup warmed my bones, and my stomach welcomed it. I was recovering.

The snow continued, and Joe stoked the fires as evening faded into night. Alice and Mother went about encasing our beds in thick winter quilts and preparing the bed warmers as the fires burned bright.

I climbed the stairs to don warm nightclothes and settle into my own bedroom again. But I would not sleep. The major hadn't left my mind all day, and as much as I feared the worst, I had to know what happened to him.

I called for Mother and insisted she take the chair near the fire. I closed the door and sat on the stool at her feet.

"I know you have information about the major, and I understand that you may not wish to tell me." My eyes filled with tears. "Yet I must know the truth."

Her own tears welled up. "Yes, you must be told. I wish I had a better explanation because you deserve to hear the full story, yet I will say what I know."

She took both my hands in hers, keeping her eyes down. "After your arrest, I went to Mr. Rivington to seek his advice because Robert was gone. He assured me he was aware of what happened to you and was making certain inquiries."

I wondered with whom Mr. Rivington may have spoken on my behalf. Senior officers, perhaps. And Culper Senior.

I urged her to continue, wrapping her fingers in mine.

"I also asked him if he knew anything regarding Major André." She turned to stare into the fire, then faced me again. "He didn't know all that transpired, other than that the major was charged as a spy. Apparently, General Washington might have traded him for General Arnold due to Arnold's treason, although I do not know the details of that. For whatever reason, General Clinton thought better of it and would not make the trade."

Her lips trembled as tears rolled down her cheeks. "Elizabeth, Mr. Rivington informed me that on 2 October in Tappan, your Major André was hanged for spying."

Long after Mother finally kissed my forehead and closed my door, I lingered at the fireside, unable to move. I cried for John André and for myself. I tried to sort out what happened, what I knew and what I missed, despite the futility and the utter senselessness of it all.

At last, I rose and went to the window, retrieved my paper Major André and propped it on my desk. I had so much to say to him. With pen and paper, I told him everything.

My dearest John,

It snows tonight. In silence, it blankets the hard ground, the bare trees, and the houses with their glowing candles at dark windows. I am reminded of the night we rode through the falling snow to the Yuletide Frolic and of our cold, moon-lit walks in the Common.

It is time for me to divulge a secret. I often wondered how or when I might tell you, and now this letter is the only way for me to explain.

Not long after the evening of our first dance at the Kennedy mansion, I joined a group of Patriot spies. That is why I always reacted in disgust when you tried to enlist me to do the same for the Crown.

My reason is simple. I believe America must be free. During our time together, I conveyed to my contacts whatever I could glean from you and others that might aid in our war for freedom. I deeply regret not learning more of your plans regarding WP because I might have prevented your travels there, or perhaps the outcome for you would have been different.

Please know that there always existed a tension between my desire to serve my country and my growing and absolute desire and love for you. I might compare it to having two opposing roles in the same play, yet it was all too real. While I continued in my duties, I always longed for the day when things might change and I could simply be myself with you.

I expect to discover what took place on your trip north and what led to your parting this life. During your captivity, my actions or words apparently raised suspicions and I was sent to the hell ship. Through determination, help from others, and a miracle or two, I survived. My heart is utterly broken in learning you did not.

Knowing you, I assume you died as you lived—a gentleman, honorable and forthright. I pray you will be remembered so. I do not pretend to believe no other woman caught your eye in the time we knew each other—yet I am certain you would not have lavished your attentions on me if you hadn't truly wished to do so.

I will forever hold dear the fact that we were "more than friends." And I shall not forget your quick wit, your kind smile, your generosity, and your sweet insecurities that few others, if any, were aware of in a man so outwardly self-assured.

Thank you for allowing me to know a part of the real John André. And thank you for showing me that I could be

*extraordinary. I will treasure our love story until we meet
again.*

> *Toujours,*
> *Betty*

Sobbing and shaking, I folded the letter and kissed it. I clutched
it to my chest, walked to the blazing fire, and cast it into the flames.

Self-portrait by Major André, on the day before he was executed.

Forty-Five

I lay awake long into the night until sleep finally pulled me under. When I woke, the day had warmed enough to turn the overnight snow into slush. Wrapping a shawl over my dressing gown, I made my way to the pantry.

Alice was there, humming random notes. She took one look at me and fumbled for her handkin. "Oh, Miss Betty, what a shame about the major. A horrible shame! Your mother told me jus' yesterday."

I did not wish to talk but I reached out to rub her arm. "Thank you, Alice."

She sniffed and wiped her nose. "You want somethin' to eat? I can fix—"

"No, just some tea, if there's any left."

She motioned to the teapot on the worktable. "Gimme jus' a minute. You want to sit down?"

Standing there and waiting took all my effort. "I think I'll take it with me, if you don't mind."

As soon as she poured the tea, I took the cup and went to the stairs. All I wanted was to be alone. If only Celeste wasn't coming, yet it was probably better that I see her and prevent any rumors circulating about my arrest among our acquaintances.

Mother had asked the night before if I wanted her and Alice to stay home that afternoon rather than go as they'd planned to the Dicksons' to help with candle-making. I didn't want them fussing over me and preferred some time alone. I assured her I would be all right.

Later, I watched from the parlor window as Marcus held the carriage door open for Celeste and assisted her onto our wet path. She lifted her skirts to avoid the pooling slush. I adjusted my cap and opened the door.

She entered the foyer and held out her arms. "Oh, Betty . . ."

"Thank you for coming." I fell into her embrace, biting back tears.

"I was so worried!" She held me at arm's length. "Your hair— what happened?"

I glanced toward the parlor. "Would you like to sit down?"

"Yes, of course. I don't mean to rush you." She removed her gloves and cape and hung them over the stairway banister. "I can see you've been crying."

I led the way into the parlor, and she took a seat beside me on the settee. I grasped her hands. "I assume you've been given the news of the major."

She frowned, squeezing my hands. "Father told me. I still cannot believe it."

I was at a loss as to what to say, even to my dearest friend. "'Tis difficult . . ."

"All of New York is in mourning." Celeste shook her head. "Every ball and party has been postponed indefinitely."

I swallowed and willed myself to simply breathe.

We sat that way for a bit, until Celeste took her hands away and rearranged the folds of her dark woolen gown. "Betty, I wanted to see you, not only to grieve with you and tell you how thankful I am that you're safe but . . . I came for another reason."

I searched her eyes. "Yes?"

"This won't be easy, but I must be direct." She bit her lower lip, clearly uncomfortable. "Please believe me when I say that I had absolutely no idea you would be arrested, let alone sent to that ship."

I didn't understand. "I beg your pardon?"

Her eyes glistened with unshed tears. "You've never been the least bit secretive with me until sometime over a year ago. There were moments . . . I sensed you were hiding something, but I could never determine what it might be. Then, when the major was arrested, you sounded as though you knew more than anyone else. And I couldn't understand why you were angry with Benedict Arnold for trying to hand over West Point."

What was she trying to say?

She took a long pause, then continued, her voice cracking.

"Finally, I decided to mention it to Captain Hollingsworth. I assumed he might tell me I was imagining things. Yet he was much more interested than I expected." Her eyes met mine. "I attempted to explain to him that I trust you and he needn't take it so seriously. However, he passed on my unease to his—"

I could not fathom what I was hearing. "Are you saying that you and Hollingsworth were behind my arrest?"

"No, Betty, I'm—"

"Yet you spoke to him with your concerns." I paused, thinking back to the day of my arrest. "Do you have any notion at all what that moment was like for me?"

"I never thought—"

Anger surged through me like flames. I was on my feet. "What in God's name *were* you thinking? You were fully aware they're constantly looking for anyone they can stop and arrest, and they hardly need a reason. Did it not occur to you that he would follow orders and turn in anyone that raised suspicions, especially yours?" My voice was hoarse. "We've been friends for years, Celeste. Why didn't you simply come and ask me to explain?"

She rose and faced me, her hands in the air. "You've been so evasive. How could I know if you would speak the truth?"

"Stop minimizing it. You raised his suspicions enough for him to have me arrested!"

"I did not think he'd—"

I turned away and marched to the window. "Let me describe for you exactly what the *Jersey* is, Celeste, in case you and Hollingsworth and all those self-righteous pigs masquerading as officers choose to think otherwise."

I whirled around and took slow, deliberate steps toward her. "The rumors are correct. It is the closest thing to hell on this earth. One small bowl a day consisting of bits of rancid meat in stinking broth, moldy bread on occasion, complete with maggots. Locked in the pitch-dark hold at night with the rats.

"Yet I hid on the open deck, even during freezing rain. I slept beside a dead woman so her body wouldn't be thrown into the river with all the others. And the only way to relieve myself was to squat over a bucket in broad daylight while other women stood guard . . ."

Celeste covered her ears. "I don't need to hear this."

I pulled her hands down. "You're going to hear it."

I lowered my voice but there was no denying the rage rising to the surface. I had bottled it for too long, and it poured out now.

"You need to hear that the wretched food made me so ill that if it weren't for my brother gathering a rescue party, I would surely be dead by now. Yet to escape, I had to pretend I was dead and endure the prisoners' and guards' dirty hands all over me, no matter how much I wanted to scream and slap them."

I let go of her hands and yanked off my cap. "My hair and clothes were so infested with lice and caked with my own filth that they had to be burned."

She turned pale and whimpered. "Betty . . ."

I pointed at her face. "I witnessed unspeakable evils you should hope you never see, all because you couldn't deal with my *evasiveness*, as you put it, so you took it into your own hands and tattled to the person you *knew* would do something about it!"

She dissolved into tears. "I made a terrible, horrible mistake. Dear God, please forgive me!"

I breathed hard, fighting the urge to slap her, not knowing what to do next. I sank to the nearest chair, heart pounding. All that I'd endured welled up inside me, not only my time aboard the *Jersey* but the senseless deaths of Christopher Martin and John André. I could bear it no longer.

I hollered at the top of my voice. "As God is my witness, I did nothing wrong."

Her voice trembled. "I hope you will forgive me, Betty."

I was spent. "It's too late. The damage is done." I rose in desperation, not knowing if I should stand or run. I turned toward the window again but fell to the rug, shaking from outrage and sadness and so much impossible loss. I was raw. I wept and screamed from the depths of my stomach until I retched.

When I sat up at last, Celeste had gone.

Forty-Six

November 1780

The snow melted as if it had never fallen. It would return soon in great quantities, and winter would lock us in once again. For now, New York City lay still, holding its breath, grieving the death of the man it had so loved and admired and wondering when and how the war would ever end.

I continued to recover physically and gradually resumed the never-ending household chores and tutoring Joe. And regardless of Celeste's revelation, I forced my heart to begin the process of healing as well. It fought me, beating normally one minute and breaking into pieces the next. But as in the past, I saw no alternative other than clawing my way up and out of the pit of despair.

Long nights were spent grieving for the major, recalling our conversations, and lambasting my inability to piece together the clues that may have prevented his death. Was the Culper Ring still in operation and in what capacity? Did General Washington know I was safe? Were my services still required with Robert gone and Major André dead?

Joe came in one afternoon and found me in the pantry, preparing squash for roasting. Triple lay wrapped around his neck like a fur scarf. Although Mother had decreed that the cat was not welcome in the house, she and Alice were occupied above stairs, unpacking the trunks that held our heavy quilts once again. I chose not to mention Joe's infraction. After all, I owed him my life. And I had to admit, I *did* like Triple.

He helped himself to the last of the spoon bread in the bowl on the table. "I heard officers talking in the Square today. General Arnold is here in New York now. He plans to hunt down all the spies he can find. They said he's trying to earn Clinton's favor, but no one wants anything to do with him after what happened."

As I'd suspected. "'Tis wise of them. Benedict Arnold is nothing but a conniving, selfish traitor."

Even if no one was cooperating, I wondered if Arnold had any knowledge of my association with John André.

Joe may have been reading my thoughts. He whispered, "Will that be a problem?"

I wiped my hands on my apron and embraced him. "No, of course not." In any case, I reminded myself that Betty Floyd had been listed as dead on the *Jersey*.

The other Ring members were surely aware of Arnold's plans. They would stay quiet for now and take extra precautions. While I pondered the fate of the Culpers and what General Washington might do, three letters arrived over the span of seven days. As letters often do, they provided answers. And raised more questions.

The first was from Robert, addressed to Mother. He had settled once again near Oyster Bay "for the time being." In typical Robert Townsend fashion, he gave no return address, no elaboration. In a separate, sealed note to me, he expressed his relief at hearing of my escape from the death ship.

He added, "Acquaintances may contact you; however, I advise great caution. As for myself, I have retired." He included a short condolence at the bottom: "Regret the loss of J.A."

I speculated as to how word of my liberation had reached him. Perhaps Mr. Rivington had been informed and alerted the Ring. I hoped Robert would return to New York when he thought it safe. There was much I wished to tell him, and he would be pleased to learn that his young cousin James had redeemed himself after the debacle of last winter by aiding in my rescue. I imagined General Washington would be as well.

Aunt Hannah sent the second letter to Mother.

"She writes that your cousin Mary and Ben Tallmadge are courting," Mother said. "It's a shame he didn't become a minister like his father, although apparently he's become a trusted aide to General Washington."

I marveled at the thought of my own cousin possibly marrying one of the Culper Ring leaders. Did she have an inkling as to her future husband's role in the saga surrounding Benedict Arnold?

Perhaps soon there would be a wedding or a family gathering, and I would meet Ben Tallmadge again, and he might tell me of John André's last days on earth. Uncle William would be present, and he could freely explain to me all that Congress had undergone since they had signed the Declaration of Independence. Yet I was getting ahead of myself: There was still a war to be fought.

The last letter came the next day. It had been months since I'd heard from Jacob, and I savored his news.

> *With winter's approach, the Straits will soon be frozen over again, slowing the construction on Fort Mackinac. I have been reassigned to Fort George in New York for the winter months, and shall return here in the spring, when construction of the fort will resume at full pace.*
>
> *I pray we may renew our friendship and put our dancing abilities to the test. I trust you will overlook my lack of practice, as the only dancing here occurs after a great deal of rum consumption, and I am not often one to imbibe.*

Celeste had been right in guessing that one day Jacob might be transferred to New York. It would be wonderful to see him again; however, I could not imagine when it would be safe for me to appear in public. I would need to be on guard for the time being, lest the news that Betty Floyd was alive reached the wrong ears.

A week later, I penned a message and paid for its delivery. I had not ventured from home since my rescue; however, there was an important matter to address and I felt it must be settled face to face.

Given the fact that I didn't dare to be recognized, it would have made sense to hire a carriage. Yet a walk had always helped me gather my thoughts. So, as the late autumn sun teased the birds into song, I donned my hooded cape and set out.

Not far from home, I waited at a distance as a group of eight soldiers marched past, led by a young lieutenant. They each wore a band of black on their upper left arm, a sign of mourning for the fallen Major André.

I pulled my hood lower over my eyes and continued on, reflecting on all that had taken place since I said yes to Robert Townsend and joined the Culper Ring. Regardless of the way I'd suffered aboard the *Jersey*, I did not regret serving my country for a single moment. I could only pray it made a small difference toward a favorable outcome in a most horrid war.

Was I like Esther, chosen for such a time as this? I knew not. I had simply been willing. And I had done what I could.

Robert had always insisted America would prevail. Good would triumph over evil, and freedom over tyranny, because as the Declaration states, God gives freedom. The stakes were high— impossibly high. It would take a miracle from heaven and great courage not only to defeat the British but also to forge ahead into the future.

I crossed the Broadway behind a waiting carriage, just as a door opened at the entrance to the home nearest the Kennedy mansion. A young woman carrying a baby descended the steps, wearing a beaver-trimmed black hat atop her honey-colored, wavy hair. She glanced my way as she adjusted the baby's blanket.

But for the black cape and the shadows beneath her eyes, she was the exact image of the major's drawing I'd once admired in the *Royal Gazette*—the woman I'd wondered about ever since I'd first heard her name—Peggy Shippen Arnold.

At the shock of seeing her, I lost my footing and stumbled over a stone. She paused, perhaps thinking I twisted an ankle. Recovering, I nodded to her briefly. She returned my nod, then accepted the hand of someone inside the carriage. Was it her traitor husband? I wouldn't look, for fear of him having me followed.

What might I have said to her, if I could speak the truth? Had she prior knowledge of her husband's treason, and did her black attire indicate her grief for the major? She would never know how I shared in her mourning.

I approached Number One Broadway, remembering the warm

evening I arrived in Celeste's crimson gown to meet the dashing John André and enter the lions' den. What an evening it was, where I dined with New York's elite and first heard General Clinton remark that "the road to victory runs through West Point."

Now, I took in the tall windows, recalling the view from inside the grand dining room. *I'm afraid that road is closed to you, General.*

At last, around the bend, the Walkers' pine trees reached higher than I had ever noticed. Sunlight beamed through the branches as I walked to Celeste's door. I shielded my eyes and watched her pull aside the curtain.

I would hold fast to the promise I made to my country and see what God had in store for us. And I would forgive. Only then could I begin again.

The End

Epilogue

Mackinac Island, Michigan
Present Day

A nne Price, senior researcher and specialist in eighteenth-century studies for Michigan State University's archaeology department, hunched over a battered and dirt-encrusted tin box recently discovered during the college's excavation at Fort Mackinac.

With gloved hands, she held the shoebox-sized container to the light. By the looks of it, she doubted it was of any great value. So far, other than a few Revolutionary War–era buttons and a broken inkwell, the dig hadn't uncovered much of interest. Still, something shifted inside the box as she tilted it. She'd get it open, then call it a day.

Anne used her brushes to sweep loose dirt from the top and sides of the box, then wiped it gently with a clean cloth. As she thought—it bore no imprints or anything remarkable. Most likely, it belonged to one of the hundreds of enlisted men stationed at the fort after construction was completed in the 1780s.

She coaxed the lid free of the sides with a pair of small pliers until it was loose enough to pull back. Inside lay random items—a quill pen, a folded piece of tan leather, a straight razor, and a pair of tattered black woolen socks.

Anne reached for her camera and photographed the contents, then noted her findings on a pad at the desk. She poked around the thread-bare socks with her tweezers in case she'd missed anything. Her intern could handle the measuring and cataloging the next day.

But something was inside the ragged toe of one sock. She reached in with the tweezers until she located a wad of crumpled paper. Laying the sock back in the box, Anne grabbed another pair of tweezers and slowly opened the yellowed, disintegrating piece of paper.

Several lines of barely legible numbers and letters were written in ink on one side. She set the tweezers down and searched the desk for her magnifying glass and a small pencil brush to gently sweep away the accumulated dirt and dust.

Even under magnification, not one word made sense. And the interspersed numbers—what did they signify?

Then, at the very bottom in the right-hand corner, once boldly written yet now barely visible, was a number that took Anne's breath away.

355.

"I intend to visit New York before long and think by the assistance of a lady of my acquaintance, shall be able to outwit them all."

—Abraham Woodhull to Major Benjamin Tallmadge
August 15, 1779

Author's Note

This is a work of fiction, and the identity of the Culper Ring spy known as 355 remains a mystery. Perhaps she truly was Robert Townsend's cousin Betty or another woman entirely. Whoever she was, 355 played a vital role in the Ring's efforts to infiltrate the plans of the British in New York during the American Revolution. Like the other Culper Ring members, she did not seek recognition after the war or wish her name to be known.

As Jacob's letters to Betty state, construction of Fort Mackinac (pronounced Mackinaw) began on Mackinac Island, Michigan, following a move from Michilimackinac, in present-day Mackinaw City. After the war, the fort became a United States Army outpost, closing in 1895. Today, it operates as a tourist attraction and is part of Mackinac Island State Park.

Elizabeth Burgin did take food and supplies to Americans imprisoned on the ships in Wallabout Bay, assisted by a man named George Higday, and perhaps others. They helped more than two hundred prisoners to escape the ships. Burgin avoided capture by fleeing to Philadelphia, then returned to New York briefly to recover her three children. She was one of a few women who were later granted a pension from Congress.

Major John André contacted Benedict Arnold after the American general had suggested to General Clinton in May 1779 that he might be of service. They corresponded for more than a year until the ploy to deliver Fort West Point into Britain's hands took shape during the following summer. On his return to New York after meeting with General Arnold, André was stopped by American militiamen and taken to a nearby camp, despite holding a pass from Arnold. Major Benjamin Tallmadge and General Washington soon learned of the situation, and Arnold's treasonous scheme unraveled.

Meanwhile, Arnold had escaped. Washington wished to release André in exchange for Arnold, but General Clinton refused. Washington then made the difficult decision to hang André as a spy in Tappan, New Jersey. Forty years later, his remains were taken to London's Westminster Abbey for a military burial.

Benedict Arnold's escape to New York put the Ring in greater danger, although they managed to resume some of their usual activities. Abraham Woodhull sent reports to Washington, and Robert Townsend returned to his shop in the city. A plan to kidnap Arnold failed, and General Clinton sent him to a post in Virginia. In 1782, he and his family left for London.

As the tide began to turn in the Patriots' favor and the war came to a close, the Ring members wanted no public recognition. Robert Townsend in particular did not want his name ever to be connected with the Ring. It was not until the 1920s that he was identified as the unassuming, meticulous Culper Junior.

From 1779 to 1782, the Culper Ring provided crucial intelligence to General Washington to aid in his battle against the British. In letters to Tallmadge, the general himself praised the Ring for their work, despite the constant risks they faced. However, he would often become frustrated with the length of time it took for intelligence to reach him. Overall, historians agree that the Ring played a vital role in America's fight for independence.

The war officially came to an end in 1783 with the signing of the Treaty of Paris. General Washington rode triumphantly into New York City on November 25, and days later, bid an emotional farewell to his officers in an upstairs room in Fraunces Tavern. He would be unanimously elected by Congress as the first president of the United States in 1789.

As Americans, we are forever indebted to the Culper Ring and to all the men and women who so courageously worked in secret in the battle for freedom.

Bibliography and Resources

Allen, Thomas B. *George Washington, Spymaster*. National Geographic Society, 2004.

Andrlik, Todd. *Reporting the Revolutionary War: Before It Was History, It Was News*. Sourcebooks, 2012.

Baber, Jean. *The World of Major John André, an Accomplished Man and Gallant Officer*. The Copy Factory, Inc., 1994.

Bleyer, Bill. *George Washington's Long Island Spy Ring*. History Press, 2021.

Burrows, Edwin G. *Forgotten Patriots: The Untold Story of American Prisoners During the Revolution*. Basic Books, 2008.

Daughan, George C. *Revolution on the Hudson*. W. W. Norton & Company, 2016.

Fisher, David. *Bill O'Reilly's Legends and Lies: The Patriots*. Henry Holt & Company, 2016.

Fredrikson, John C. *Revolutionary War Almanac*. Infobase Publishing, 2006.

Gunn, Cameron. *Ben and Me*, Penguin Group, 2010.

Hensley, Jeannine, ed. *The Works of Anne Bradstreet*. President and Fellows of Harvard College, 1967.

Homberger, Eric. *The Historical Atlas of New York City*. Henry Holt & Company, 2005.

Ketchum, Richard M. *Divided Loyalties*. Henry Holt & Company, 2002.

Kilmeade, Brian, and Don Yaeger. *George Washington's Secret Six*. Penguin Group, 2013.

Maxwell, William. *A Portrait of William Floyd, Long Islander*. Society for the Preservation of Long Island Antiquities, 1956.

Nagy, John A. *Invisible Ink: Spycraft of the American Revolution*. Westholme Publishing, 2011.

Norton, Mary Beth. *Liberty's Daughters*. Scott, Foresman and Company, 1980.

O'Reilly, Bill, and Martin Dugard. *Killing England*. Henry Holt and Company, 2017.

Raphael, Ray. *A People's History of the American Revolution*. The New Press, 2002.

Rose, Alexander. *Washington's Spies*. Bantam Dell, 2007.

Volo, Dorothy Deneen, and James M. Volo. *Daily Life During the American Revolution*. Greenwood Press, 2003.

Weitenbaker, Thomas J. *Father Knickerbocker Rebels*. Chas. Scribner & Sons, 1948.

Widder, Keith R. *Reveille Till Taps*. Mackinac State Historic Parks, 1972.

Wilcoxson, Samantha. *Women of the American Revolution*. Pen and Sword Books, 2022.

Articles

"Dances of Colonial America," mountvernon.org, https://www.mountvernon.org/library/digitalhistory/colonial-music-institute/essays/dances-of-colonial-america.

"Deliver the Goods," *Trend & Tradition*, Winter, 2016.

"Descendants and Ancestors of Richard Floyd." Long Island Genealogy. https://www.longislandgenealogy.com/floyd.html.

Hellier, Cathy. "The Perfection of All Dancing: The Minuet." *Colonial Williamsburg Journal*, Autumn, 2015.

"History's Women: Hannah Jones Floyd." Historyswomen.com. https://historyswomen.com/early-america/hannah-jones-floyd/.

"Myths of the American Revolution." smithsonianmag.com. 2010. https://www.smithsonianmag.com/history/myths-of-the-american-revolution-10941835/.

"Signers of the Declaration of Independence: William Floyd." ushistory.org. https://www.ushistory.org/declaration/signers/floyd.html.

Stallings, Amy. "Stepping on Toes: The Political Statements of 17th- and 18th-Century Dance." *Trend & Tradition*, Summer, 2016.

"Sugar House Prisons in New York City." Wikipedia.org. 2018. https://en.wikipedia.org/wiki/Sugar_house_prisons_in_New_York_City.

Trifone, Nicole. "The Spices of Colonial Life: Sowing the Seeds of 18th-Century Herbal Remedies." *Trend & Tradition*, Spring, 2017.

Pamphlet

National Park Service. *George Washington's New York*. 2018.

Play

The Recruiting Officer. Edited by Simon Trussler. Nick Hern Books, 1997.

Tours

Fort Mackinac, Mackinac Island, MI.
Fraunces Tavern Museum, 54 Pearl Street, New York, NY.
George Washington's New York Official Walking Tour, New York, NY.
Patriot Tours, New York, NY.
Tri-Spy Tours, Setauket, NY.

Websites

"Benjamin Franklin's Famous Quotes." Franklin Institute. https://fi.edu/en/science-and-education/benjamin-franklin/famous-quotes.
Fashion History Timeline. https:fashionhistory.fitnyc.edu/1770-1779/.
History.com. https://www.history.com/articles/culper-spy-ring.
Long Island Genealogy. https://www.longislandgenealogy.com/floyd.html.
Museum of the American Revolution. www.amrevmuseum.org.
Three Villages Historical Society. https://www.tvhs.org/.

Illustration Credits

1. Map of New York City. Wikimedia Commons. Public Domain. File: Map of City of New York published in 1834.jpg.

2. Portrait of Major John André. Wikimedia Commons. Public Domain. File: George Engleheart - Major André - B1974.2.33 - Yale Center for British Art.jpg

3. William Floyd. Reference: William Floyd, Wikimedia Commons, Asher Brown Durand, CC0, via Wikimedia Commons, https://commons.wikimedia.org/wiki/File:William_Floyd_MET_DP837755.jpg.

4. Drawing of Robert Townsend. Wikimedia Commons. Public Domain. File: Robert-Townsend.jpg.

5. Portrait of James Rivington. Wikimedia Commons. Public Domain. File: James Rivington - Engraved by A. H. Ritchie. LCCN2005688191.jpg.

6. Peggy Shippen. Wikimedia Commons. Public Domain. File: Margaret Shippen by Major John André (page 159 crop).jpg.

7. Page of the Culper Spy Ring Code. Wikimedia Commons. Public Domain. File: Culper Ring code, rendered.jpg.

8. Benedict Arnold. Wikimedia Commons. Public Domain. File: Benedict Arnold illustration.jpg.

9. The Jersey Prison Ship. Wikimedia Commons. Public Domain. File: HMS Jersey Prison Ship 1782.jpg.

10. Self Portrait by Major John André. Wikimedia Commons. Public Domain. File: John Andre self-portrait 1780-10-01.jpg.

About the Author

Peggy Wirgau loves true stories from the past and writes through the eyes of unsung women in history who faced extraordinary challenges and became heroes.

Her debut novel, *The Stars in April* (Iron Stream Media, March 2021), is based on the true story of a twelve-year-old *Titanic* survivor. The book is the recipient of several awards and honors, including a Starred Review from School Library Journal, the Southern Christian Writers Conference Notable Book Award, and the Pageturner Award Longlist.

A Michigan native, she moved with her husband to Colorado in 2023. They have two adult children and three grandchildren. When not in her vegetable garden or baking bread, Peggy enjoys traveling and speaking at conferences and book clubs.

She is an active member of American Christian Fiction Writers, Colorado Authors League, and Historical Novel Society. You can reach her at https://www.peggywirgau.com.

If you enjoyed this book, will you consider sharing the message with others?

Let us know your thoughts. You can let the author know by visiting or sharing a photo of the cover on our social media pages or leaving a review at a retailer's site. All of it helps us get the message out!

Email: info@ironstreammedia.com

 @ironstreammedia

Iron Stream, Iron Stream Fiction, Iron Stream Kids, and Brookstone Publishing Group, are imprints of Iron Stream Media, which derives its name from Proverbs 27:17, "As iron sharpens iron, so one person sharpens another." This sharpening describes the process of discipleship, one to another. With this in mind, Iron Stream Media provides a variety of solutions for churches, ministry leaders, and nonprofits ranging from in-depth Bible study curriculum and Christian book publishing to custom publishing and consultative services.

For more information on ISM and its imprints, please visit
IronStreamMedia.com